DIE VOLUME 3:
THE GREAT GAME

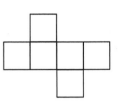

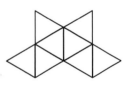

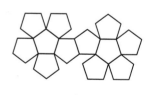

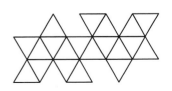

DIE VOLUME 3:
THE GREAT GAME

KIERON GILLEN
Writer

STEPHANIE HANS
Artist

CLAYTON COWLES
Letterer

RIAN HUGHES
Designer

CHRISSY WILLIAMS
Editor

IMAGE COMICS, INC.
Todd McFarlane: President • **Jim Valentino**: Vice President
Marc Silvestri: Chief Executive Officer • **Erik Larsen**: Chief
Financial Officer • **Robert Kirkman**: Chief Operating Officer
Eric Stephenson: Publisher/Chief Creative Officer
Shanna Matuszak: Editorial Coordinator • **Marla Eizik**: Talent
Liaison • **Nicole Lapalme**: Controller • **Leanna Caunter**:
Accounting Analyst • **Sue Korpela**: Accounting & HR Manager
Jeff Boison: Director of Sales & Publishing Planning
Dirk Wood: Director of International Sales & Licensing
Alex Cox: Director of Direct Market & Specialty Sales
Chloe Ramos-Peterson: Book Market & Library Sales Manager
Emilio Bautista: Digital Sales Coordinator • **Kat Salazar**:
Director of PR & Marketing • **Drew Fitzgerald**: Marketing
Content Associate • **Heather Doornink**: Production Director
Drew Gill: Art Director • **Hilary DiLoreto**: Print Manager
Tricia Ramos: Traffic Manager • **Erika Schnatz**: Senior
Production Artist • **Ryan Brewer**: Production Artist
Deanna Phelps: Production Artist • **IMAGECOMICS.COM**

ISBN: 978-1-5343-1716-1

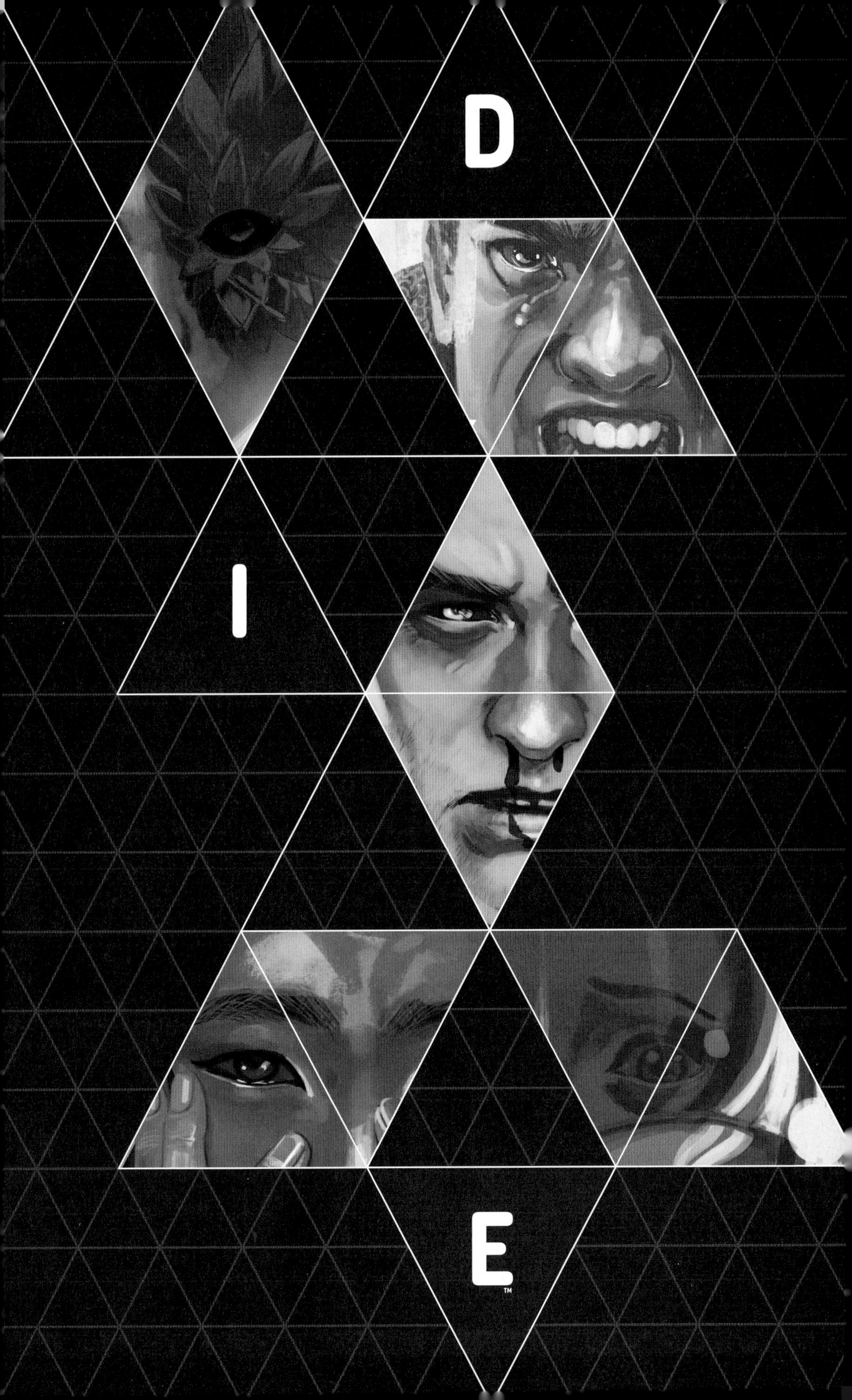
D
I
E™

In 1991, six teenagers disappeared into a fantasy role-playing game. Only five returned.

In 2018, they're dragged back in. They can't go home until six agree. They don't. It is 2019, and the Party wars.

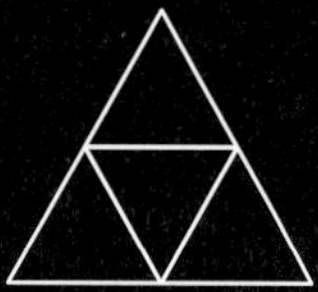

D4
ASH
Dictator

Dominic Ash in the real world, Ash in the world of Die. Married. Sol's best friend. Presently Queen of Angria.

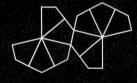

D6
CHUCK
Fool

Fantasy novelist with multiple ex-wives, no tact, and a film franchise. Has a fatal disease.

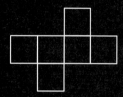

D8
MATT
Grief Knight

Parent and husband. Statistics professor at the local university.

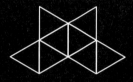

D10
ANGELA
Neo

Coder and parent on the outside, going through an ugly divorce. Ash's sister.

D12
ISABELLE
Godbinder

Divorced school-teacher with aggressively bilingual intelligence.

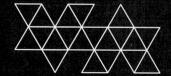

D20
SOL
Grandmaster

Solomon made the game but never made it out. Murdered by Ash and is now one of the Fallen.

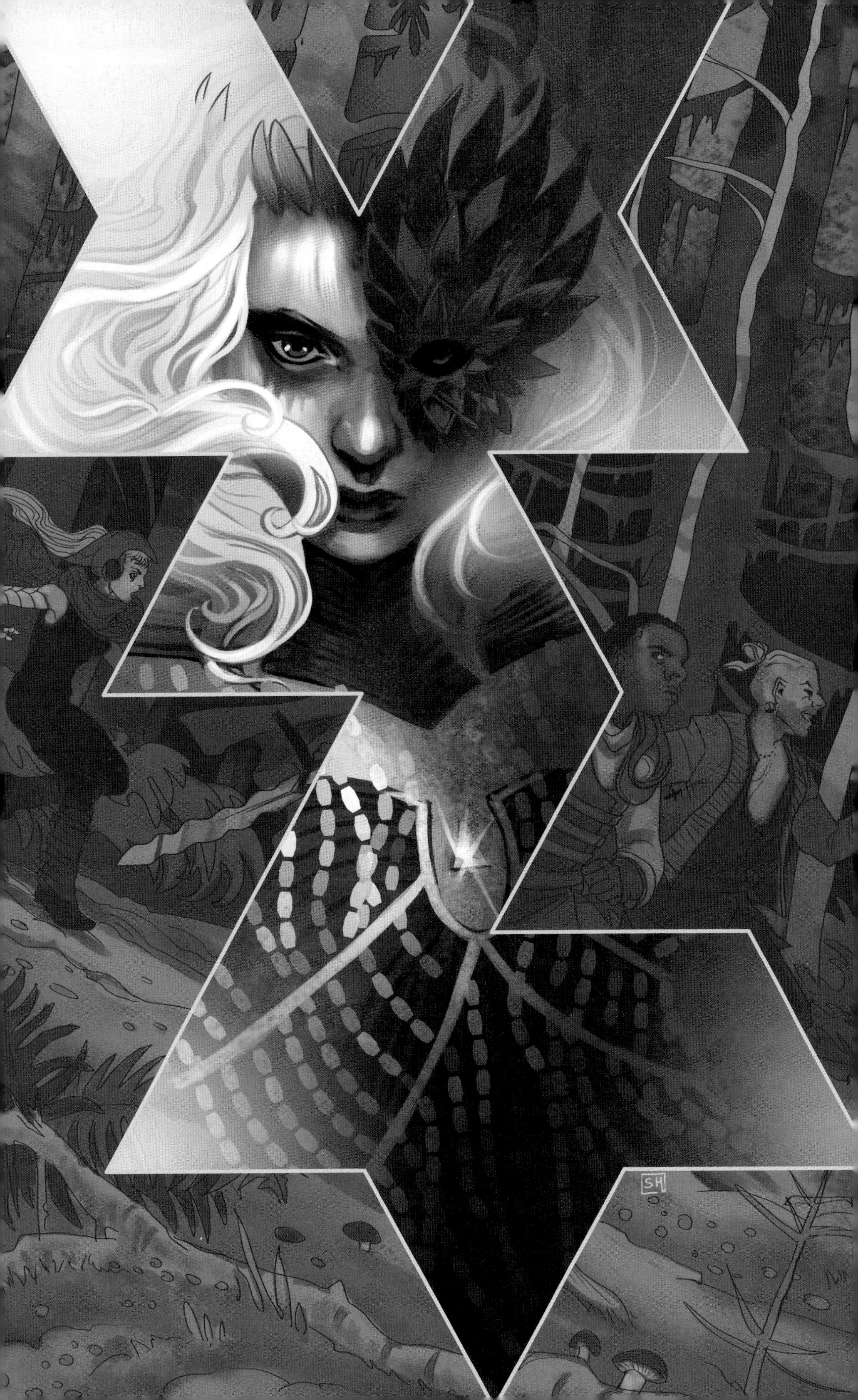
SH

11:
RISK

"Peace is maintained by the equilibrium of forces, and will continue just as long as this equilibrium exists, and no longer."
– *Carl von Clausewitz,* On War

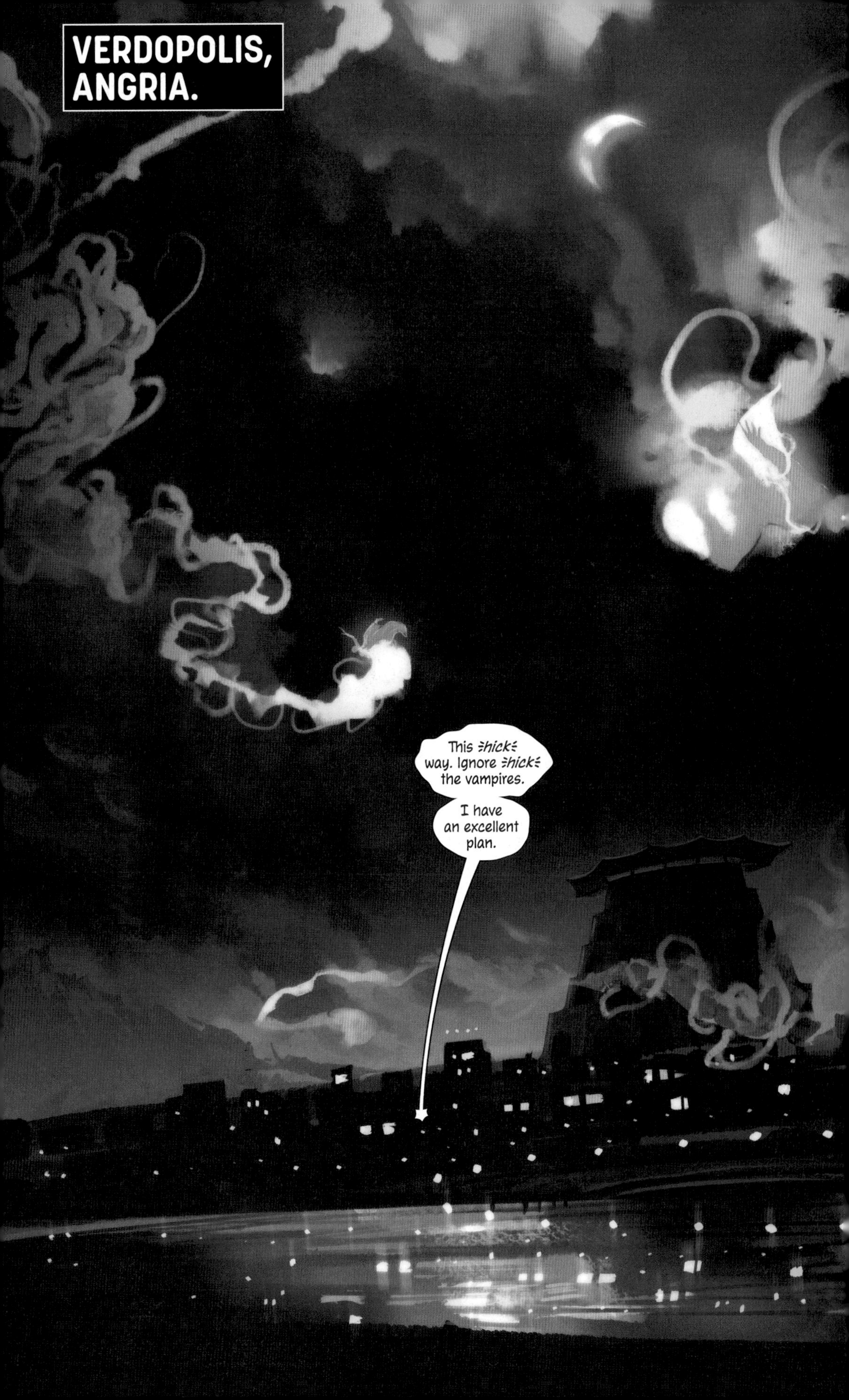
VERDOPOLIS, ANGRIA.
This ≈hick≈ way. Ignore ≈hick≈ the vampires.
I have an excellent plan.

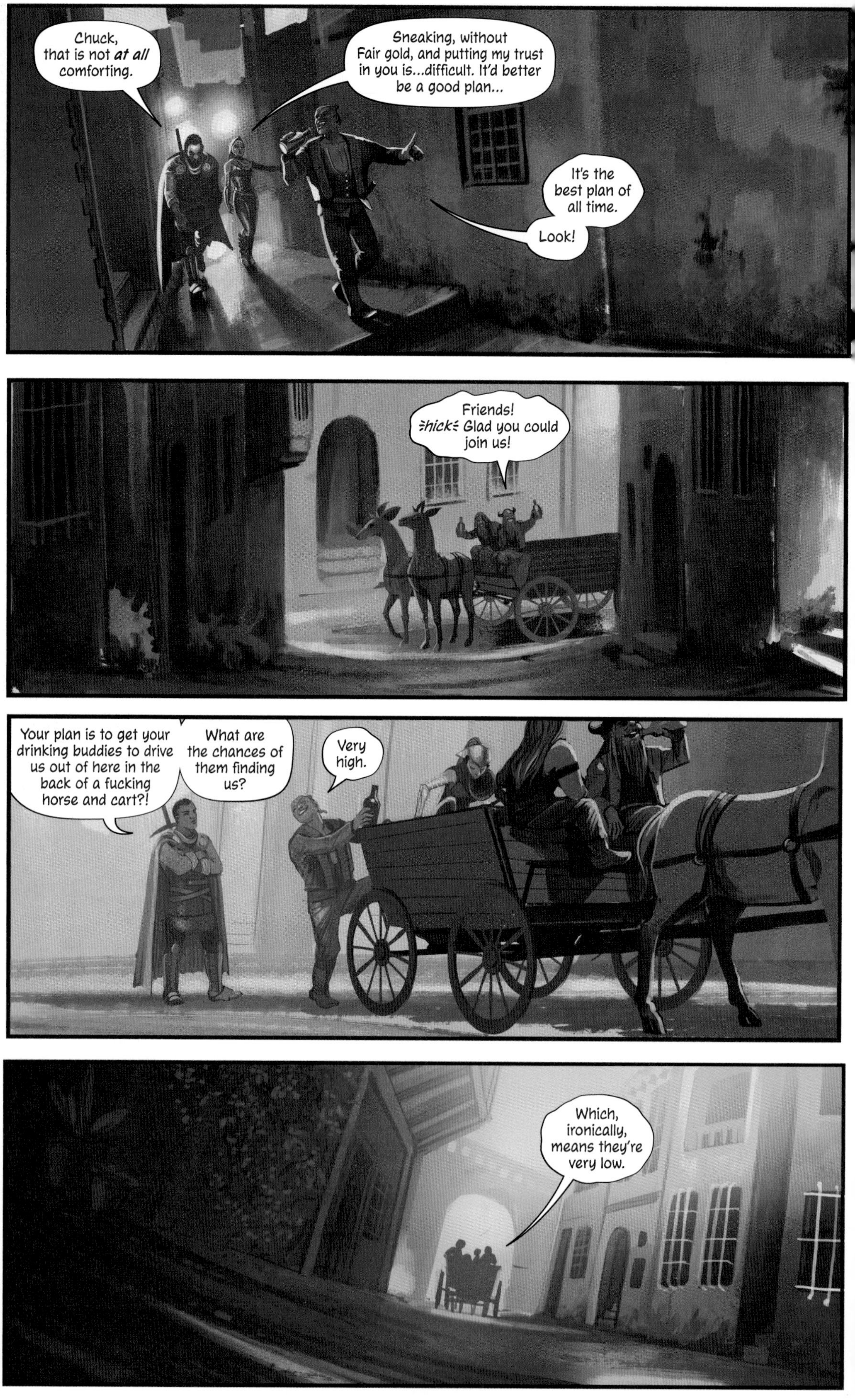
Chuck, that is not *at all* comforting.
Sneaking, without Fair gold, and putting my trust in you is...difficult. It'd better be a good plan...
It's the best plan of all time.
Look!
Friends! =*hick*= Glad you could join us!
Your plan is to get your drinking buddies to drive us out of here in the back of a fucking horse and cart?!
What are the chances of them finding us?
Very high.
Which, ironically, means they're very low.

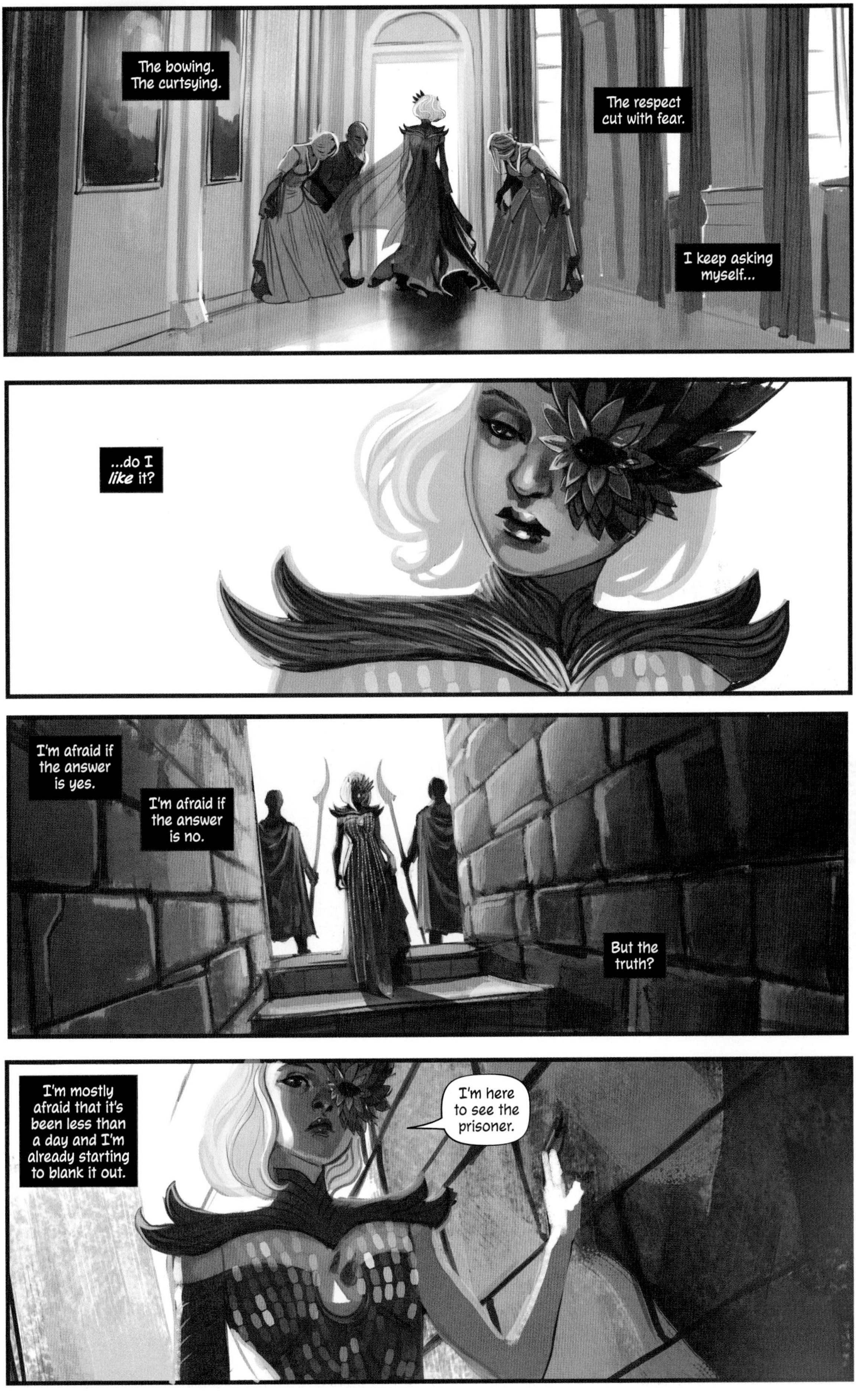
The bowing. The curtsying.
The respect cut with fear.
I keep asking myself...
...do I *like* it?
I'm afraid if the answer is yes.
I'm afraid if the answer is no.
But the truth?
I'm mostly afraid that it's been less than a day and I'm already starting to blank it out.
I'm here to see the prisoner.

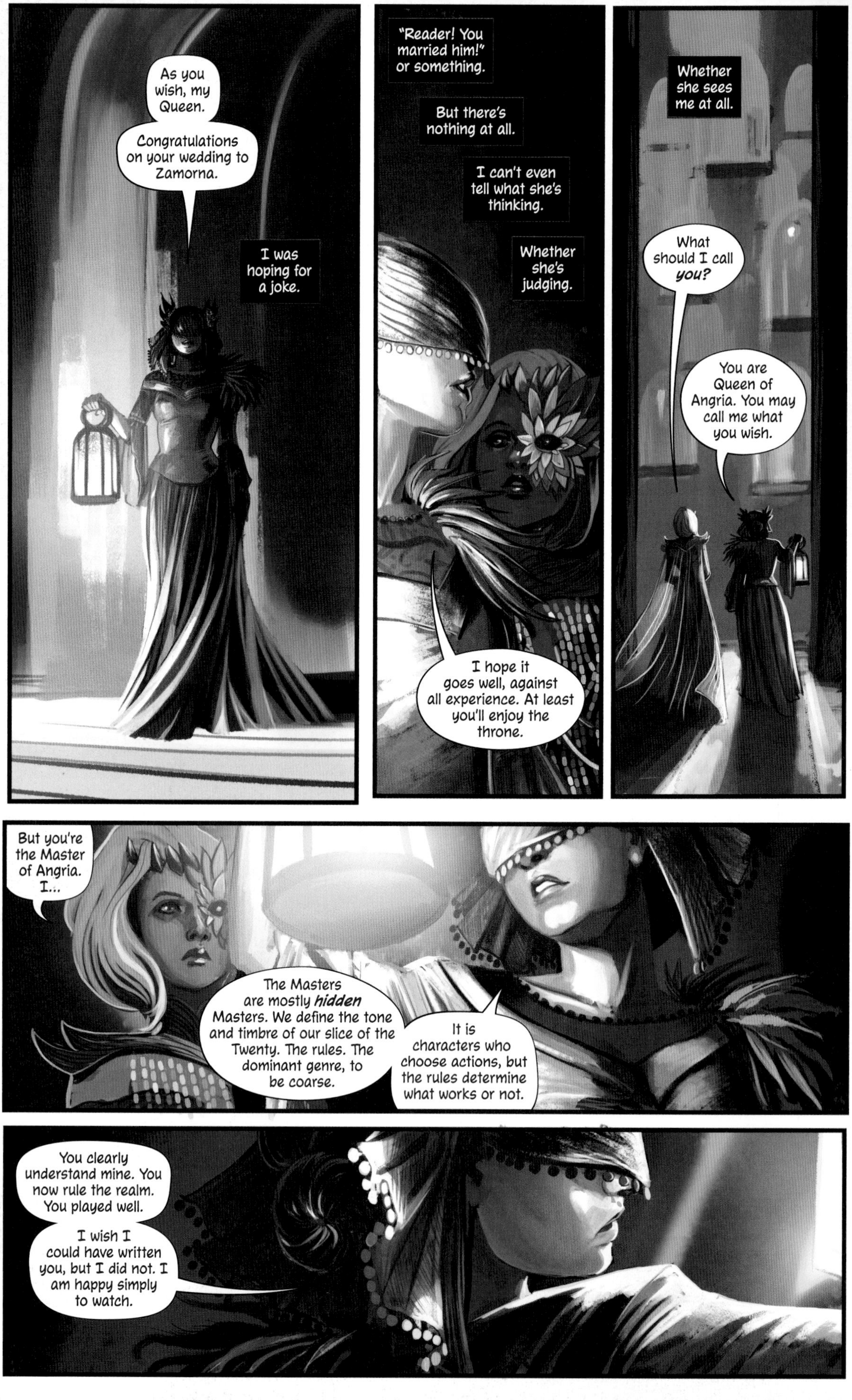
As you wish, my Queen.
Congratulations on your wedding to Zamorna.
I was hoping for a joke.
"Reader! You married him!" or something.
But there's nothing at all.
I can't even tell what she's thinking.
Whether she's judging.
I hope it goes well, against all experience. At least you'll enjoy the throne.
Whether she sees me at all.
What should I call *you?*
You are Queen of Angria. You may call me what you wish.
But you're the Master of Angria. I...
The Masters are mostly *hidden* Masters. We define the tone and timbre of our slice of the Twenty. The rules. The dominant genre, to be coarse.
It is characters who choose actions, but the rules determine what works or not.
You clearly understand mine. You now rule the realm. You played well.
I wish I could have written you, but I did not. I am happy simply to watch.

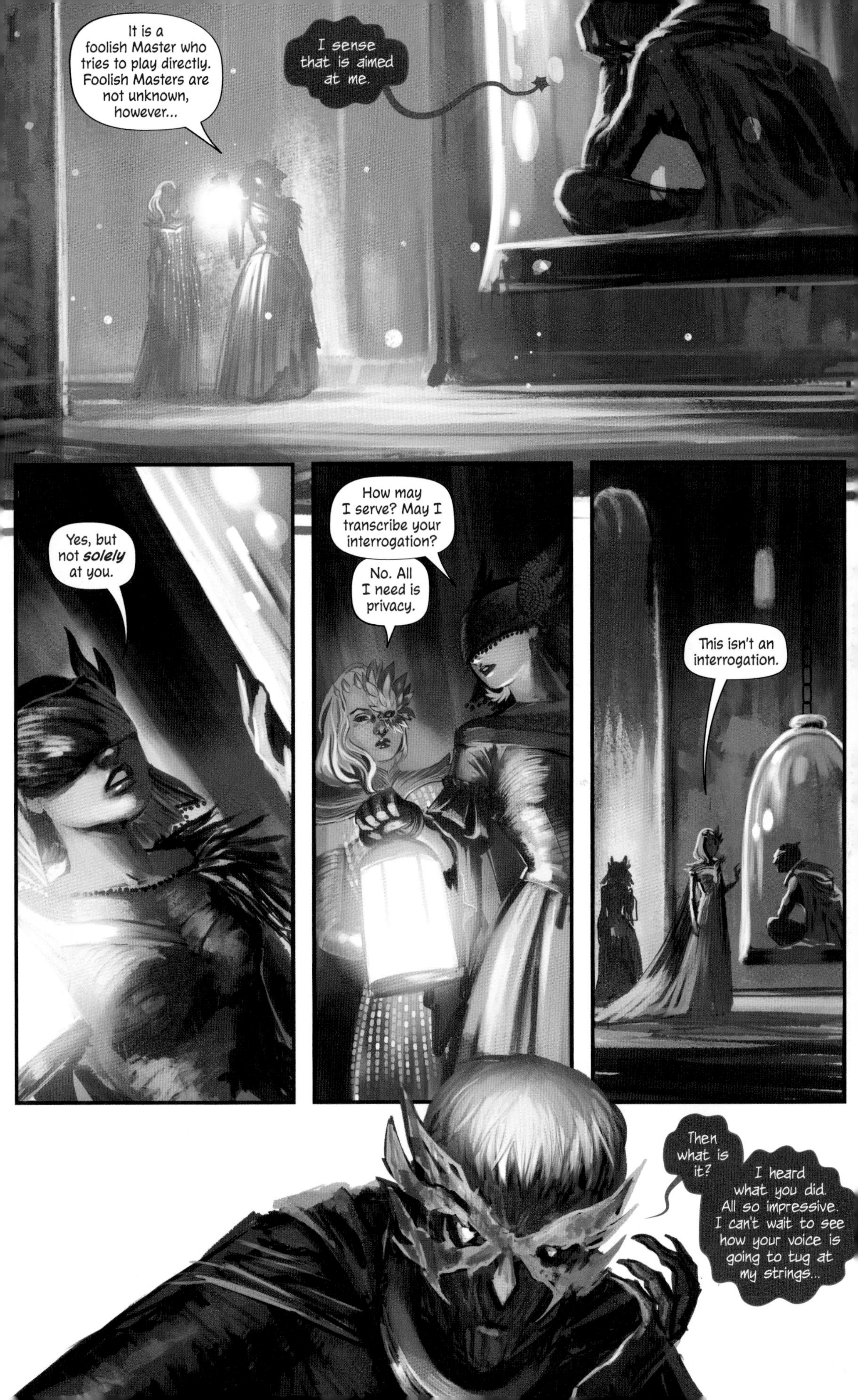
It is a foolish Master who tries to play directly. Foolish Masters are not unknown, however...
I sense that is aimed at me.
Yes, but not *solely* at you.
How may I serve? May I transcribe your interrogation?
No. All I need is privacy.
This isn't an interrogation.
Then what is it?
I heard what you did. All so impressive. I can't wait to see how your voice is going to tug at my strings...

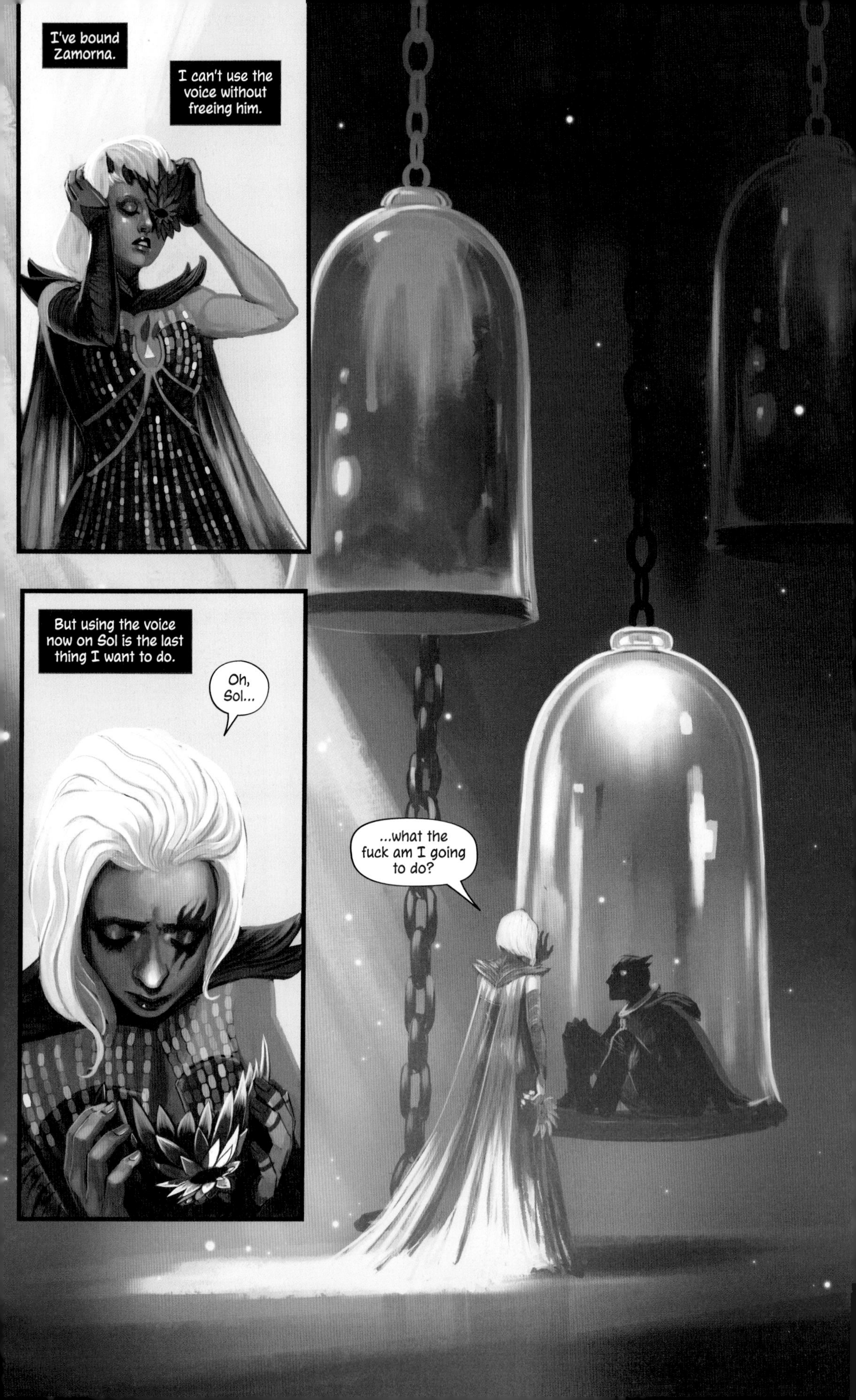
I've bound Zamorna.
I can't use the voice without freeing him.
But using the voice now on Sol is the last thing I want to do.
Oh, Sol...
...what the fuck am I going to do?

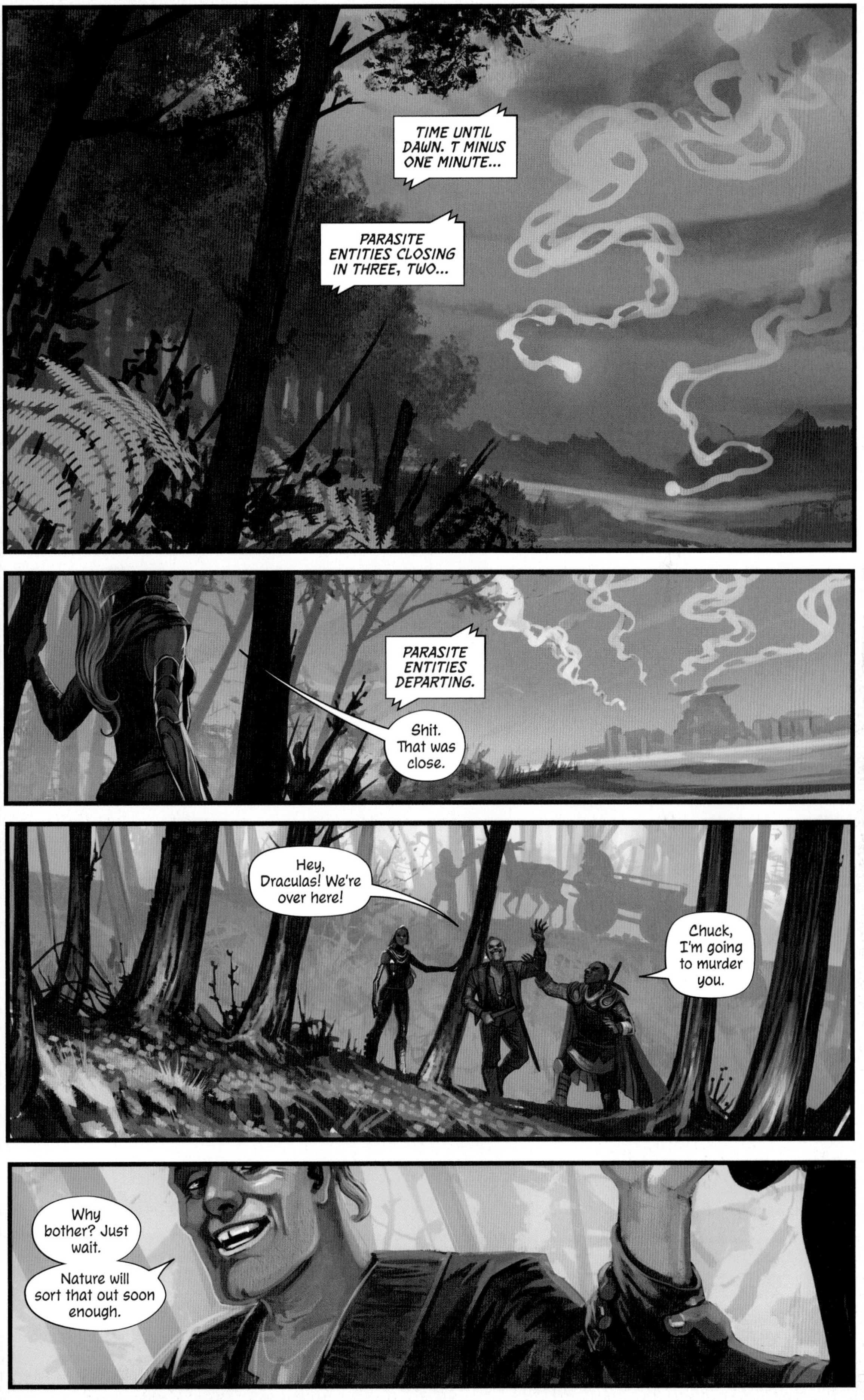
TIME UNTIL DAWN. T MINUS ONE MINUTE...
PARASITE ENTITIES CLOSING IN THREE, TWO...
PARASITE ENTITIES DEPARTING.
Shit. That was close.
Hey, Draculas! We're over here!
Chuck, I'm going to murder you.
Why bother? Just wait.
Nature will sort that out soon enough.

Chuck...you said you were dying. What do you actually mean? This isn't stuff you should joke about.

Well, one day I woke up, went to the bathroom and pissed blood...

"A few weeks later, when I decided it wasn't a one-off thing and the fear got worse, I finally went to a doctor."

"The next day they rushed me in for tests."

The week after, I have less than a year to live.

"Struck down in his prime. All his fans will cry. Won't be a dry eye on Twitter, mark my words."

Chuck, listen to yourself!

You're going to die. If you can't take it seriously, I will.

I'm sorry.

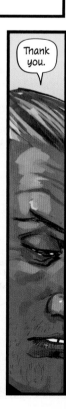

Thank you.

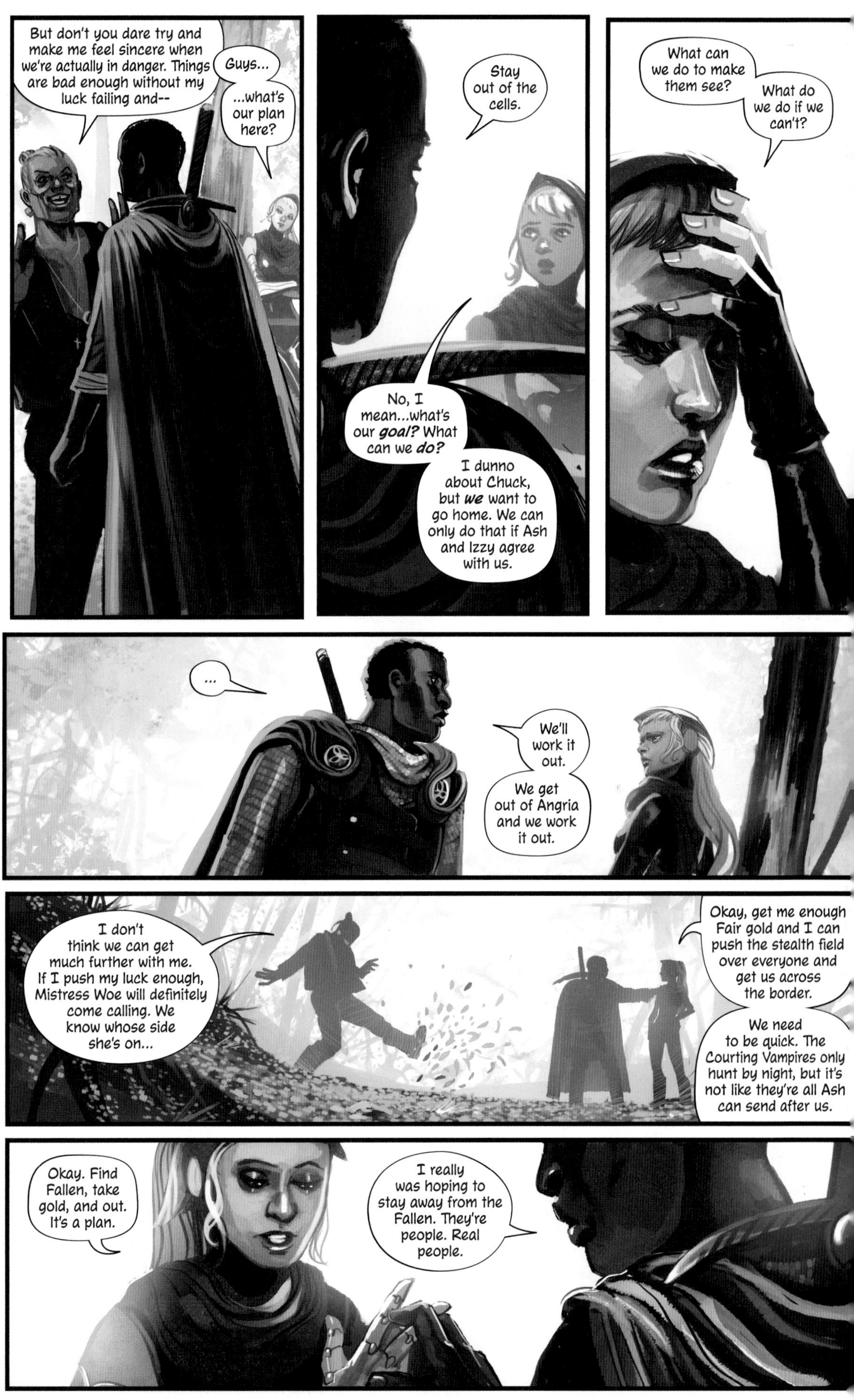
But don't you dare try and make me feel sincere when we're actually in danger. Things are bad enough without my luck failing and--
Guys...
...what's our plan here?
Stay out of the cells.
No, I mean...what's our ***goal?*** What can we ***do?***
I dunno about Chuck, but ***we*** want to go home. We can only do that if Ash and Izzy agree with us.
What can we do to make them see?
What do we do if we can't?
...
We'll work it out.
We get out of Angria and we work it out.
I don't think we can get much further with me. If I push my luck enough, Mistress Woe will definitely come calling. We know whose side she's on...
Okay, get me enough Fair gold and I can push the stealth field over everyone and get us across the border.
We need to be quick. The Courting Vampires only hunt by night, but it's not like they're all Ash can send after us.
Okay. Find Fallen, take gold, and out. It's a plan.
I really was hoping to stay away from the Fallen. They're people. Real people.

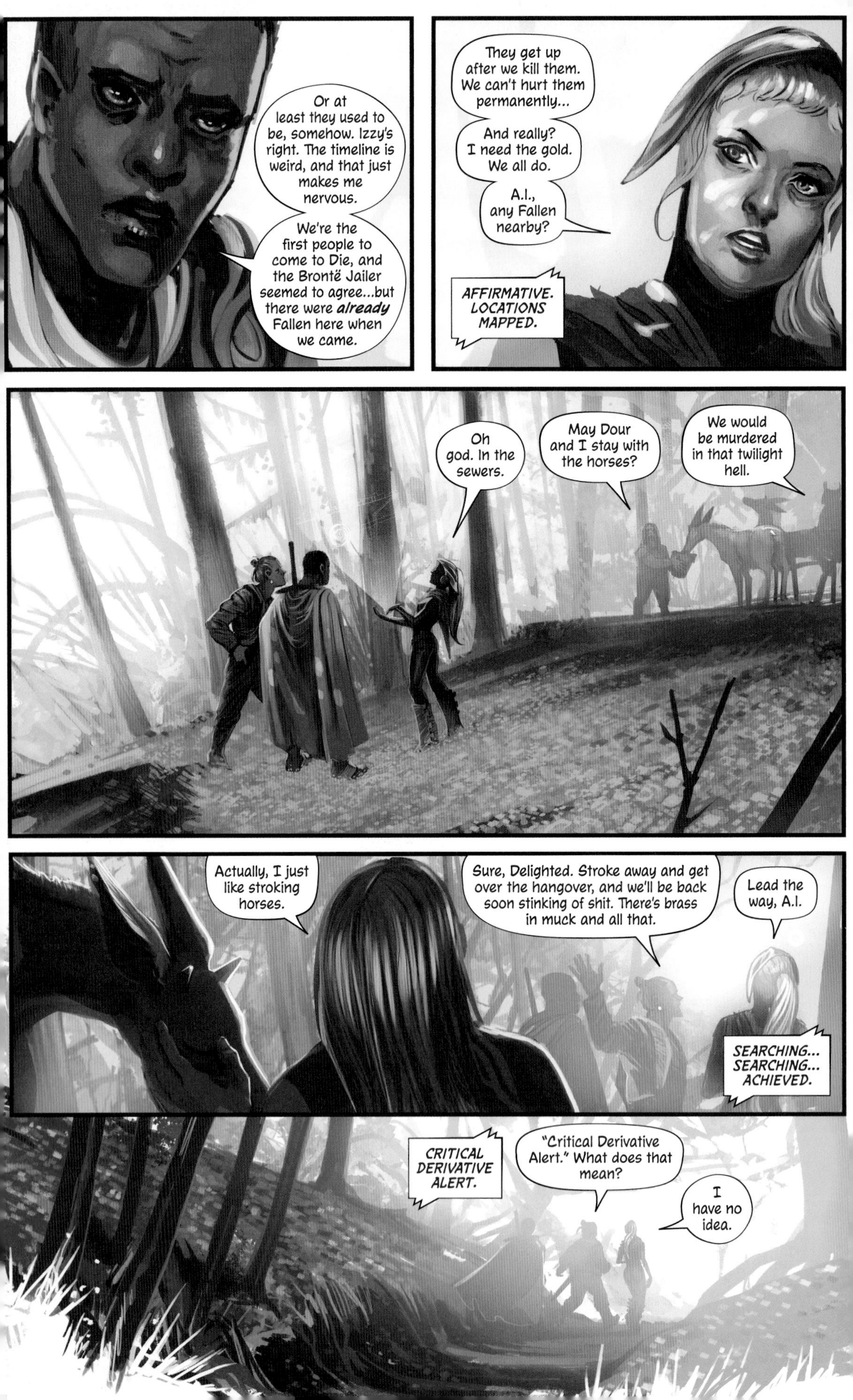
Or at least they used to be, somehow. Izzy's right. The timeline is weird, and that just makes me nervous.
We're the first people to come to Die, and the Brontë Jailer seemed to agree...but there were *already* Fallen here when we came.
They get up after we kill them. We can't hurt them permanently...
And really? I need the gold. We all do.
A.I., any Fallen nearby?
AFFIRMATIVE. LOCATIONS MAPPED.
Oh god. In the sewers.
May Dour and I stay with the horses?
We would be murdered in that twilight hell.
Actually, I just like stroking horses.
Sure, Delighted. Stroke away and get over the hangover, and we'll be back soon stinking of shit. There's brass in muck and all that.
Lead the way, A.I.
SEARCHING... SEARCHING... ACHIEVED.
CRITICAL DERIVATIVE ALERT.
"Critical Derivative Alert." What does that mean?
I have no idea.

You really don't want to ask any questions?

No. I don't. I need a break from that. I just...

Ask *me* something. Don't tell me something. Please.

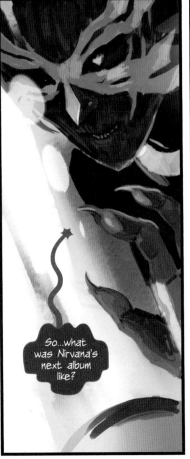

So...what was Nirvana's next album like?

And for a second, I can feel the child I was scream with joy.

Sol asked for my opinion on something.

It was great. It was really dark, but--

And then I remember.

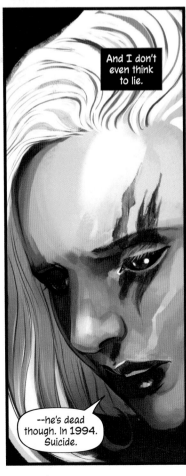

And I don't even think to lie.

--he's dead though. In 1994. Suicide.

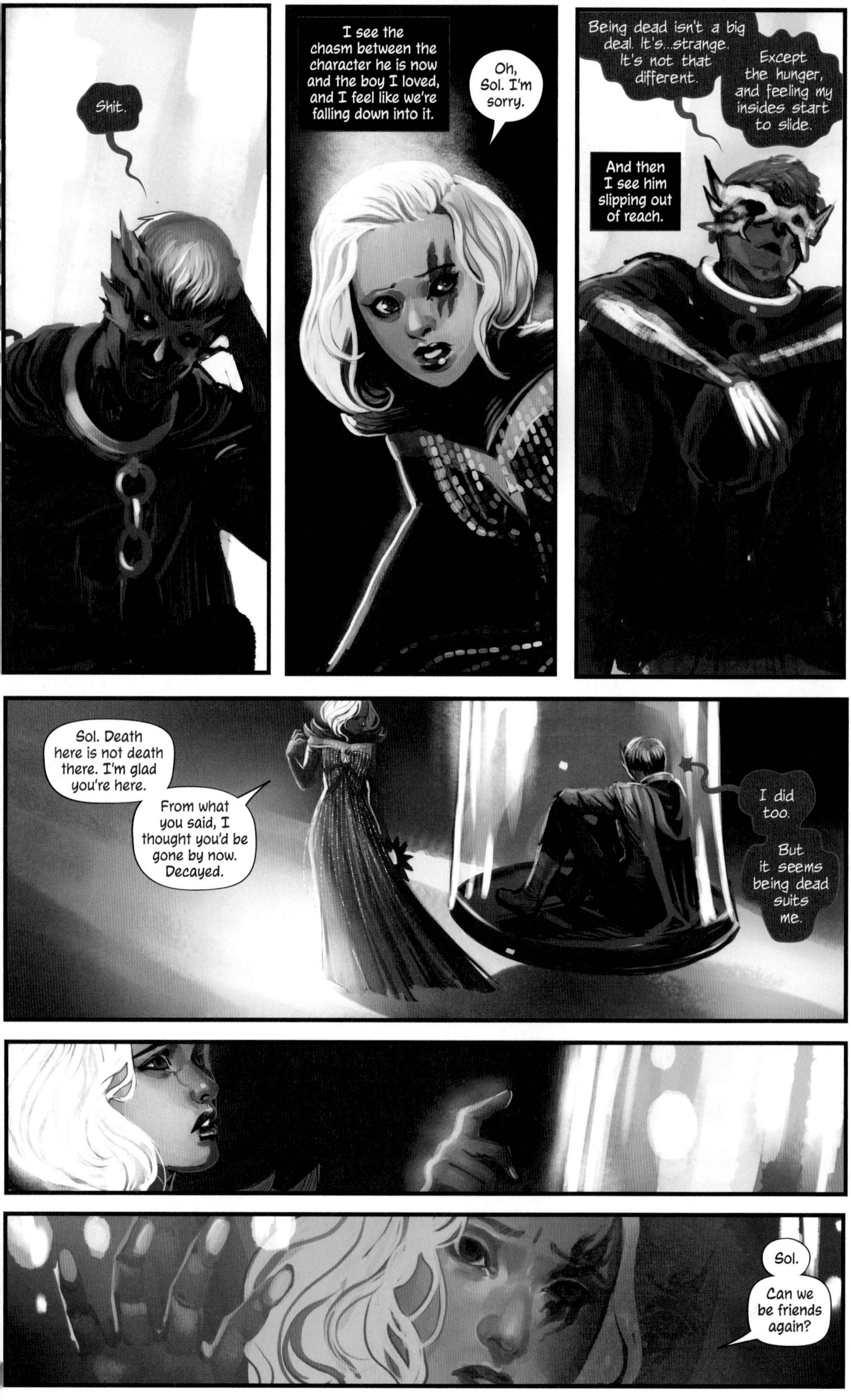
Shit.
I see the chasm between the character he is now and the boy I loved, and I feel like we're falling down into it.
Oh, Sol. I'm sorry.
Being dead isn't a big deal. It's...strange. It's not that different.
Except the hunger, and feeling my insides start to slide.
And then I see him slipping out of reach.
Sol. Death here is not death there. I'm glad you're here.
From what you said, I thought you'd be gone by now. Decayed.
I did too.
But it seems being dead suits me.
Sol.
Can we be friends again?

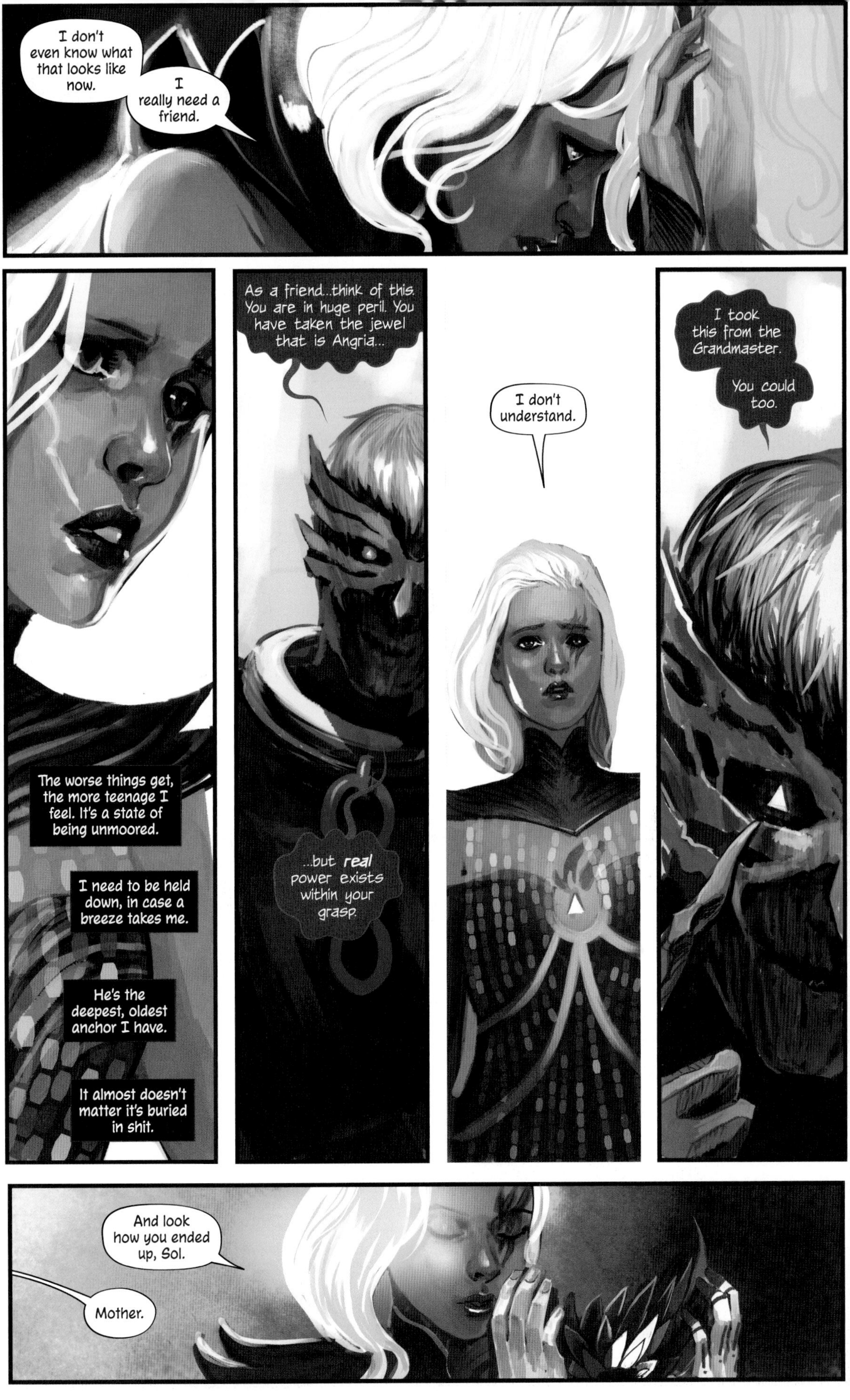
I don't even know what that looks like now.
I really need a friend.
The worse things get, the more teenage I feel. It's a state of being unmoored.
I need to be held down, in case a breeze takes me.
He's the deepest, oldest anchor I have.
It almost doesn't matter it's buried in shit.
As a friend...think of this. You are in huge peril. You have taken the jewel that is Angria...
...but **real** power exists within your grasp.
I don't understand.
I took this from the Grandmaster.
You could too.
And look how you ended up, Sol.
Mother.

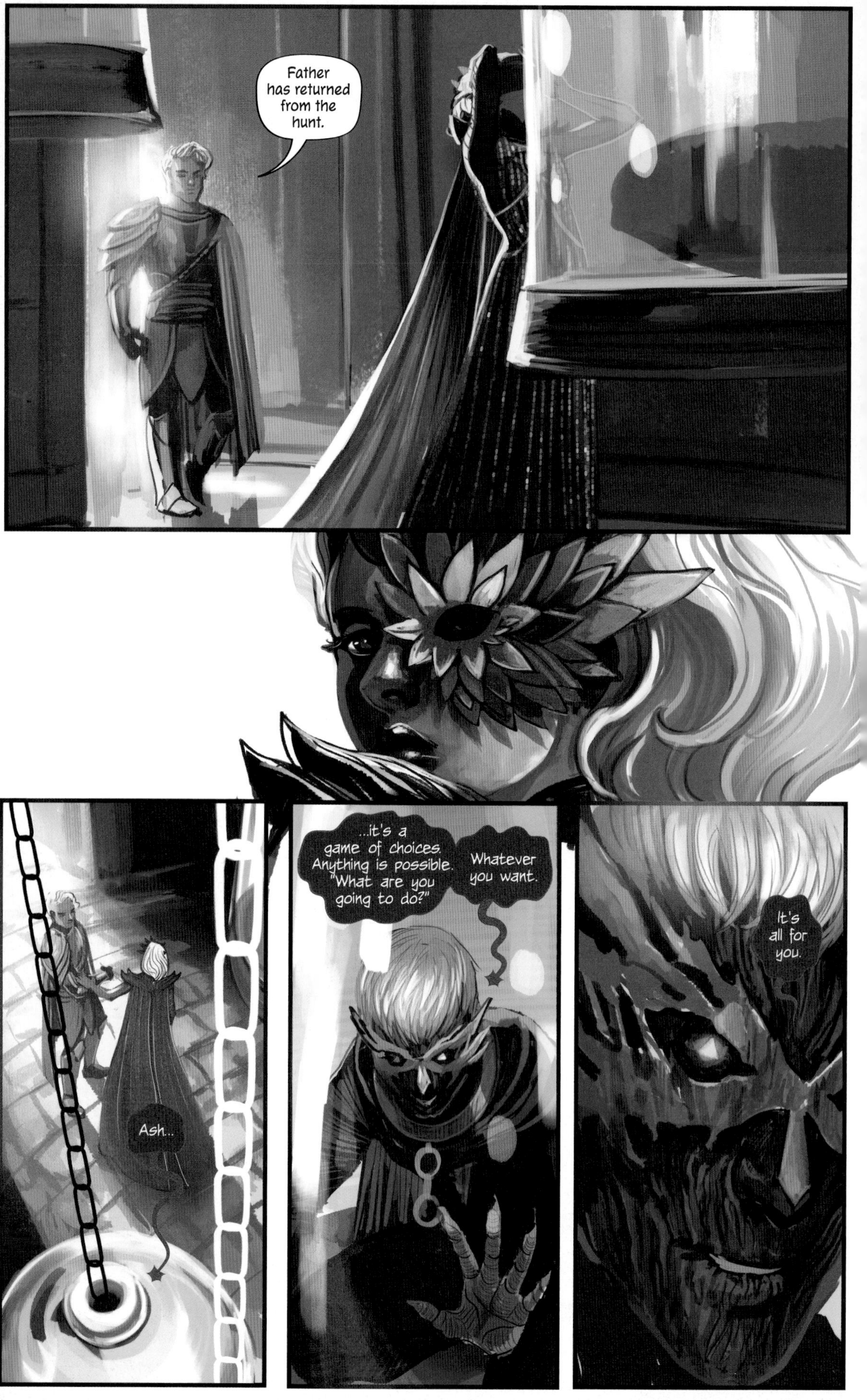
Father has returned from the hunt.
Ash...
...it's a game of choices. Anything is possible. "What are you going to do?"
Whatever you want.
It's all for you.

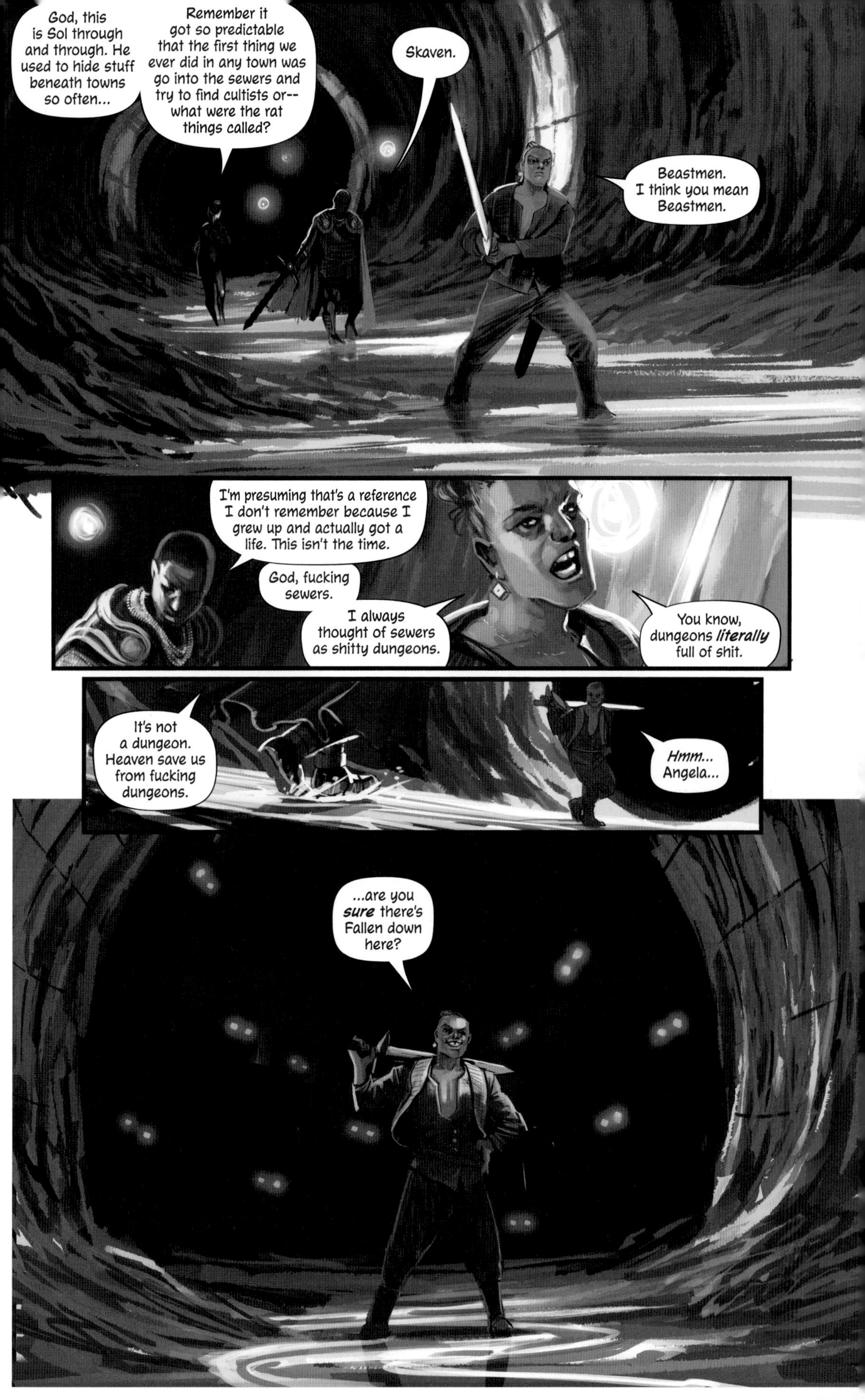
God, this is Sol through and through. He used to hide stuff beneath towns so often...
Remember it got so predictable that the first thing we ever did in any town was go into the sewers and try to find cultists or-- what were the rat things called?
Skaven.
Beastmen. I think you mean Beastmen.
I'm presuming that's a reference I don't remember because I grew up and actually got a life. This isn't the time.
God, fucking sewers.
I always thought of sewers as shitty dungeons.
You know, dungeons *literally* full of shit.
It's not a dungeon. Heaven save us from fucking dungeons.
Hmm... Angela...
...are you *sure* there's Fallen down here?

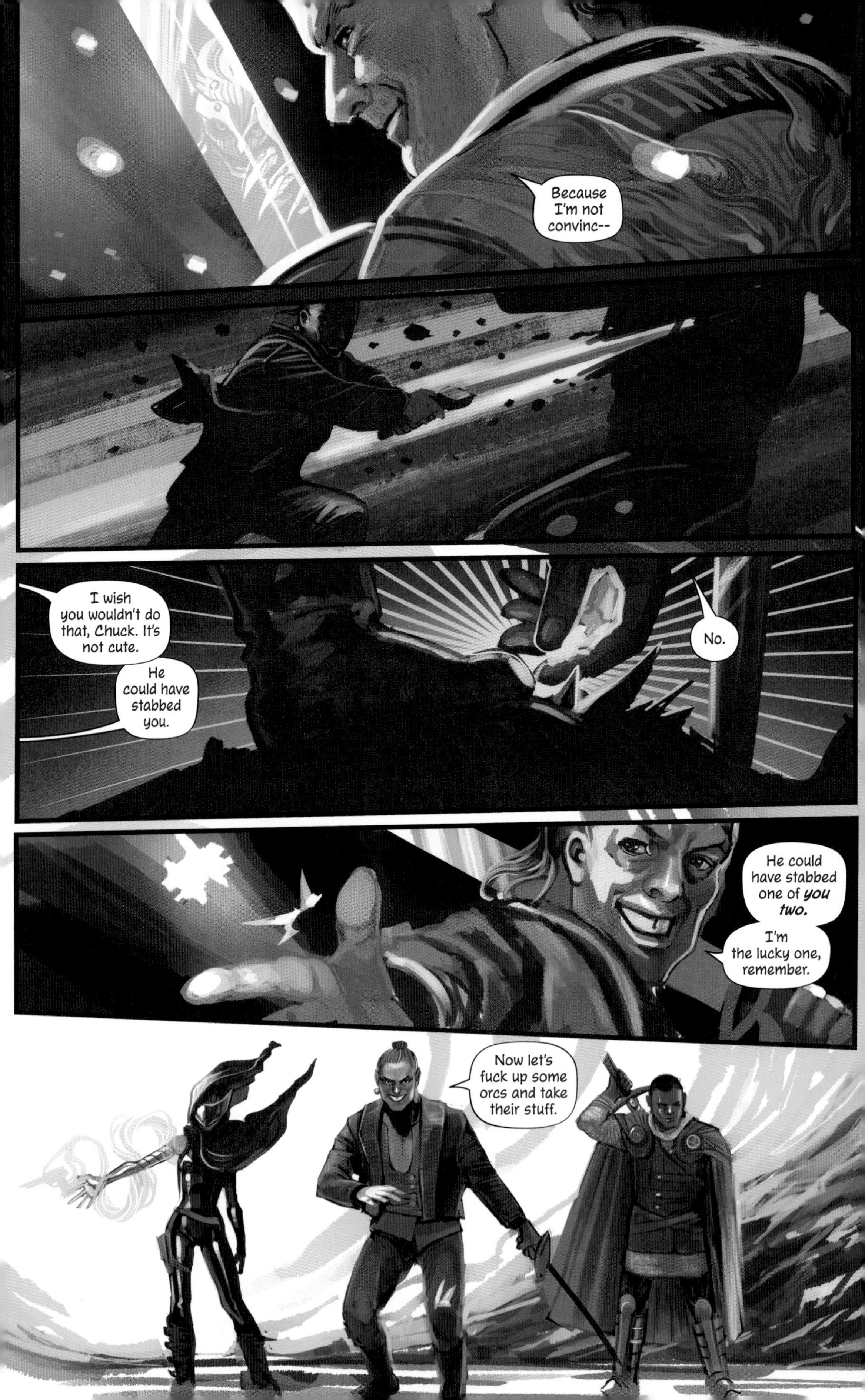
Because I'm not convinc--
I wish you wouldn't do that, Chuck. It's not cute.
He could have stabbed you.
No.
He could have stabbed one of ***you two.***
I'm the lucky one, remember.
Now let's fuck up some orcs and take their stuff.

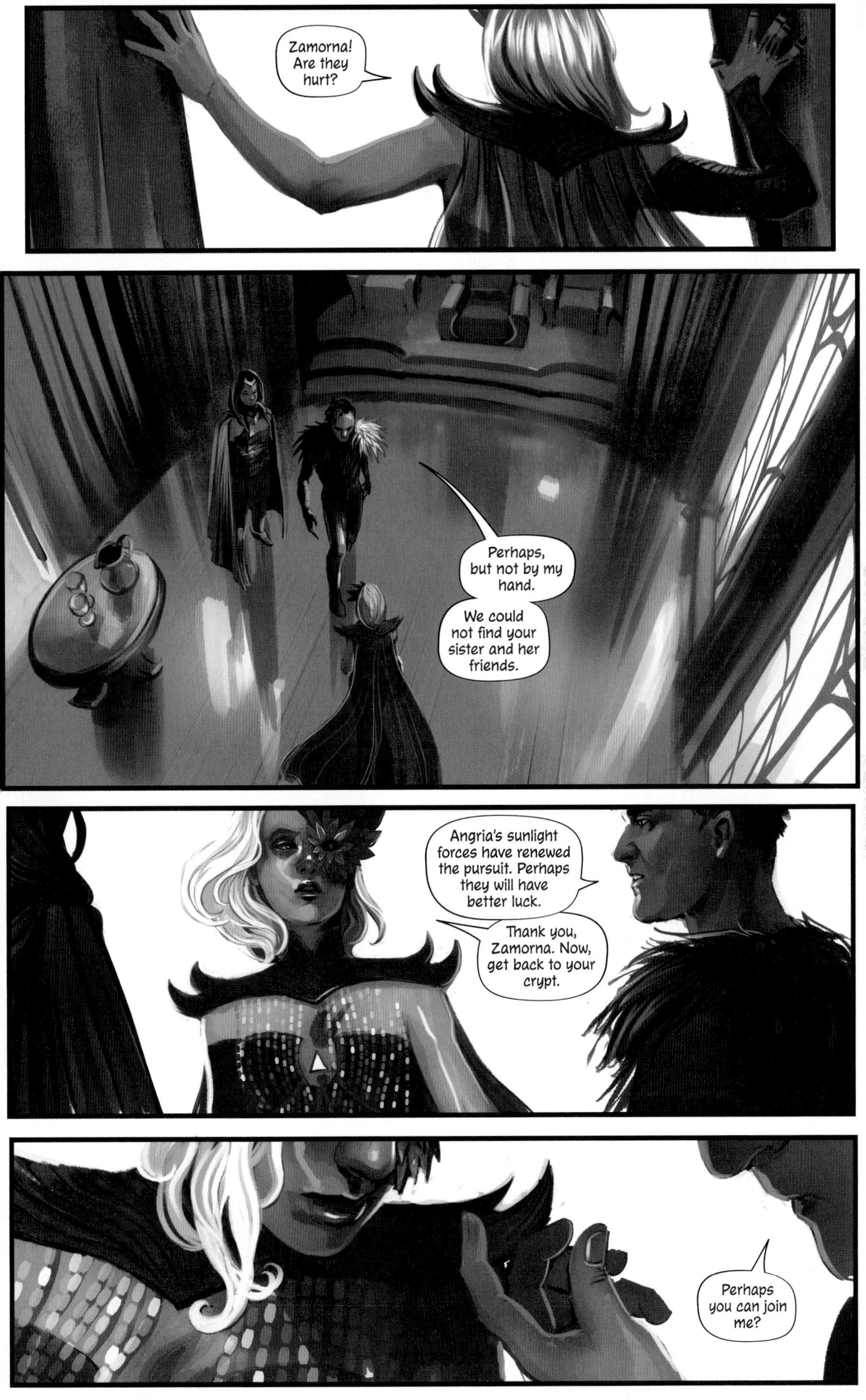
Zamorna! Are they hurt?
Perhaps, but not by my hand.
We could not find your sister and her friends.
Angria's sunlight forces have renewed the pursuit. Perhaps they will have better luck.
Thank you, Zamorna. Now, get back to your crypt.
Perhaps you can join me?

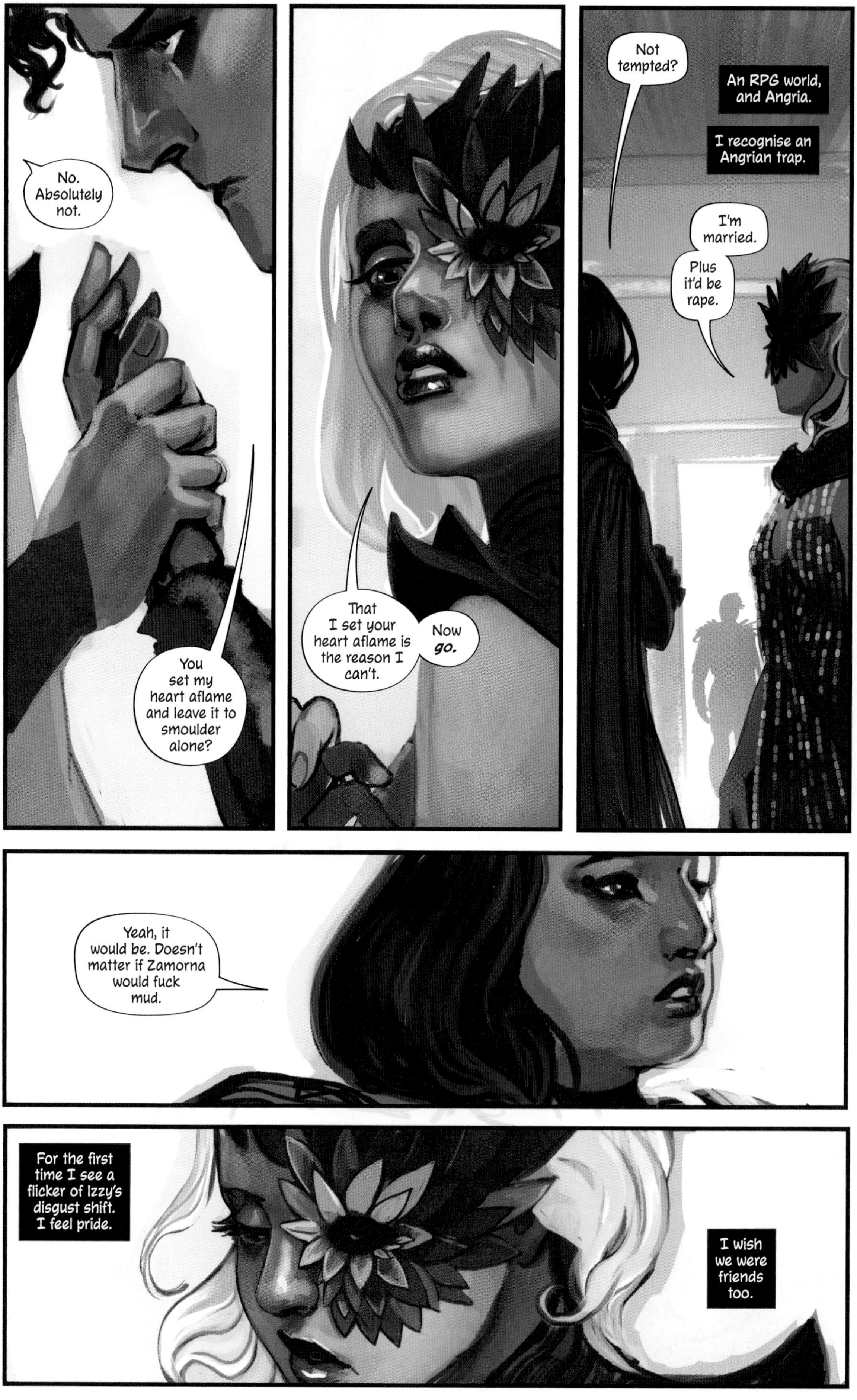
No. Absolutely not.
You set my heart aflame and leave it to smoulder alone?
That I set your heart aflame is the reason I can't.
Now *go.*
Not tempted?
An RPG world, and Angria.
I recognise an Angrian trap.
I'm married.
Plus it'd be rape.
Yeah, it would be. Doesn't matter if Zamorna would fuck mud.
For the first time I see a flicker of Izzy's disgust shift. I feel pride.
I wish we were friends too.

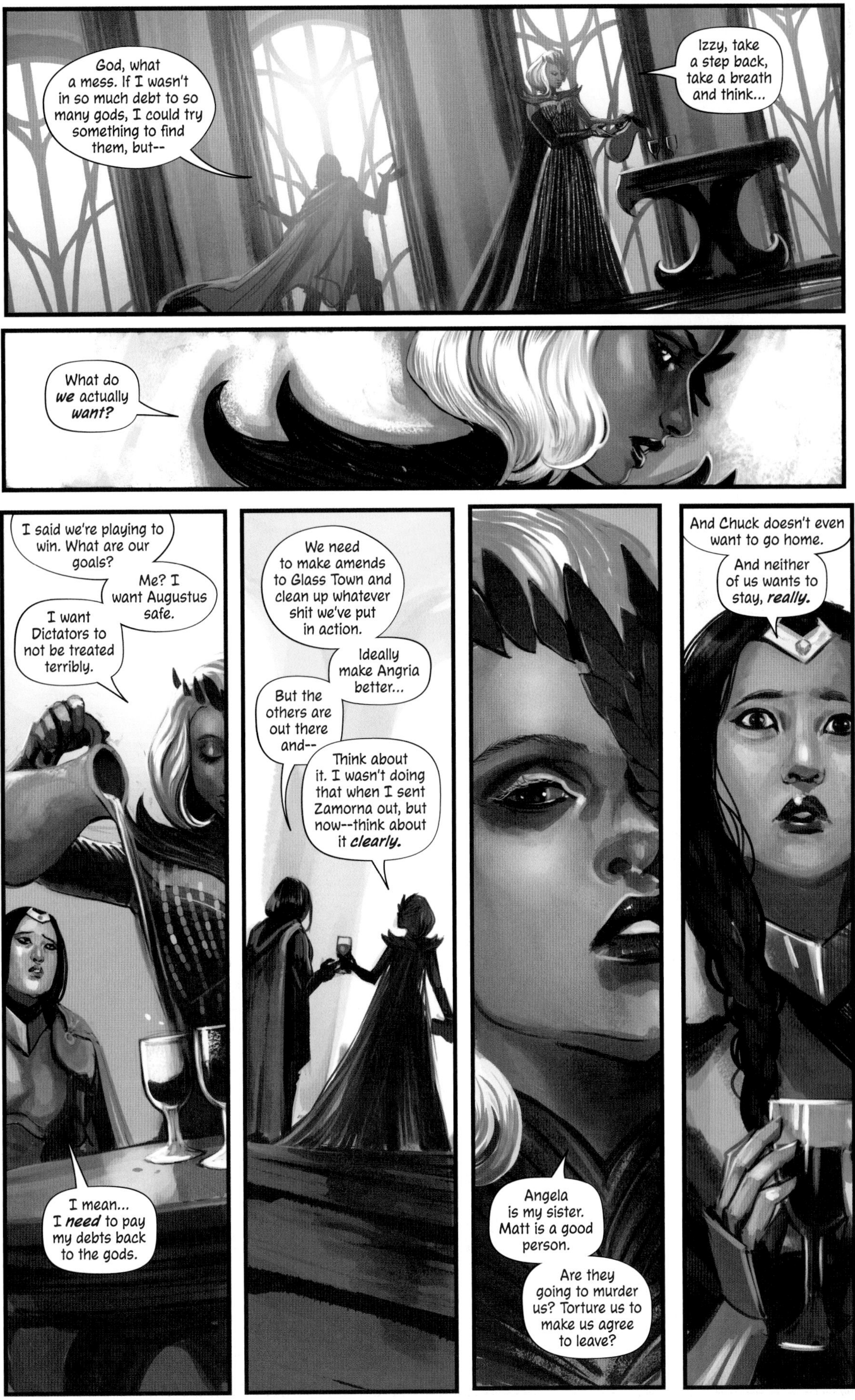
God, what a mess. If I wasn't in so much debt to so many gods, I could try something to find them, but--
Izzy, take a step back, take a breath and think...
What do *we* actually *want?*
I said we're playing to win. What are our goals?
Me? I want Augustus safe.
I want Dictators to not be treated terribly.
I mean... I *need* to pay my debts back to the gods.
We need to make amends to Glass Town and clean up whatever shit we've put in action.
Ideally make Angria better...
But the others are out there and--
Think about it. I wasn't doing that when I sent Zamorna out, but now--think about it *clearly.*
Angela is my sister. Matt is a good person.
Are they going to murder us? Torture us to make us agree to leave?
And Chuck doesn't even want to go home.
And neither of us wants to stay, *really.*

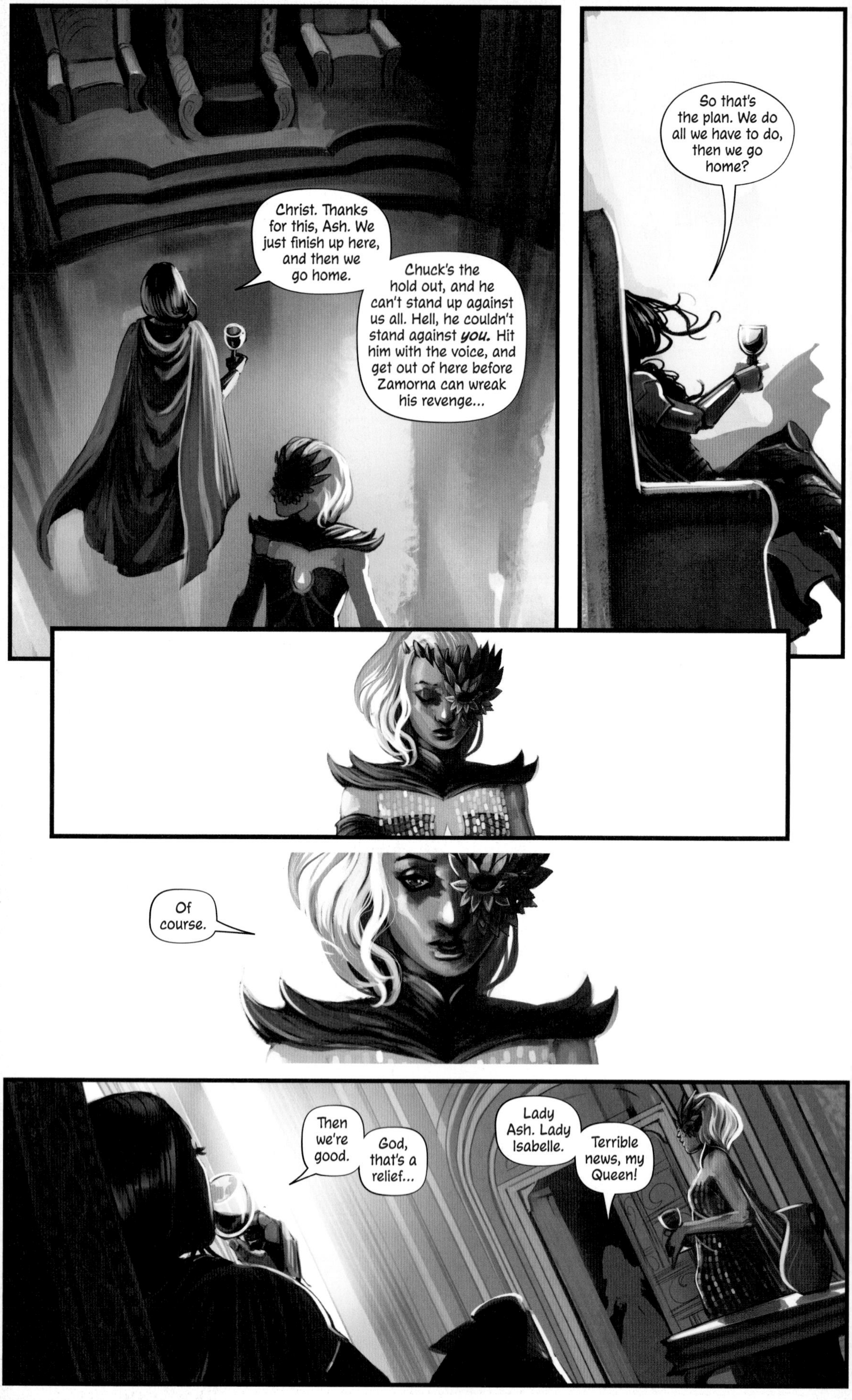
Christ. Thanks for this, Ash. We just finish up here, and then we go home.
Chuck's the hold out, and he can't stand up against us all. Hell, he couldn't stand against ***you.*** Hit him with the voice, and get out of here before Zamorna can wreak his revenge...
So that's the plan. We do all we have to do, then we go home?
Of course.
Then we're good.
God, that's a relief...
Lady Ash. Lady Isabelle.
Terrible news, my Queen!

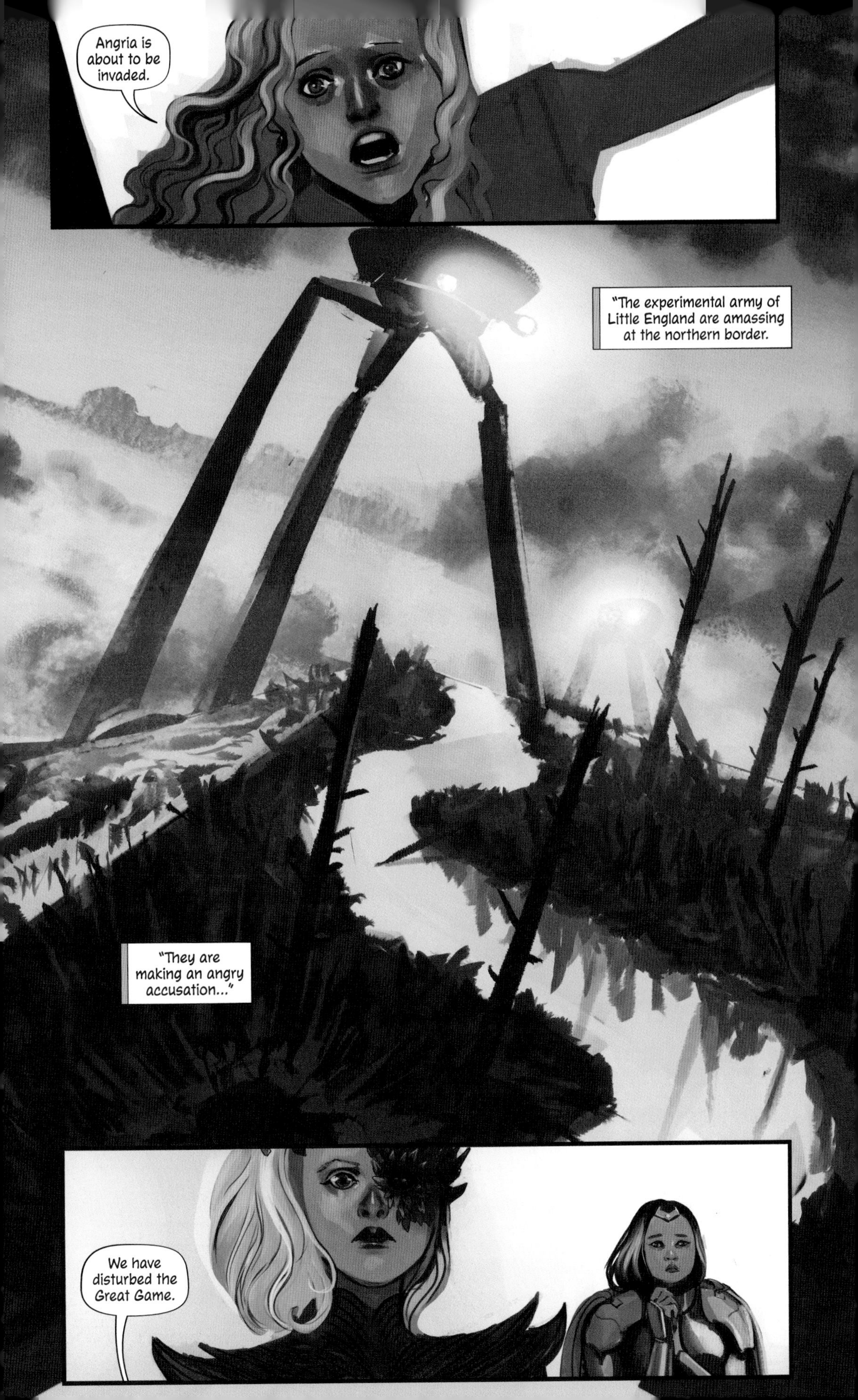
Angria is about to be invaded.
"The experimental army of Little England are amassing at the northern border.
"They are making an angry accusation..."
We have disturbed the Great Game.

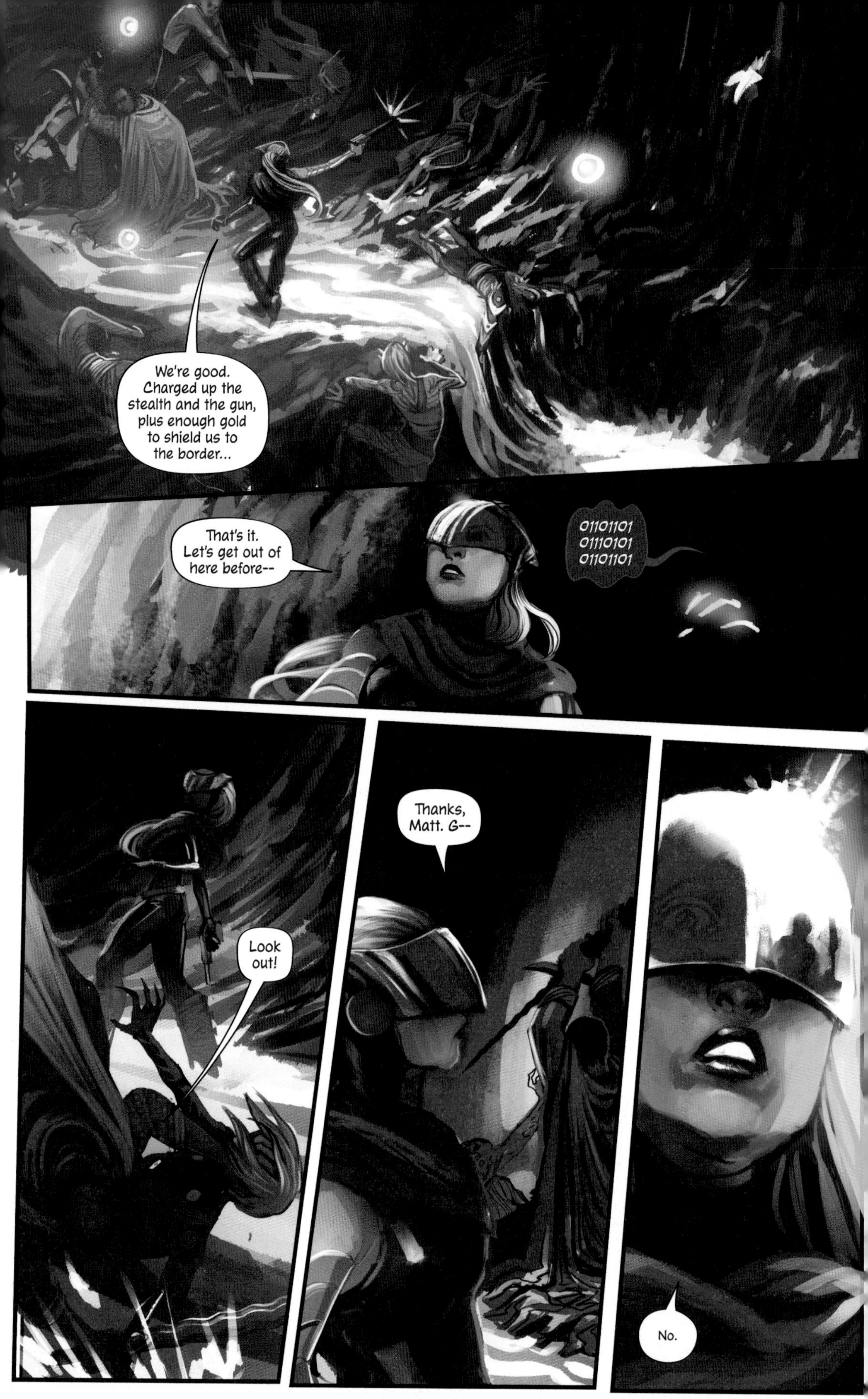
We're good. Charged up the stealth and the gun, plus enough gold to shield us to the border...
That's it. Let's get out of here before--
01101101 01110101 01101101
Look out!
Thanks, Matt. G--
No.

Angela?

Fucking hell, Angela!

Please, please, it can't be.

01101101
01110101
01101101

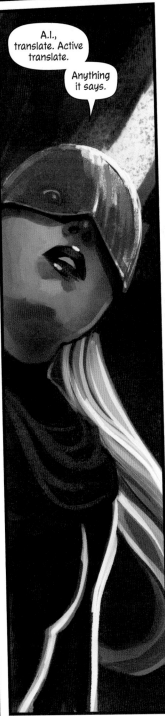

A.I., translate. Active translate.

Anything it says.

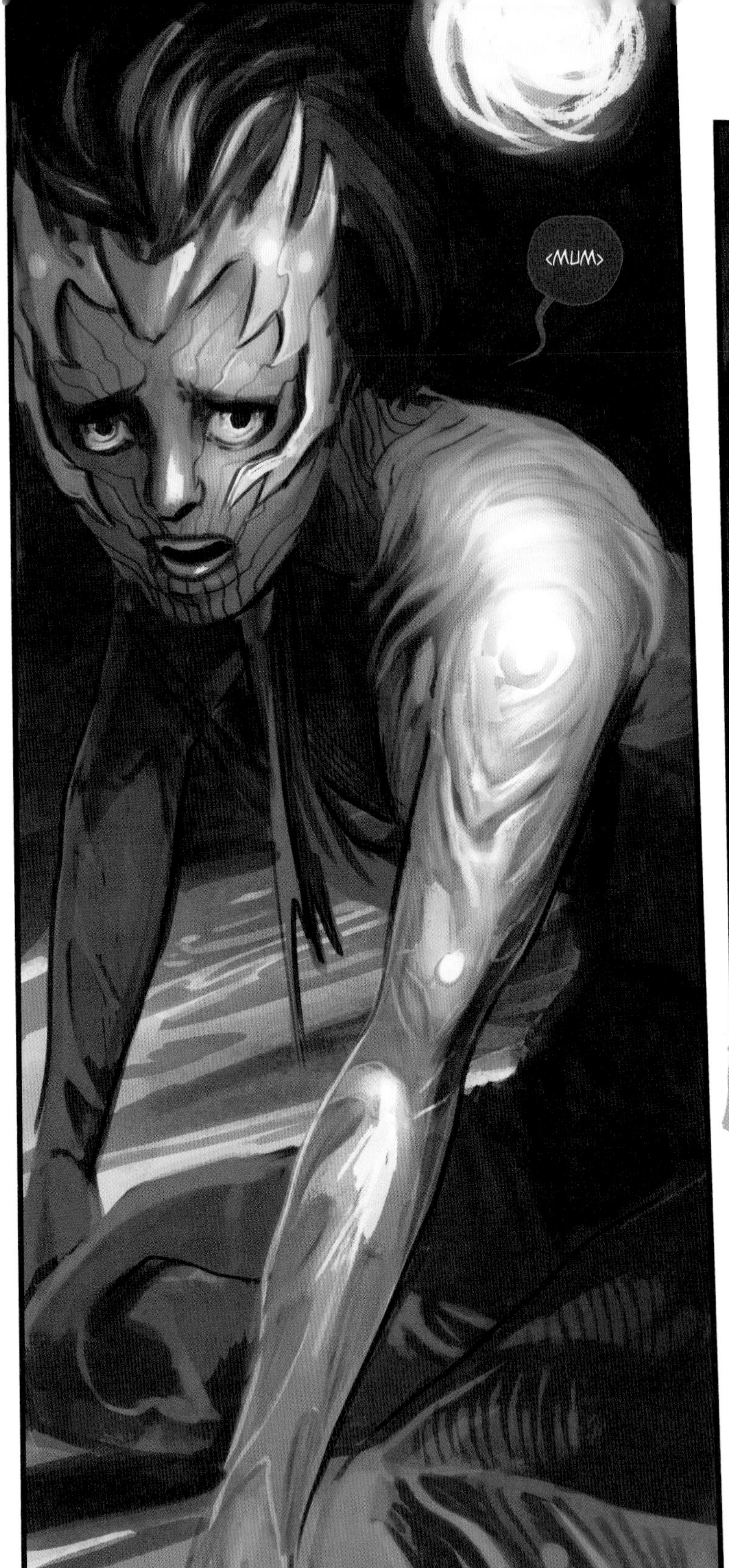
<MUM>

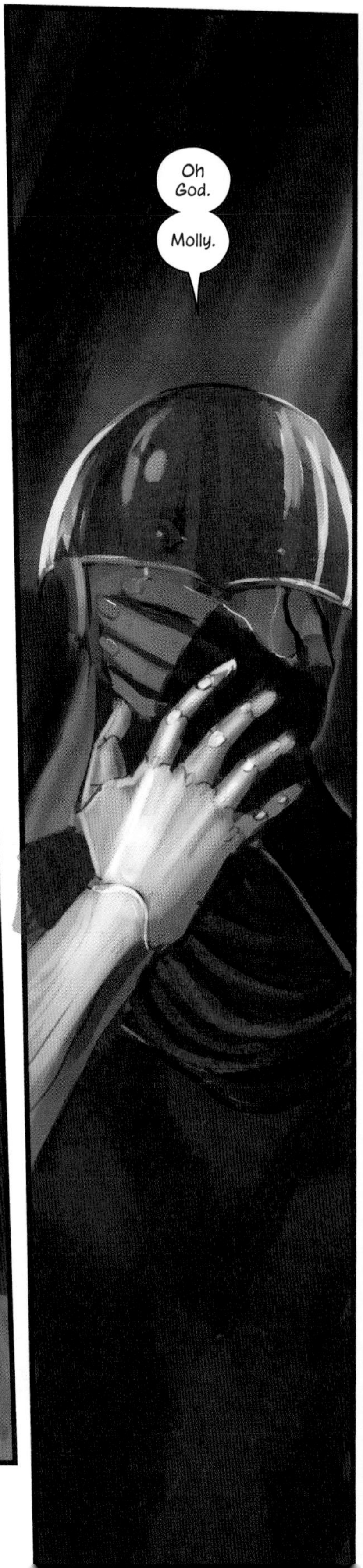
Oh God.
Molly.

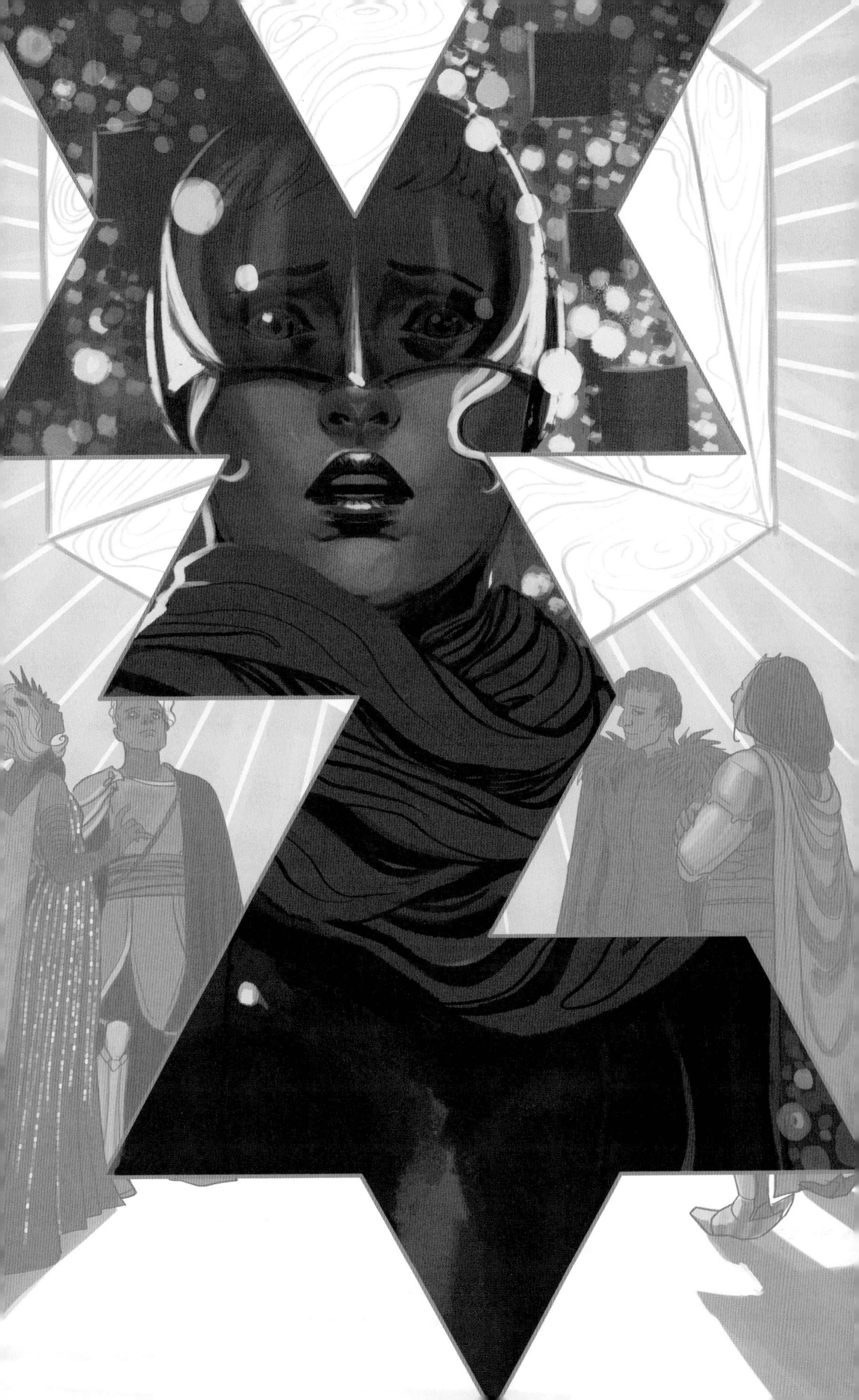

12:
HIDDEN
ROLE

"I wouldn't mind being a Pawn ... though of course I should like to be a Queen, best."
– *Lewis Carroll*, Through the Looking-Glass

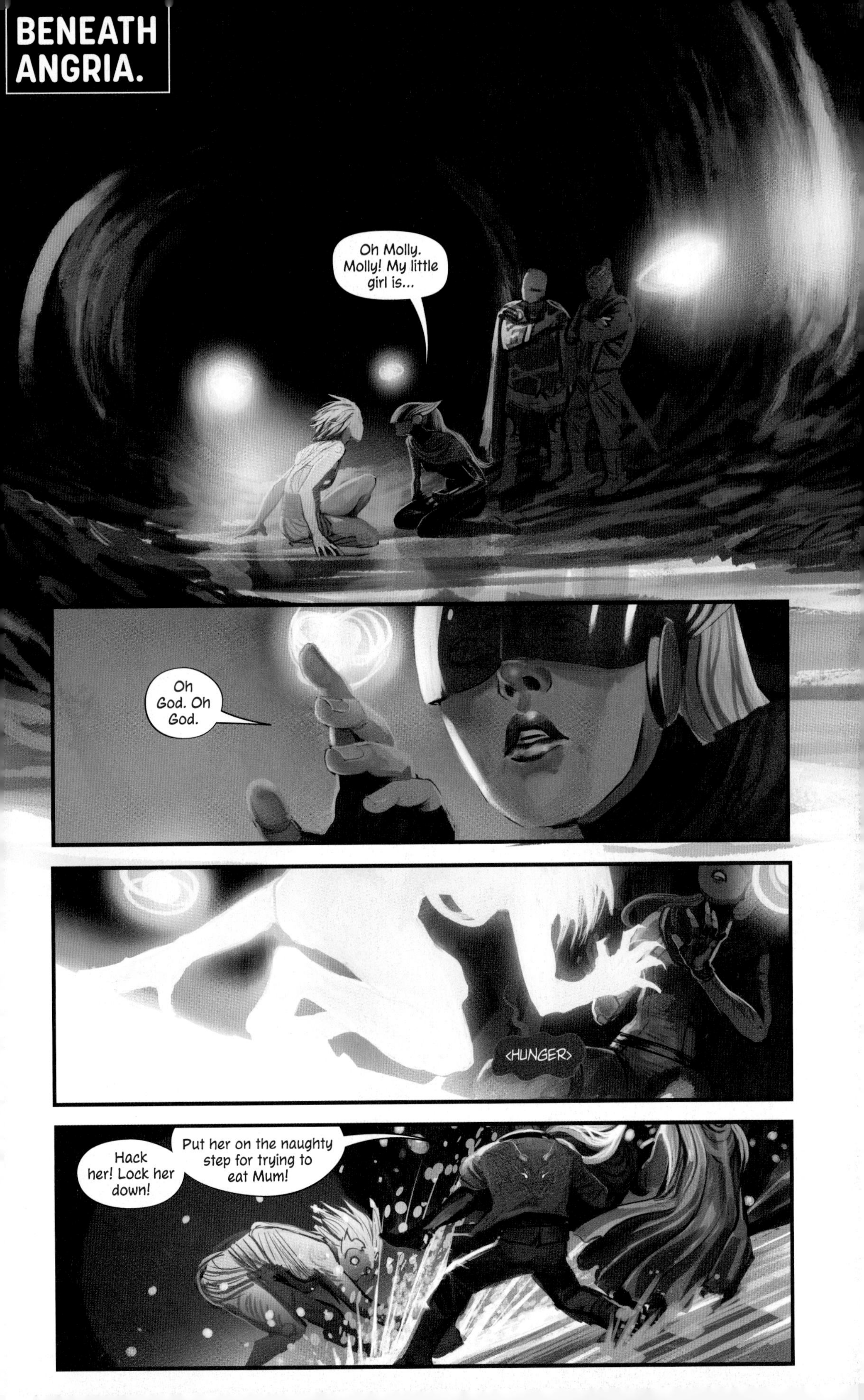
BENEATH ANGRIA.
Oh Molly. Molly! My little girl is...
Oh God. Oh God.
<HUNGER>
Hack her! Lock her down!
Put her on the naughty step for trying to eat Mum!

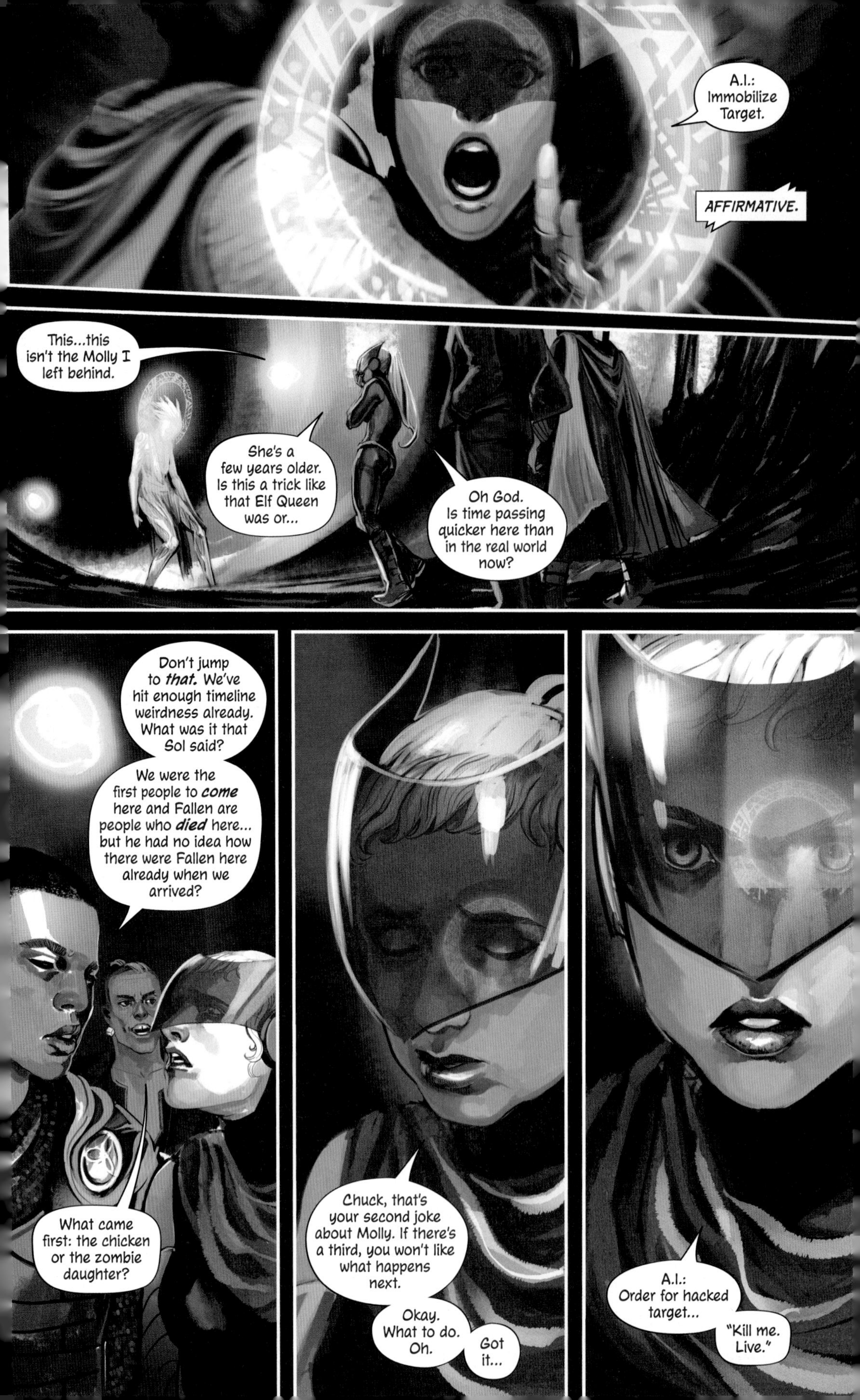
A.I.: Immobilize Target.
AFFIRMATIVE.
This...this isn't the Molly I left behind.
She's a few years older. Is this a trick like that Elf Queen was or...
Oh God. Is time passing quicker here than in the real world now?
Don't jump to *that.* We've hit enough timeline weirdness already. What was it that Sol said?
We were the first people to *come* here and Fallen are people who *died* here... but he had no idea how there were Fallen here already when we arrived?
What came first: the chicken or the zombie daughter?
Chuck, that's your second joke about Molly. If there's a third, you won't like what happens next.
Okay. What to do. Oh.
Got it...
A.I.: Order for hacked target...
"Kill me. Live."

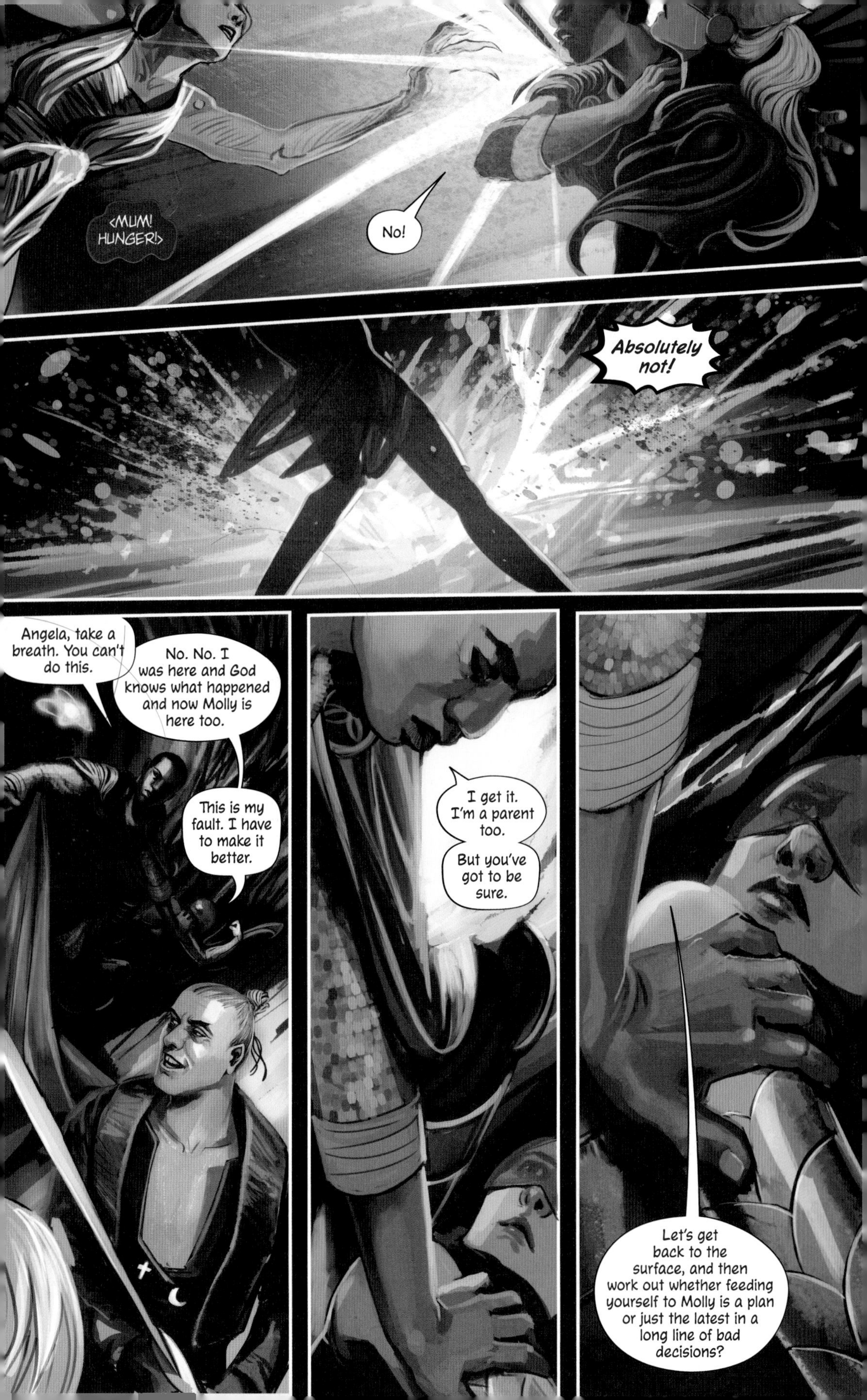
<MUM! HUNGER!>
No!
Absolutely not!
Angela, take a breath. You can't do this.
No. No. I was here and God knows what happened and now Molly is here too.
This is my fault. I have to make it better.
I get it. I'm a parent too.
But you've got to be sure.
Let's get back to the surface, and then work out whether feeding yourself to Molly is a plan or just the latest in a long line of bad decisions?

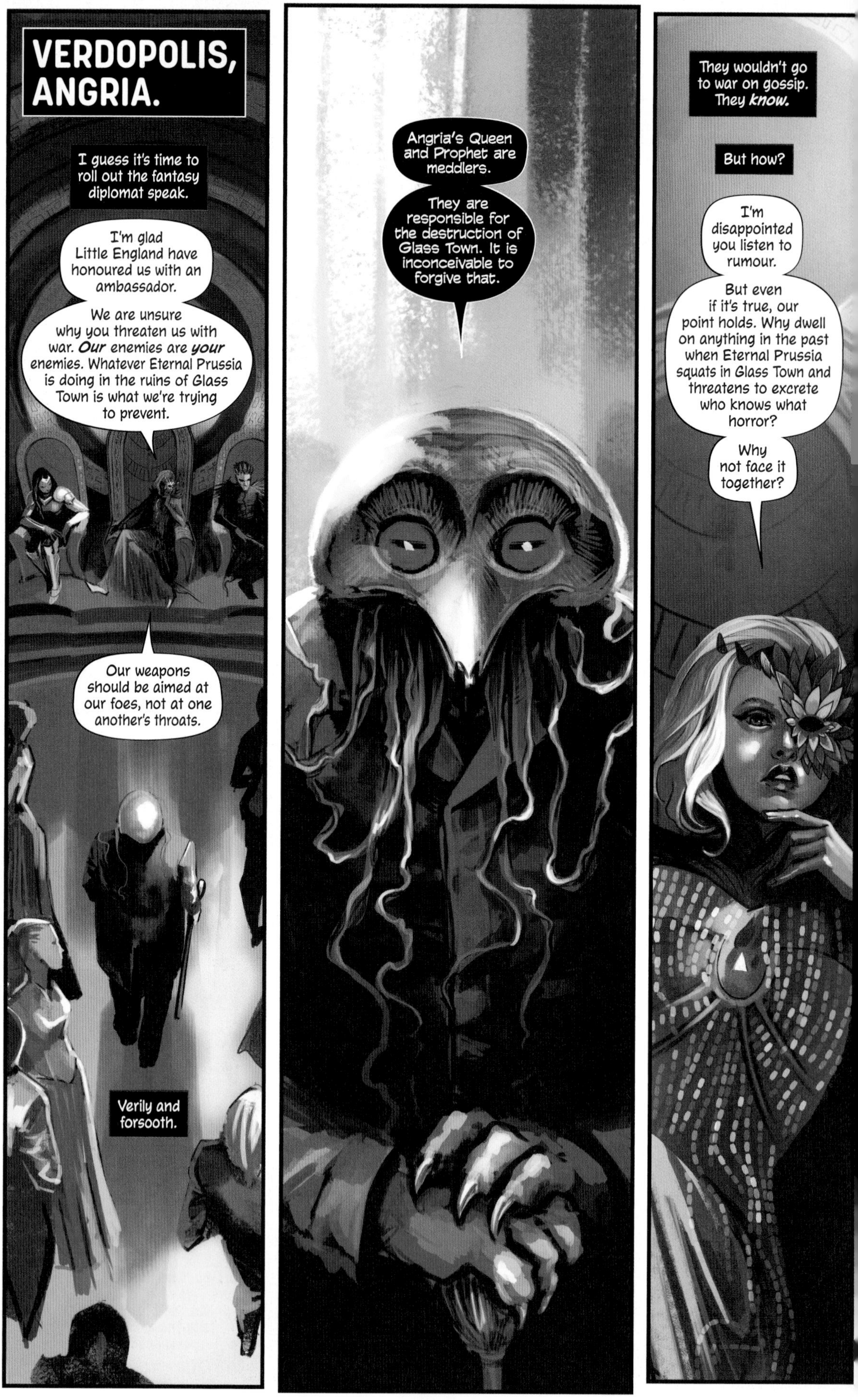
VERDOPOLIS, ANGRIA.
I guess it's time to roll out the fantasy diplomat speak.
I'm glad Little England have honoured us with an ambassador.
We are unsure why you threaten us with war. Our enemies are your enemies. Whatever Eternal Prussia is doing in the ruins of Glass Town is what we're trying to prevent.
Our weapons should be aimed at our foes, not at one another's throats.
Verily and forsooth.
Angria's Queen and Prophet are meddlers.
They are responsible for the destruction of Glass Town. It is inconceivable to forgive that.
They wouldn't go to war on gossip. They know.
But how?
I'm disappointed you listen to rumour.
But even if it's true, our point holds. Why dwell on anything in the past when Eternal Prussia squats in Glass Town and threatens to excrete who knows what horror?
Why not face it together?

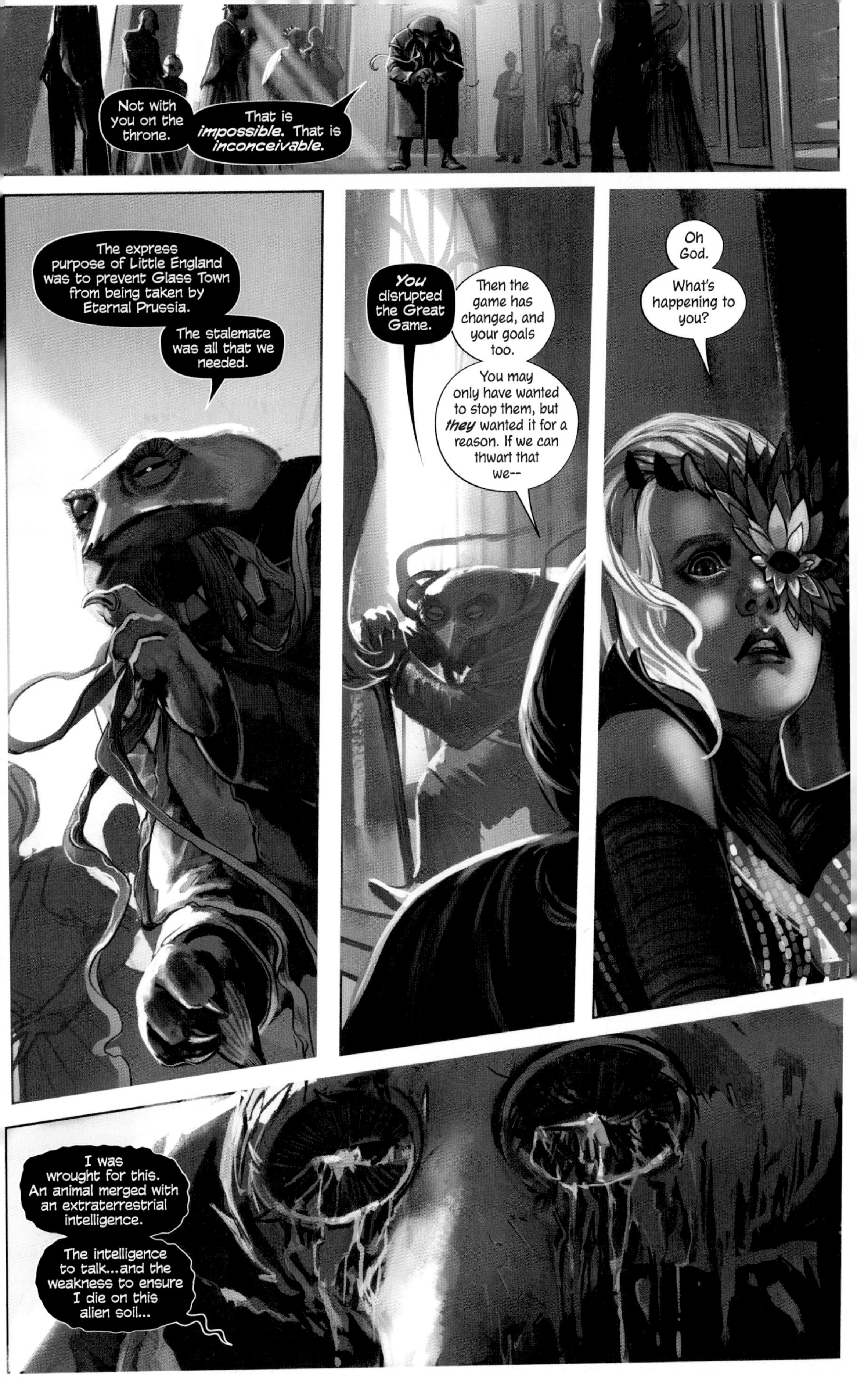
Not with you on the throne.
That is *impossible.* That is *inconceivable.*
The express purpose of Little England was to prevent Glass Town from being taken by Eternal Prussia.
The stalemate was all that we needed.
You disrupted the Great Game.
Then the game has changed, and your goals too.
You may only have wanted to stop them, but *they* wanted it for a reason. If we can thwart that we--
Oh God.
What's happening to you?
I was wrought for this. An animal merged with an extraterrestrial intelligence.
The intelligence to talk...and the weakness to ensure I die on this alien soil...

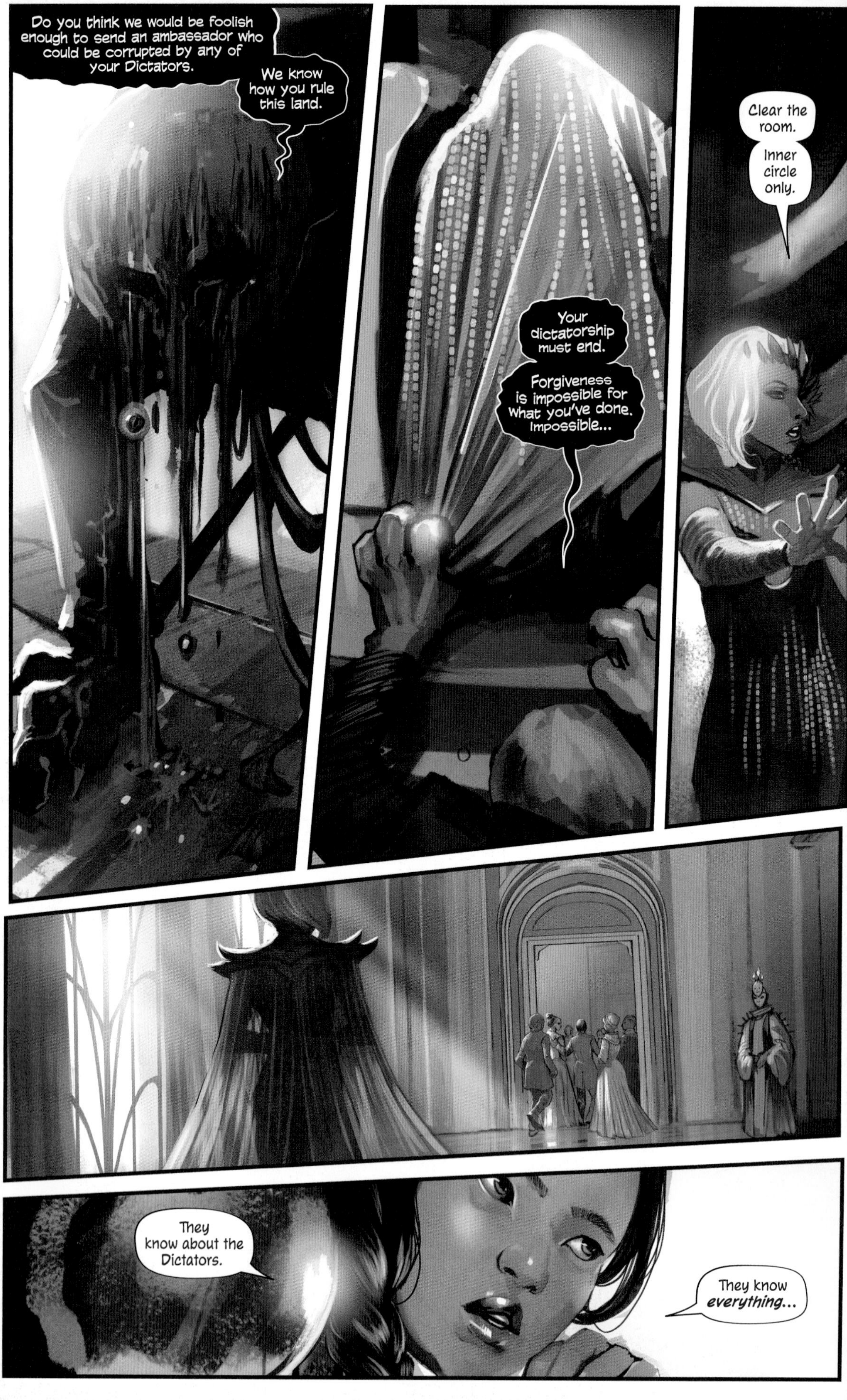
Do you think we would be foolish enough to send an ambassador who could be corrupted by any of your Dictators.
We know how you rule this land.
Your dictatorship must end.
Forgiveness is impossible for what you've done. Impossible...
Clear the room.
Inner circle only.
They know about the Dictators.
They know *everything...*

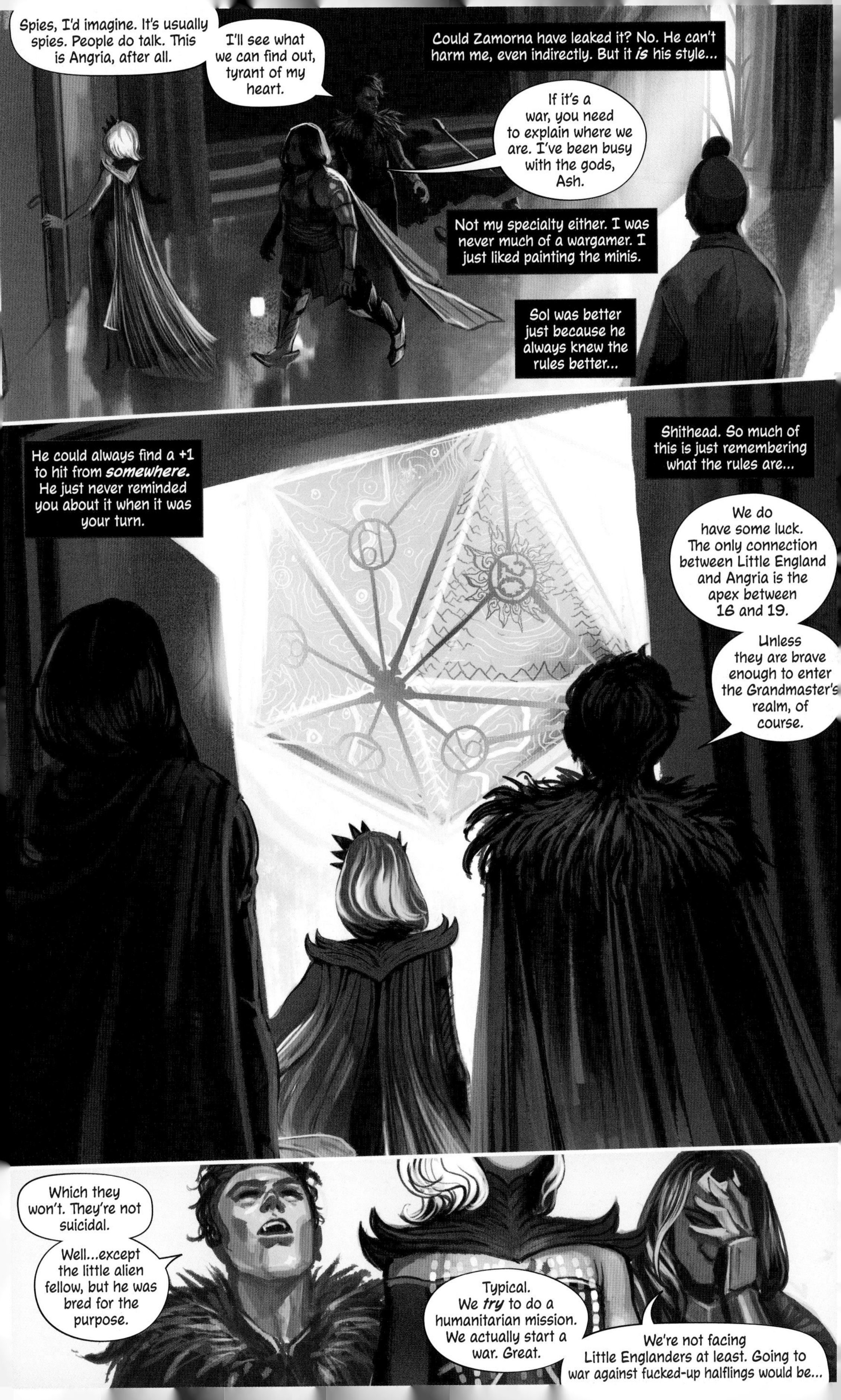

Spies, I'd imagine. It's usually spies. People do talk. This is Angria, after all.
I'll see what we can find out, tyrant of my heart.
Could Zamorna have leaked it? No. He can't harm me, even indirectly. But it *is* his style...
If it's a war, you need to explain where we are. I've been busy with the gods, Ash.
Not my specialty either. I was never much of a wargamer. I just liked painting the minis.
Sol was better just because he always knew the rules better...
He could always find a +1 to hit from ***somewhere.*** He just never reminded you about it when it was your turn.
Shithead. So much of this is just remembering what the rules are...
We do have some luck. The only connection between Little England and Angria is the apex between 16 and 19.
Unless they are brave enough to enter the Grandmaster's realm, of course.
Which they won't. They're not suicidal.
Well...except the little alien fellow, but he was bred for the purpose.
Typical. We *try* to do a humanitarian mission. We actually start a war. Great.
We're not facing Little Englanders at least. Going to war against fucked-up halflings would be...

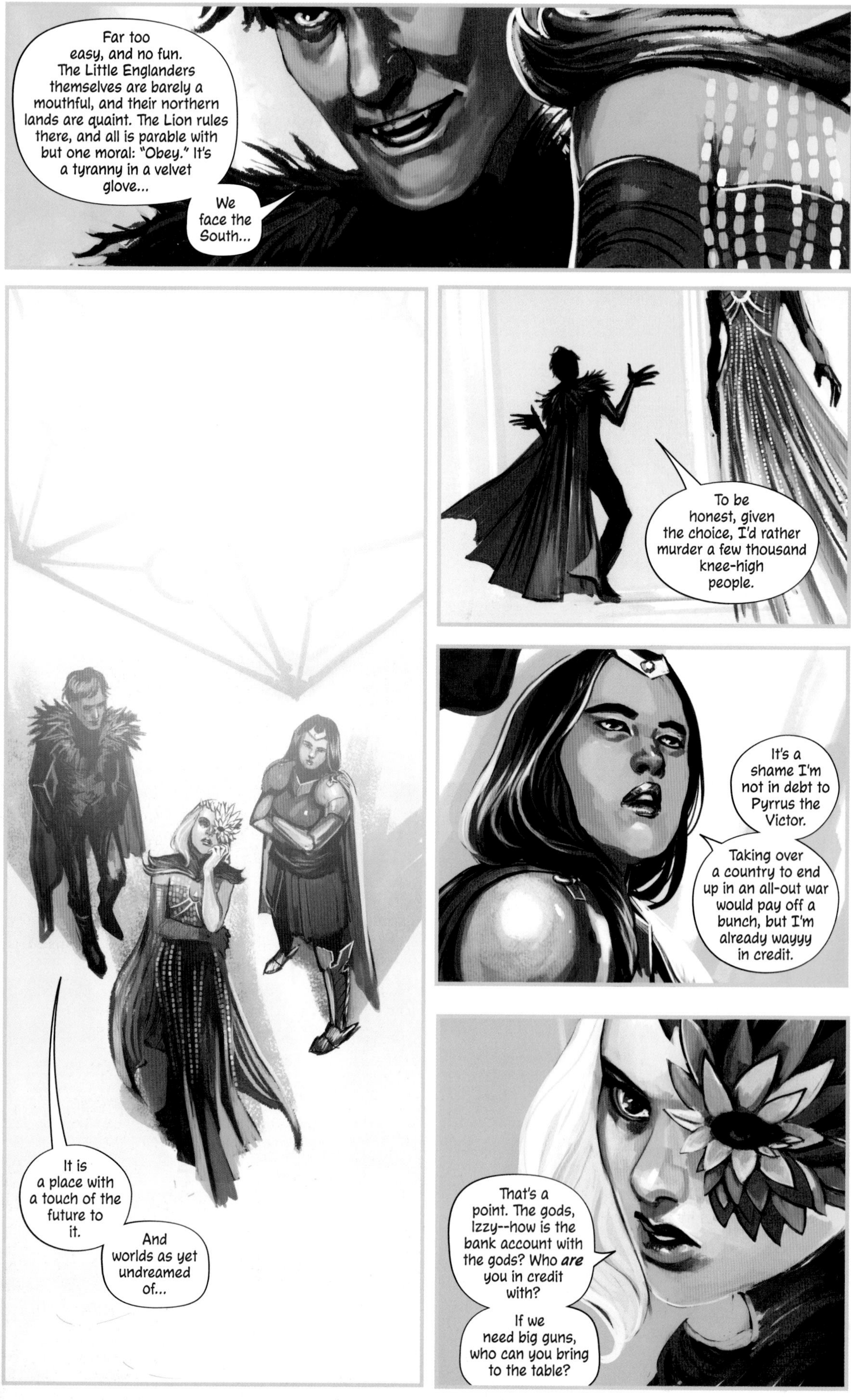
Far too easy, and no fun. The Little Englanders themselves are barely a mouthful, and their northern lands are quaint. The Lion rules there, and all is parable with but one moral: "Obey." It's a tyranny in a velvet glove...
We face the South...
It is a place with a touch of the future to it.
And worlds as yet undreamed of...
To be honest, given the choice, I'd rather murder a few thousand knee-high people.
It's a shame I'm not in debt to Pyrrus the Victor.
Taking over a country to end up in an all-out war would pay off a bunch, but I'm already wayyy in credit.
That's a point. The gods, Izzy--how is the bank account with the gods? Who *are* you in credit with?
If we need big guns, who can you bring to the table?

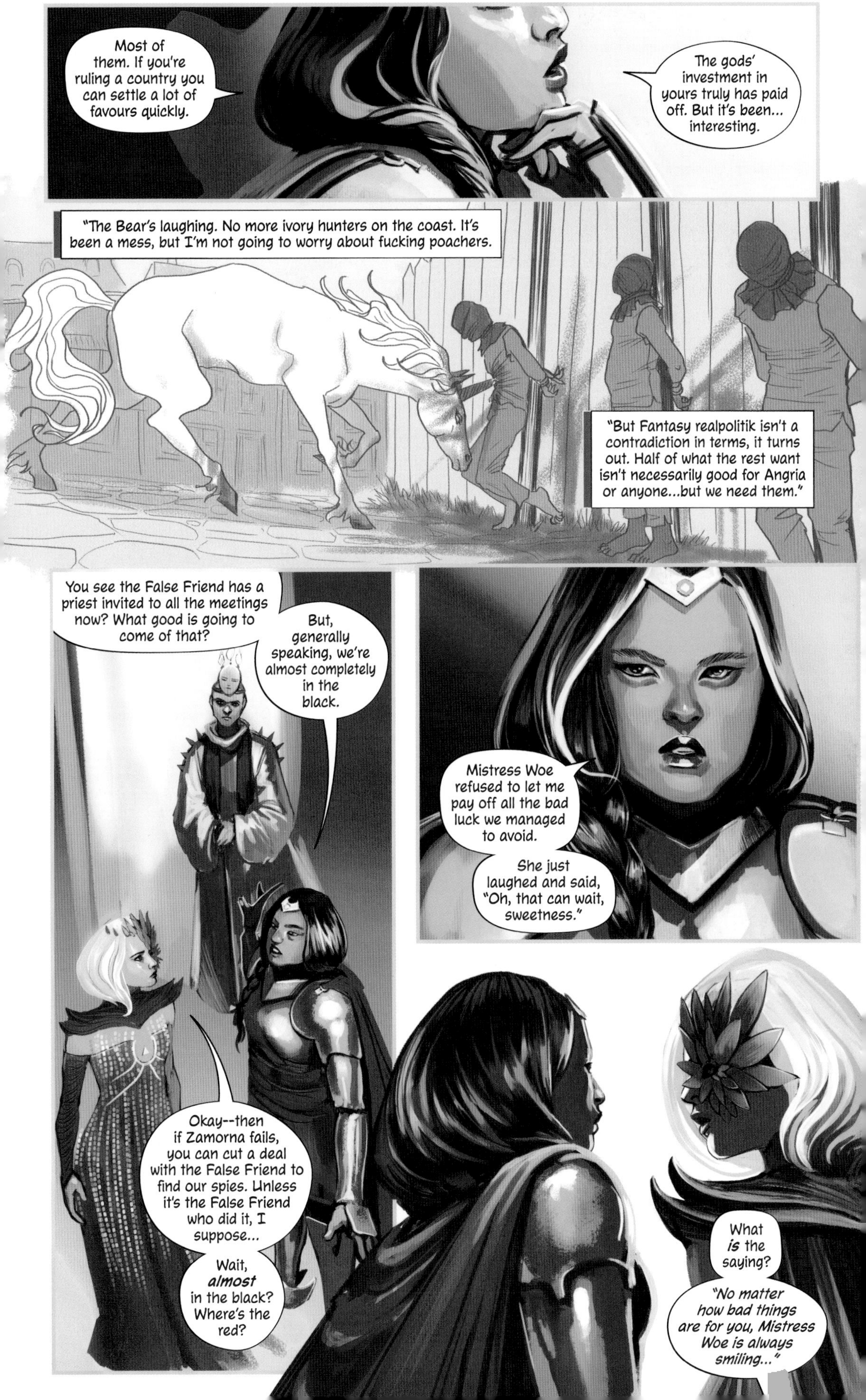
Most of them. If you're ruling a country you can settle a lot of favours quickly.
The gods' investment in yours truly has paid off. But it's been... interesting.
"The Bear's laughing. No more ivory hunters on the coast. It's been a mess, but I'm not going to worry about fucking poachers.
"But Fantasy realpolitik isn't a contradiction in terms, it turns out. Half of what the rest want isn't necessarily good for Angria or anyone...but we need them."
You see the False Friend has a priest invited to all the meetings now? What good is going to come of that?
But, generally speaking, we're almost completely in the black.
Mistress Woe refused to let me pay off all the bad luck we managed to avoid.
She just laughed and said, "Oh, that can wait, sweetness."
Okay--then if Zamorna fails, you can cut a deal with the False Friend to find our spies. Unless it's the False Friend who did it, I suppose...
Wait, ***almost*** in the black? Where's the red?
What ***is*** the saying?
"No matter how bad things are for you, Mistress Woe is always smiling..."

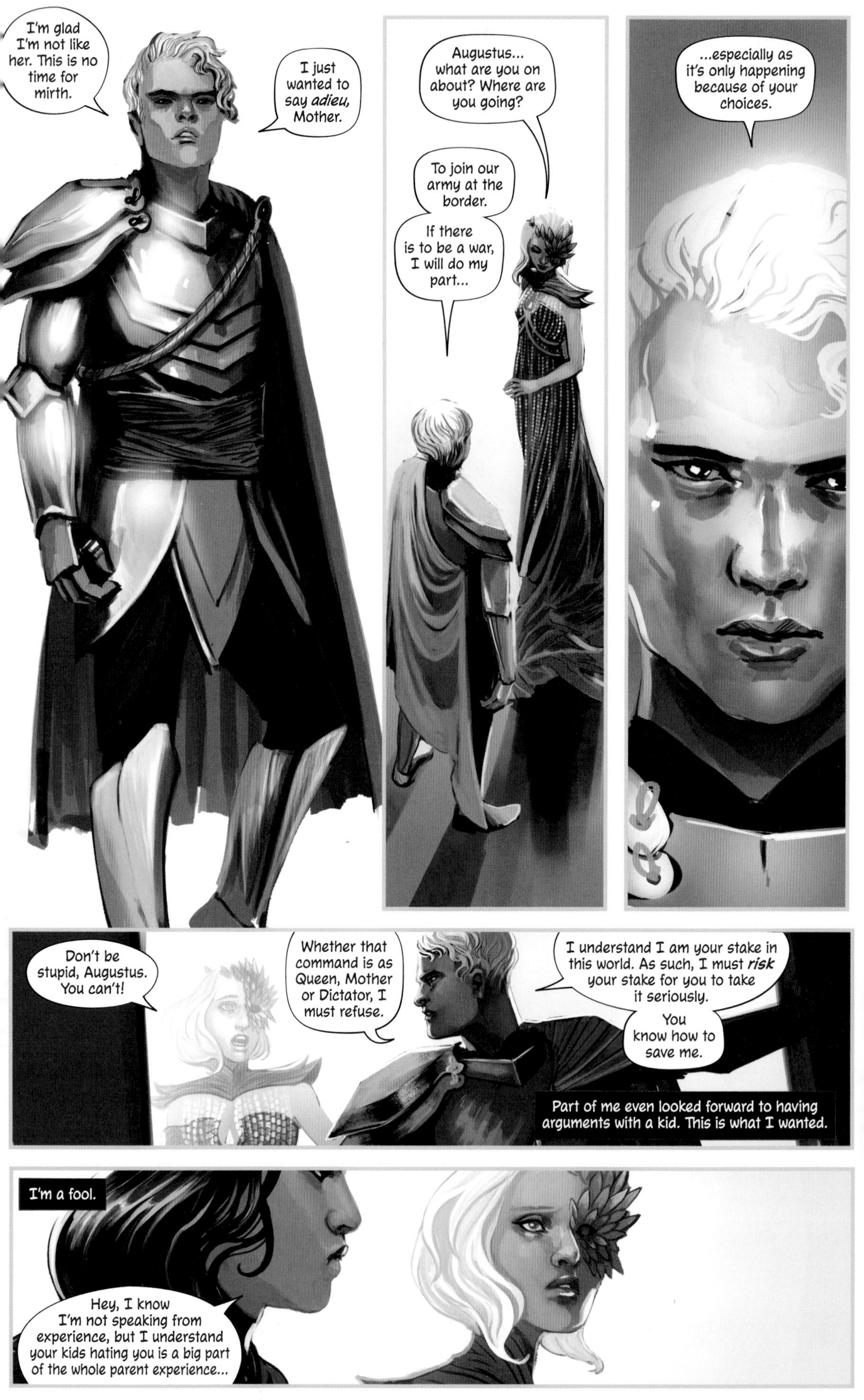
I'm glad I'm not like her. This is no time for mirth.
I just wanted to say *adieu,* Mother.
Augustus... what are you on about? Where are you going?
To join our army at the border.
If there is to be a war, I will do my part...
...especially as it's only happening because of your choices.
Don't be stupid, Augustus. You can't!
Whether that command is as Queen, Mother or Dictator, I must refuse.
I understand I am your stake in this world. As such, I must *risk* your stake for you to take it seriously.
You know how to save me.
Part of me even looked forward to having arguments with a kid. This is what I wanted.
I'm a fool.
Hey, I know I'm not speaking from experience, but I understand your kids hating you is a big part of the whole parent experience...

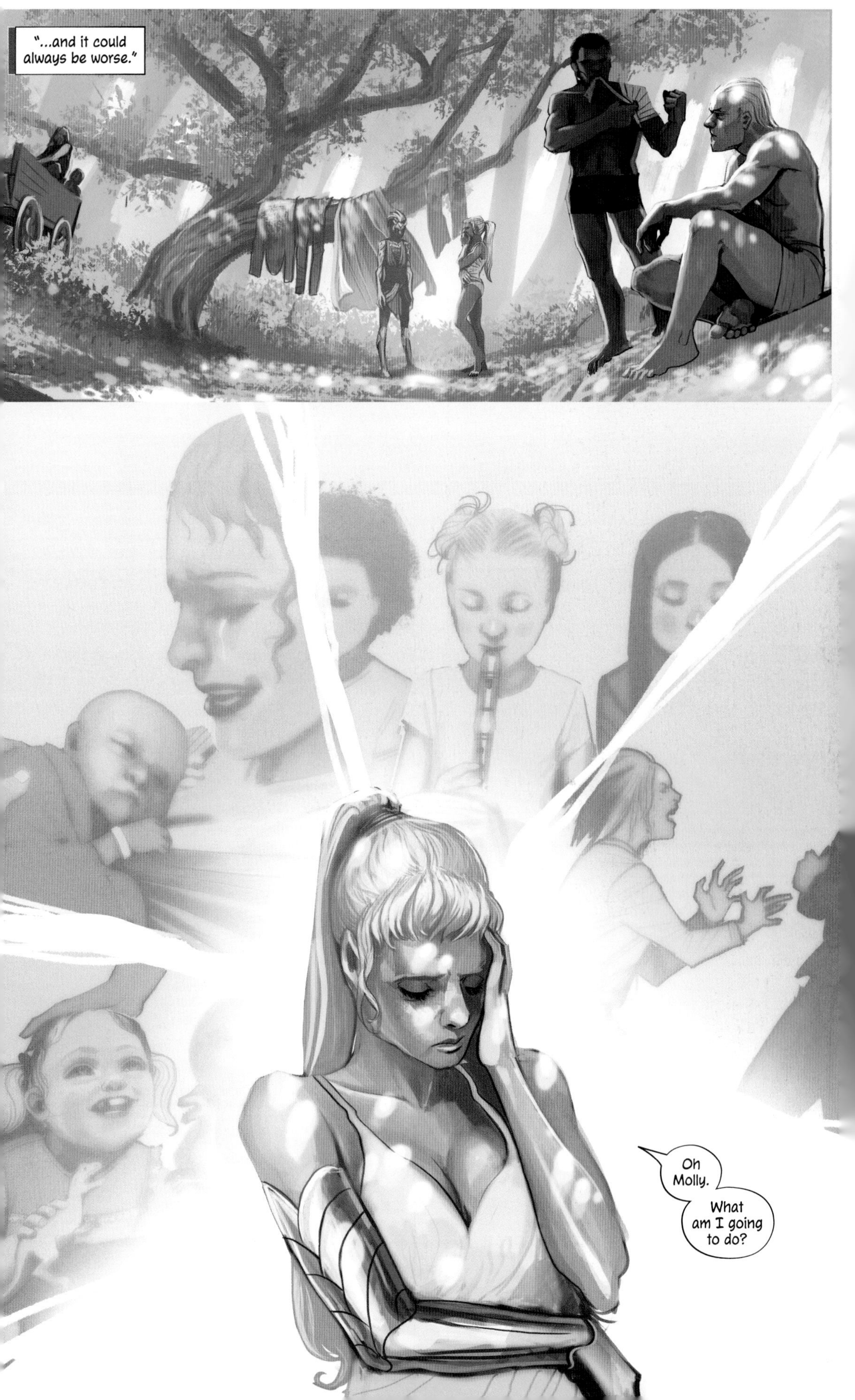
"...and it could always be worse."
Oh Molly.
What am I going to do?

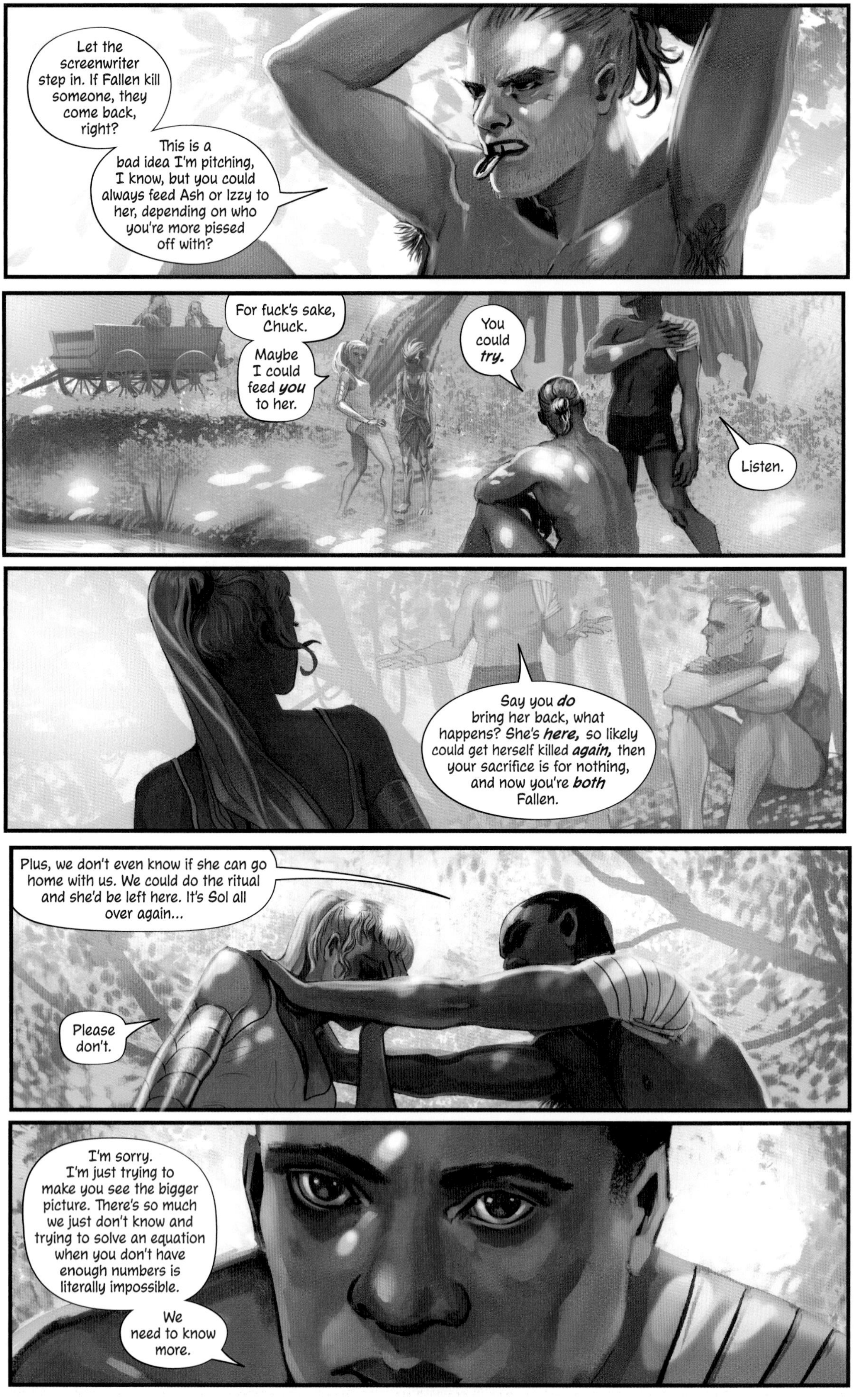

Let the screenwriter step in. If Fallen kill someone, they come back, right?
This is a bad idea I'm pitching, I know, but you could always feed Ash or Izzy to her, depending on who you're more pissed off with?
For fuck's sake, Chuck.
Maybe I could feed ***you*** to her.
You could ***try.***
Listen.
Say you ***do*** bring her back, what happens? She's ***here,*** so likely could get herself killed ***again,*** then your sacrifice is for nothing, and now you're ***both*** Fallen.
Plus, we don't even know if she can go home with us. We could do the ritual and she'd be left here. It's Sol all over again...
Please don't.
I'm sorry. I'm just trying to make you see the bigger picture. There's so much we just don't know and trying to solve an equation when you don't have enough numbers is literally impossible.
We need to know more.

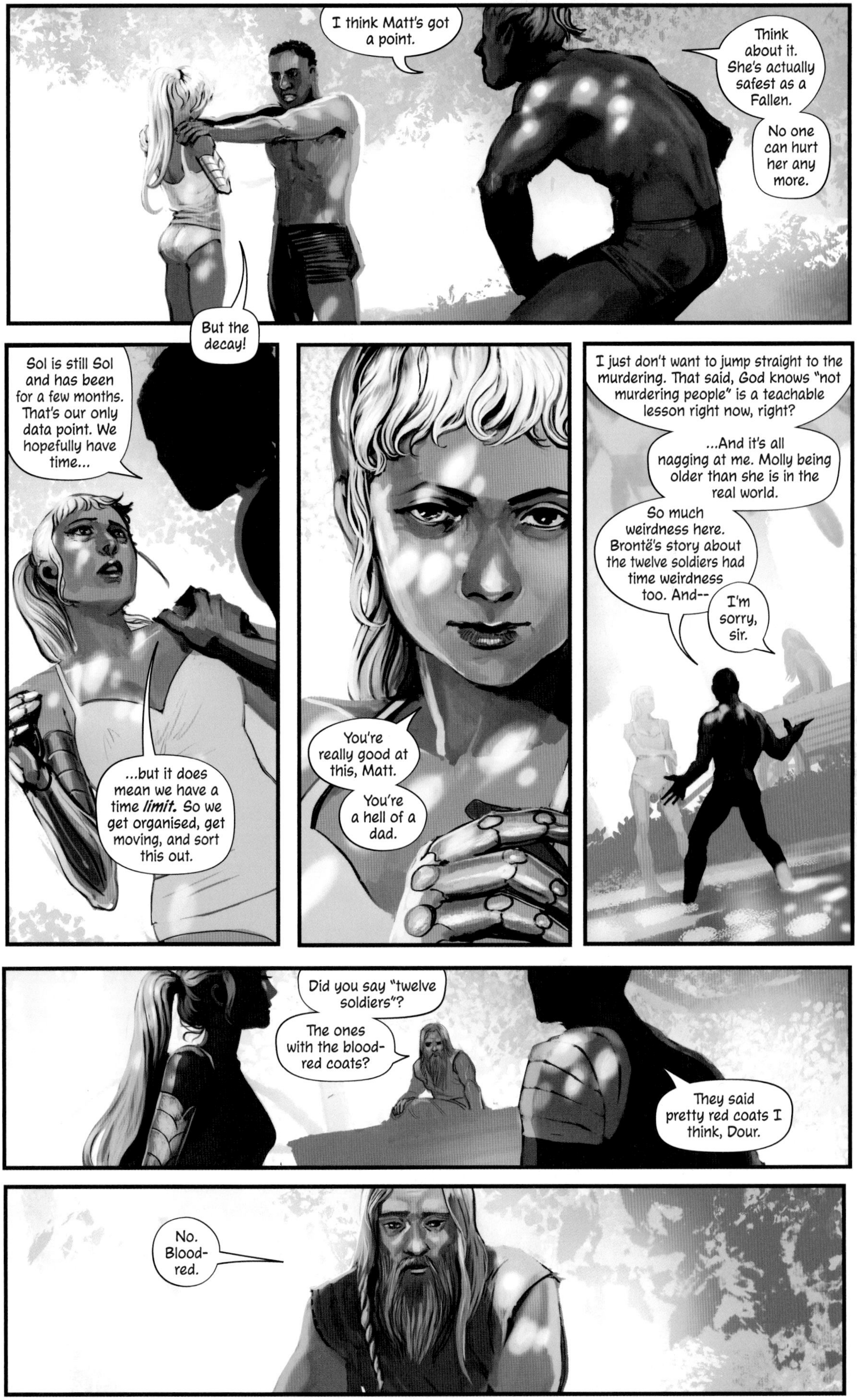
I think Matt's got a point.
Think about it. She's actually safest as a Fallen.
No one can hurt her any more.
But the decay!
Sol is still Sol and has been for a few months. That's our only data point. We hopefully have time...
...but it does mean we have a time *limit.* So we get organised, get moving, and sort this out.
You're really good at this, Matt.
You're a hell of a dad.
I just don't want to jump straight to the murdering. That said, God knows "not murdering people" is a teachable lesson right now, right?
...And it's all nagging at me. Molly being older than she is in the real world.
So much weirdness here. Brontë's story about the twelve soldiers had time weirdness too. And--
I'm sorry, sir.
Did you say "twelve soldiers"?
The ones with the blood-red coats?
They said pretty red coats I think, Dour.
No. Blood-red.

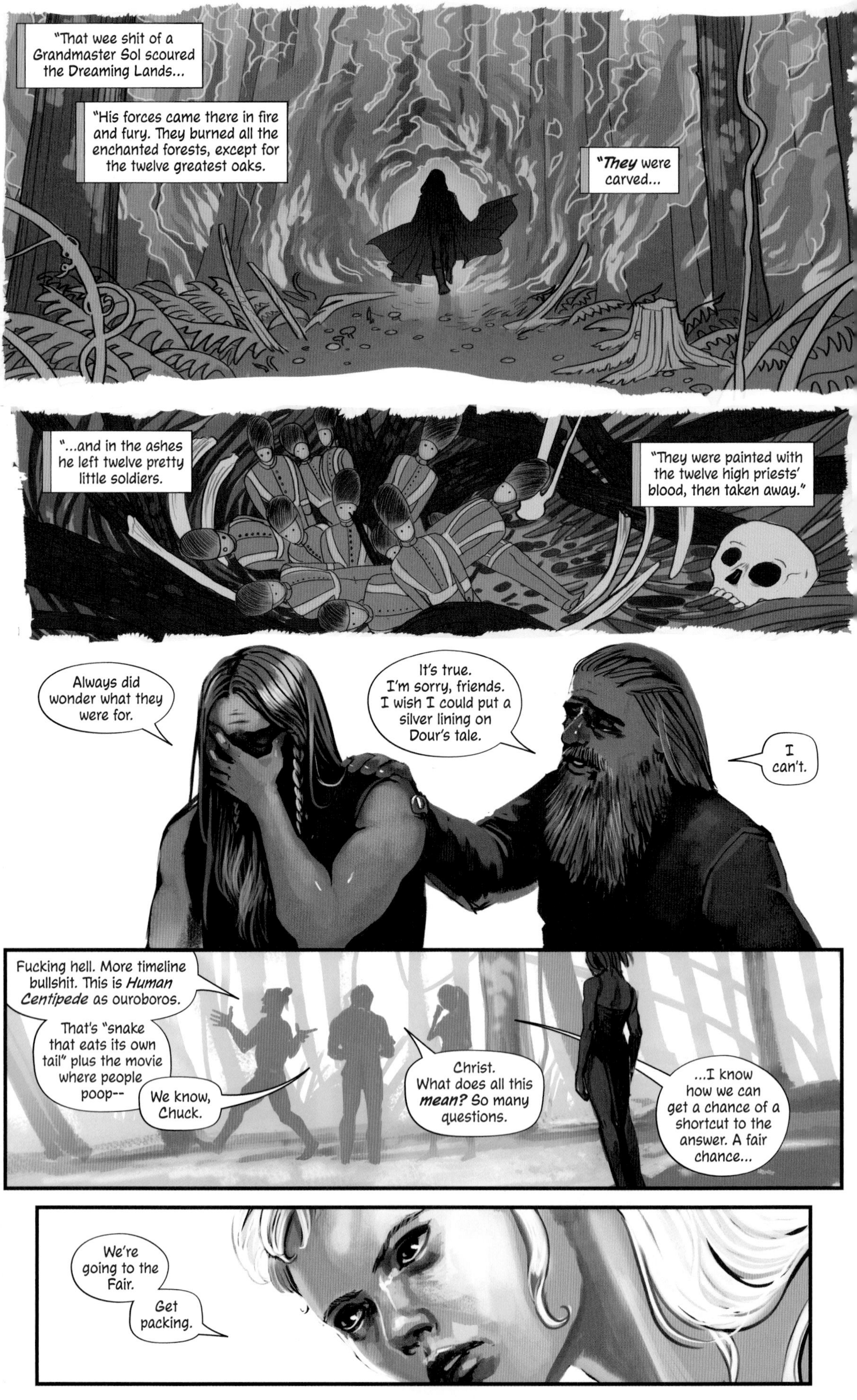
"That wee shit of a Grandmaster Sol scoured the Dreaming Lands...
"His forces came there in fire and fury. They burned all the enchanted forests, except for the twelve greatest oaks.
"*They* were carved...
"...and in the ashes he left twelve pretty little soldiers.
"They were painted with the twelve high priests' blood, then taken away."
Always did wonder what they were for.
It's true. I'm sorry, friends. I wish I could put a silver lining on Dour's tale.
I can't.
Fucking hell. More timeline bullshit. This is *Human Centipede* as ouroboros.
That's "snake that eats its own tail" plus the movie where people poop--
We know, Chuck.
Christ. What does all this *mean?* So many questions.
...I know how we can get a chance of a shortcut to the answer. A fair chance...
We're going to the Fair.
Get packing.

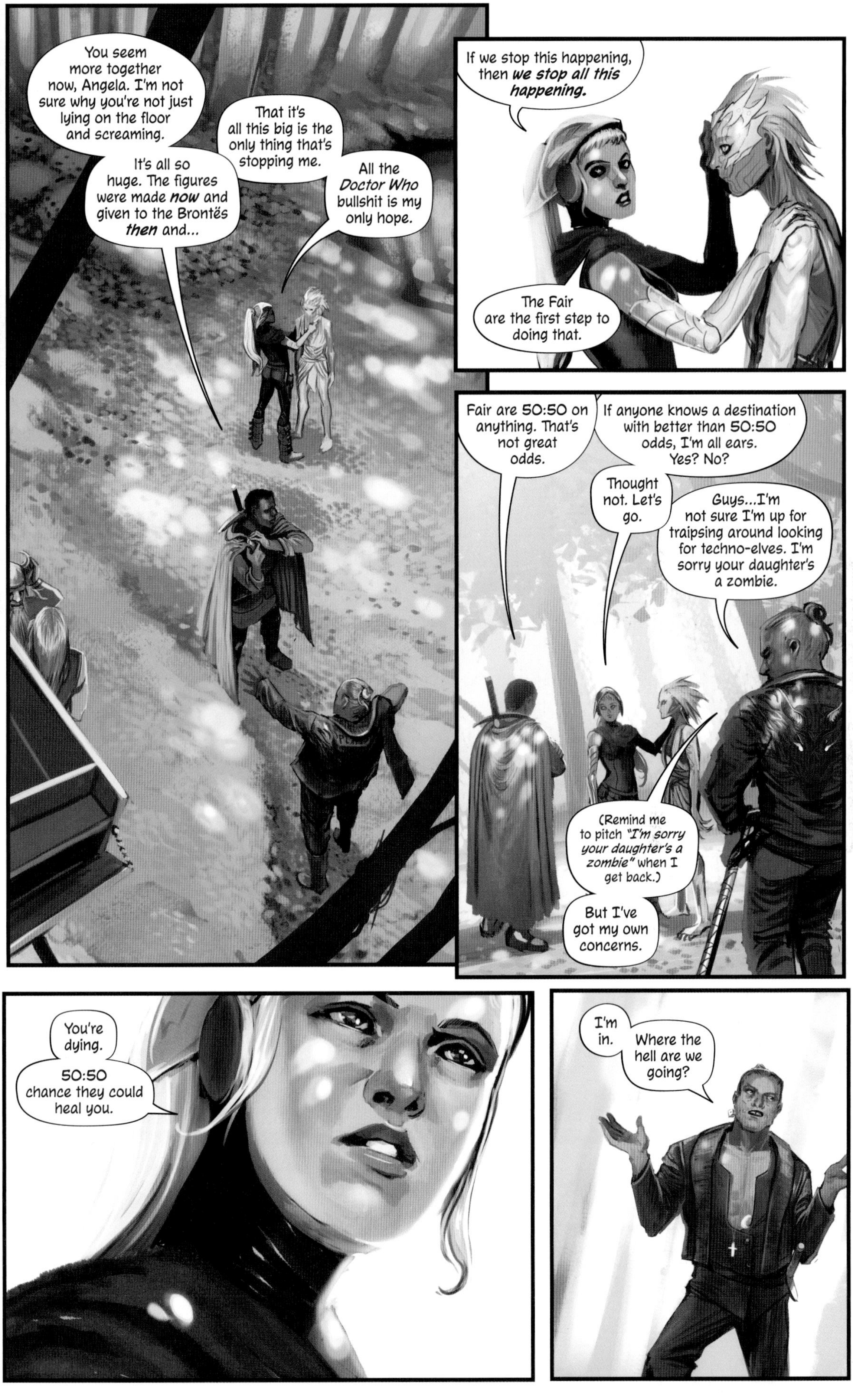
You seem more together now, Angela. I'm not sure why you're not just lying on the floor and screaming.
That it's all this big is the only thing that's stopping me.
It's all so huge. The figures were made *now* and given to the Brontës *then* and...
All the *Doctor Who* bullshit is my only hope.
If we stop this happening, then ***we stop all this happening.***
The Fair are the first step to doing that.
Fair are 50:50 on anything. That's not great odds.
If anyone knows a destination with better than 50:50 odds, I'm all ears. Yes? No?
Thought not. Let's go.
Guys...I'm not sure I'm up for traipsing around looking for techno-elves. I'm sorry your daughter's a zombie.
(Remind me to pitch *"I'm sorry your daughter's a zombie"* when I get back.)
But I've got my own concerns.
You're dying.
50:50 chance they could heal you.
I'm in.
Where the hell are we going?

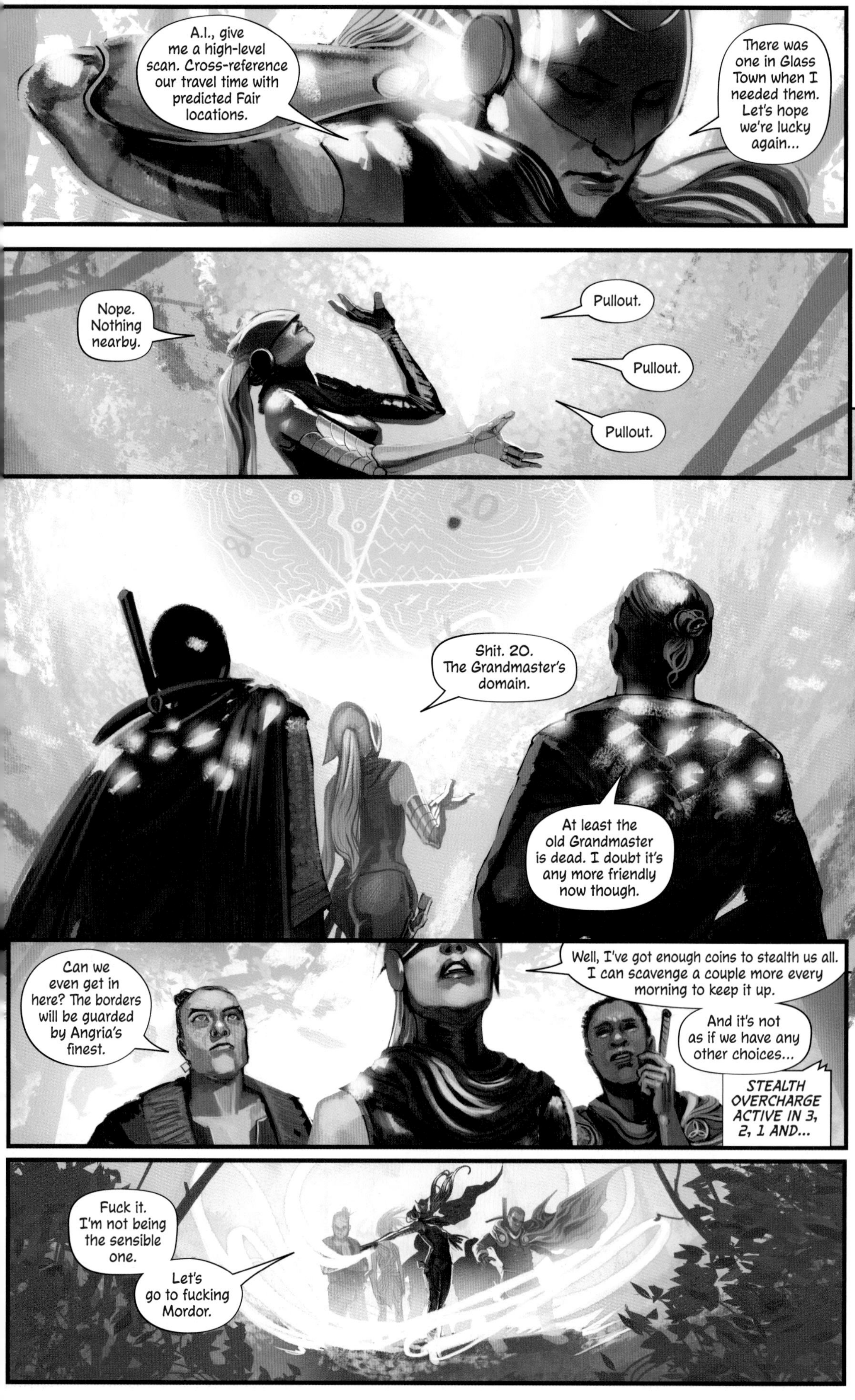

A.I., give me a high-level scan. Cross-reference our travel time with predicted Fair locations.
There was one in Glass Town when I needed them. Let's hope we're lucky again...
Nope. Nothing nearby.
Pullout.
Pullout.
Pullout.
20
Shit. 20. The Grandmaster's domain.
At least the old Grandmaster is dead. I doubt it's any more friendly now though.
Can we even get in here? The borders will be guarded by Angria's finest.
Well, I've got enough coins to stealth us all. I can scavenge a couple more every morning to keep it up.
And it's not as if we have any other choices...
STEALTH OVERCHARGE ACTIVE IN 3, 2, 1 AND...
Fuck it. I'm not being the sensible one.
Let's go to fucking Mordor.

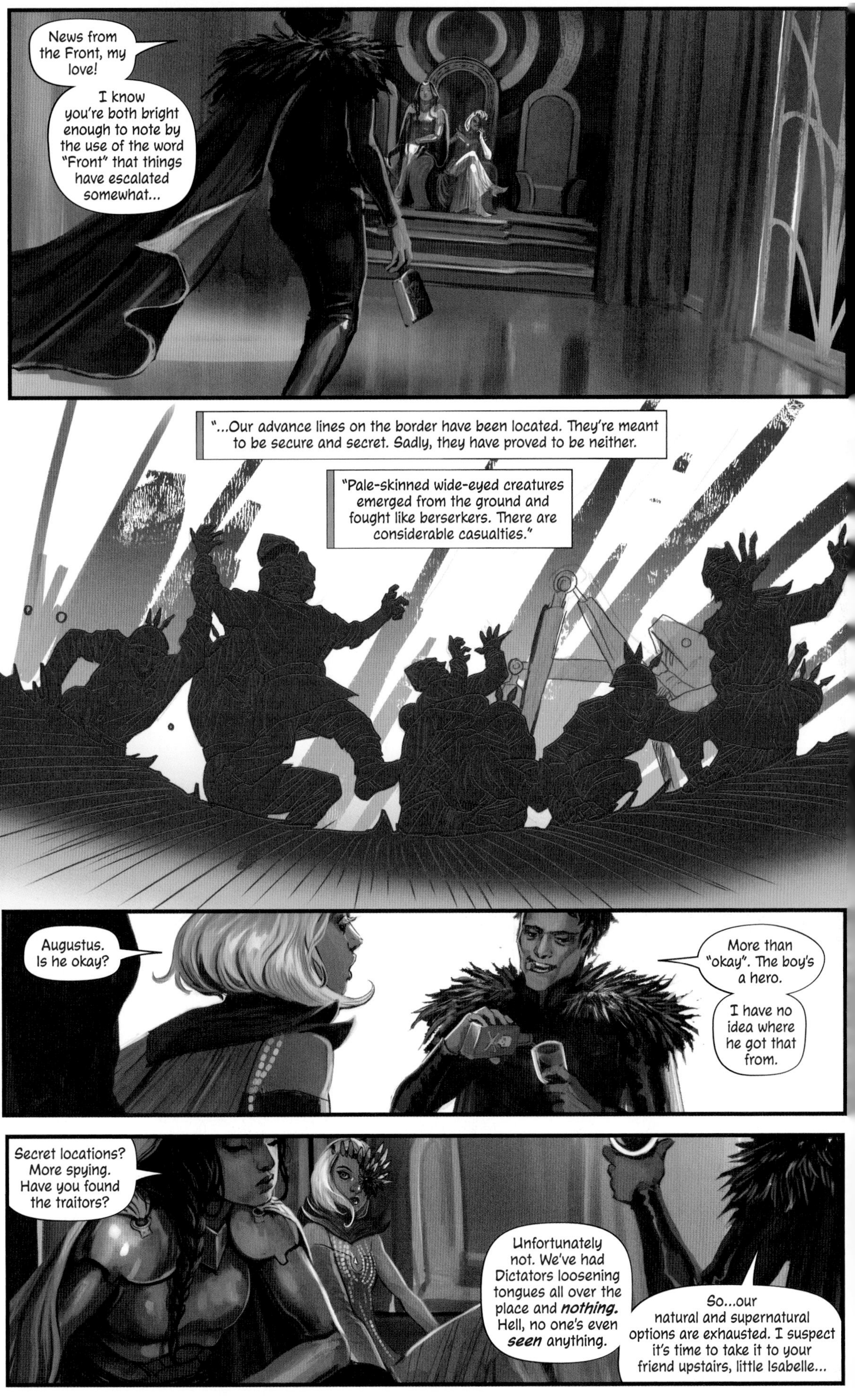
News from the Front, my love!
I know you're both bright enough to note by the use of the word "Front" that things have escalated somewhat...
"...Our advance lines on the border have been located. They're meant to be secure and secret. Sadly, they have proved to be neither.
"Pale-skinned wide-eyed creatures emerged from the ground and fought like berserkers. There are considerable casualties."
Augustus. Is he okay?
More than "okay". The boy's a hero.
I have no idea where he got that from.
Secret locations? More spying. Have you found the traitors?
Unfortunately not. We've had Dictators loosening tongues all over the place and *nothing.* Hell, no one's even *seen* anything.
So...our natural and supernatural options are exhausted. I suspect it's time to take it to your friend upstairs, little Isabelle...

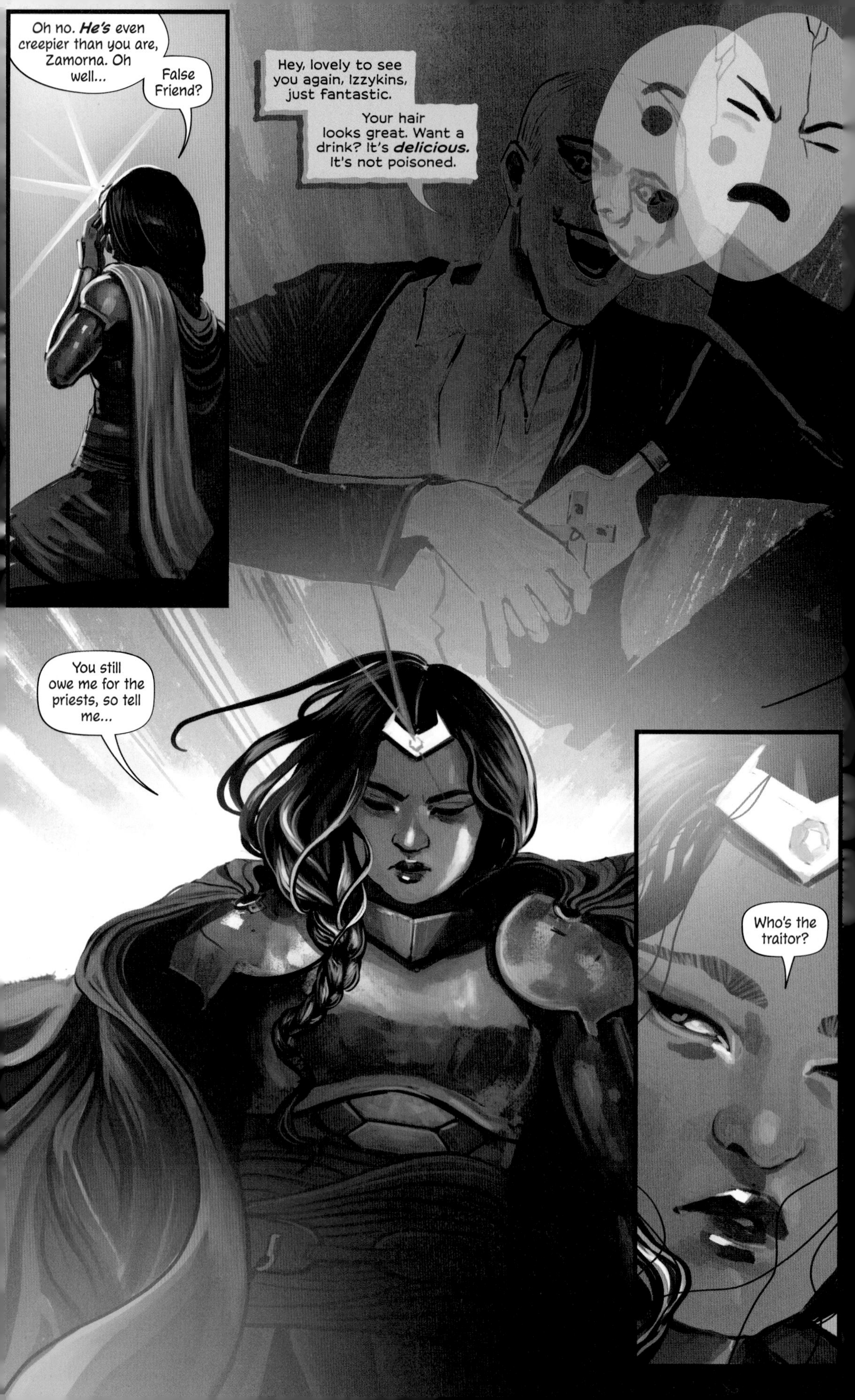

Oh no. He's even creepier than you are, Zamorna. Oh well...
False Friend?
Hey, lovely to see you again, Izzykins, just fantastic.
Your hair looks great. Want a drink? It's delicious. It's not poisoned.
You still owe me for the priests, so tell me...
Who's the traitor?

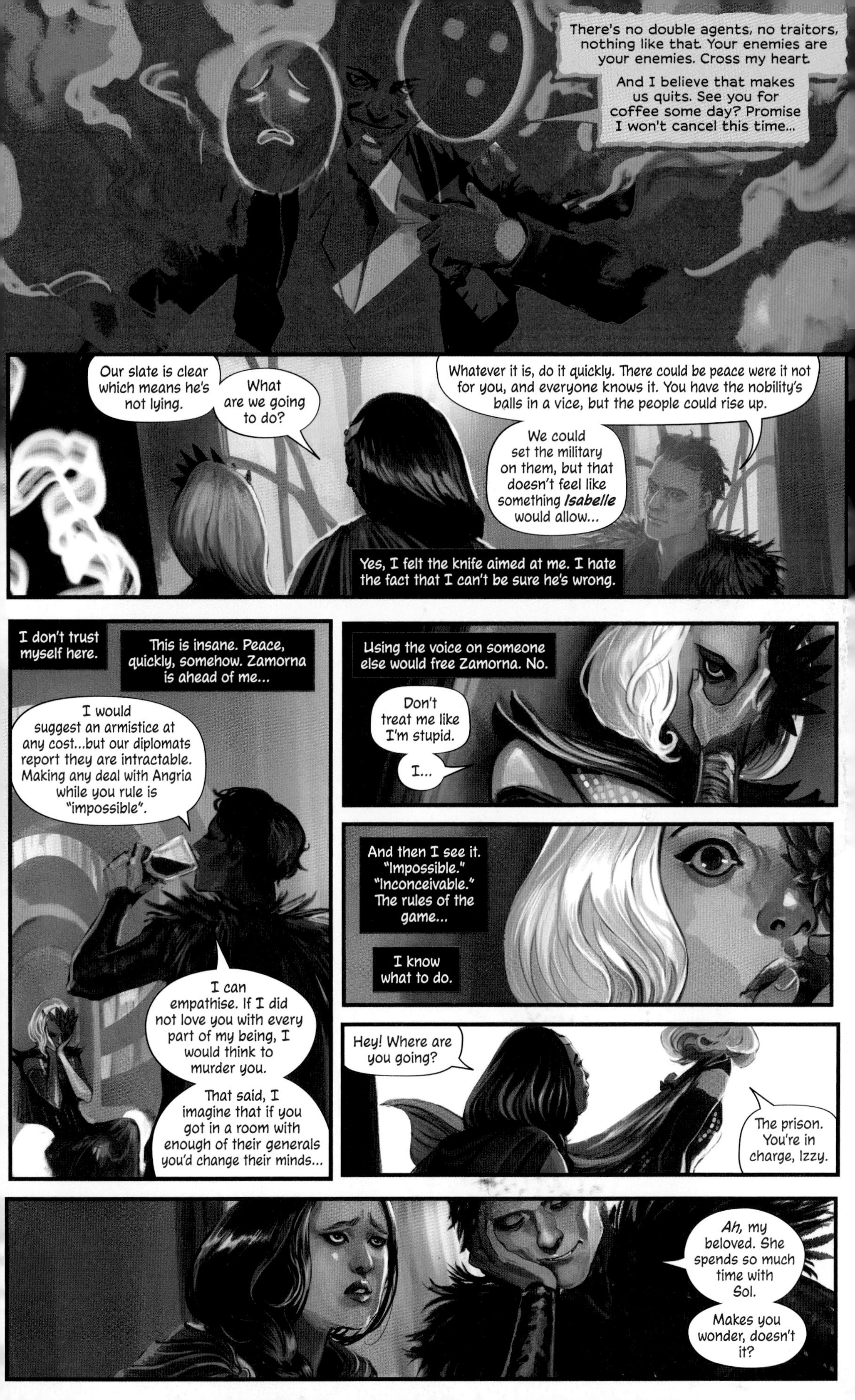
There's no double agents, no traitors, nothing like that. Your enemies are your enemies. Cross my heart.
And I believe that makes us quits. See you for coffee some day? Promise I won't cancel this time...
Our slate is clear which means he's not lying.
What are we going to do?
Whatever it is, do it quickly. There could be peace were it not for you, and everyone knows it. You have the nobility's balls in a vice, but the people could rise up.
We could set the military on them, but that doesn't feel like something *Isabelle* would allow...
Yes, I felt the knife aimed at me. I hate the fact that I can't be sure he's wrong.
I don't trust myself here.
This is insane. Peace, quickly, somehow. Zamorna is ahead of me...
I would suggest an armistice at any cost...but our diplomats report they are intractable. Making any deal with Angria while you rule is "impossible".
I can empathise. If I did not love you with every part of my being, I would think to murder you.
That said, I imagine that if you got in a room with enough of their generals you'd change their minds...
Using the voice on someone else would free Zamorna. No.
Don't treat me like I'm stupid.
I...
And then I see it. "Impossible." "Inconceivable." The rules of the game...
I know what to do.
Hey! Where are you going?
The prison. You're in charge, Izzy.
Ah, my beloved. She spends so much time with Sol.
Makes you wonder, doesn't it?

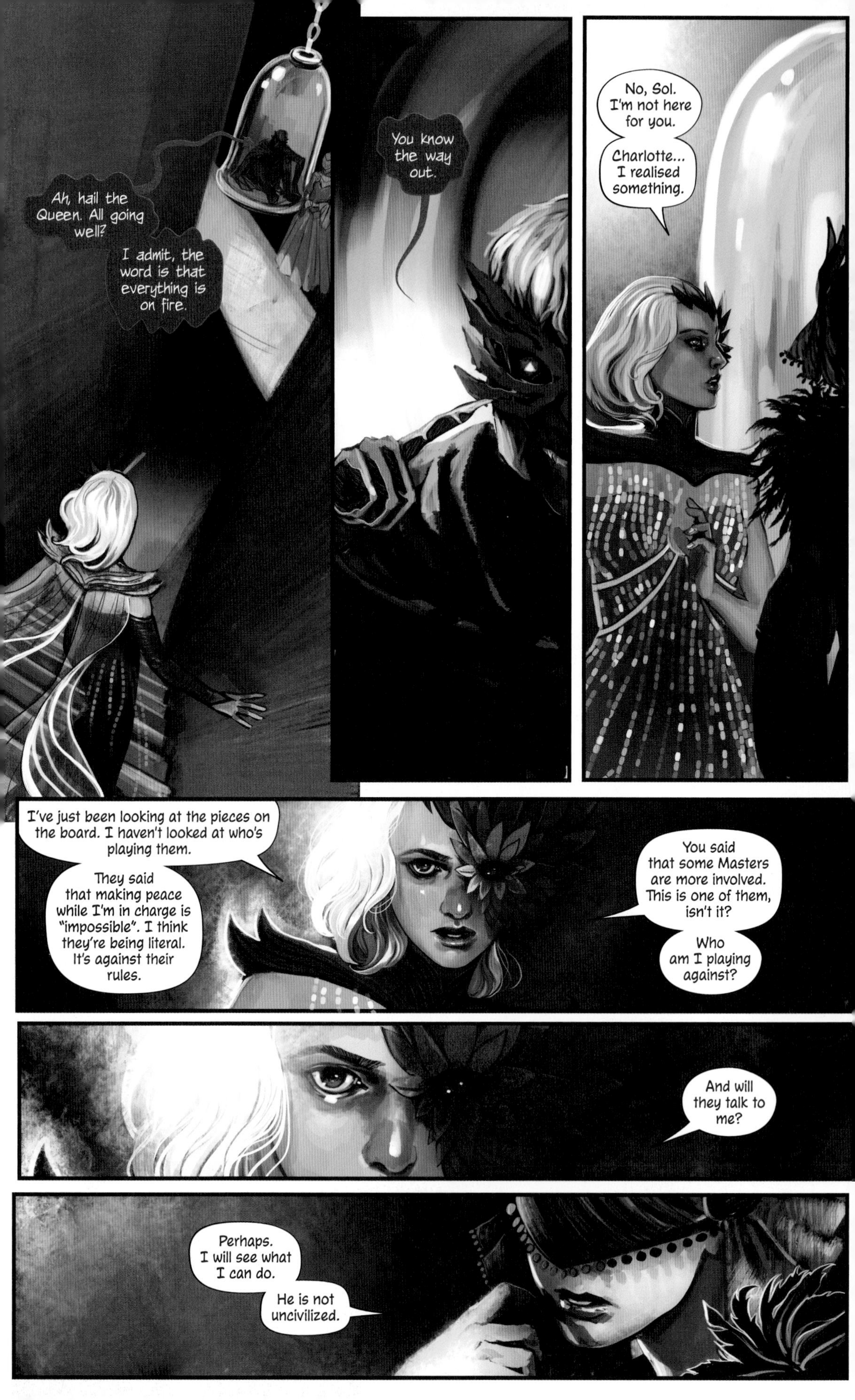
Ah, hail the Queen. All going well?
I admit, the word is that everything is on fire.
You know the way out.
No, Sol. I'm not here for you.
Charlotte... I realised something.
I've just been looking at the pieces on the board. I haven't looked at who's playing them.
They said that making peace while I'm in charge is "impossible". I think they're being literal. It's against their rules.
You said that some Masters are more involved. This is one of them, isn't it?
Who am I playing against?
And will they talk to me?
Perhaps. I will see what I can do.
He is not uncivilized.

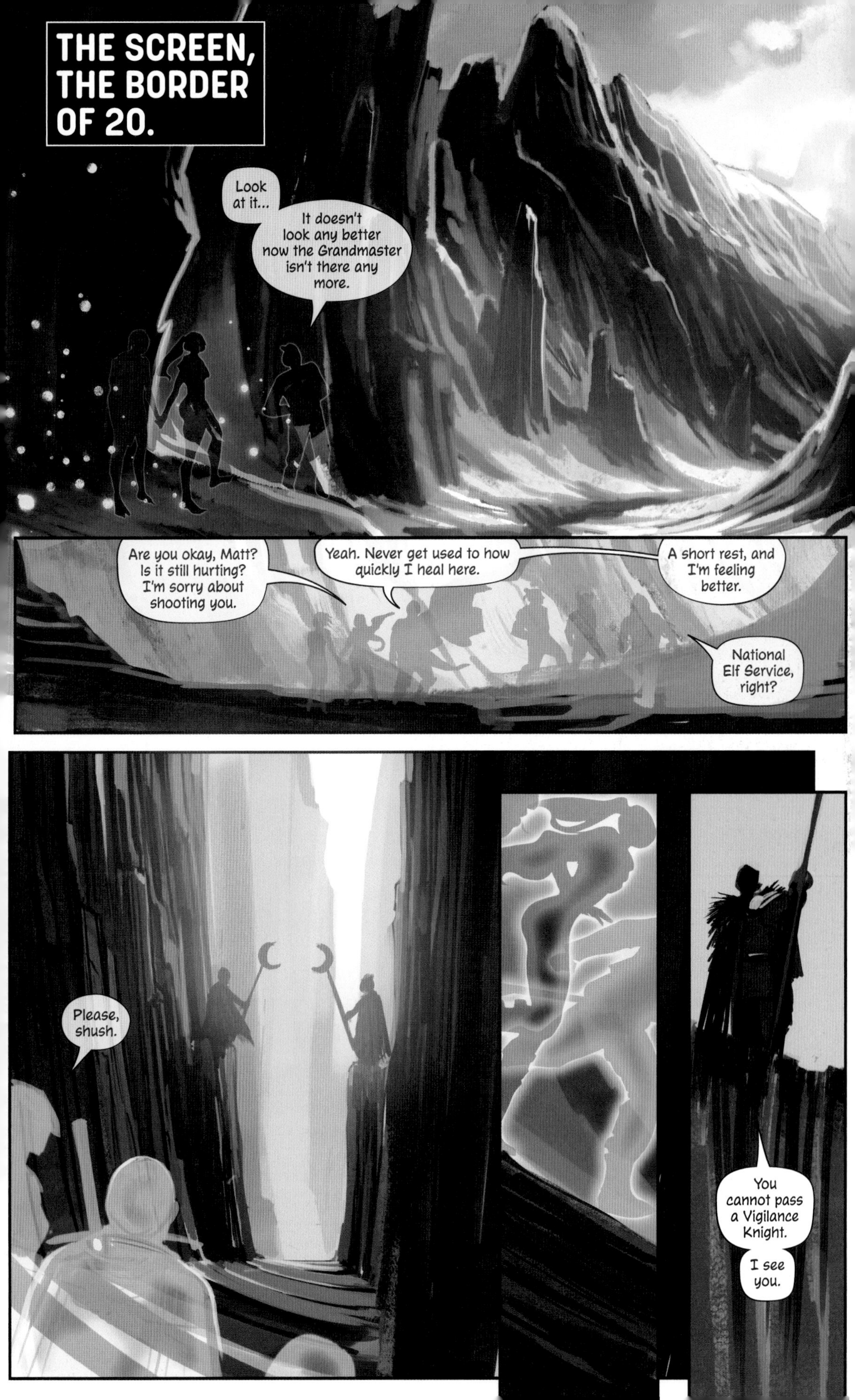
THE SCREEN, THE BORDER OF 20.
Look at it...
It doesn't look any better now the Grandmaster isn't there any more.
Are you okay, Matt? Is it still hurting? I'm sorry about shooting you.
Yeah. Never get used to how quickly I heal here.
A short rest, and I'm feeling better.
National Elf Service, right?
Please, shush.
You cannot pass a Vigilance Knight.
I see you.

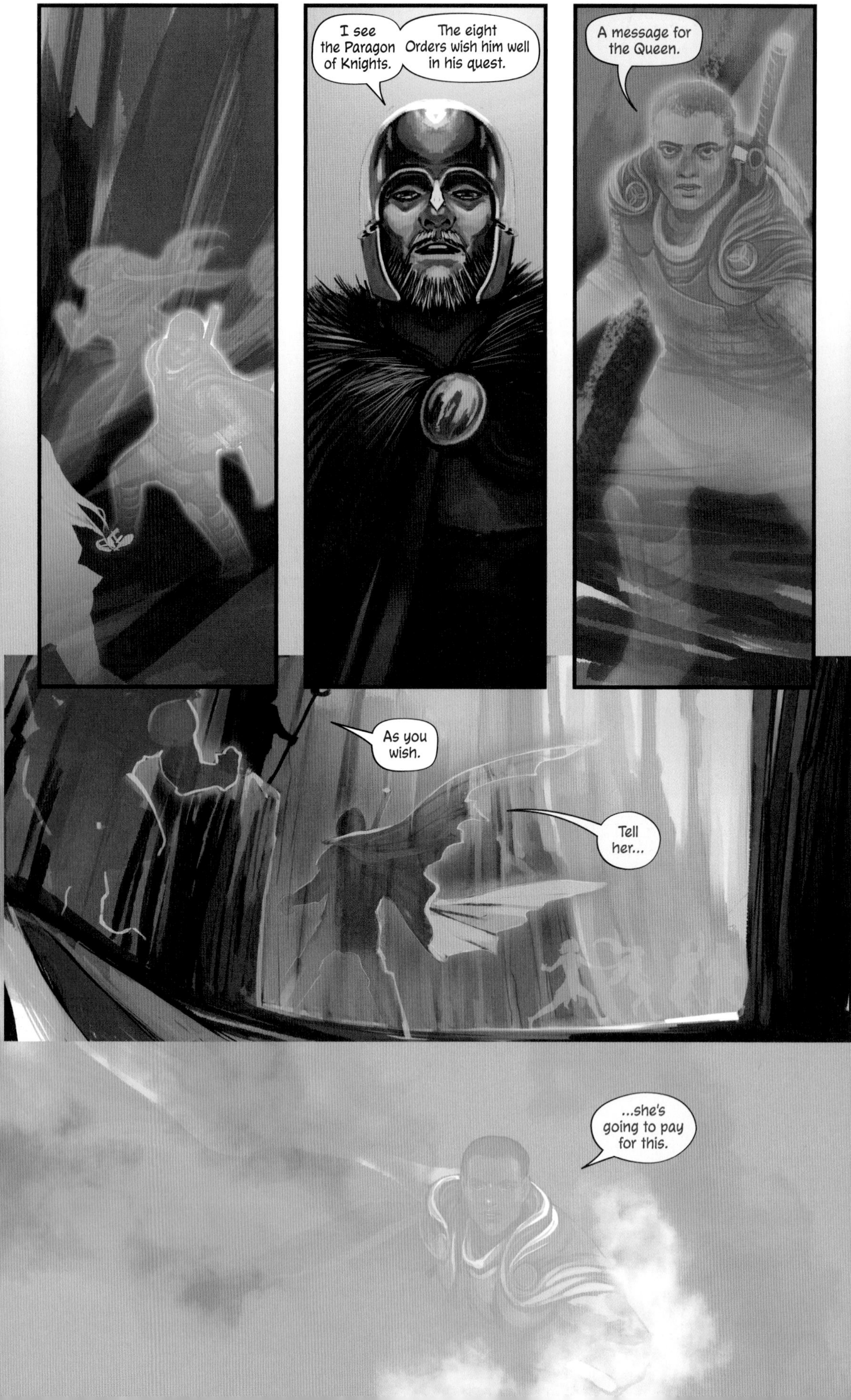
I see the Paragon of Knights.
The eight Orders wish him well in his quest.
A message for the Queen.
As you wish.
Tell her...
...she's going to pay for this.

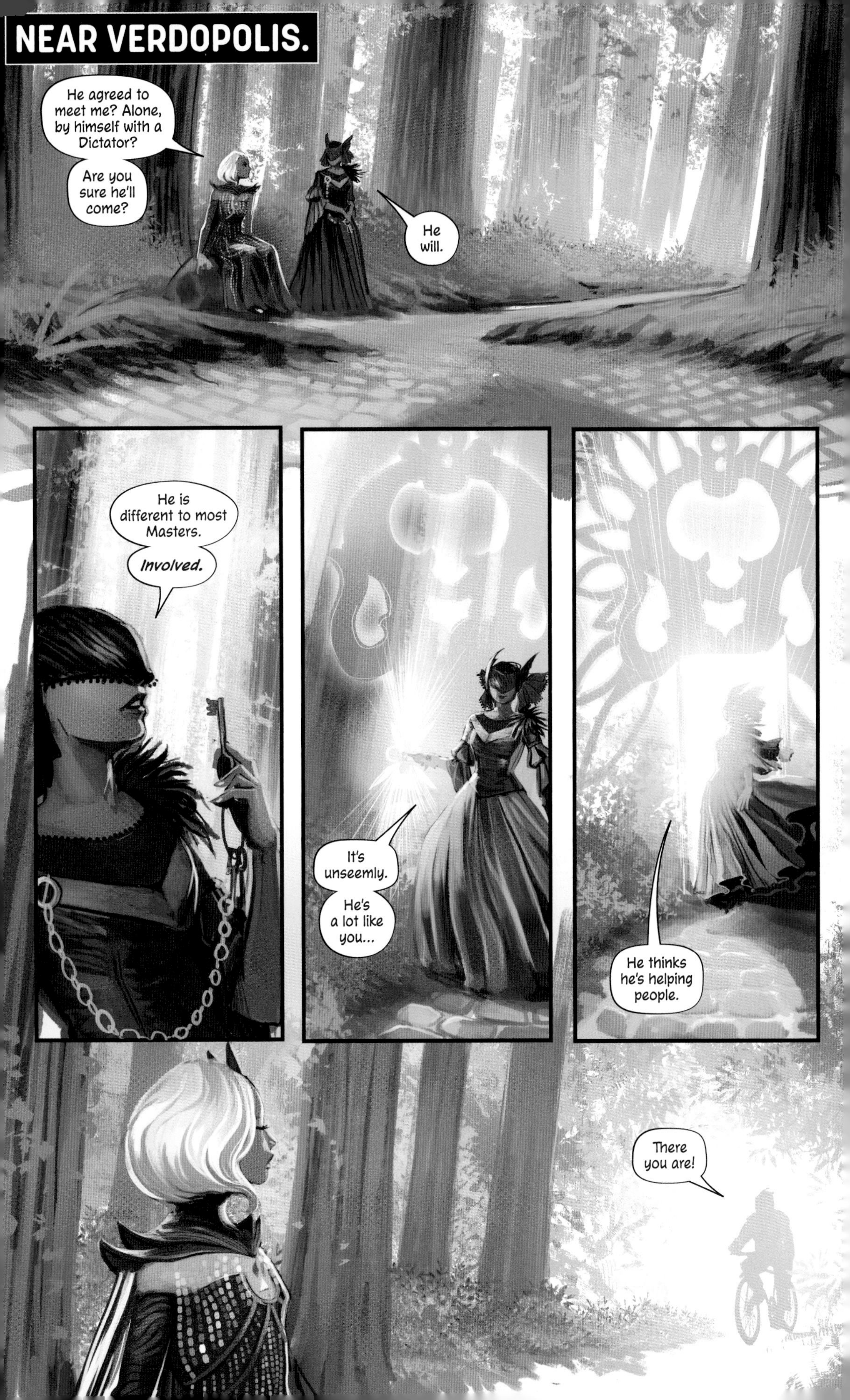
NEAR VERDOPOLIS.
He agreed to meet me? Alone, by himself with a Dictator?
Are you sure he'll come?
He will.
He is different to most Masters.
Involved.
It's unseemly.
He's a lot like you...
He thinks he's helping people.
There you are!

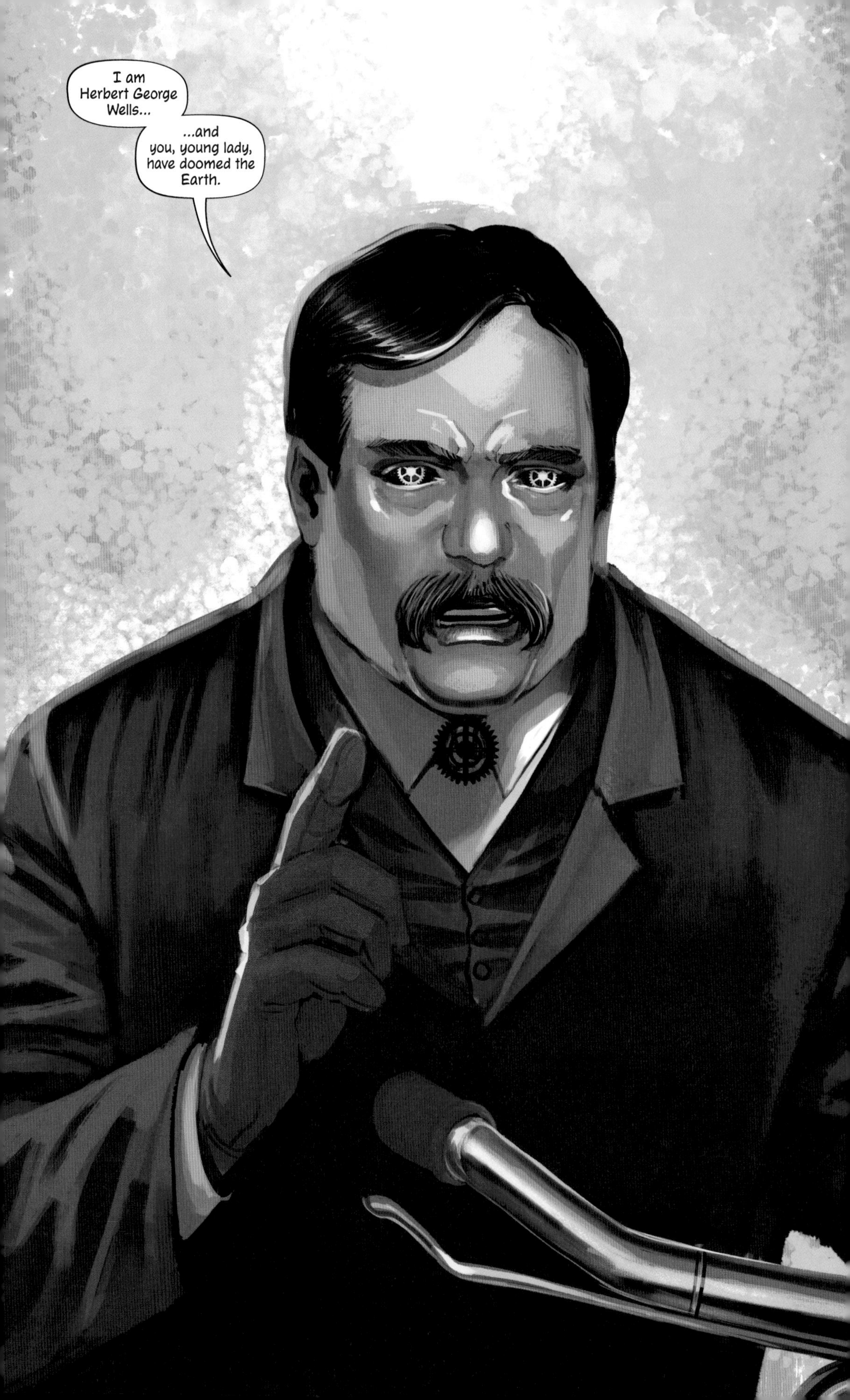
I am Herbert George Wells...
...and you, young lady, have doomed the Earth.

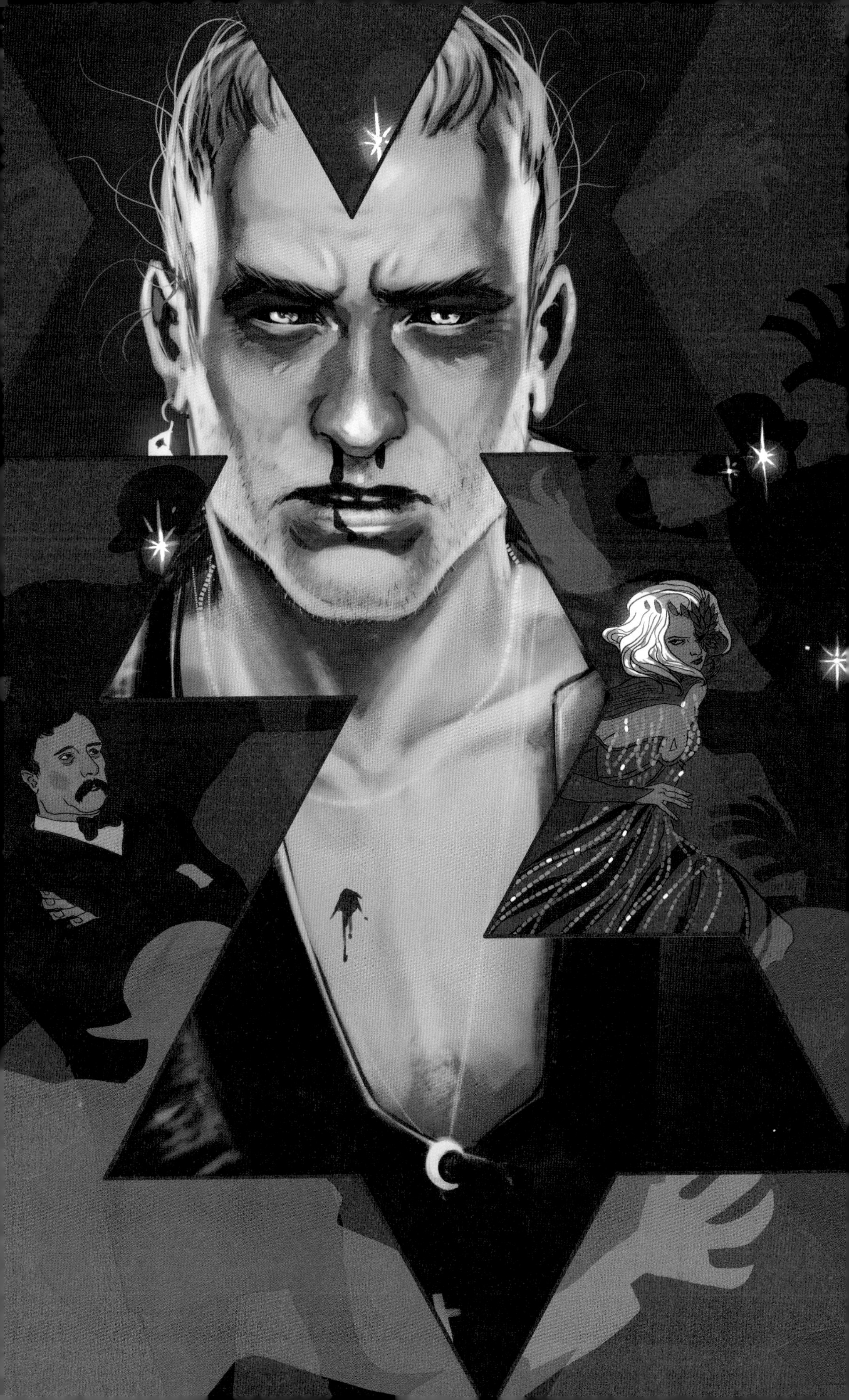

13:
LITTLE WARS

"Behind the fantasy real wills and powers exist, independent of the minds and purposes of men."
– *JRR Tolkien*

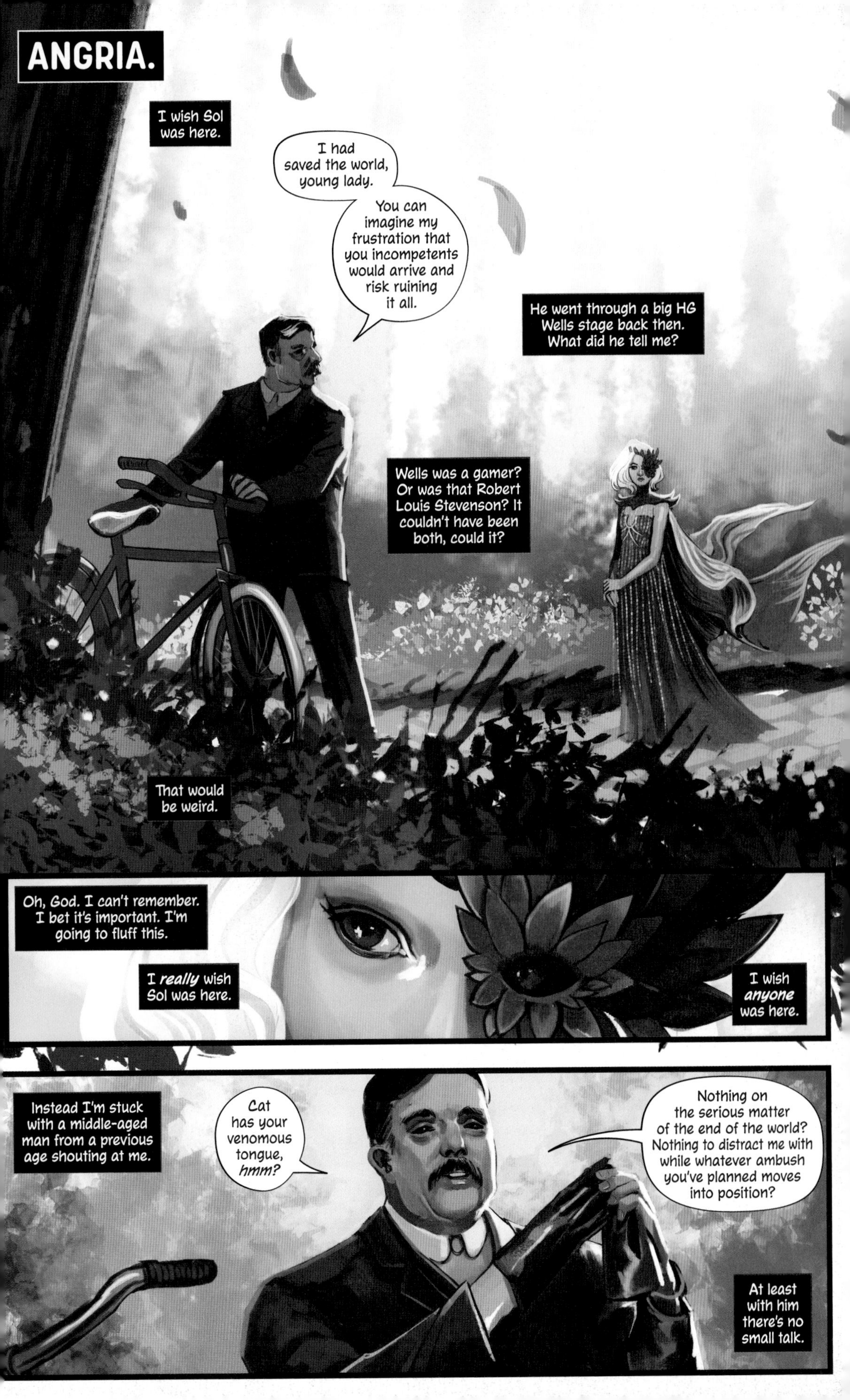
ANGRIA.
I wish Sol was here.
I had saved the world, young lady.
You can imagine my frustration that you incompetents would arrive and risk ruining it all.
He went through a big HG Wells stage back then. What did he tell me?
Wells was a gamer? Or was that Robert Louis Stevenson? It couldn't have been both, could it?
That would be weird.
Oh, God. I can't remember. I bet it's important. I'm going to fluff this.
I *really* wish Sol was here.
I wish *anyone* was here.
Instead I'm stuck with a middle-aged man from a previous age shouting at me.
Cat has your venomous tongue, *hmm?*
Nothing on the serious matter of the end of the world? Nothing to distract me with while whatever ambush you've planned moves into position?
At least with him there's no small talk.

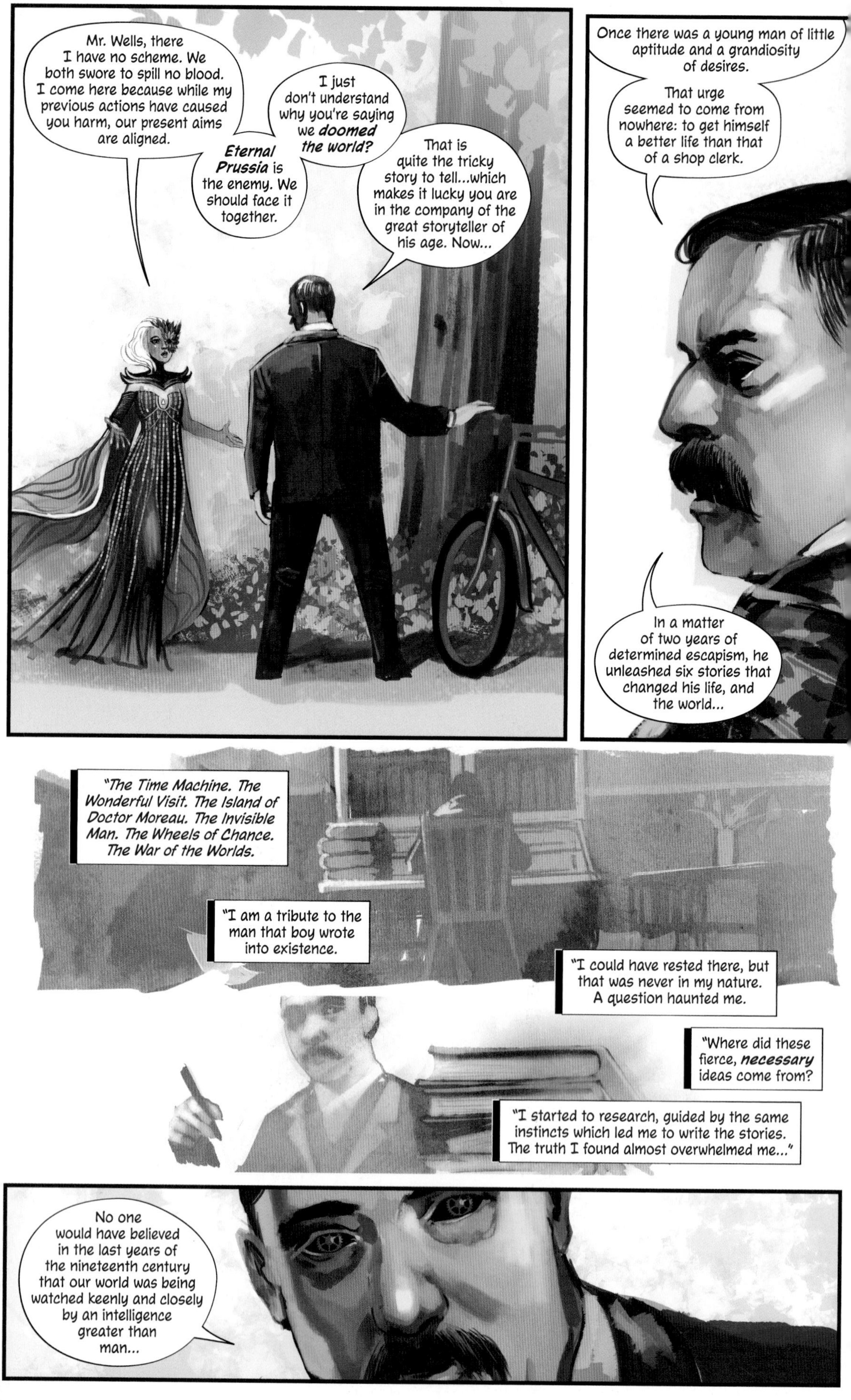

Mr. Wells, there I have no scheme. We both swore to spill no blood. I come here because while my previous actions have caused you harm, our present aims are aligned.
I just don't understand why you're saying we **doomed the world?**
Eternal Prussia is the enemy. We should face it together.
That is quite the tricky story to tell...which makes it lucky you are in the company of the great storyteller of his age. Now...
Once there was a young man of little aptitude and a grandiosity of desires.
That urge seemed to come from nowhere: to get himself a better life than that of a shop clerk.
In a matter of two years of determined escapism, he unleashed six stories that changed his life, and the world...
"*The Time Machine. The Wonderful Visit. The Island of Doctor Moreau. The Invisible Man. The Wheels of Chance. The War of the Worlds.*
"I am a tribute to the man that boy wrote into existence.
"I could have rested there, but that was never in my nature. A question haunted me.
"Where did these fierce, ***necessary*** ideas come from?
"I started to research, guided by the same instincts which led me to write the stories. The truth I found almost overwhelmed me..."
No one would have believed in the last years of the nineteenth century that our world was being watched keenly and closely by an intelligence greater than man...

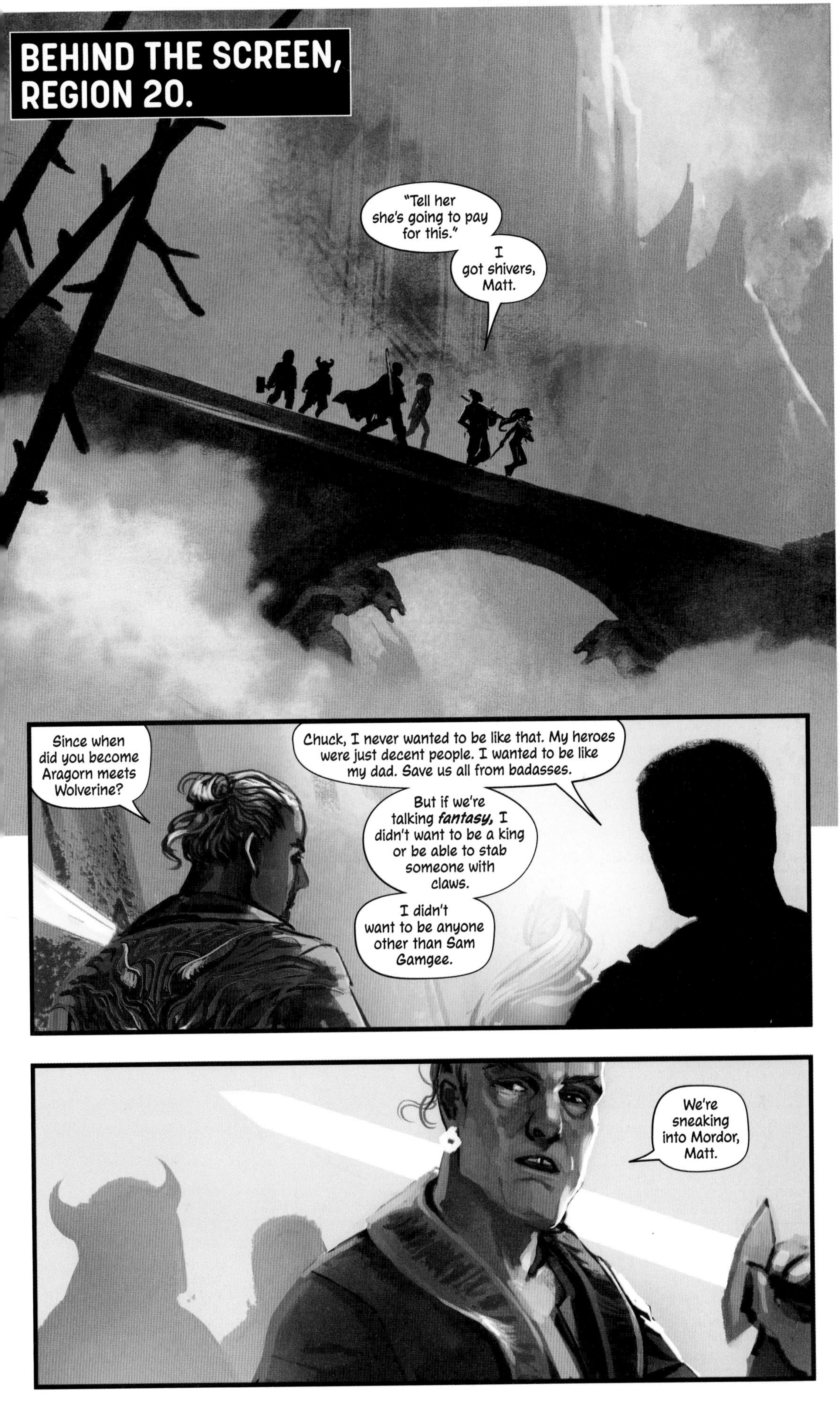
BEHIND THE SCREEN, REGION 20.
"Tell her she's going to pay for this."
I got shivers, Matt.
Since when did you become Aragorn meets Wolverine?
Chuck, I never wanted to be like that. My heroes were just decent people. I wanted to be like my dad. Save us all from badasses.
But if we're talking *fantasy,* I didn't want to be a king or be able to stab someone with claws.
I didn't want to be anyone other than Sam Gamgee.
We're sneaking into Mordor, Matt.

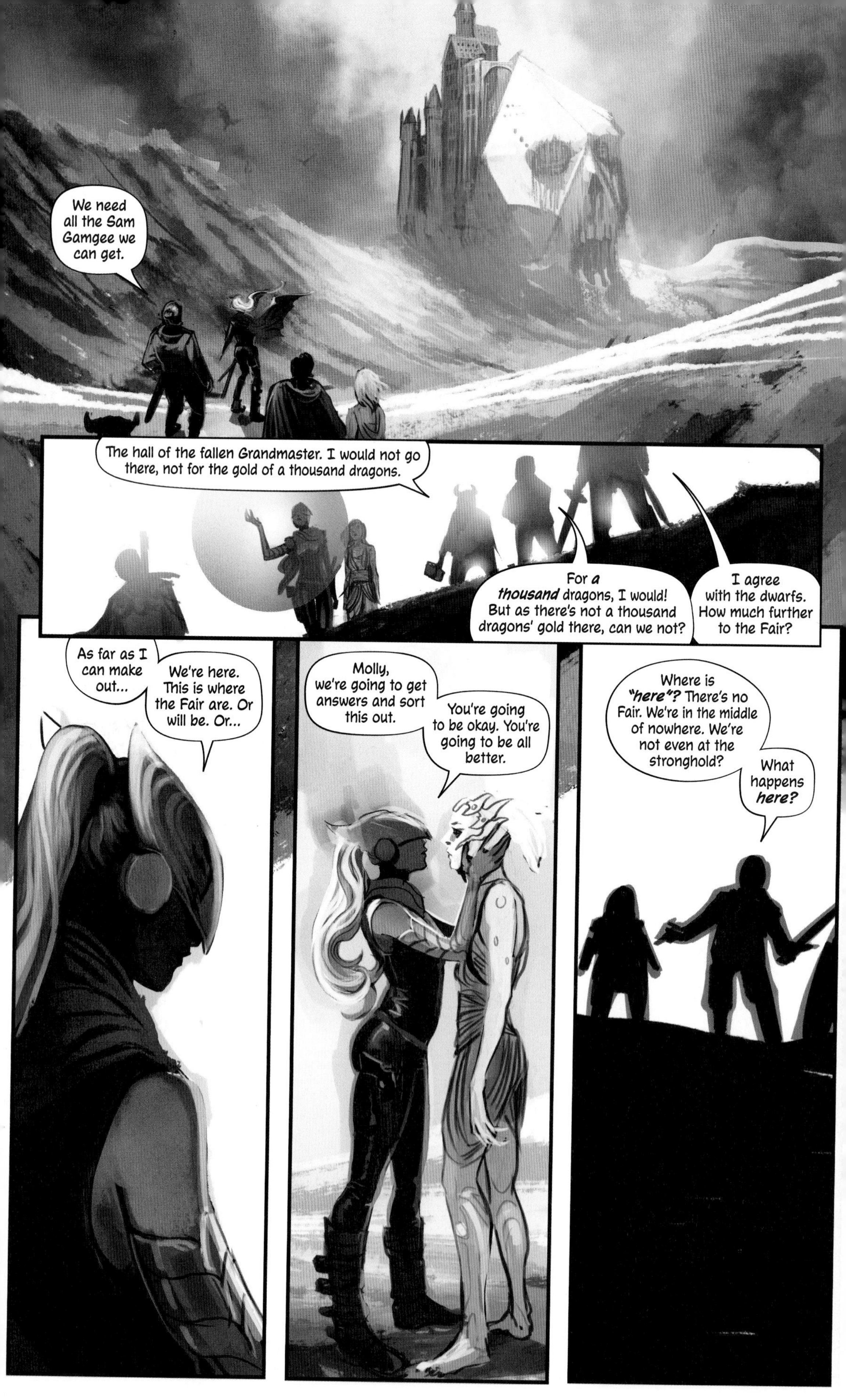
We need all the Sam Gamgee we can get.
The hall of the fallen Grandmaster. I would not go there, not for the gold of a thousand dragons.
For *a thousand* dragons, I would! But as there's not a thousand dragons' gold there, can we not?
I agree with the dwarfs. How much further to the Fair?
As far as I can make out...
We're here. This is where the Fair are. Or will be. Or...
Molly, we're going to get answers and sort this out.
You're going to be okay. You're going to be all better.
Where is *"here"?* There's no Fair. We're in the middle of nowhere. We're not even at the stronghold?
What happens *here?*

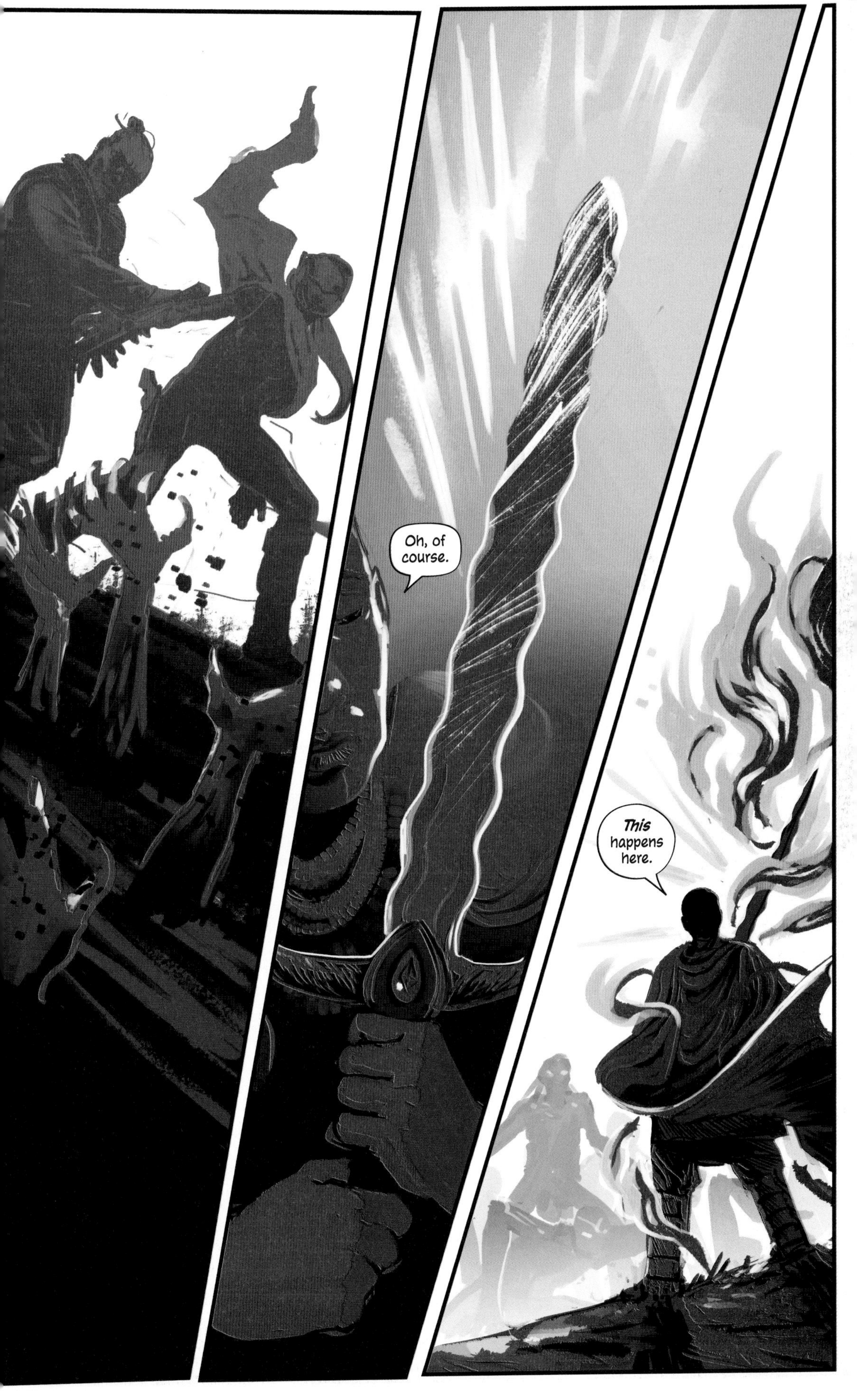
Oh, of course.
This happens here.

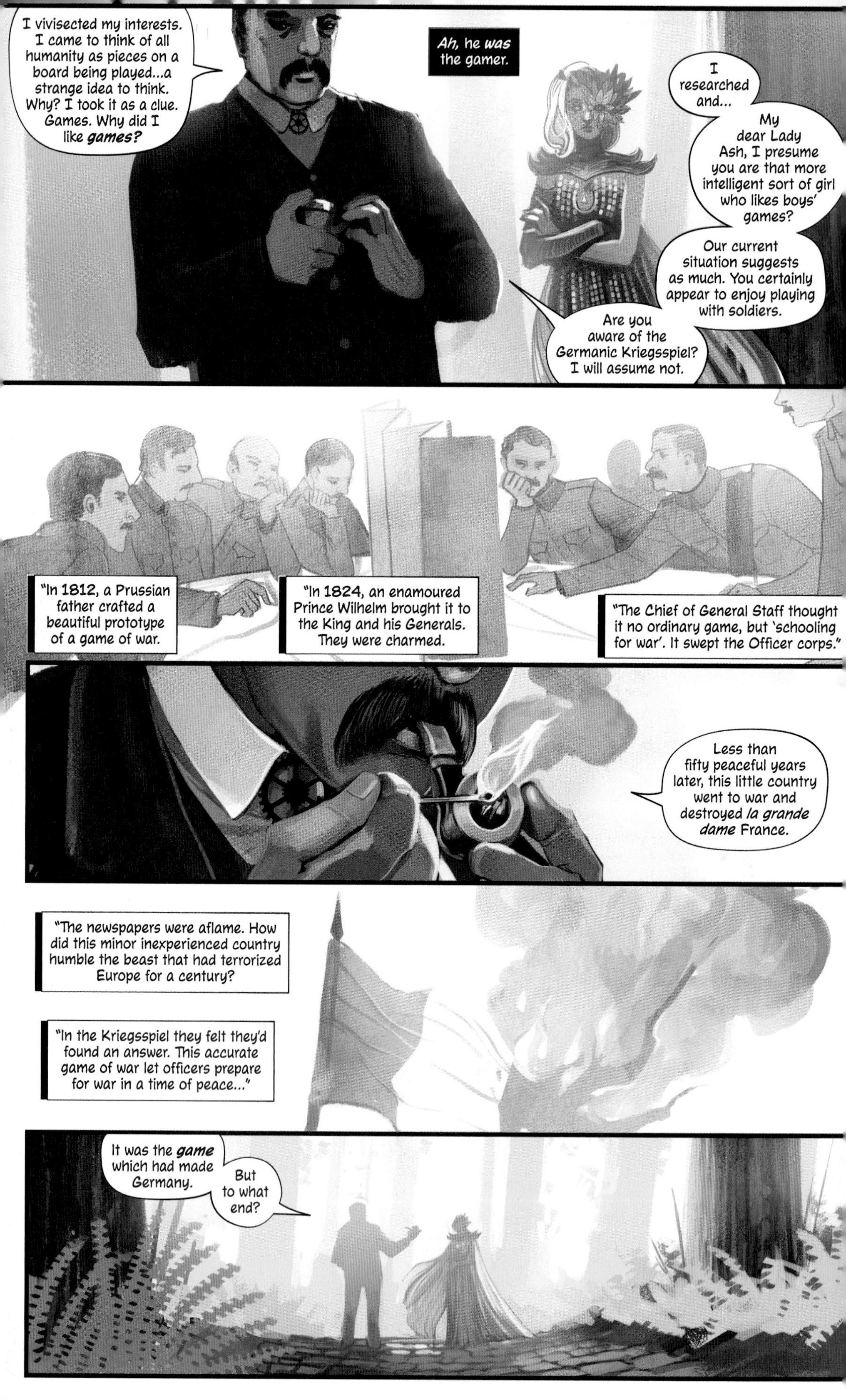
I vivisected my interests. I came to think of all humanity as pieces on a board being played...a strange idea to think. Why? I took it as a clue. Games. Why did I like *games?*
Ah, he *was* the gamer.
I researched and...
My dear Lady Ash, I presume you are that more intelligent sort of girl who likes boys' games?
Our current situation suggests as much. You certainly appear to enjoy playing with soldiers.
Are you aware of the Germanic Kriegsspiel? I will assume not.
"In 1812, a Prussian father crafted a beautiful prototype of a game of war.
"In 1824, an enamoured Prince Wilhelm brought it to the King and his Generals. They were charmed.
"The Chief of General Staff thought it no ordinary game, but 'schooling for war'. It swept the Officer corps."
Less than fifty peaceful years later, this little country went to war and destroyed *la grande dame* France.
"The newspapers were aflame. How did this minor inexperienced country humble the beast that had terrorized Europe for a century?
"In the Kriegsspiel they felt they'd found an answer. This accurate game of war let officers prepare for war in a time of peace..."
It was the *game* which had made Germany.
But to what end?

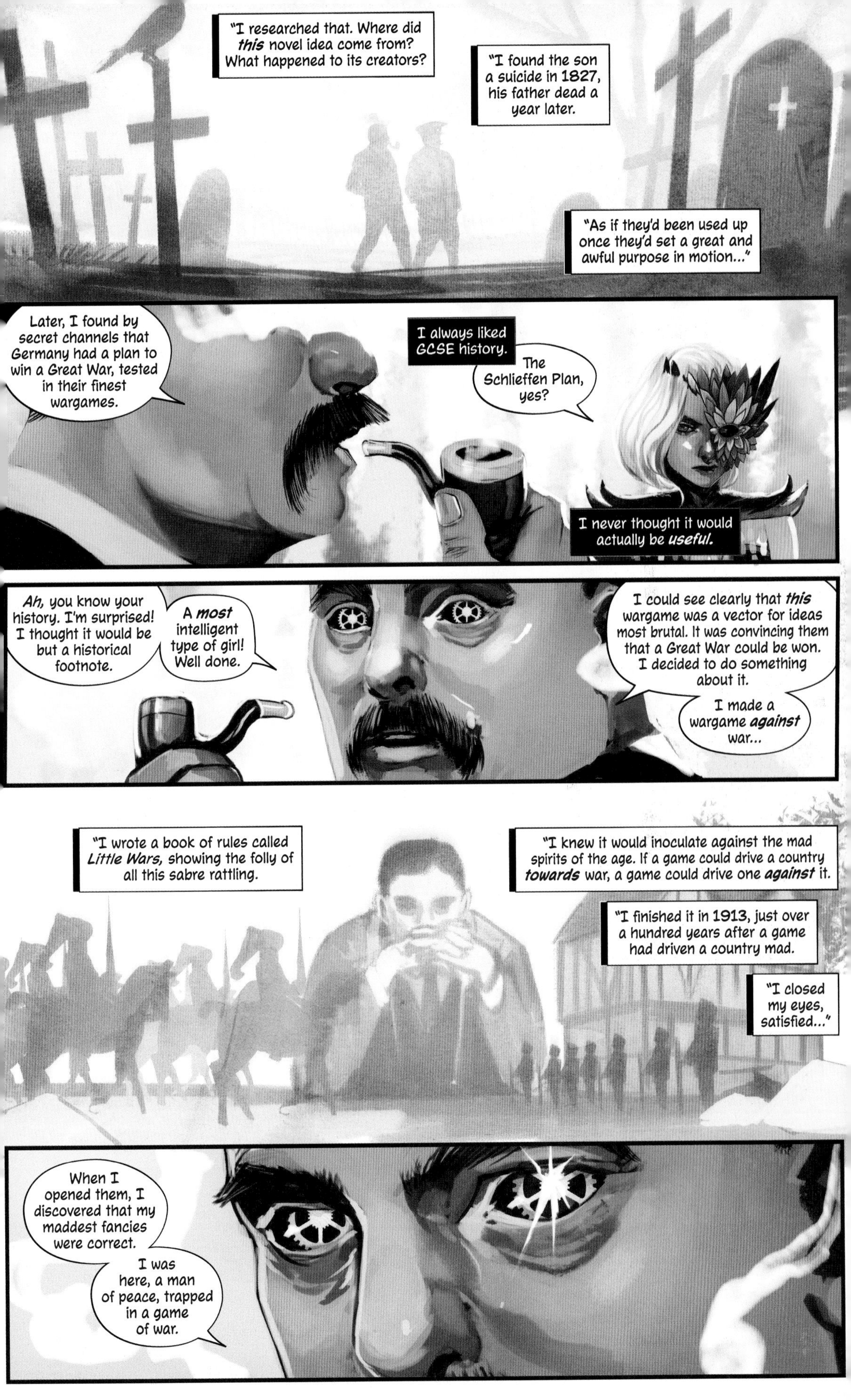
"I researched that. Where did *this* novel idea come from? What happened to its creators?
"I found the son a suicide in 1827, his father dead a year later.
"As if they'd been used up once they'd set a great and awful purpose in motion..."
Later, I found by secret channels that Germany had a plan to win a Great War, tested in their finest wargames.
I always liked GCSE history.
The Schlieffen Plan, yes?
I never thought it would actually be *useful.*
Ah, you know your history. I'm surprised! I thought it would be but a historical footnote.
A *most* intelligent type of girl! Well done.
I could see clearly that *this* wargame was a vector for ideas most brutal. It was convincing them that a Great War could be won. I decided to do something about it.
I made a wargame *against* war...
"I wrote a book of rules called *Little Wars,* showing the folly of all this sabre rattling.
"I knew it would inoculate against the mad spirits of the age. If a game could drive a country *towards* war, a game could drive one *against* it.
"I finished it in 1913, just over a hundred years after a game had driven a country mad.
"I closed my eyes, satisfied..."
When I opened them, I discovered that my maddest fancies were correct.
I was here, a man of peace, trapped in a game of war.

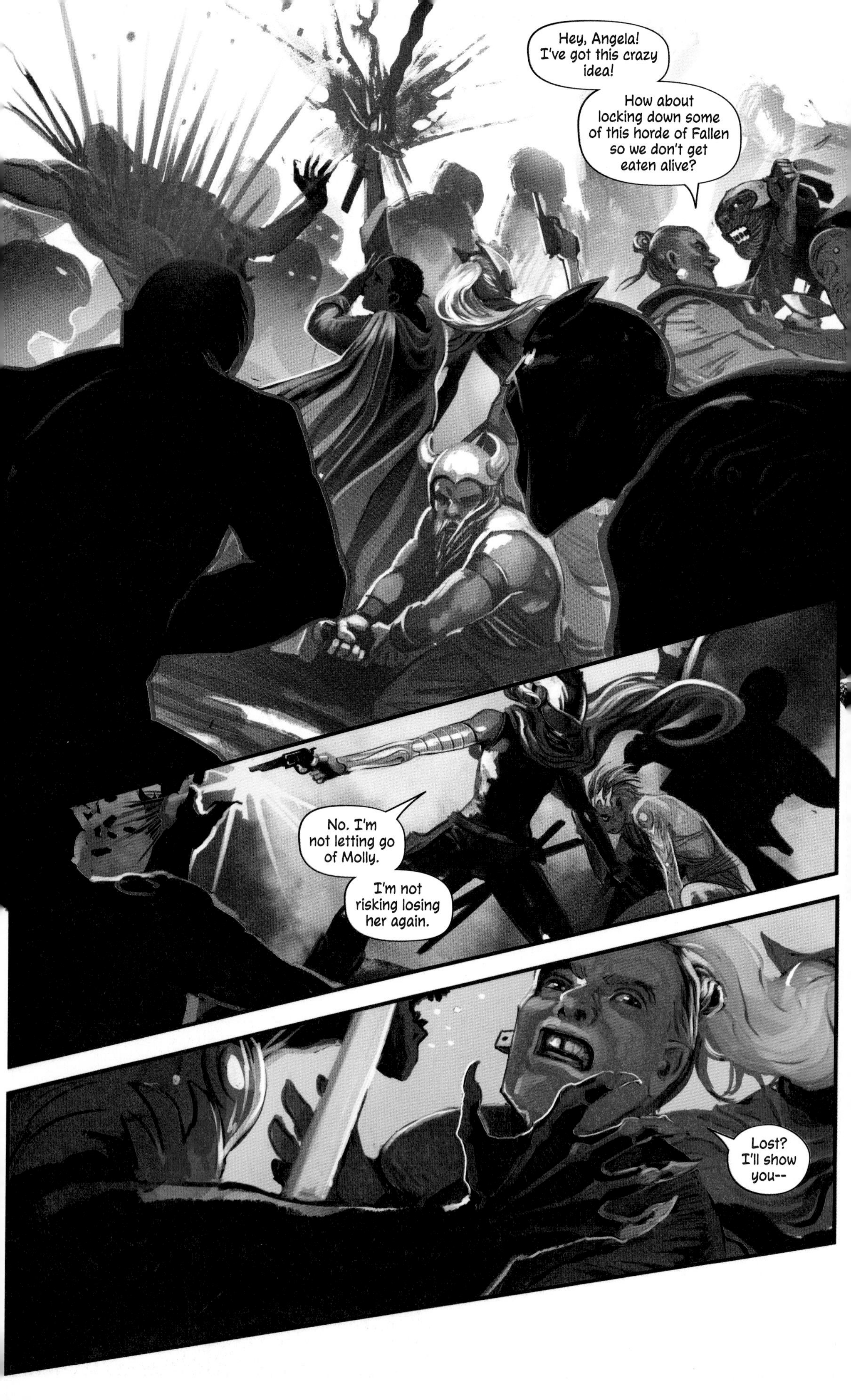
Hey, Angela! I've got this crazy idea!
How about locking down some of this horde of Fallen so we don't get eaten alive?
No. I'm not letting go of Molly.
I'm not risking losing her again.
Lost? I'll show you--

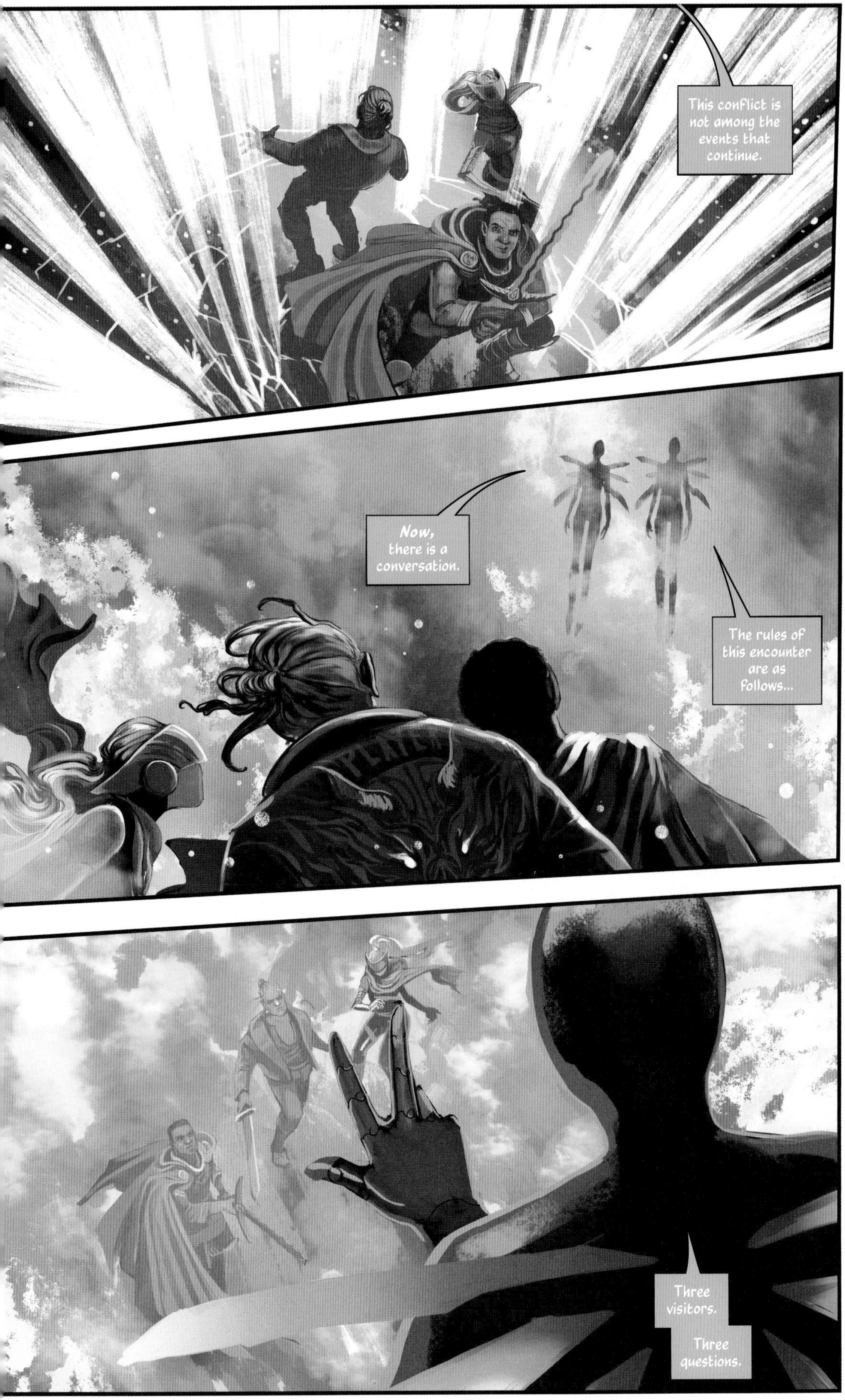
This conflict is not among the events that continue.
Now, there is a conversation.
The rules of this encounter are as follows...
Three visitors.
Three questions.

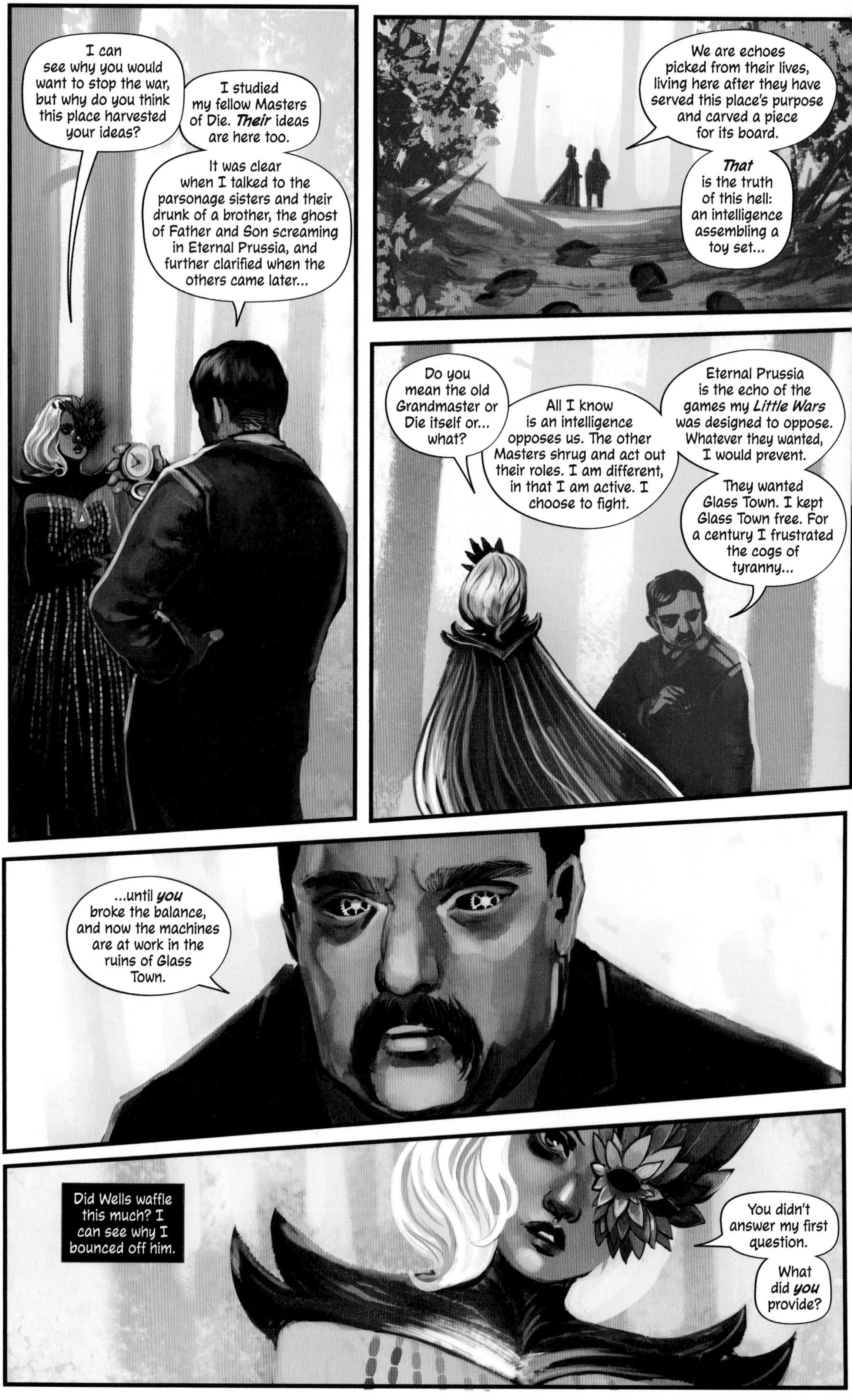
I can see why you would want to stop the war, but why do you think this place harvested your ideas?
I studied my fellow Masters of Die. **Their** ideas are here too.
It was clear when I talked to the parsonage sisters and their drunk of a brother, the ghost of Father and Son screaming in Eternal Prussia, and further clarified when the others came later...
We are echoes picked from their lives, living here after they have served this place's purpose and carved a piece for its board.
That is the truth of this hell: an intelligence assembling a toy set...
Do you mean the old Grandmaster or Die itself or... what?
All I know is an intelligence opposes us. The other Masters shrug and act out their roles. I am different, in that I am active. I choose to fight.
Eternal Prussia is the echo of the games my *Little Wars* was designed to oppose. Whatever they wanted, I would prevent.
They wanted Glass Town. I kept Glass Town free. For a century I frustrated the cogs of tyranny...
...until ***you*** broke the balance, and now the machines are at work in the ruins of Glass Town.
Did Wells waffle this much? I can see why I bounced off him.
You didn't answer my first question.
What did ***you*** provide?

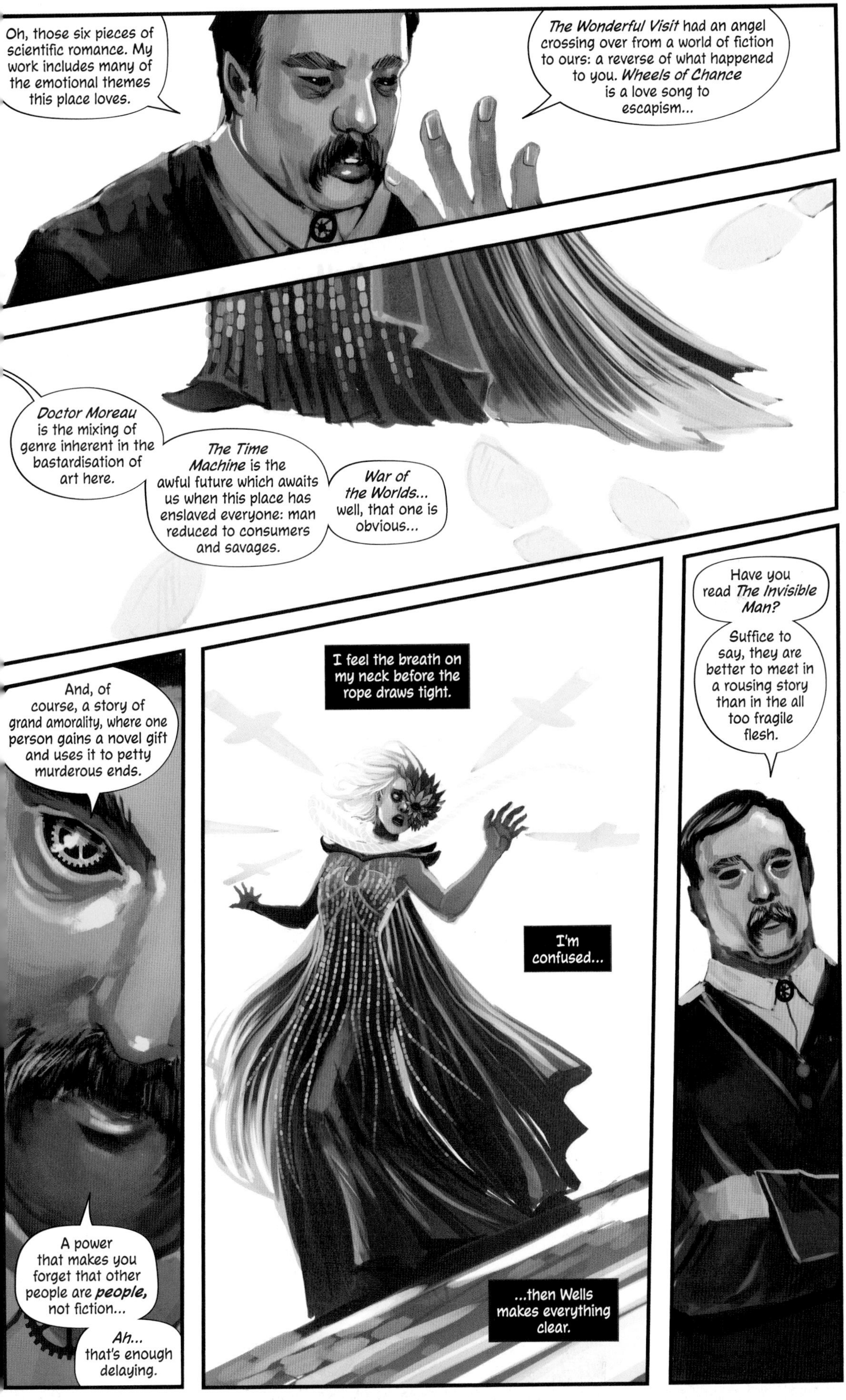
Oh, those six pieces of scientific romance. My work includes many of the emotional themes this place loves.
The Wonderful Visit had an angel crossing over from a world of fiction to ours: a reverse of what happened to you. *Wheels of Chance* is a love song to escapism...
Doctor Moreau is the mixing of genre inherent in the bastardisation of art here.
The Time Machine is the awful future which awaits us when this place has enslaved everyone: man reduced to consumers and savages.
War of the Worlds... well, that one is obvious...
And, of course, a story of grand amorality, where one person gains a novel gift and uses it to petty murderous ends.
A power that makes you forget that other people are ***people,*** not fiction...
Ah... that's enough delaying.
I feel the breath on my neck before the rope draws tight.
I'm confused...
...then Wells makes everything clear.
Have you read *The Invisible Man?*
Suffice to say, they are better to meet in a rousing story than in the all too fragile flesh.

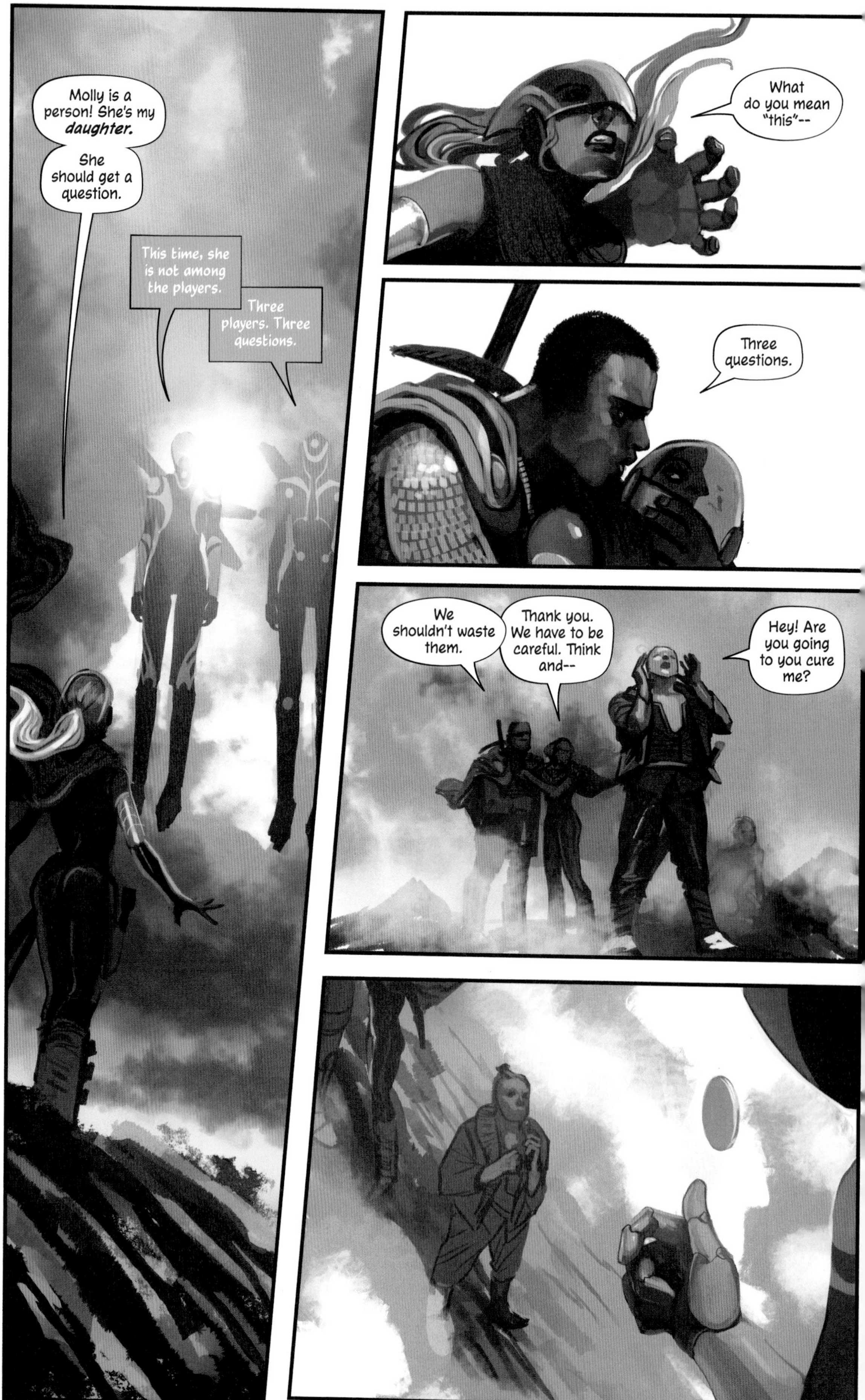
Molly is a person! She's my ***daughter.***
She should get a question.
This time, she is not among the players.
Three players. Three questions.
What do you mean "this"--
Three questions.
We shouldn't waste them.
Thank you. We have to be careful. Think and--
Hey! Are you going to you cure me?

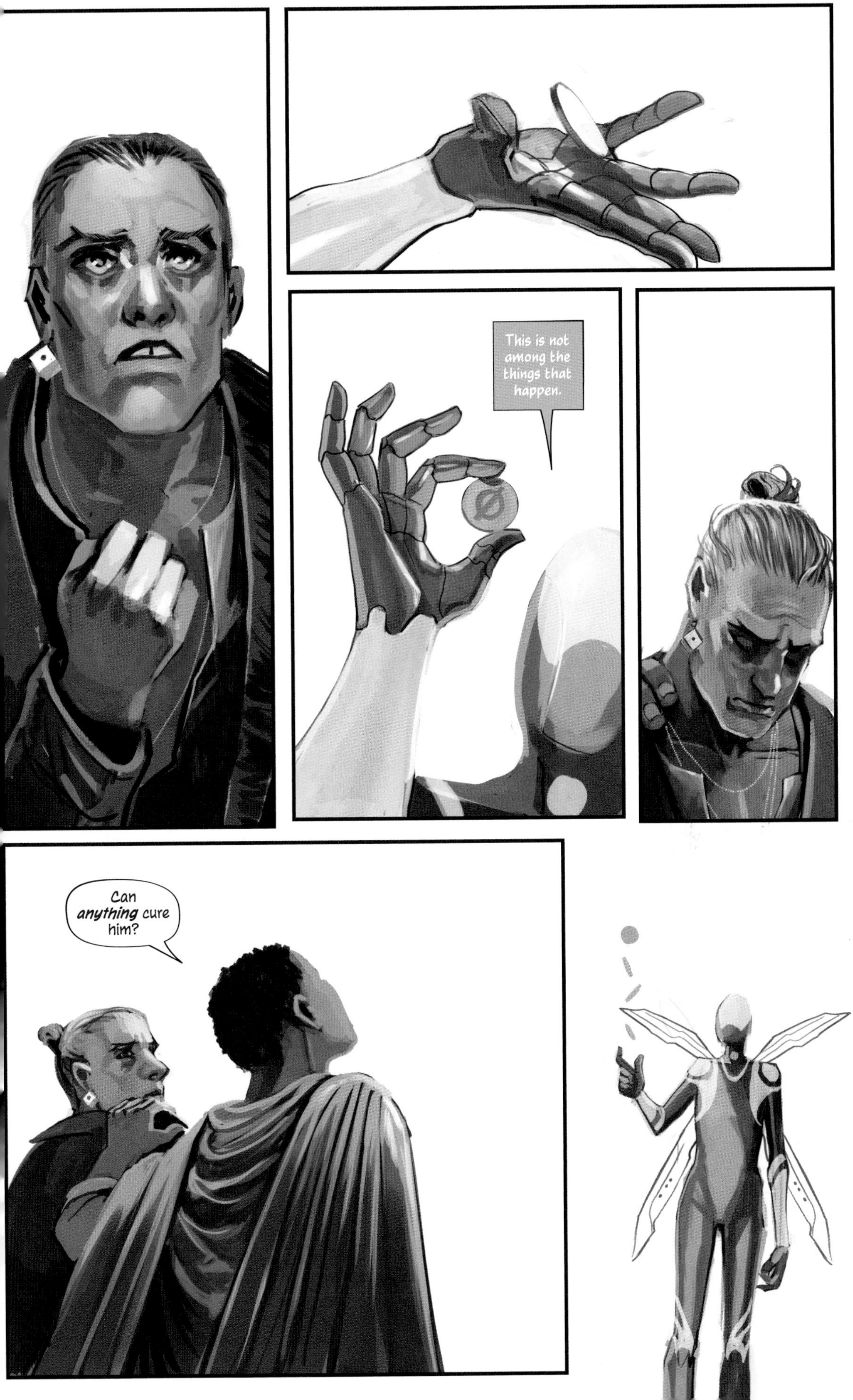
This is not among the things that happen.
Can *anything* cure him?

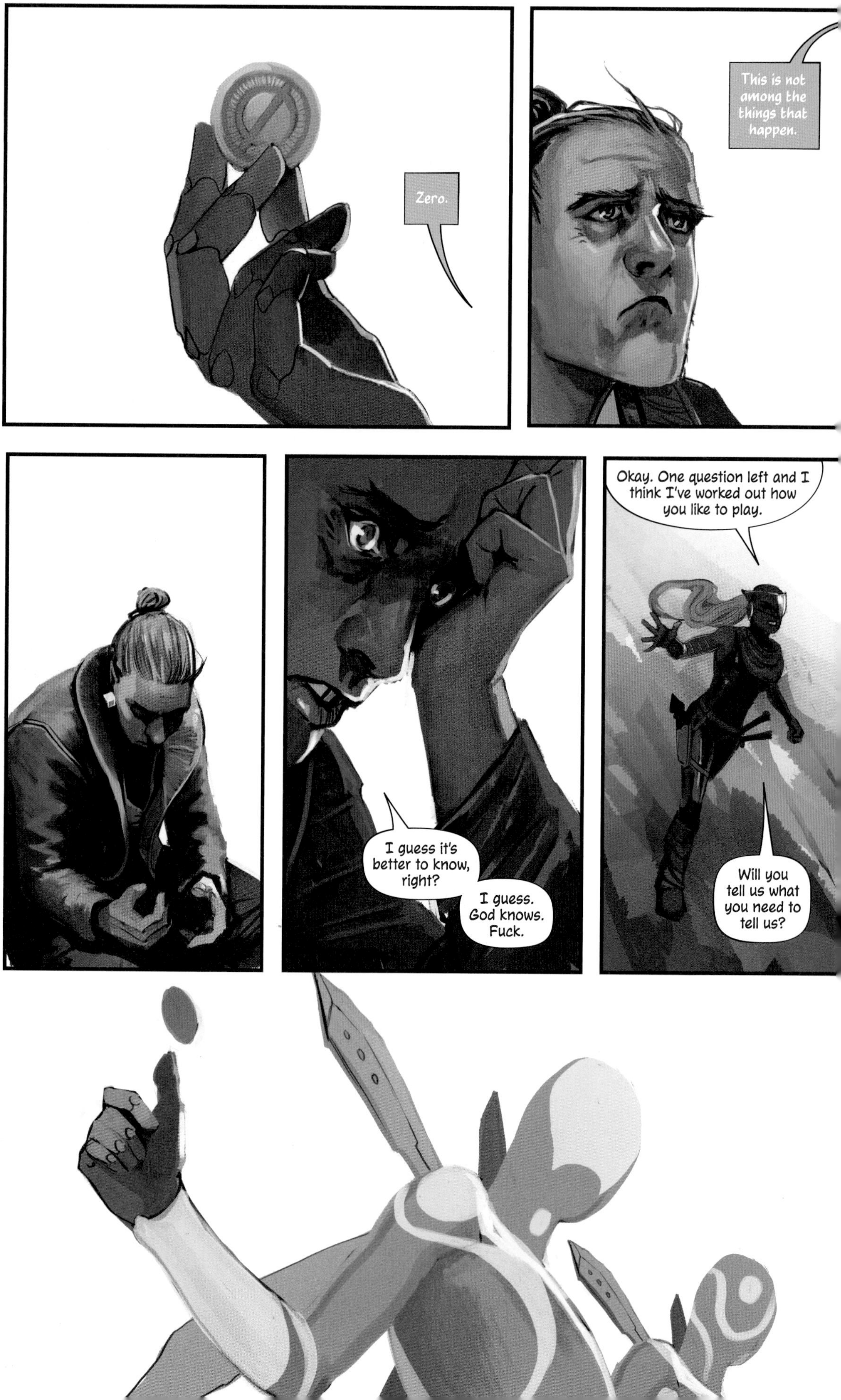
Zero.
This is not among the things that happen.
I guess it's better to know, right?
I guess. God knows. Fuck.
Okay. One question left and I think I've worked out how you like to play.
Will you tell us what you need to tell us?

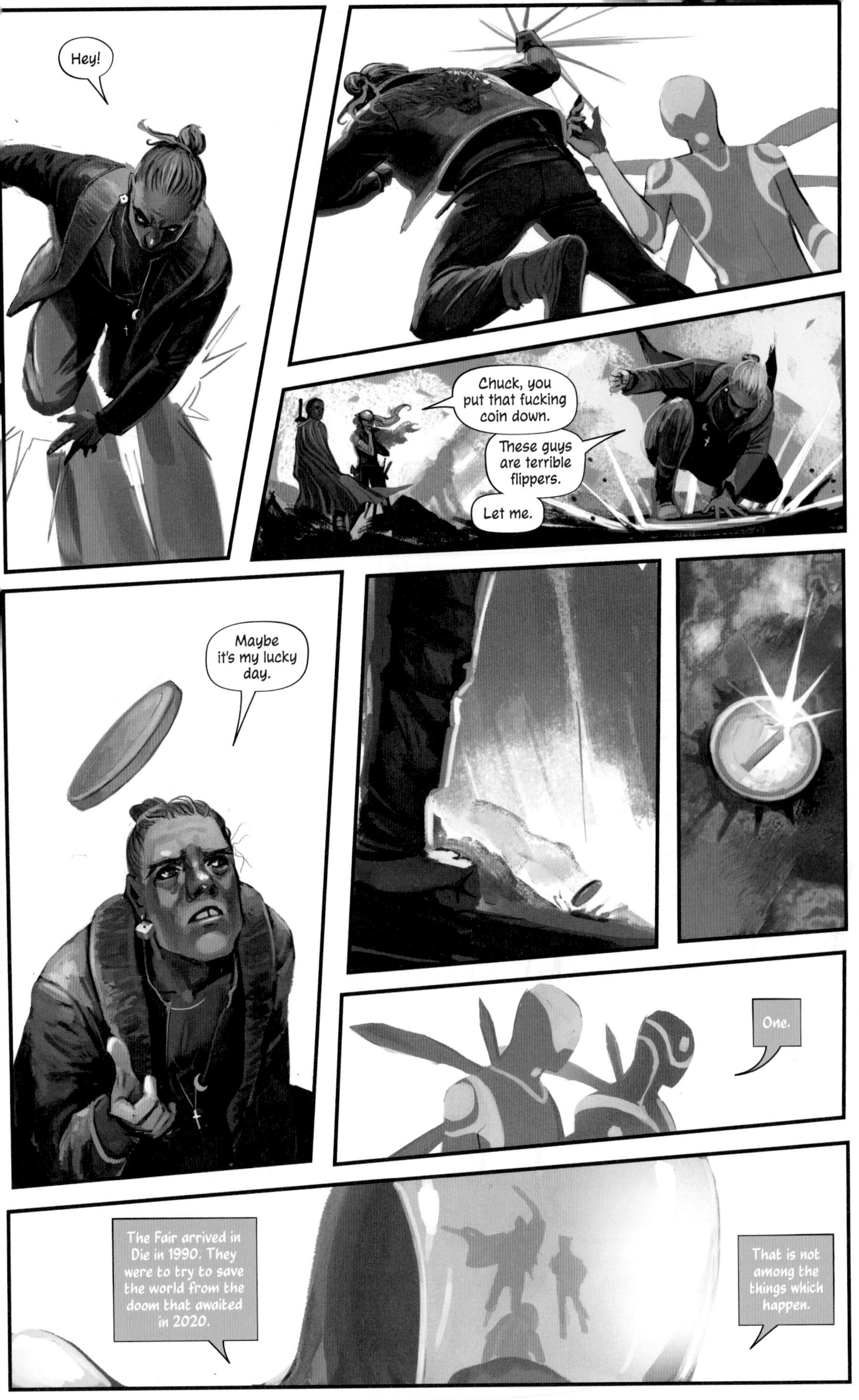

Hey!
Chuck, you put that fucking coin down.
These guys are terrible flippers.
Let me.
Maybe it's my lucky day.
One.
The Fair arrived in Die in 1990. They were to try to save the world from the doom that awaited in 2020.
That is not among the things which happen.

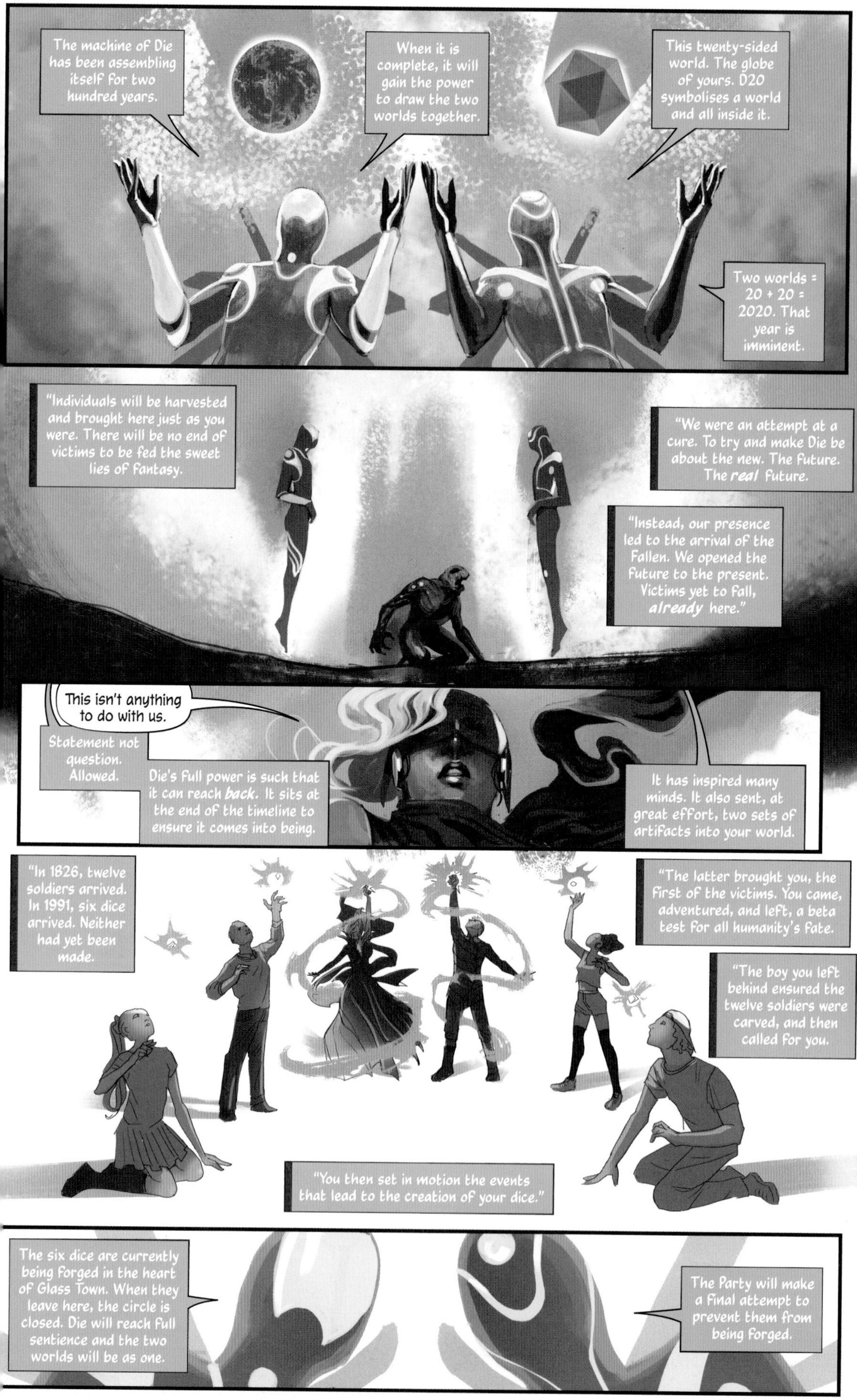

The machine of Die has been assembling itself for two hundred years.
When it is complete, it will gain the power to draw the two worlds together.
This twenty-sided world. The globe of yours. D20 symbolises a world and all inside it.
Two worlds = 20 + 20 = 2020. That year is imminent.
"Individuals will be harvested and brought here just as you were. There will be no end of victims to be fed the sweet lies of fantasy.
"We were an attempt at a cure. To try and make Die be about the new. The future. The *real* future.
"Instead, our presence led to the arrival of the Fallen. We opened the future to the present. Victims yet to fall, *already* here."
This isn't anything to do with us.
Statement not question. Allowed.
Die's full power is such that it can reach *back*. It sits at the end of the timeline to ensure it comes into being.
It has inspired many minds. It also sent, at great effort, two sets of artifacts into your world.
"In 1826, twelve soldiers arrived. In 1991, six dice arrived. Neither had yet been made.
"The latter brought you, the first of the victims. You came, adventured, and left, a beta test for all humanity's fate.
"The boy you left behind ensured the twelve soldiers were carved, and then called for you.
"You then set in motion the events that lead to the creation of your dice."
The six dice are currently being forged in the heart of Glass Town. When they leave here, the circle is closed. Die will reach full sentience and the two worlds will be as one.
The Party will make a final attempt to prevent them from being forged.

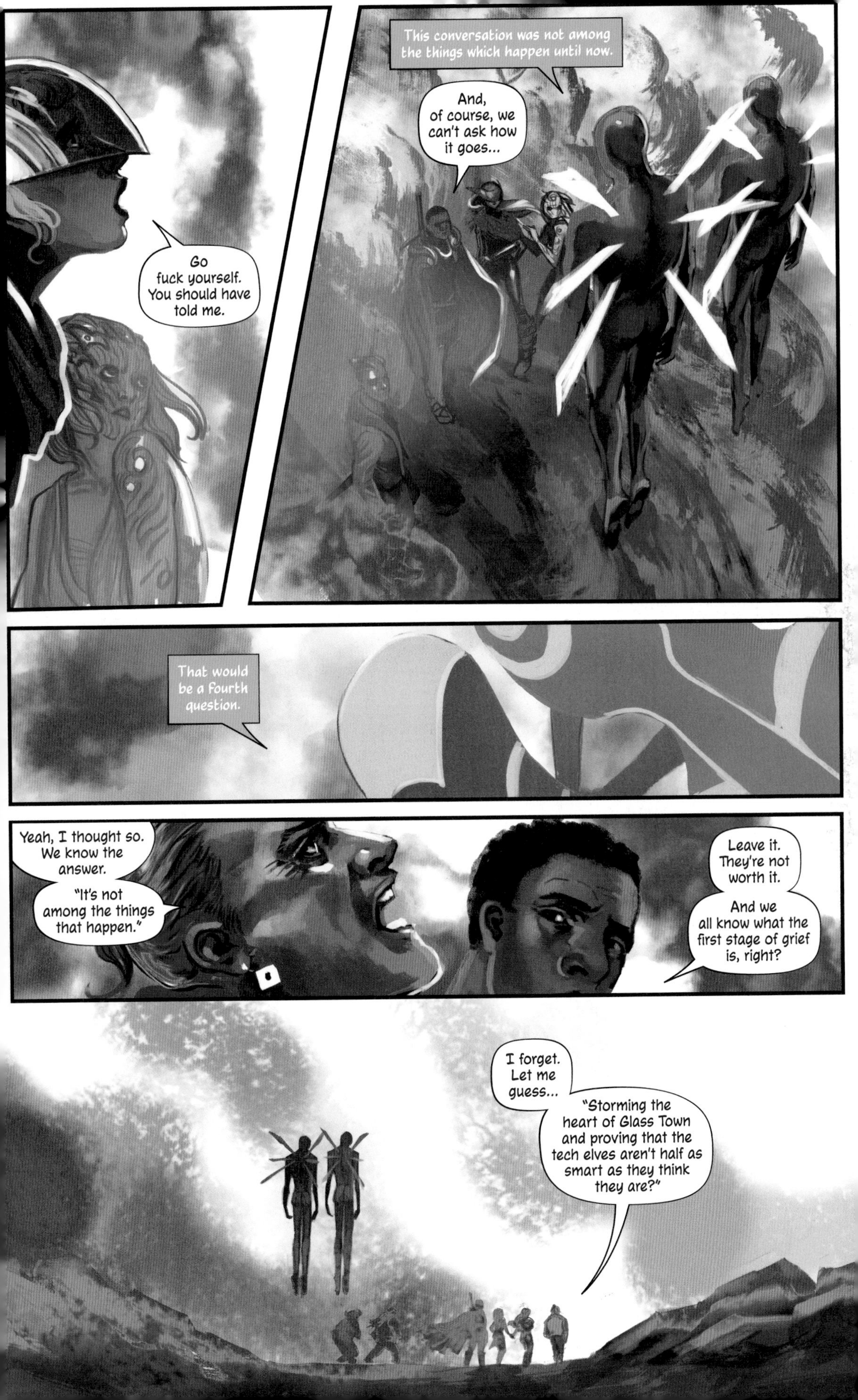

Go fuck yourself. You should have told me.
This conversation was not among the things which happen until now.
And, of course, we can't ask how it goes...
That would be a fourth question.
Yeah, I thought so. We know the answer.
"It's not among the things that happen."
Leave it. They're not worth it.
And we all know what the first stage of grief is, right?
I forget. Let me guess...
"Storming the heart of Glass Town and proving that the tech elves aren't half as smart as they think they are?"

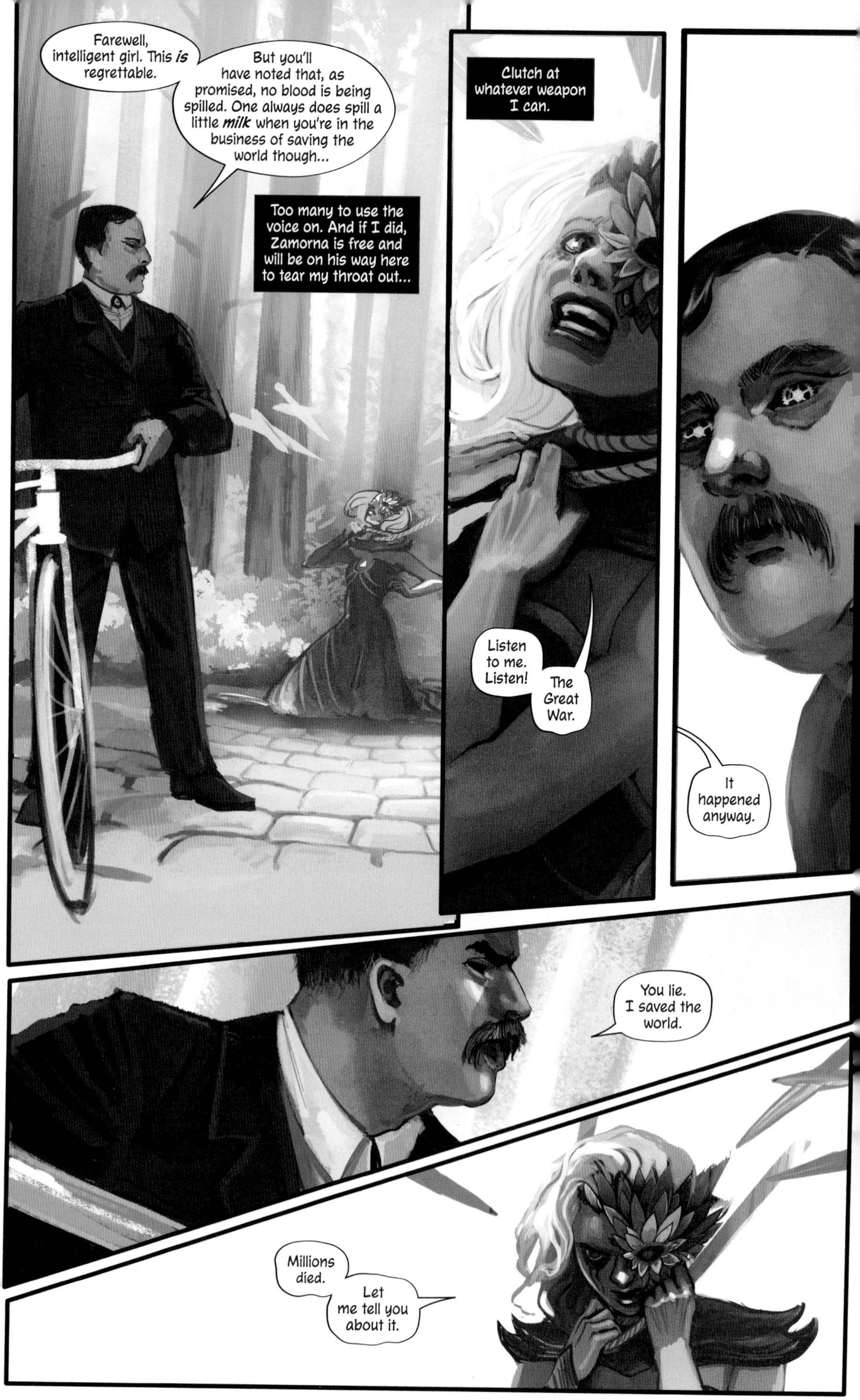
Farewell, intelligent girl. This *is* regrettable.
But you'll have noted that, as promised, no blood is being spilled. One always does spill a little *milk* when you're in the business of saving the world though...
Too many to use the voice on. And if I did, Zamorna is free and will be on his way here to tear my throat out...
Clutch at whatever weapon I can.
Listen to me. Listen!
The Great War.
It happened anyway.
You lie. I saved the world.
Millions died.
Let me tell you about it.

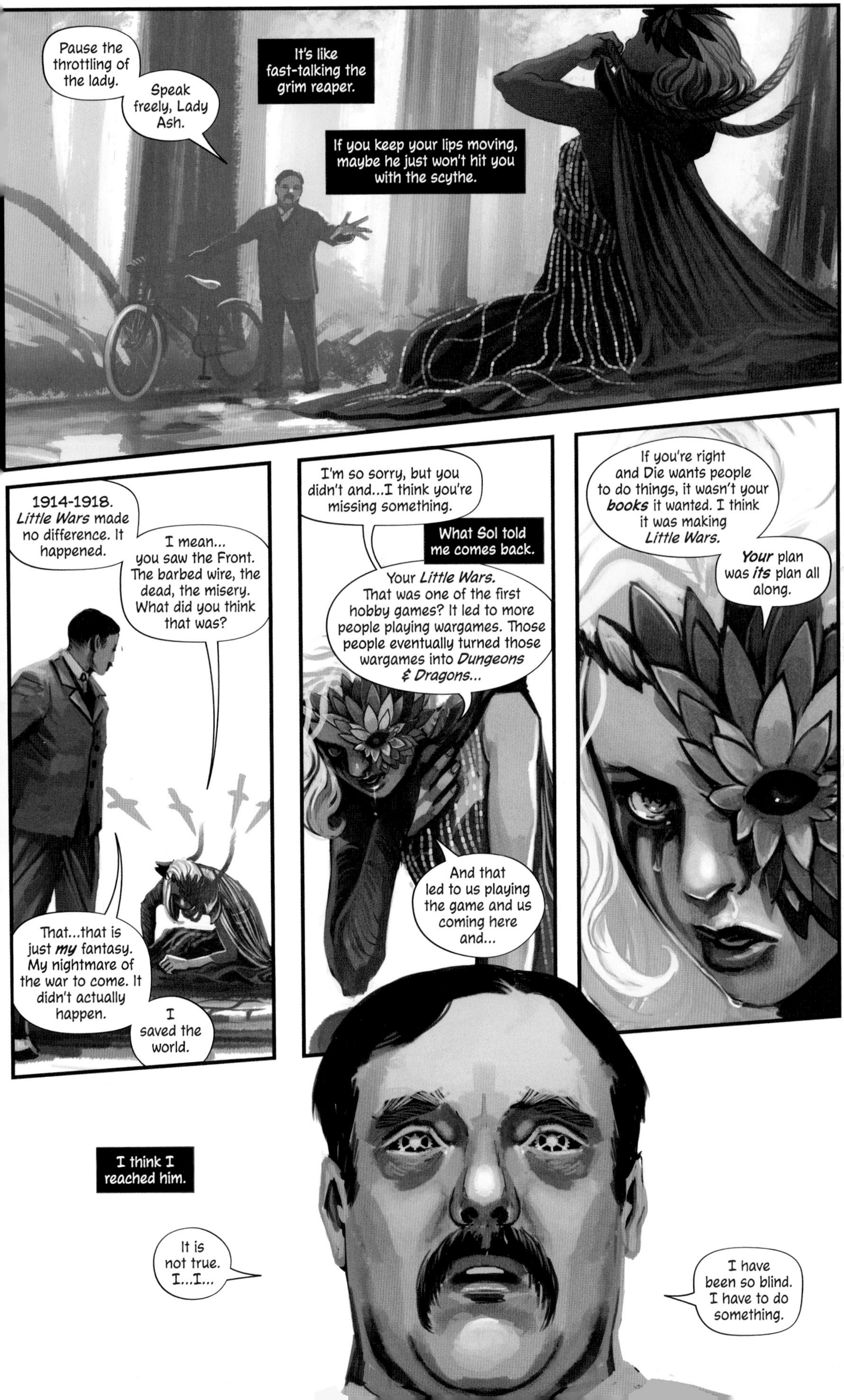

Pause the throttling of the lady.
Speak freely, Lady Ash.
It's like fast-talking the grim reaper.
If you keep your lips moving, maybe he just won't hit you with the scythe.
1914-1918. *Little Wars* made no difference. It happened.
I mean... you saw the Front. The barbed wire, the dead, the misery. What did you think that was?
That...that is just ***my*** fantasy. My nightmare of the war to come. It didn't actually happen.
I saved the world.
I'm so sorry, but you didn't and...I think you're missing something.
What Sol told me comes back.
Your *Little Wars.* That was one of the first hobby games? It led to more people playing wargames. Those people eventually turned those wargames into *Dungeons & Dragons...*
And that led to us playing the game and us coming here and...
If you're right and Die wants people to do things, it wasn't your ***books*** it wanted. I think it was making *Little Wars.*
Your plan was ***its*** plan all along.
I think I reached him.
It is not true. I...I...
I have been so blind. I have to do something.

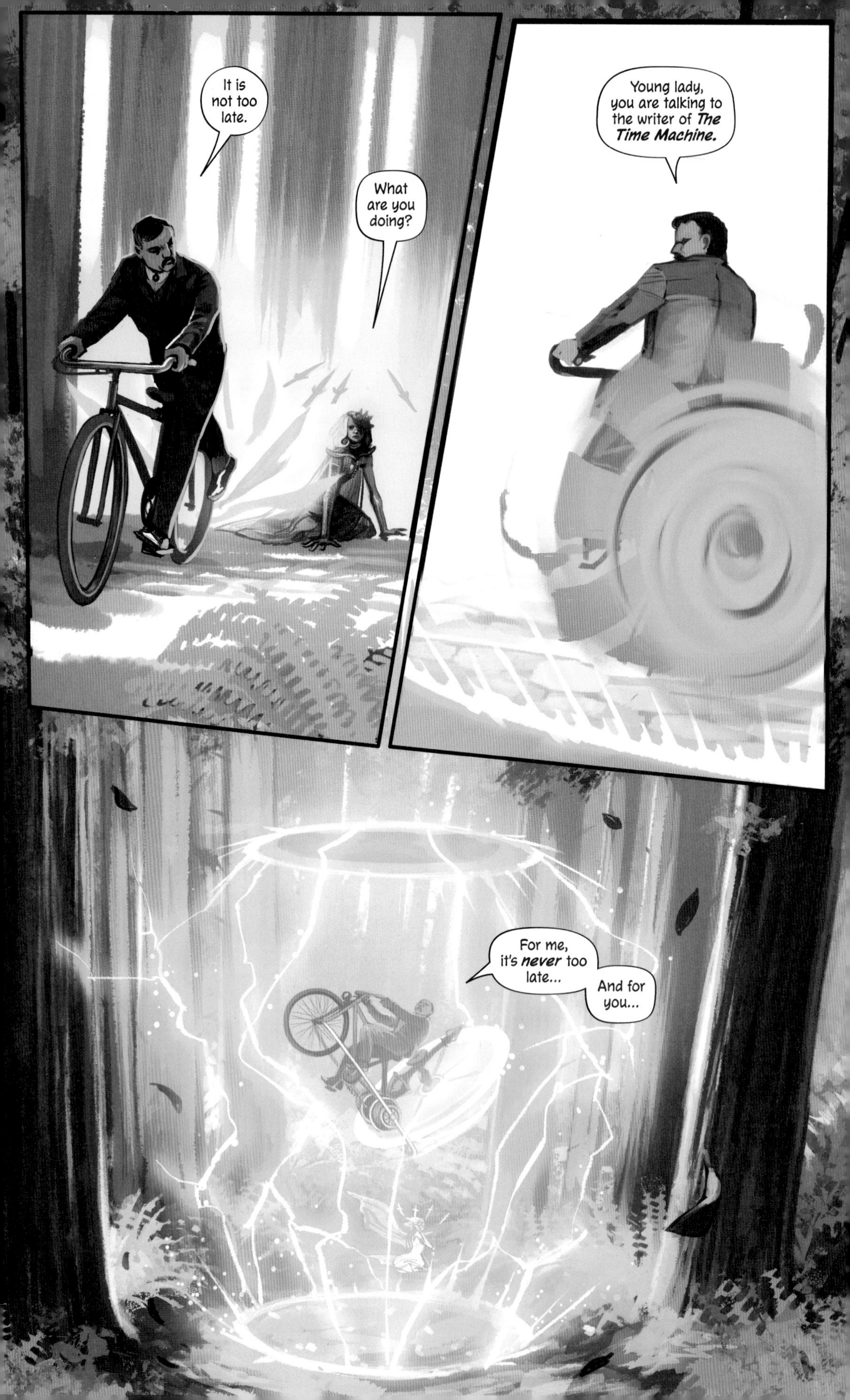
It is not too late.
What are you doing?
Young lady, you are talking to the writer of *The Time Machine.*
For me, it's *never* too late...
And for you...

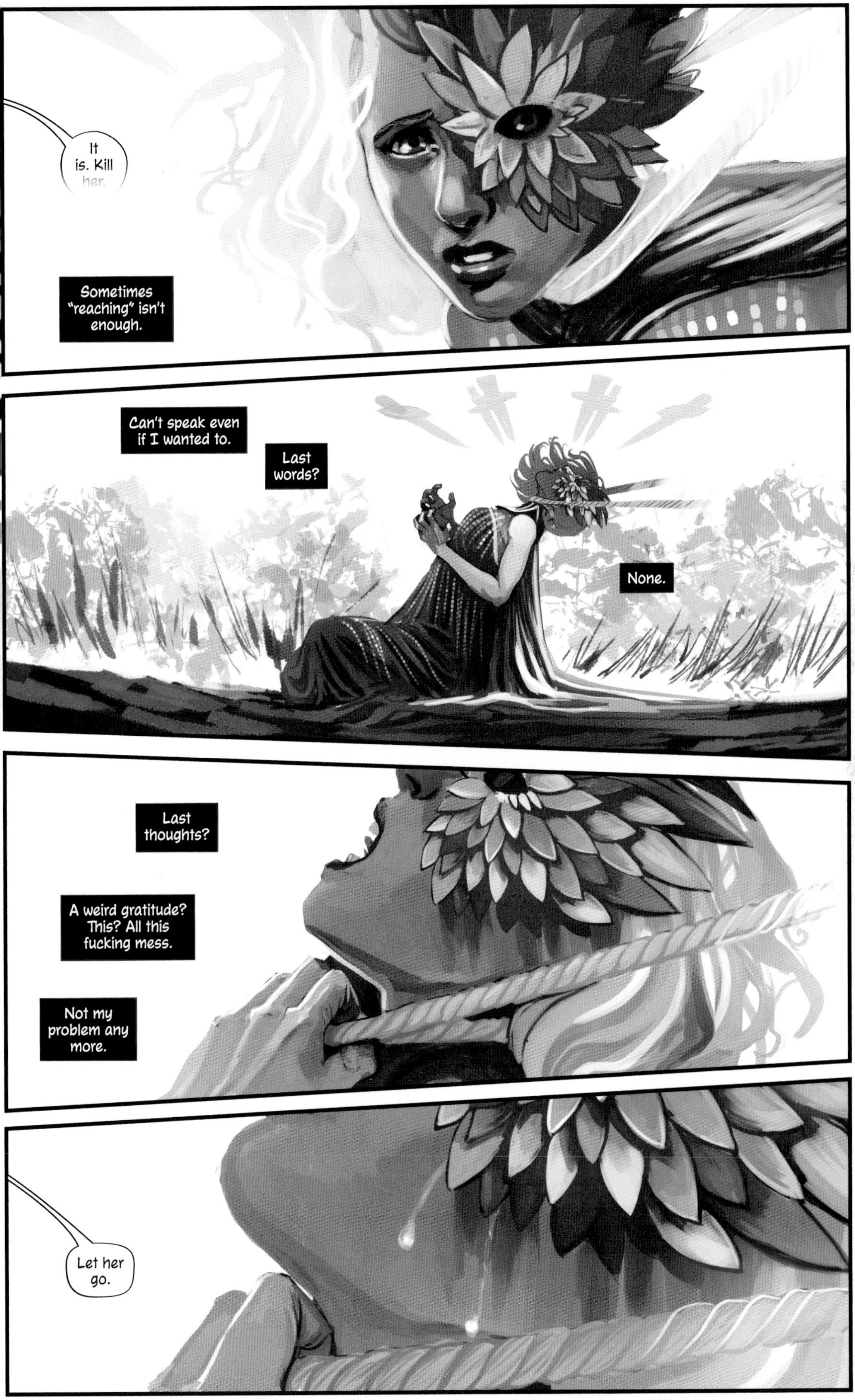
It is. Kill her.
Sometimes "reaching" isn't enough.
Can't speak even if I wanted to.
Last words?
None.
Last thoughts?
A weird gratitude? This? All this fucking mess.
Not my problem any more.
Let her go.

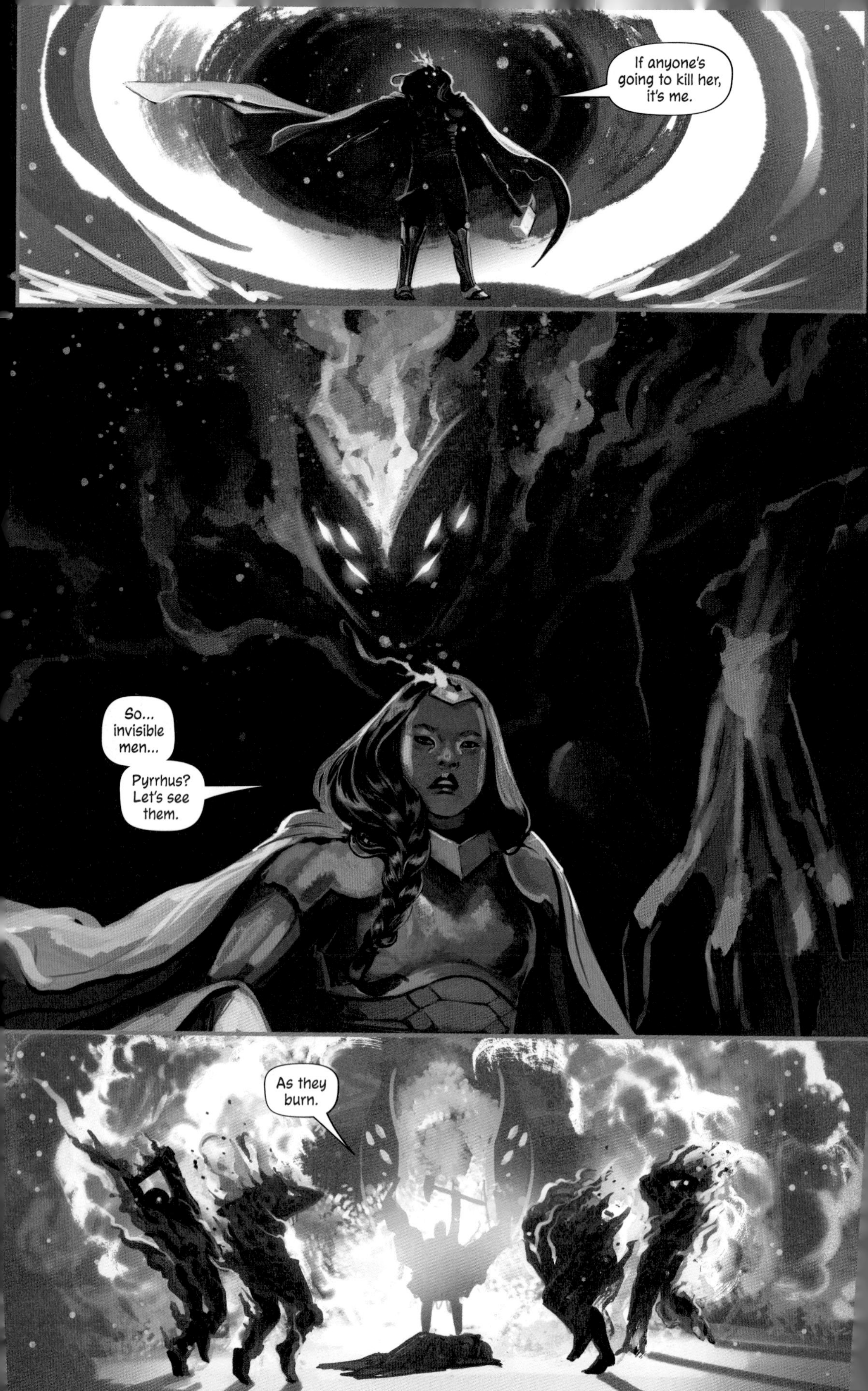
If anyone's going to kill her, it's me.
So... invisible men...
Pyrrhus? Let's see them.
As they burn.

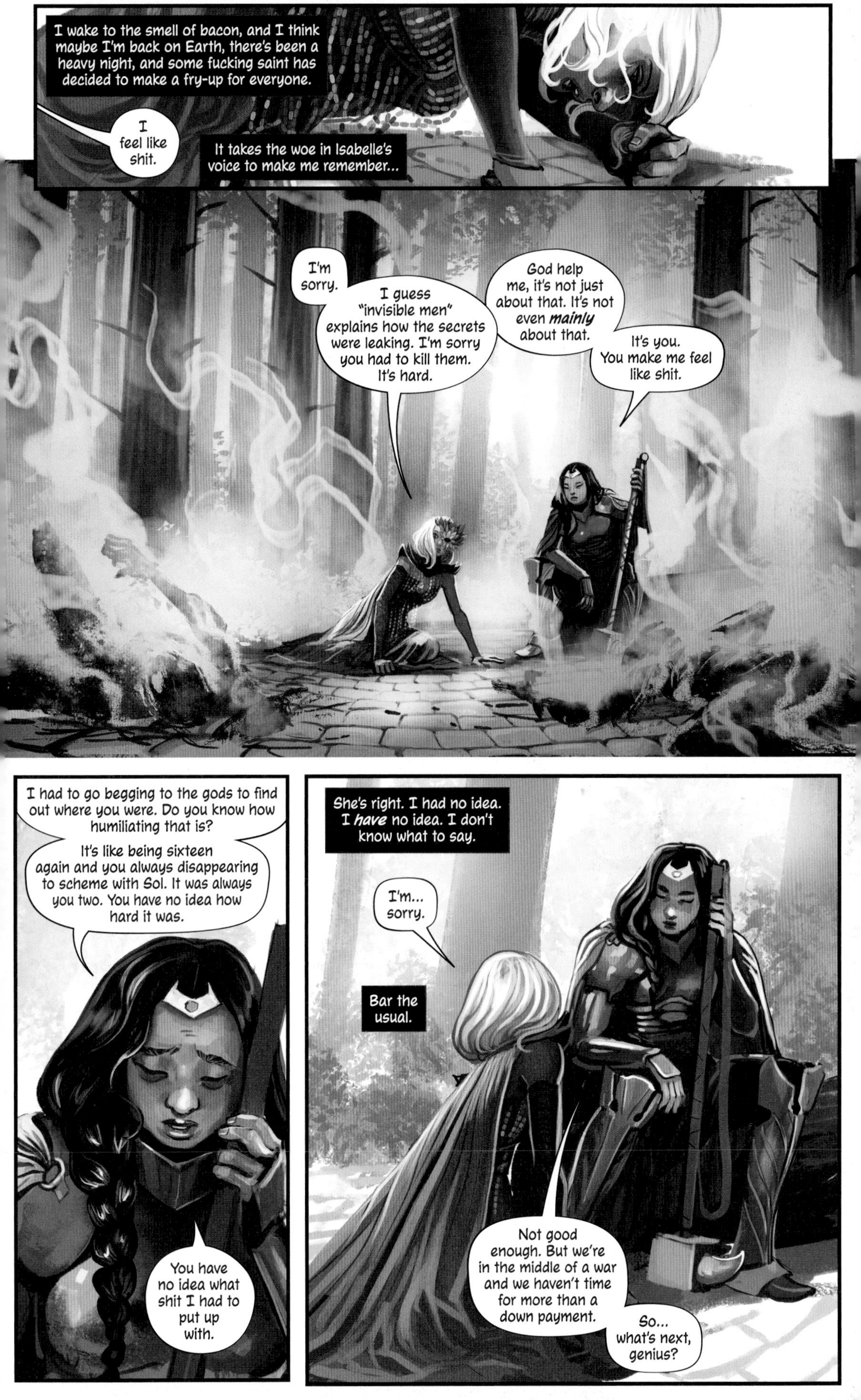
I wake to the smell of bacon, and I think maybe I'm back on Earth, there's been a heavy night, and some fucking saint has decided to make a fry-up for everyone.
I feel like shit.
It takes the woe in Isabelle's voice to make me remember...
I'm sorry.
I guess "invisible men" explains how the secrets were leaking. I'm sorry you had to kill them. It's hard.
God help me, it's not just about that. It's not even *mainly* about that.
It's you. You make me feel like shit.
I had to go begging to the gods to find out where you were. Do you know how humiliating that is?
It's like being sixteen again and you always disappearing to scheme with Sol. It was always you two. You have no idea how hard it was.
You have no idea what shit I had to put up with.
She's right. I had no idea. I *have* no idea. I don't know what to say.
I'm... sorry.
Bar the usual.
Not good enough. But we're in the middle of a war and we haven't time for more than a down payment.
So... what's next, genius?

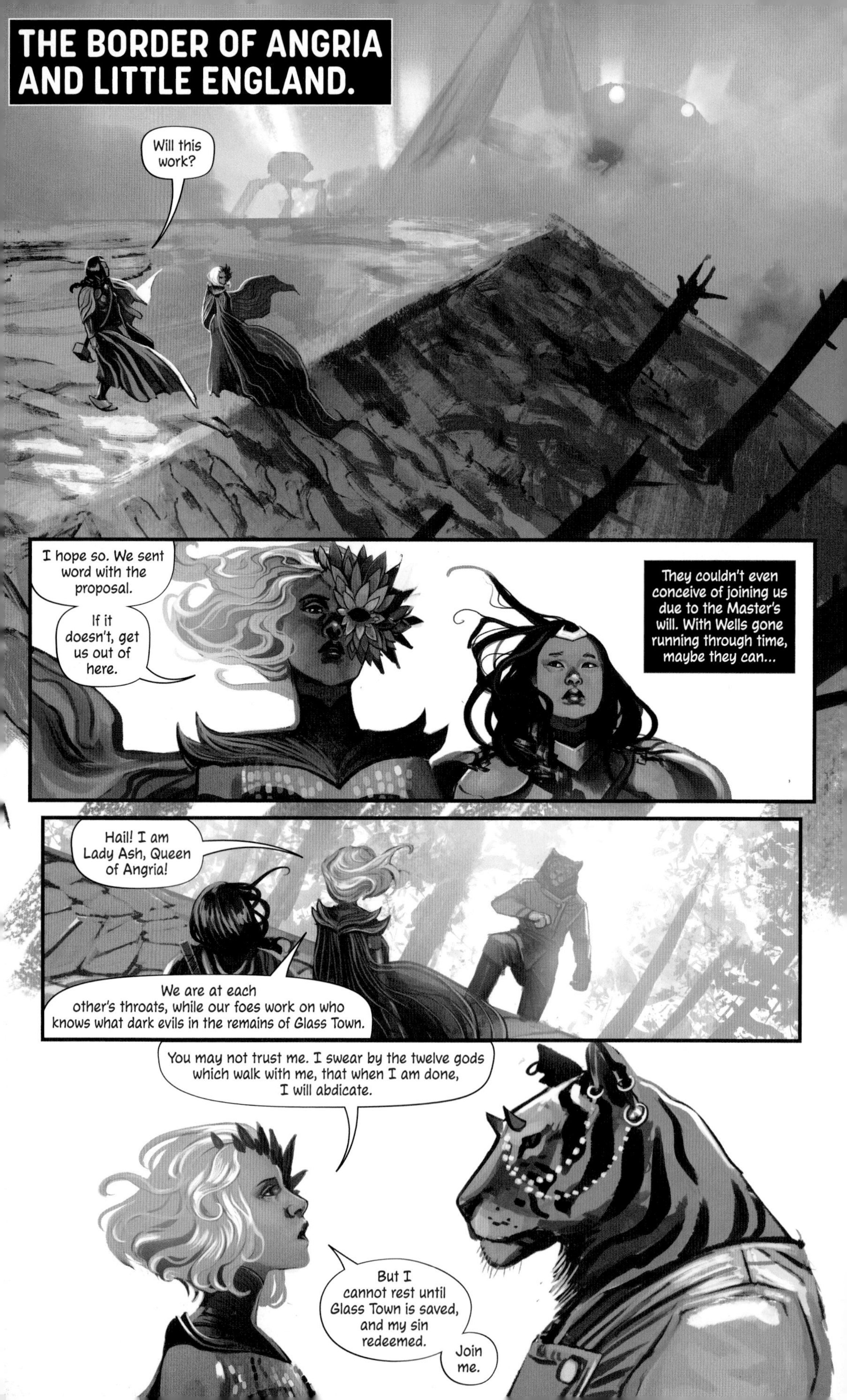
THE BORDER OF ANGRIA AND LITTLE ENGLAND.
Will this work?
I hope so. We sent word with the proposal.
If it doesn't, get us out of here.
They couldn't even conceive of joining us due to the Master's will. With Wells gone running through time, maybe they can...
Hail! I am Lady Ash, Queen of Angria!
We are at each other's throats, while our foes work on who knows what dark evils in the remains of Glass Town.
You may not trust me. I swear by the twelve gods which walk with me, that when I am done, I will abdicate.
But I cannot rest until Glass Town is saved, and my sin redeemed.
Join me.

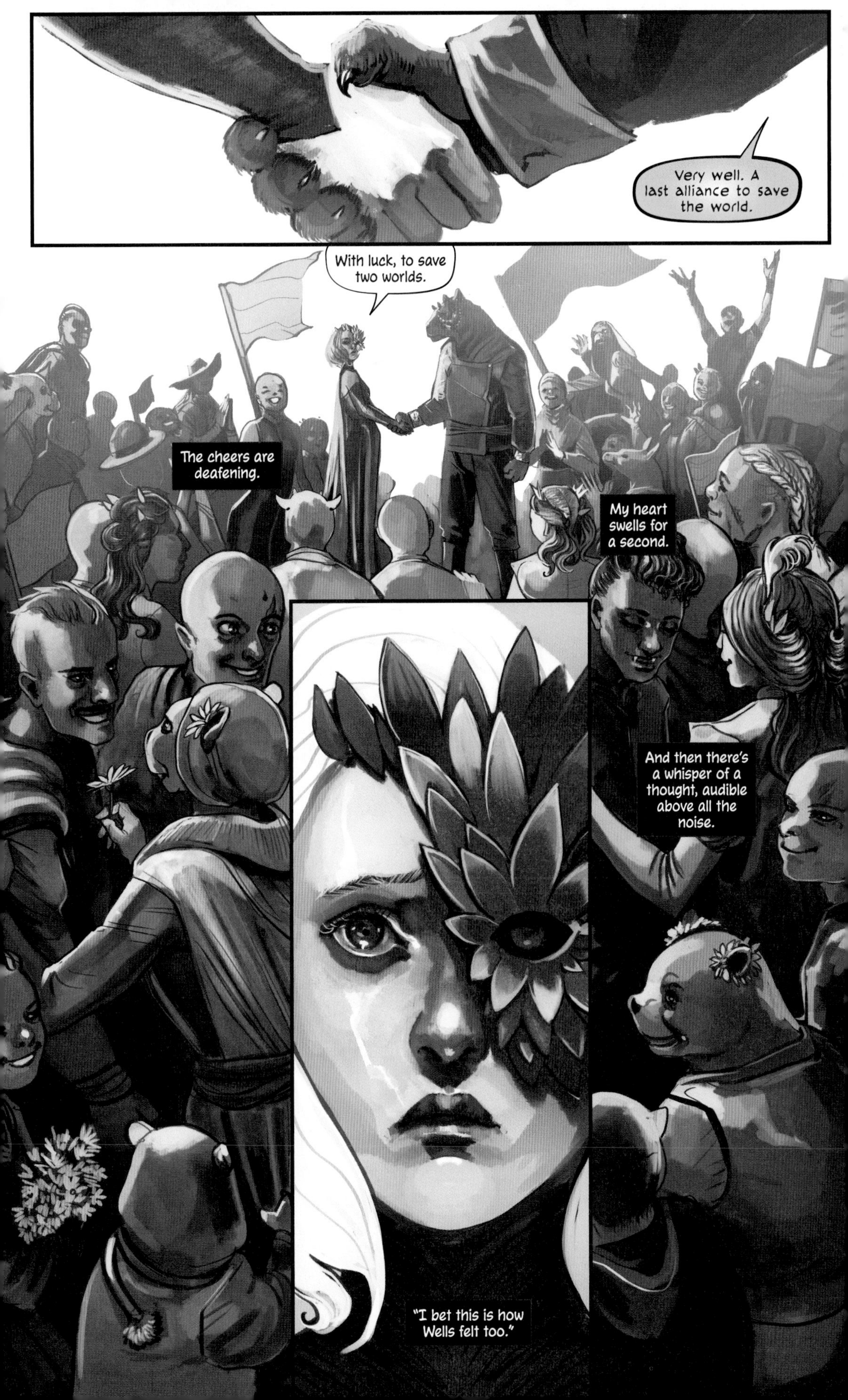
Very well. A last alliance to save the world.
With luck, to save two worlds.
The cheers are deafening.
My heart swells for a second.
And then there's a whisper of a thought, audible above all the noise.
"I bet this is how Wells felt too."

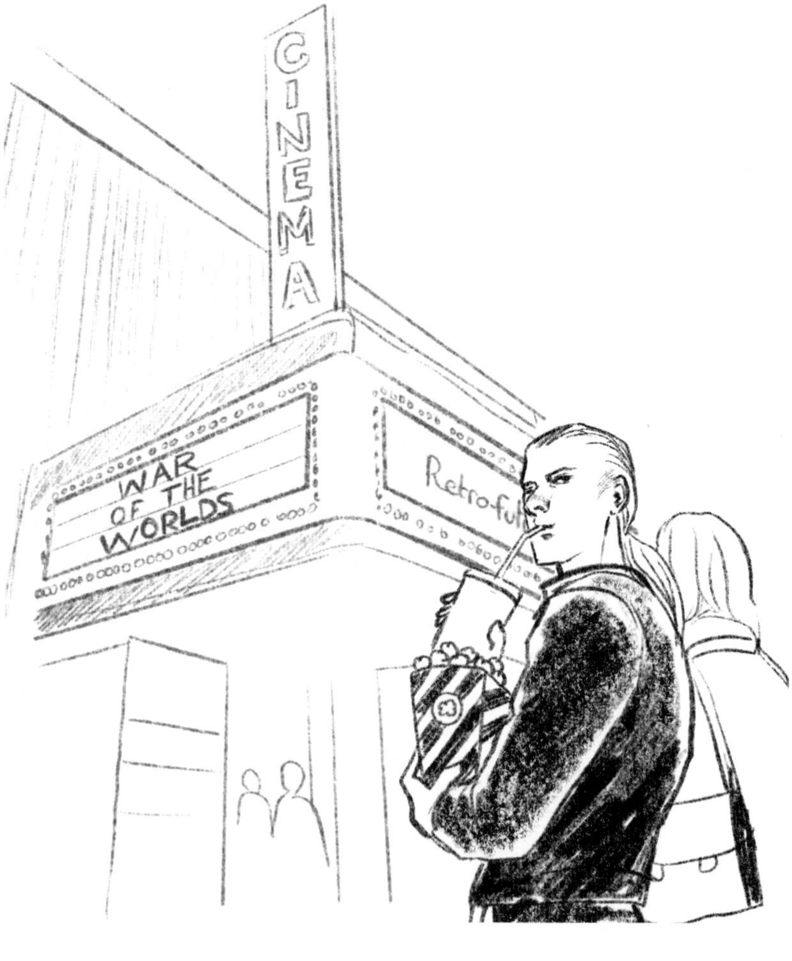
CINEMA
WAR OF THE WORLDS

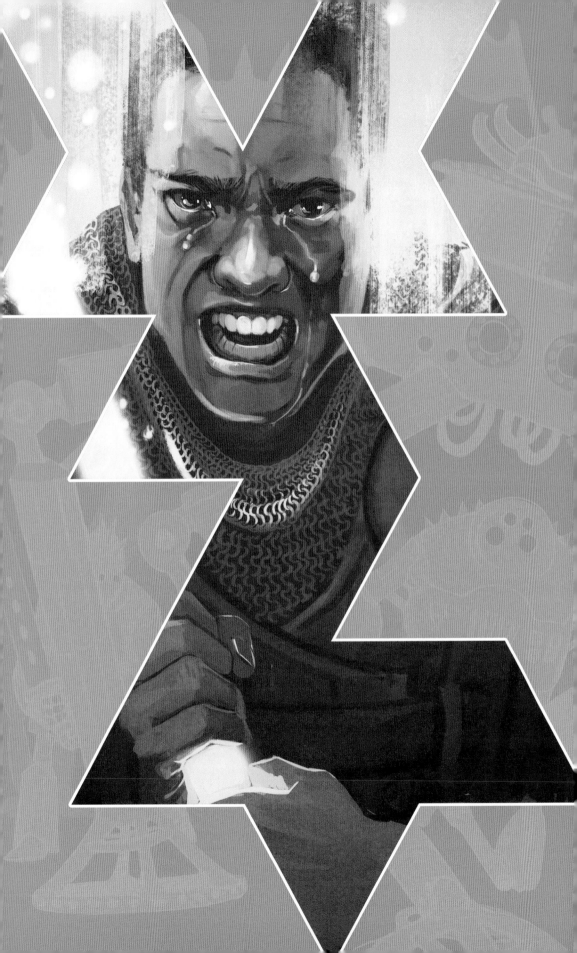

14:
DUAL WIELD

"Fools say that they learn by experience. I prefer to profit by others' experience."
– *Otto von Bismarck*

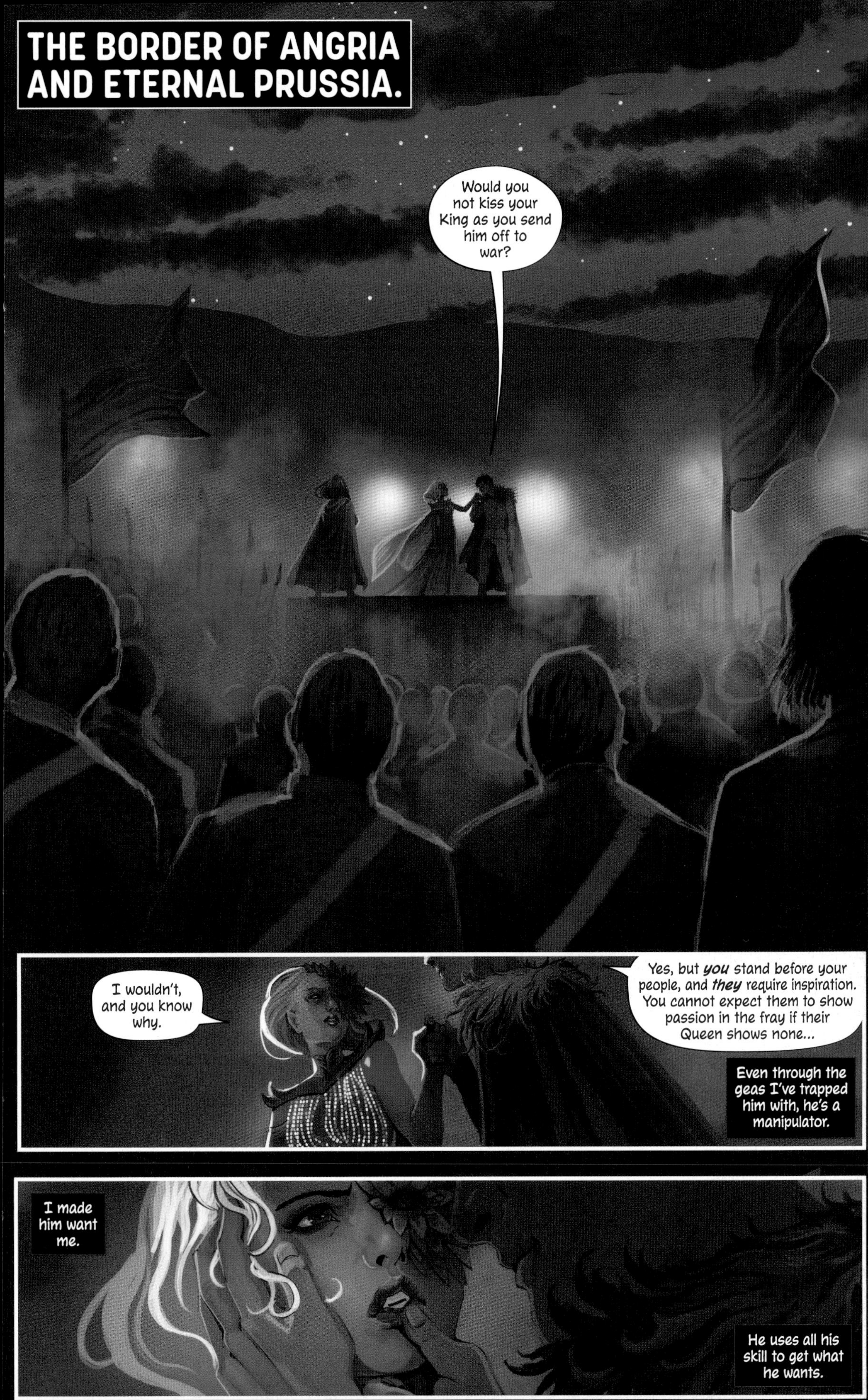
THE BORDER OF ANGRIA AND ETERNAL PRUSSIA.
Would you not kiss your King as you send him off to war?
I wouldn't, and you know why.
Yes, but *you* stand before your people, and *they* require inspiration. You cannot expect them to show passion in the fray if their Queen shows none...
Even through the geas I've trapped him with, he's a manipulator.
I made him want me.
He uses all his skill to get what he wants.

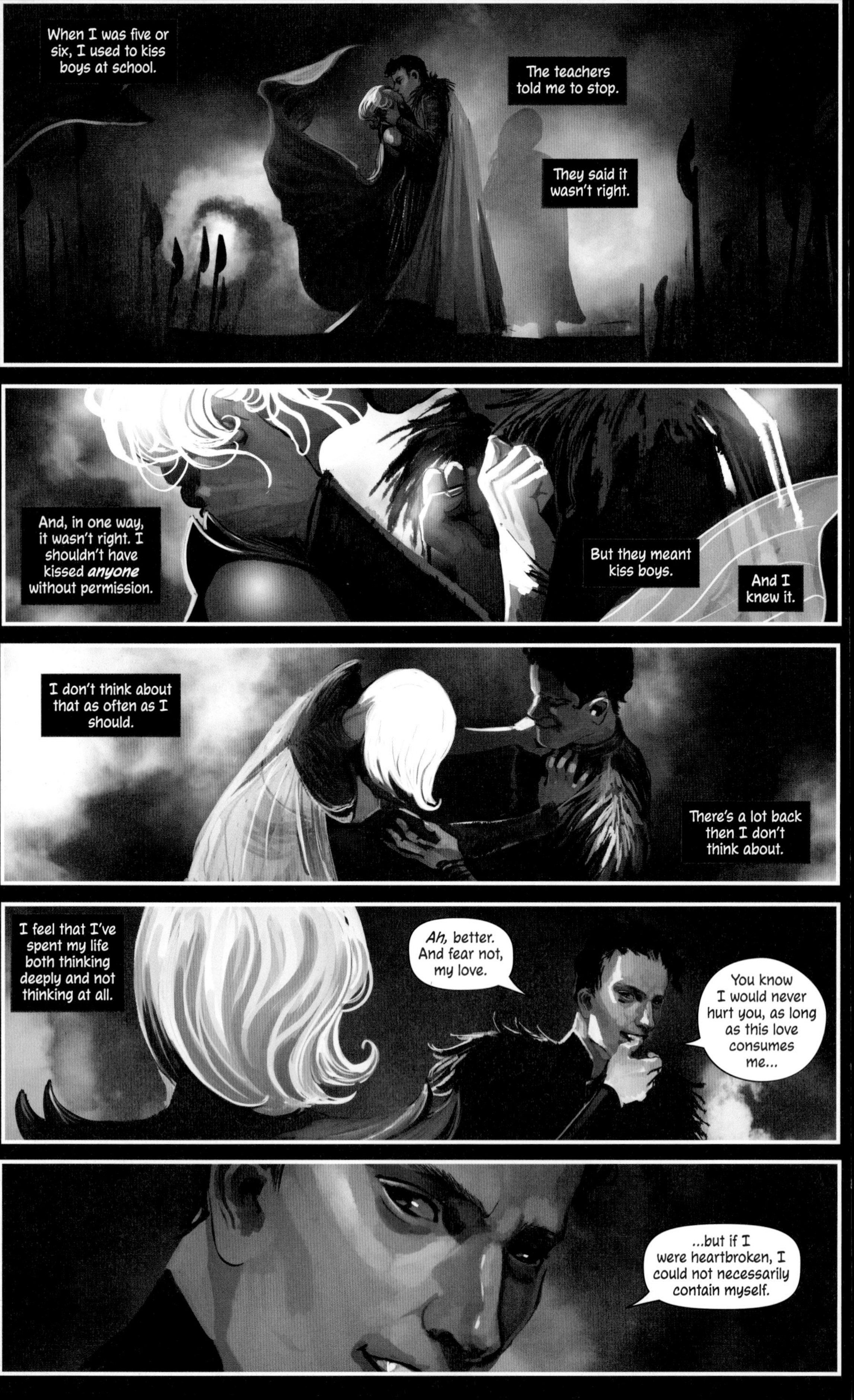
When I was five or six, I used to kiss boys at school.
The teachers told me to stop.
They said it wasn't right.
And, in one way, it wasn't right. I shouldn't have kissed *anyone* without permission.
But they meant kiss boys.
And I knew it.
I don't think about that as often as I should.
There's a lot back then I don't think about.
I feel that I've spent my life both thinking deeply and not thinking at all.
Ah, better. And fear not, my love.
You know I would never hurt you, as long as this love consumes me...
...but if I were heartbroken, I could not necessarily contain myself.

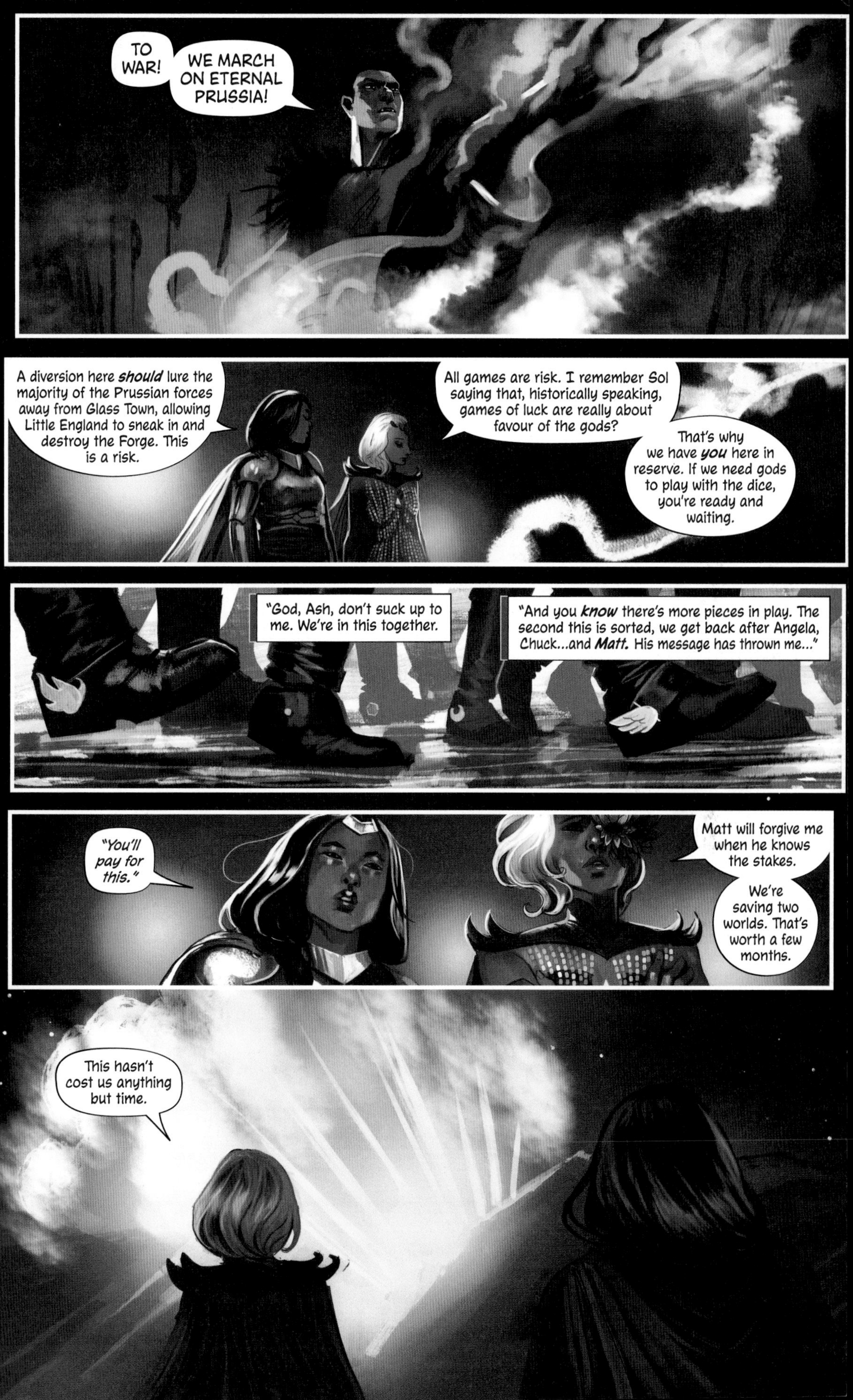
TO WAR!
WE MARCH ON ETERNAL PRUSSIA!
A diversion here *should* lure the majority of the Prussian forces away from Glass Town, allowing Little England to sneak in and destroy the Forge. This is a risk.
All games are risk. I remember Sol saying that, historically speaking, games of luck are really about favour of the gods?
That's why we have *you* here in reserve. If we need gods to play with the dice, you're ready and waiting.
"God, Ash, don't suck up to me. We're in this together.
"And you *know* there's more pieces in play. The second this is sorted, we get back after Angela, Chuck...and *Matt.* His message has thrown me..."
"You'll pay for this."
Matt will forgive me when he knows the stakes.
We're saving two worlds. That's worth a few months.
This hasn't cost us anything but time.

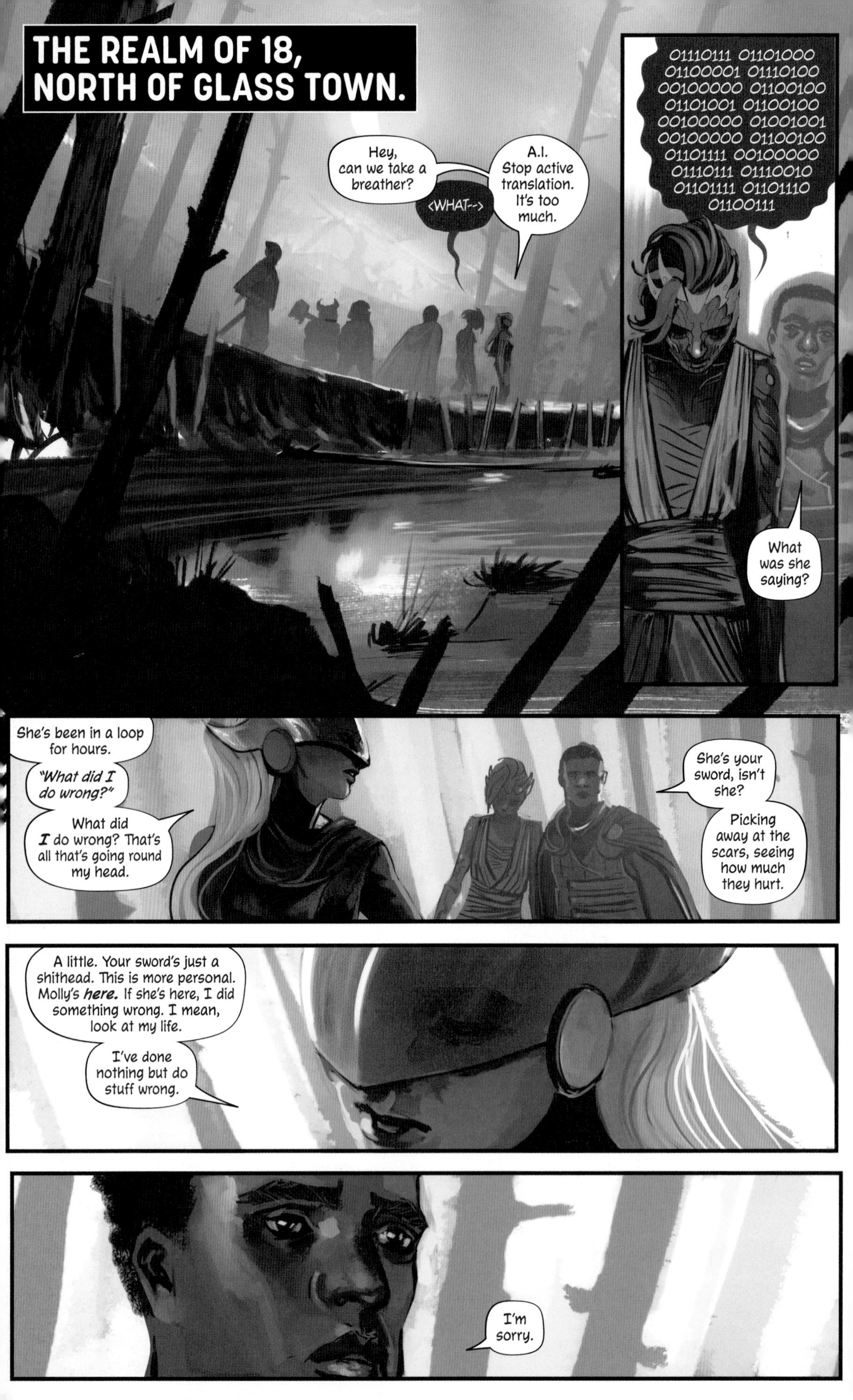
THE REALM OF 18, NORTH OF GLASS TOWN.
Hey, can we take a breather?
<WHAT-->
A.I. Stop active translation. It's too much.
01110111 01101000 01100001 01110100 00100000 01100100 01101001 01100100 00100000 01001001 00100000 01100100 01101111 00100000 01110111 01110010 01101111 01101110 01100111
What was she saying?
She's been in a loop for hours.
"What did I do wrong?"
What did I do wrong? That's all that's going round my head.
She's your sword, isn't she?
Picking away at the scars, seeing how much they hurt.
A little. Your sword's just a shithead. This is more personal. Molly's here. If she's here, I did something wrong. I mean, look at my life.
I've done nothing but do stuff wrong.
I'm sorry.

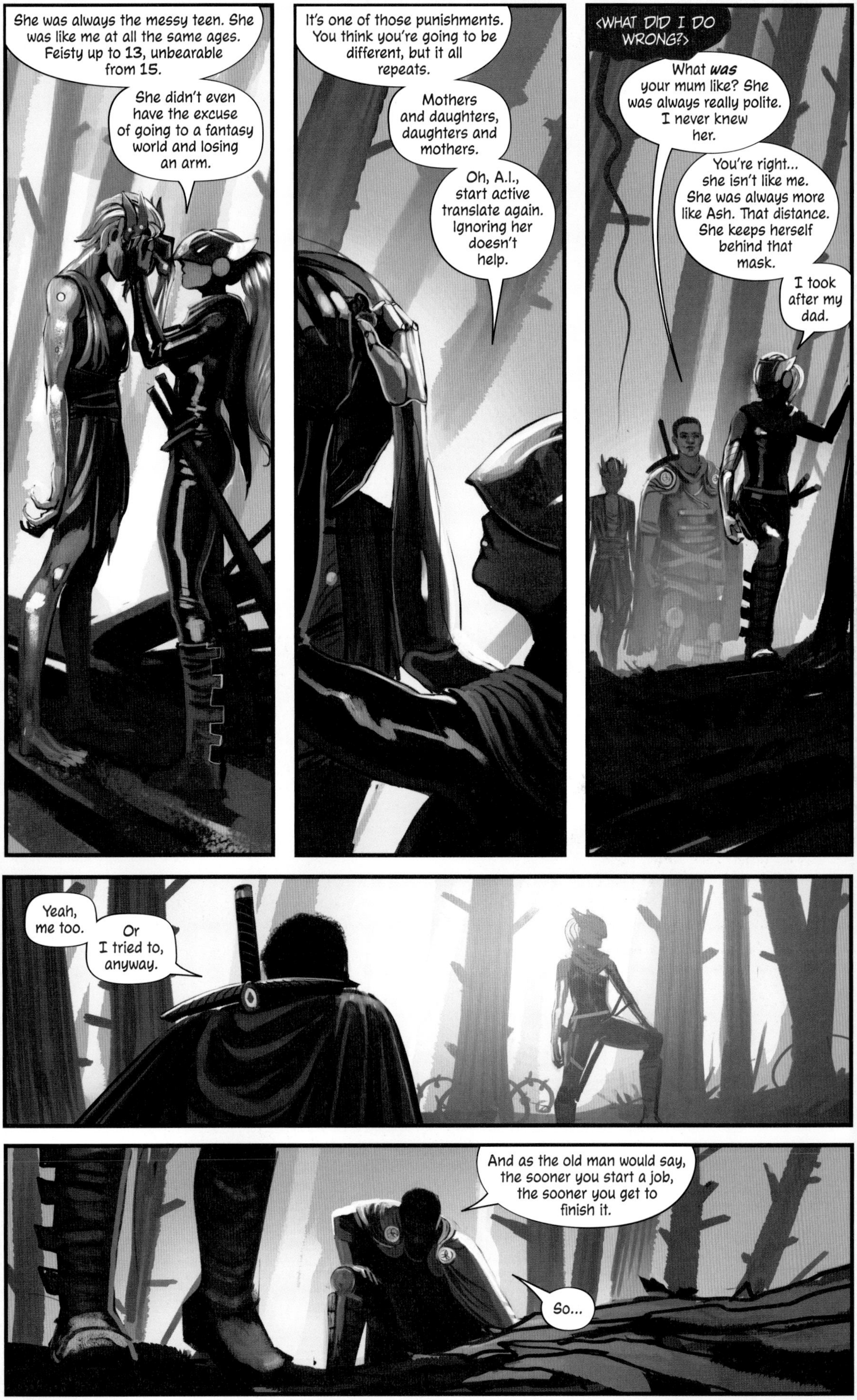

She was always the messy teen. She was like me at all the same ages. Feisty up to 13, unbearable from 15.
She didn't even have the excuse of going to a fantasy world and losing an arm.
It's one of those punishments. You think you're going to be different, but it all repeats.
Mothers and daughters, daughters and mothers.
Oh, A.I., start active translate again. Ignoring her doesn't help.
<WHAT DID I DO WRONG?>
What *was* your mum like? She was always really polite. I never knew her.
You're right... she isn't like me. She was always more like Ash. That distance. She keeps herself behind that mask.
I took after my dad.
Yeah, me too.
Or I tried to, anyway.
And as the old man would say, the sooner you start a job, the sooner you get to finish it.
So...

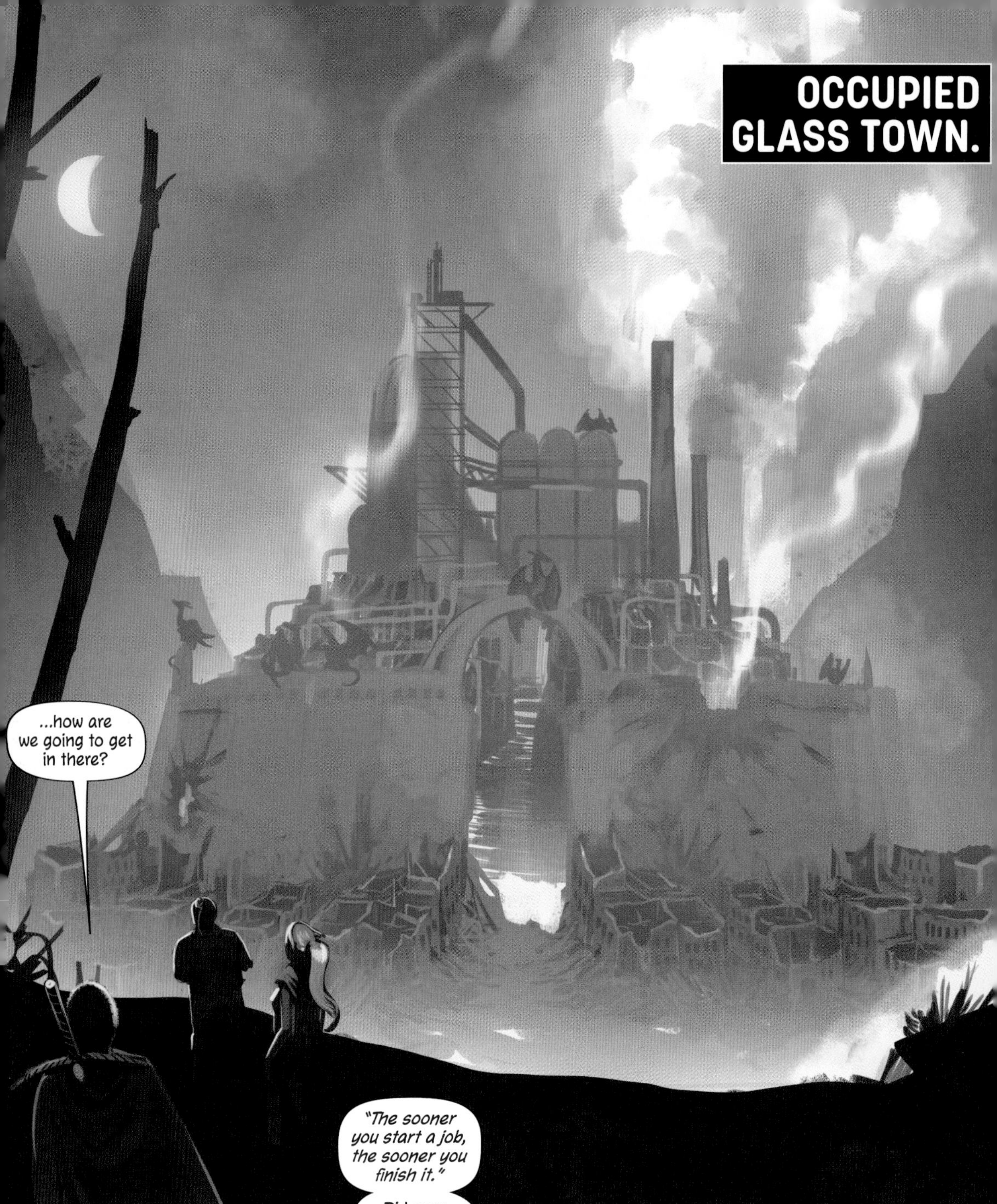
OCCUPIED GLASS TOWN.
...how are we going to get in there?

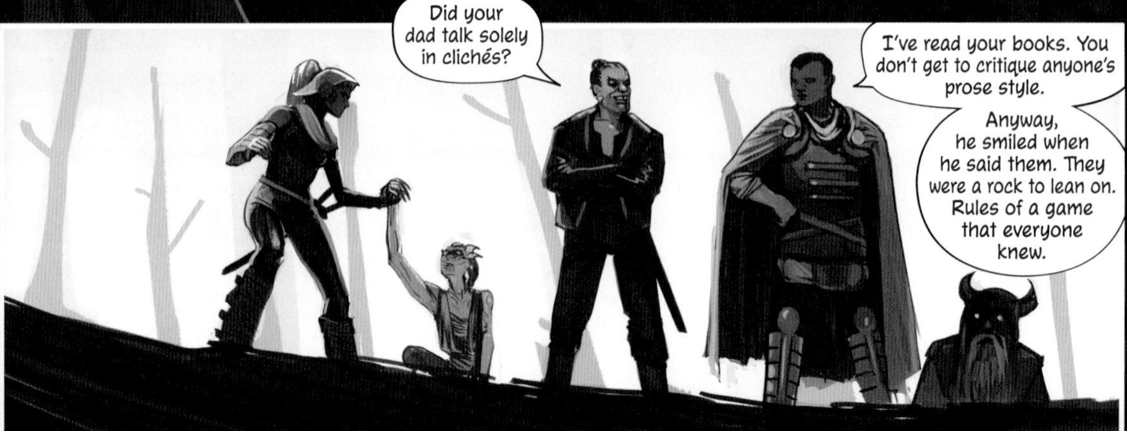
"The sooner you start a job, the sooner you finish it."
Did your dad talk solely in clichés?
I've read your books. You don't get to critique anyone's prose style.
Anyway, he smiled when he said them. They were a rock to lean on. Rules of a game that everyone knew.

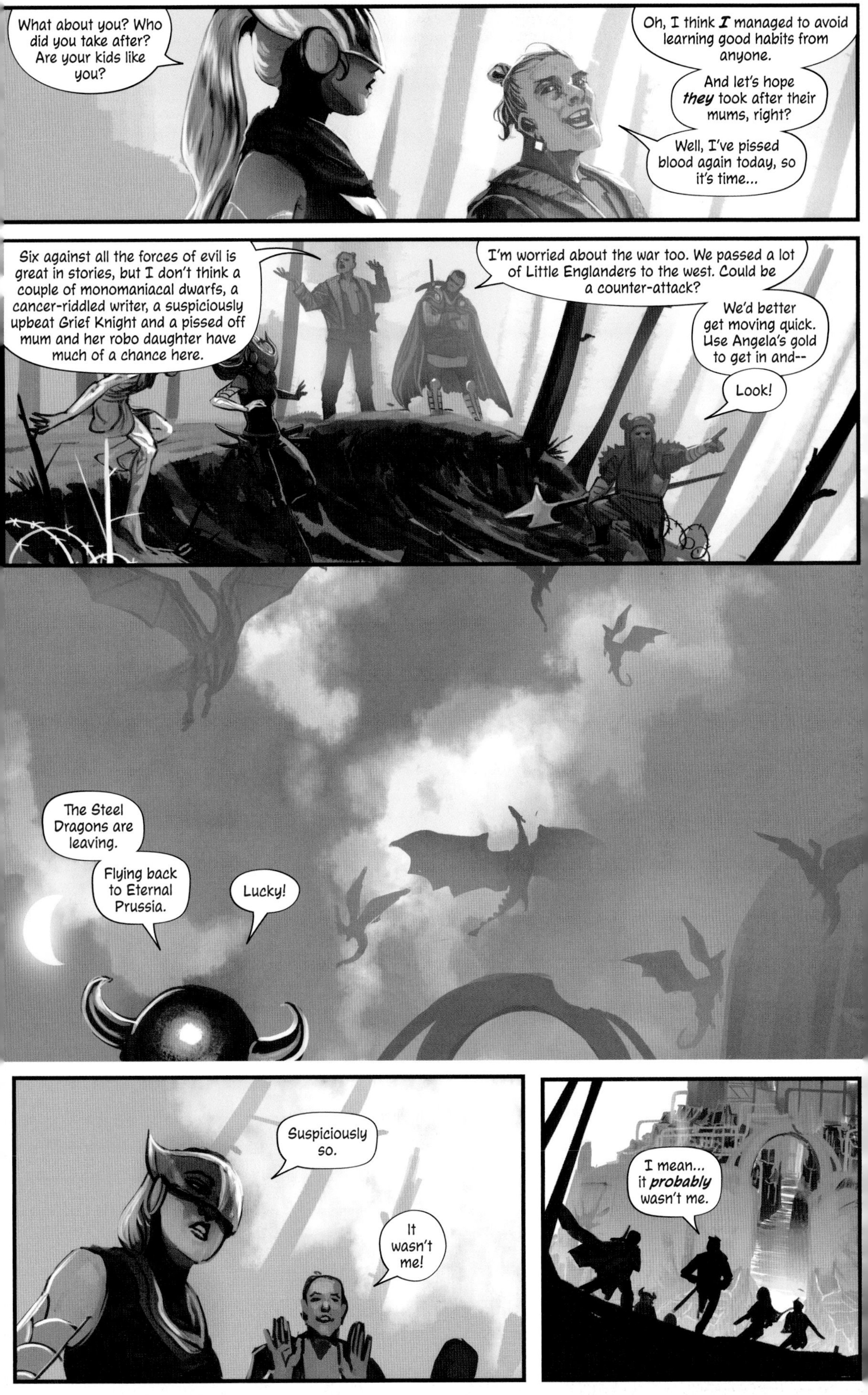
What about you? Who did you take after? Are your kids like you?
Oh, I think *I* managed to avoid learning good habits from anyone.
And let's hope *they* took after their mums, right?
Well, I've pissed blood again today, so it's time...
Six against all the forces of evil is great in stories, but I don't think a couple of monomaniacal dwarfs, a cancer-riddled writer, a suspiciously upbeat Grief Knight and a pissed off mum and her robo daughter have much of a chance here.
I'm worried about the war too. We passed a lot of Little Englanders to the west. Could be a counter-attack?
We'd better get moving quick. Use Angela's gold to get in and--
Look!
The Steel Dragons are leaving.
Flying back to Eternal Prussia.
Lucky!
Suspiciously so.
It wasn't me!
I mean... it *probably* wasn't me.

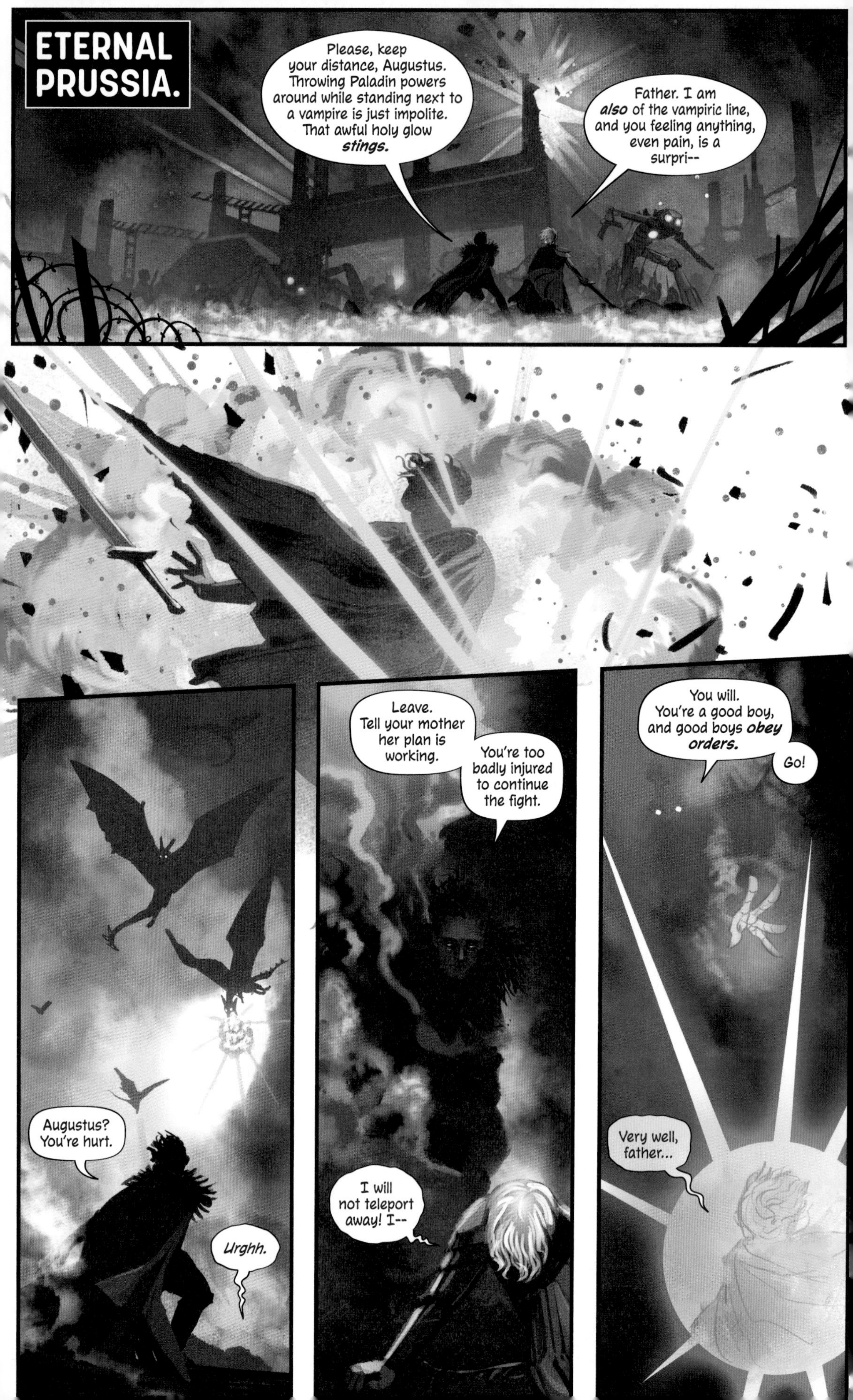

ETERNAL PRUSSIA.
Please, keep your distance, Augustus. Throwing Paladin powers around while standing next to a vampire is just impolite. That awful holy glow *stings.*
Father. I am *also* of the vampiric line, and you feeling anything, even pain, is a surpri--
Augustus? You're hurt.
Urghh.
Leave. Tell your mother her plan is working.
You're too badly injured to continue the fight.
I will not teleport away! I--
You will. You're a good boy, and good boys *obey orders.*
Go!
Very well, father...

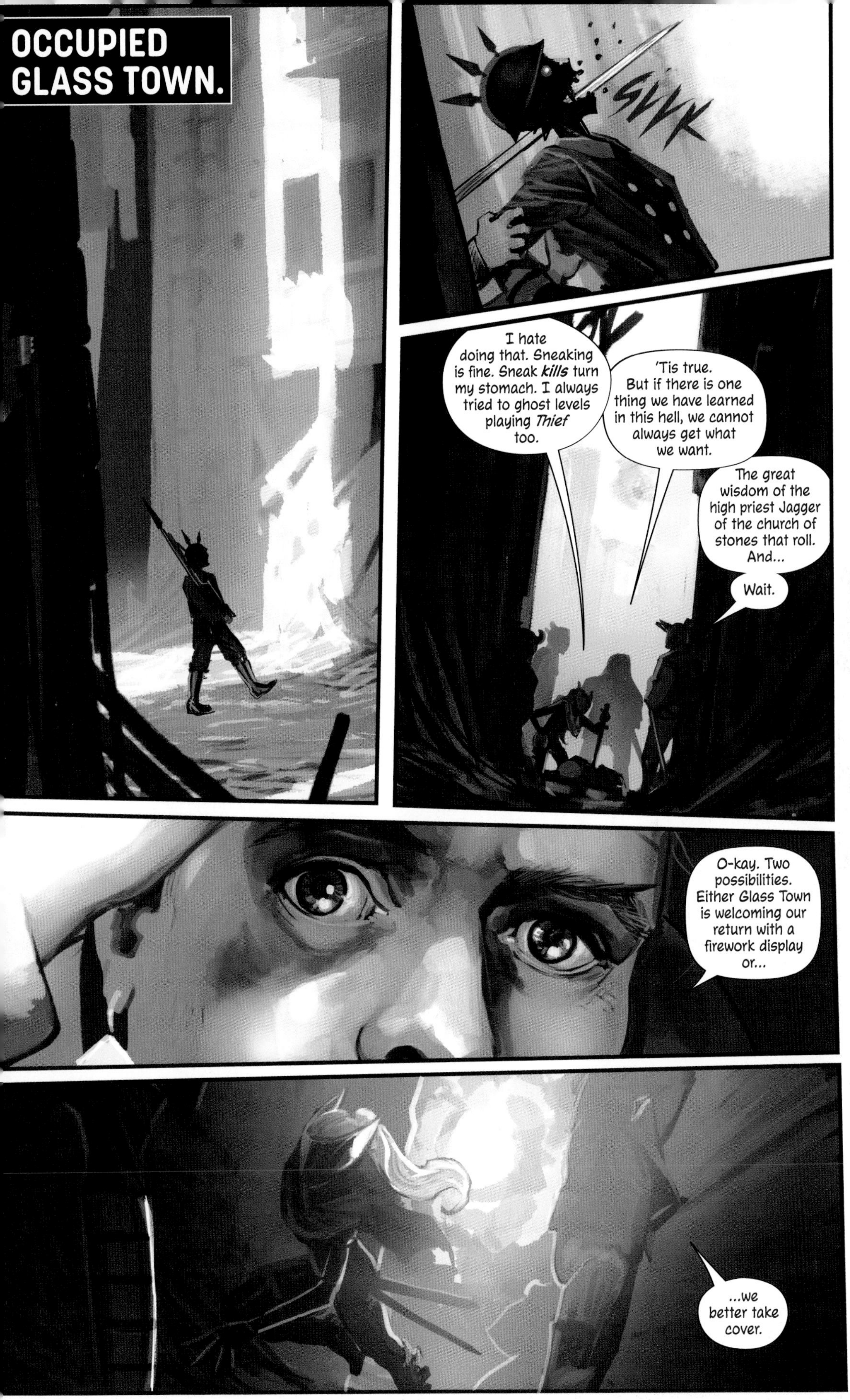
OCCUPIED GLASS TOWN.
SVVK
I hate doing that. Sneaking is fine. Sneak ***kills*** turn my stomach. I always tried to ghost levels playing *Thief* too.
'Tis true. But if there is one thing we have learned in this hell, we cannot always get what we want.
The great wisdom of the high priest Jagger of the church of stones that roll. And...
Wait.
O-kay. Two possibilities. Either Glass Town is welcoming our return with a firework display or...
...we better take cover.

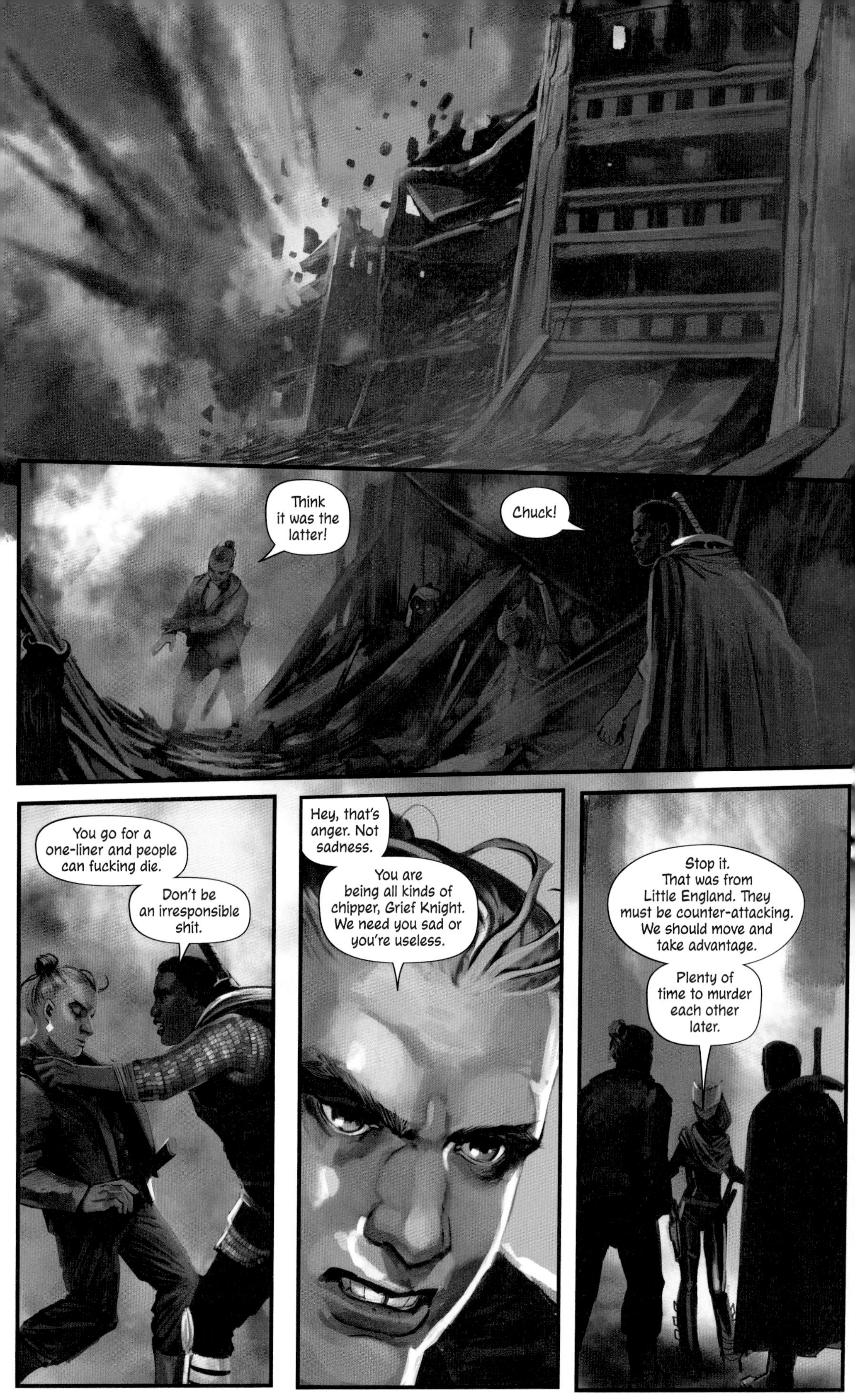
Think it was the latter!
Chuck!
You go for a one-liner and people can fucking die.
Don't be an irresponsible shit.
Hey, that's anger. Not sadness.
You are being all kinds of chipper, Grief Knight. We need you sad or you're useless.
Stop it. That was from Little England. They must be counter-attacking. We should move and take advantage.
Plenty of time to murder each other later.

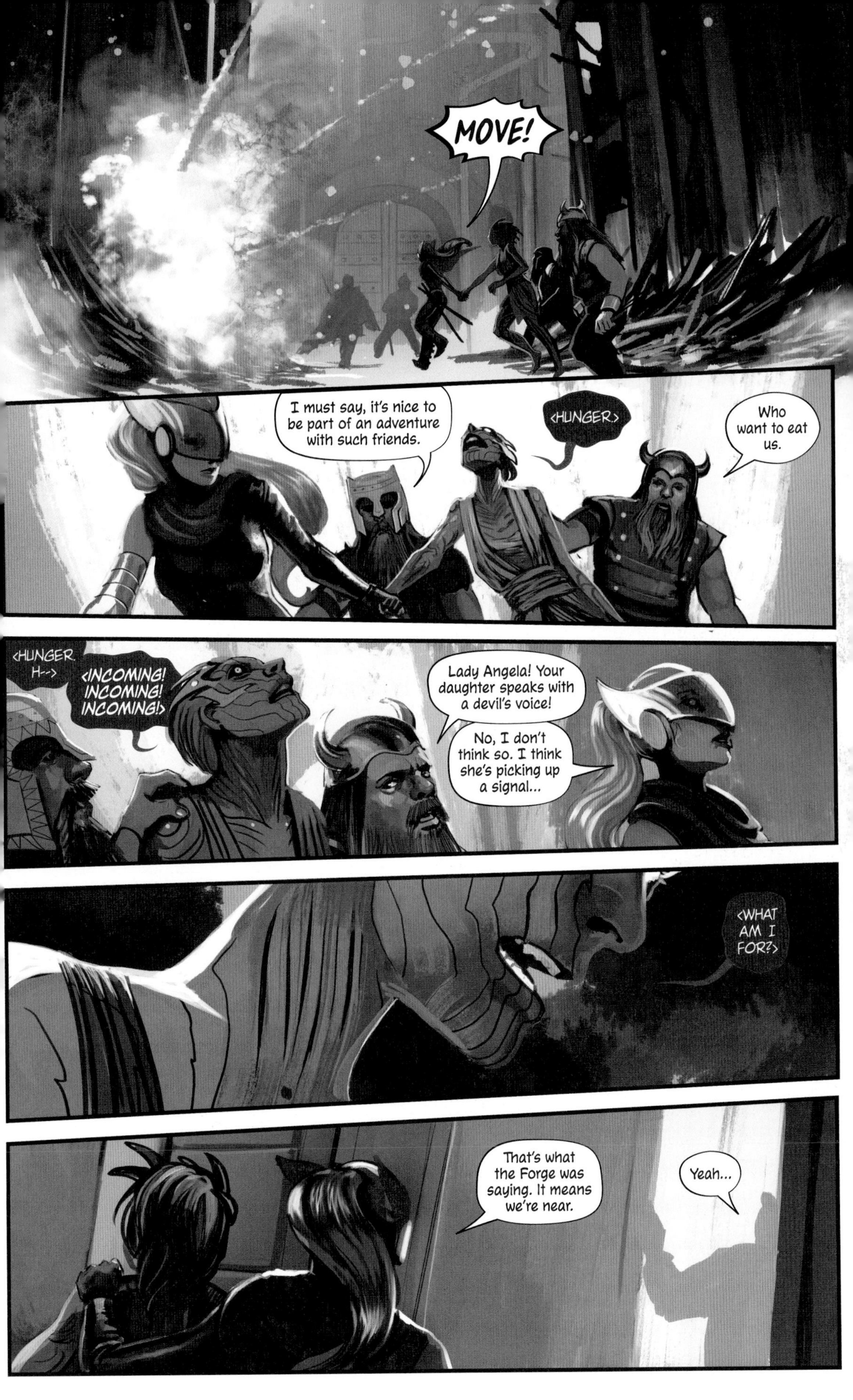
MOVE!
I must say, it's nice to be part of an adventure with such friends.
<HUNGER.>
Who want to eat us.
<HUNGER. H-->
<INCOMING! INCOMING! INCOMING!>
Lady Angela! Your daughter speaks with a devil's voice!
No, I don't think so. I think she's picking up a signal...
<WHAT AM I FOR?>
That's what the Forge was saying. It means we're near.
Yeah...

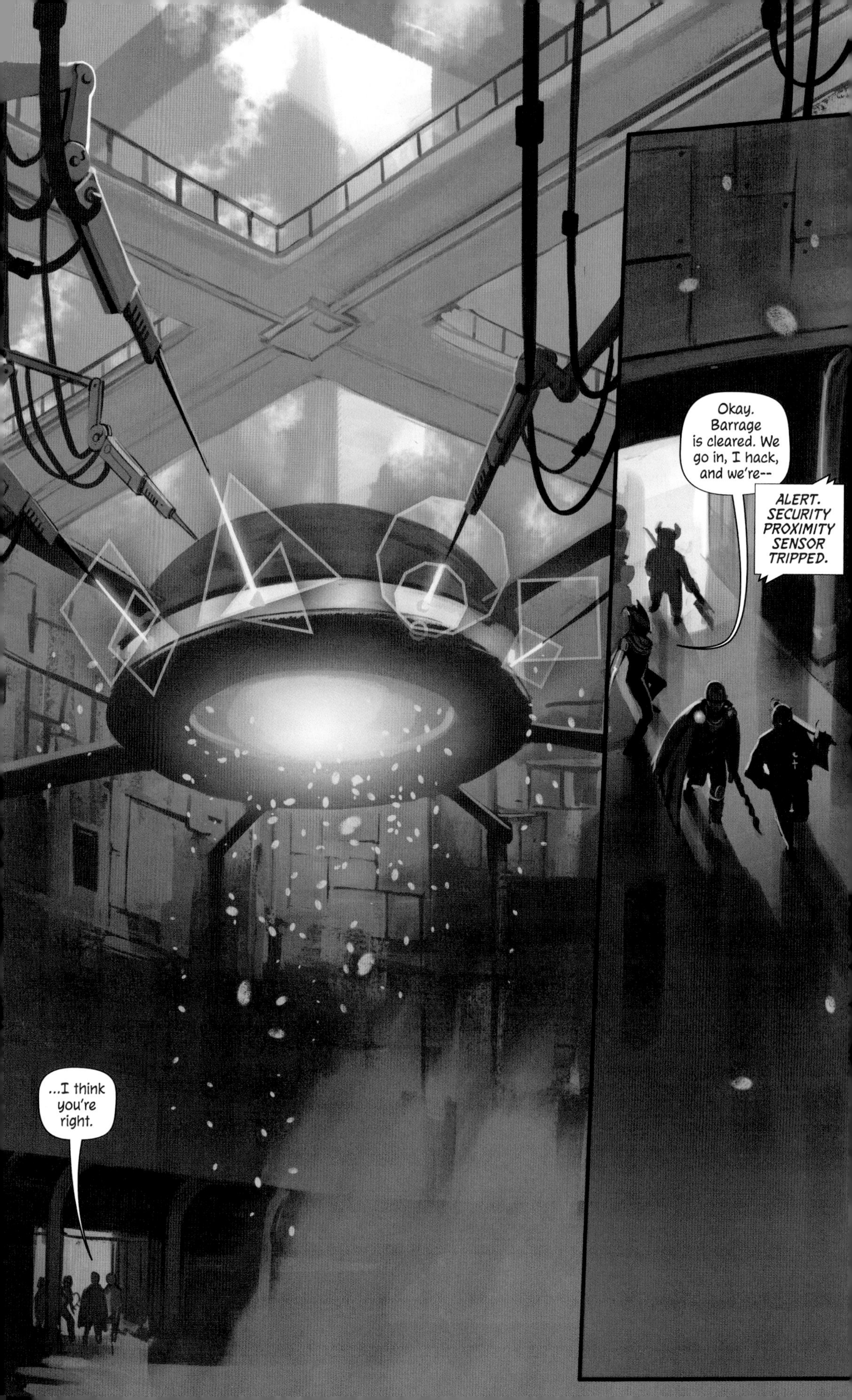
Okay. Barrage is cleared. We go in, I hack, and we're--
ALERT. SECURITY PROXIMITY SENSOR TRIPPED.
...I think you're right.

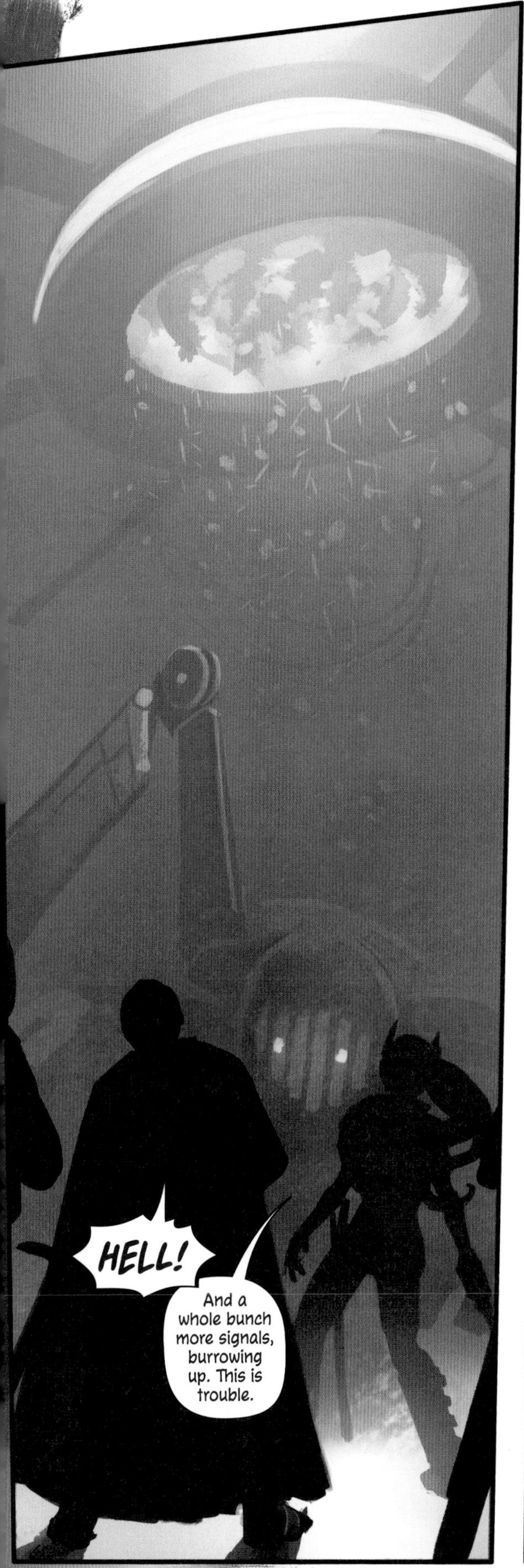
HELL!
And a whole bunch more signals, burrowing up. This is trouble.

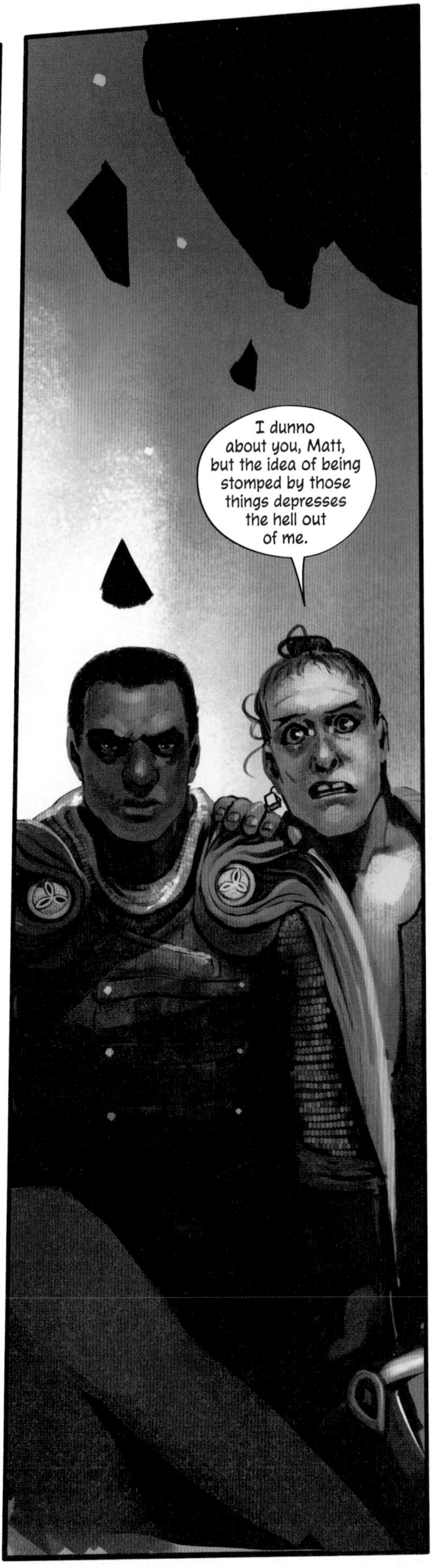
I dunno about you, Matt, but the idea of being stomped by those things depresses the hell out of me.

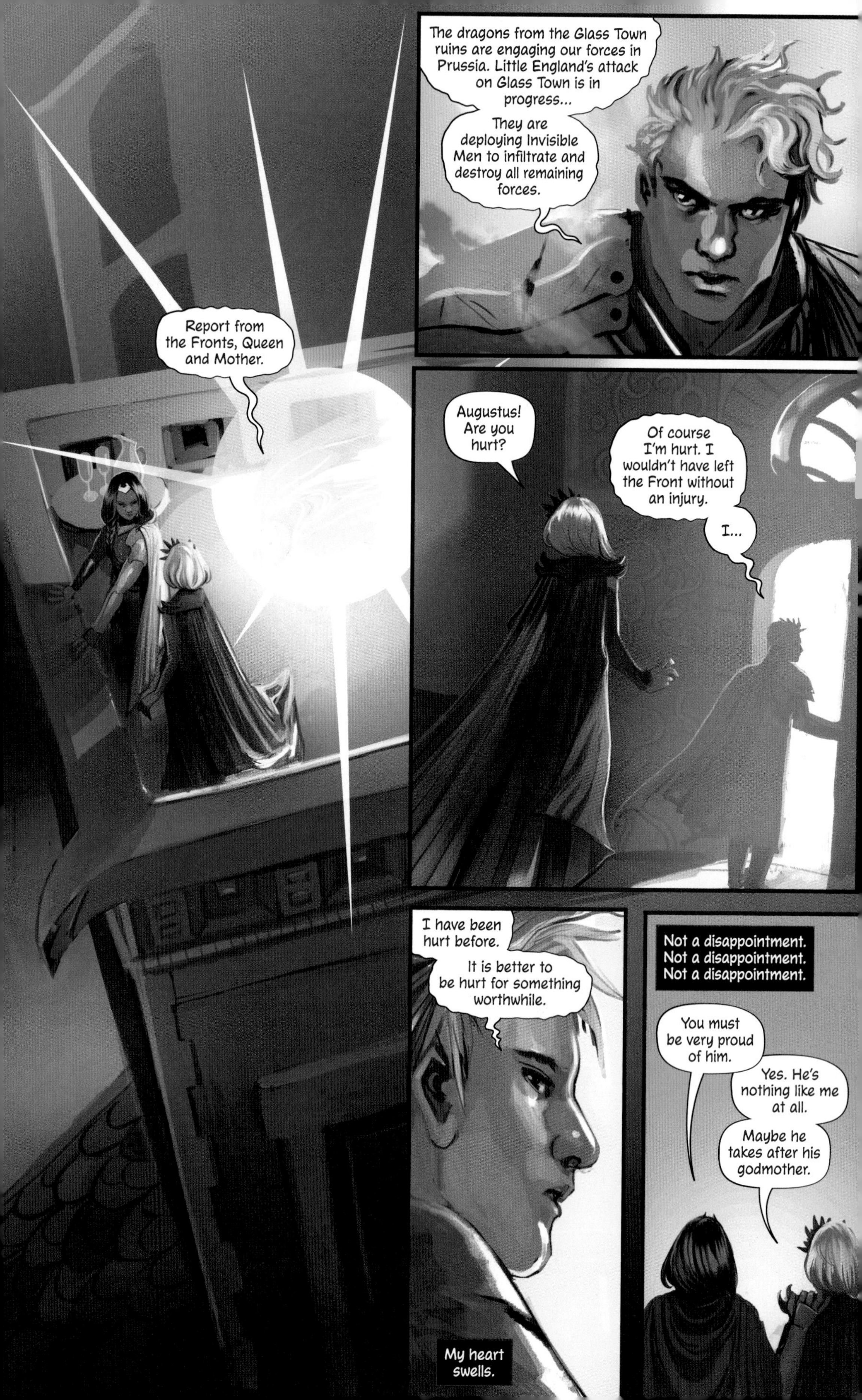
Report from the Fronts, Queen and Mother.
The dragons from the Glass Town ruins are engaging our forces in Prussia. Little England's attack on Glass Town is in progress...
They are deploying Invisible Men to infiltrate and destroy all remaining forces.
Augustus! Are you hurt?
Of course I'm hurt. I wouldn't have left the Front without an injury.
I...
I have been hurt before.
It is better to be hurt for something worthwhile.
My heart swells.
Not a disappointment.
Not a disappointment.
Not a disappointment.
You must be very proud of him.
Yes. He's nothing like me at all.
Maybe he takes after his godmother.

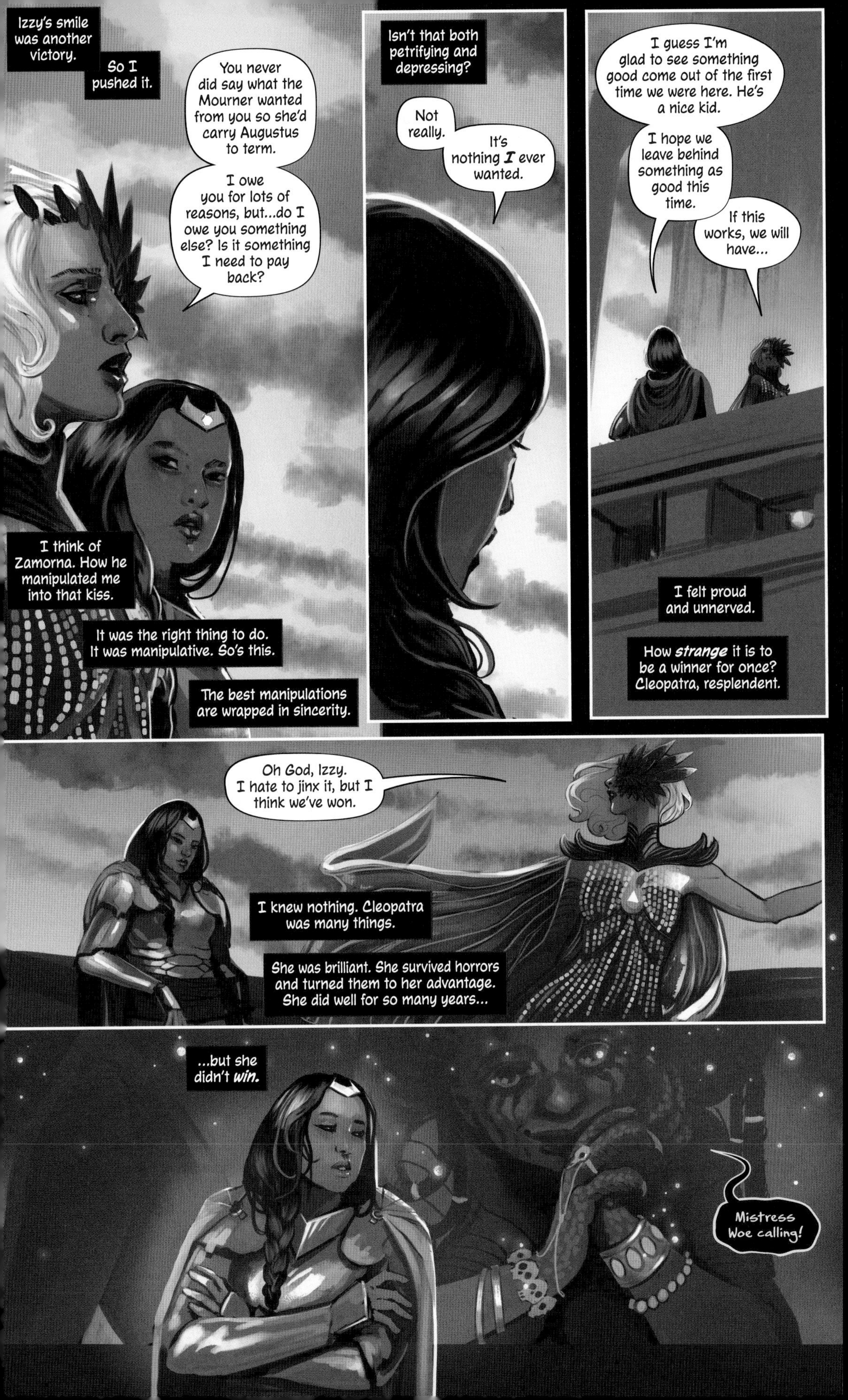
Izzy's smile was another victory.
So I pushed it.
You never did say what the Mourner wanted from you so she'd carry Augustus to term.
I owe you for lots of reasons, but...do I owe you something else? Is it something I need to pay back?
I think of Zamorna. How he manipulated me into that kiss.
It was the right thing to do. It was manipulative. So's this.
The best manipulations are wrapped in sincerity.
Isn't that both petrifying and depressing?
Not really.
It's nothing *I* ever wanted.
I guess I'm glad to see something good come out of the first time we were here. He's a nice kid.
I hope we leave behind something as good this time.
If this works, we will have...
I felt proud and unnerved.
How *strange* it is to be a winner for once? Cleopatra, resplendent.
Oh God, Izzy. I hate to jinx it, but I think we've won.
I knew nothing. Cleopatra was many things.
She was brilliant. She survived horrors and turned them to her advantage. She did well for so many years...
...but she didn't *win.*
Mistress Woe calling!

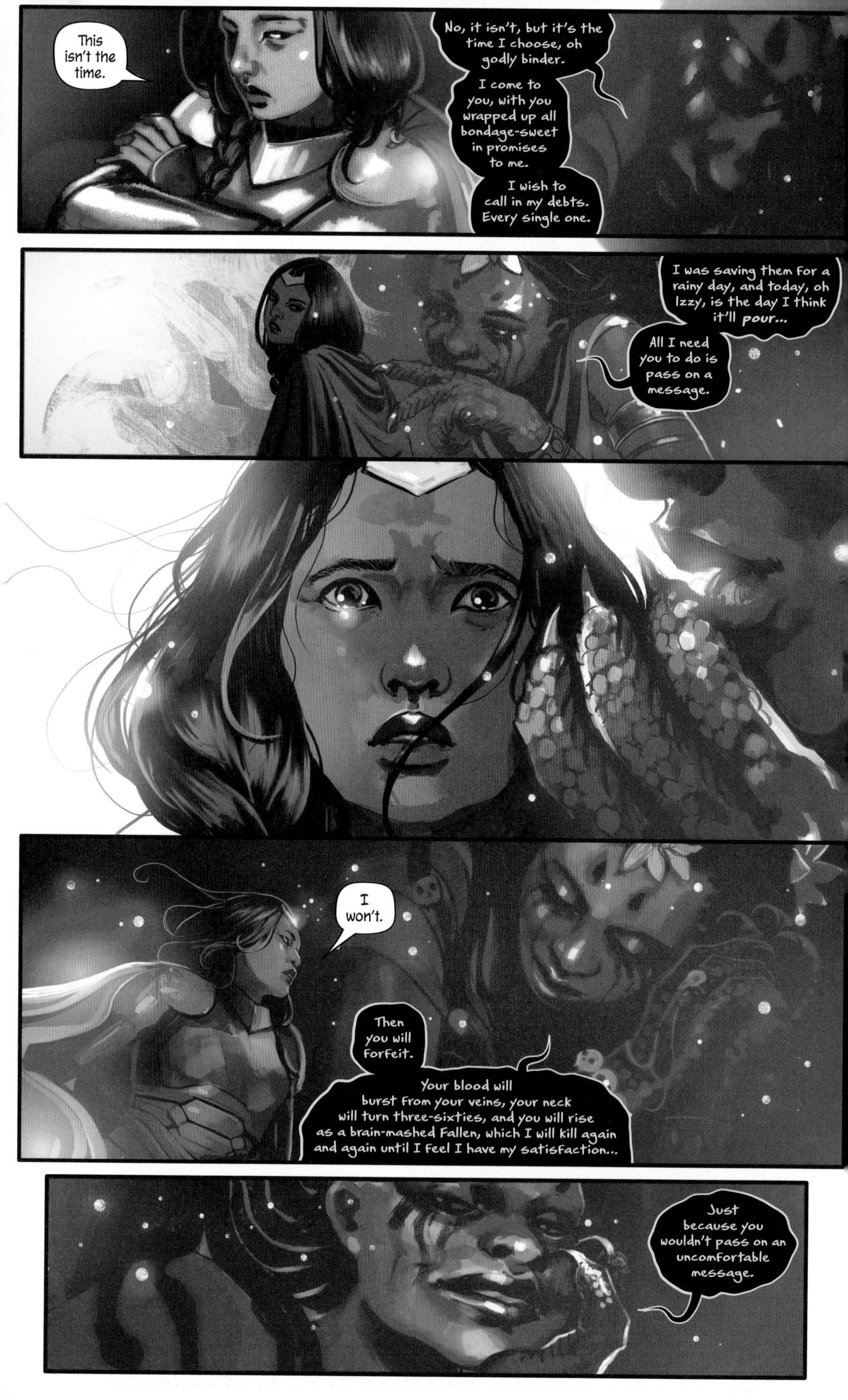
This isn't the time.
No, it isn't, but it's the time I choose, oh godly binder.
I come to you, with you wrapped up all bondage-sweet in promises to me.
I wish to call in my debts. Every single one.
I was saving them for a rainy day, and today, oh Izzy, is the day I think it'll *pour...*
All I need you to do is pass on a message.
I won't.
Then you will forfeit.
Your blood will burst from your veins, your neck will turn three-sixties, and you will rise as a brain-mashed Fallen, which I will kill again and again until I feel I have my satisfaction...
Just because you wouldn't pass on an uncomfortable message.

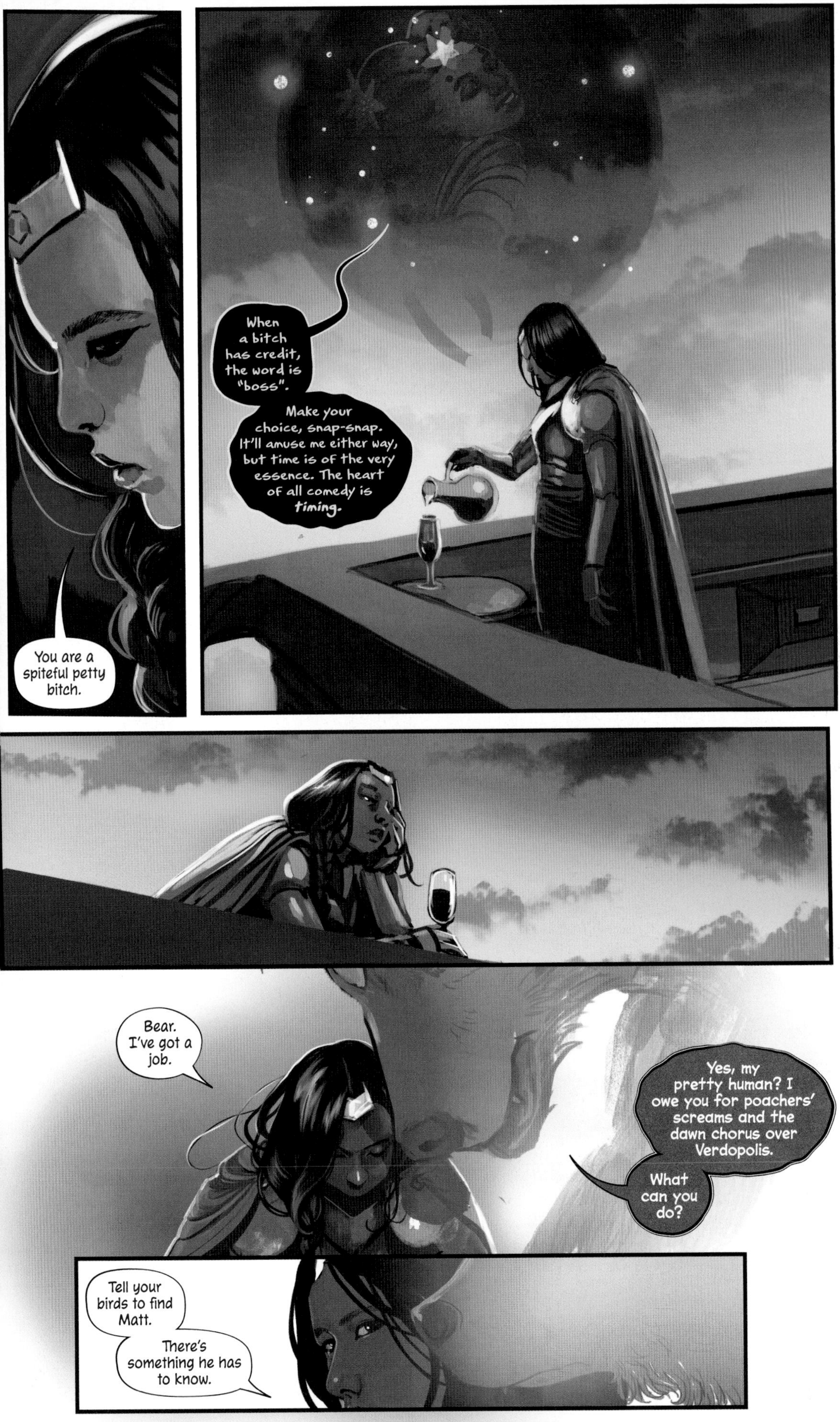
When a bitch has credit, the word is "boss".
Make your choice, snap-snap. It'll amuse me either way, but time is of the very essence. The heart of all comedy is *timing*.
You are a spiteful petty bitch.
Bear. I've got a job.
Yes, my pretty human? I owe you for poachers' screams and the dawn chorus over Verdopolis.
What can you do?
Tell your birds to find Matt.
There's something he has to know.

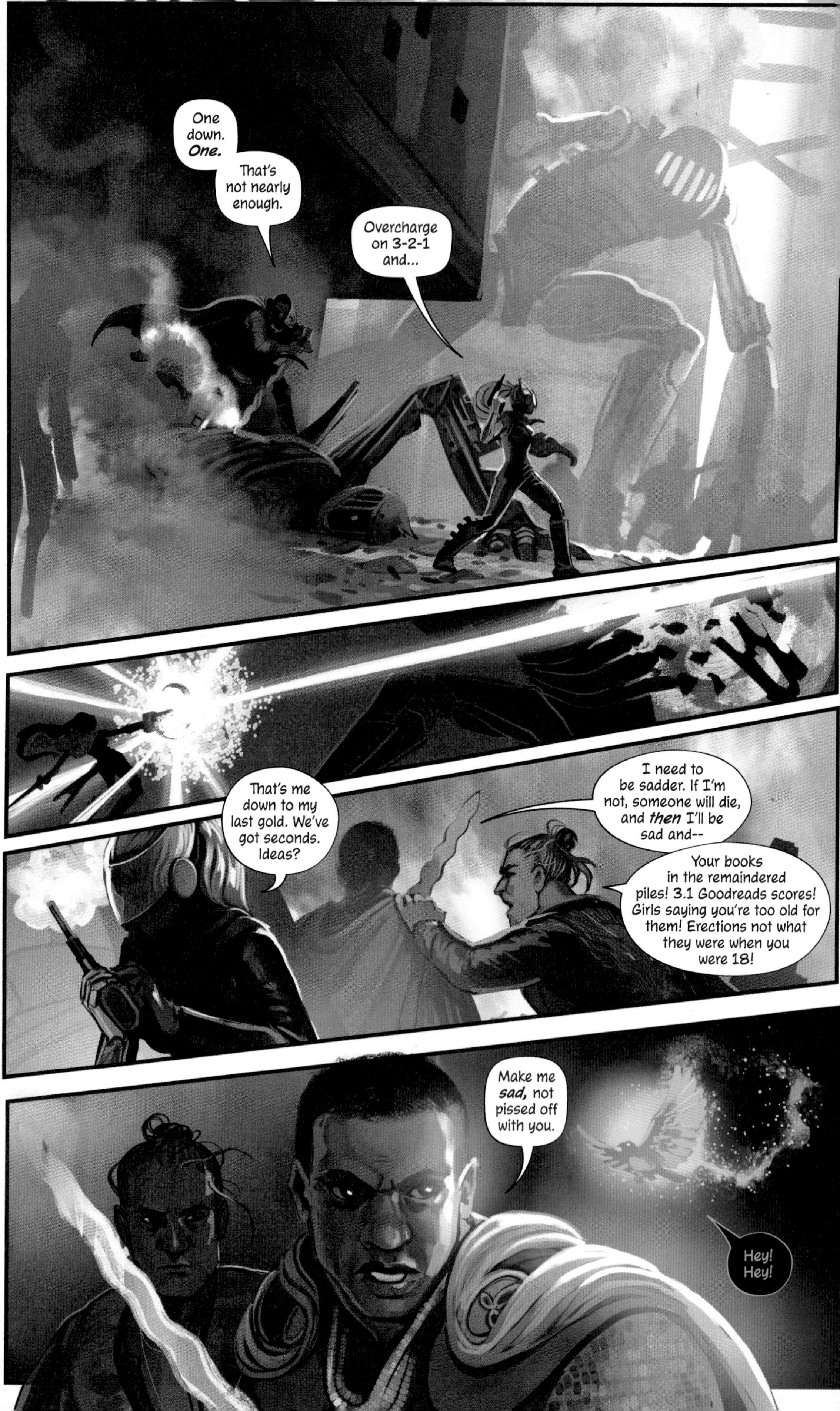
One down. *One.*
That's not nearly enough.
Overcharge on 3-2-1 and...
That's me down to my last gold. We've got seconds. Ideas?
I need to be sadder. If I'm not, someone will die, and *then* I'll be sad and--
Your books in the remaindered piles! 3.1 Goodreads scores! Girls saying you're too old for them! Erections not what they were when you were 18!
Make me *sad,* not pissed off with you.
Hey! Hey!

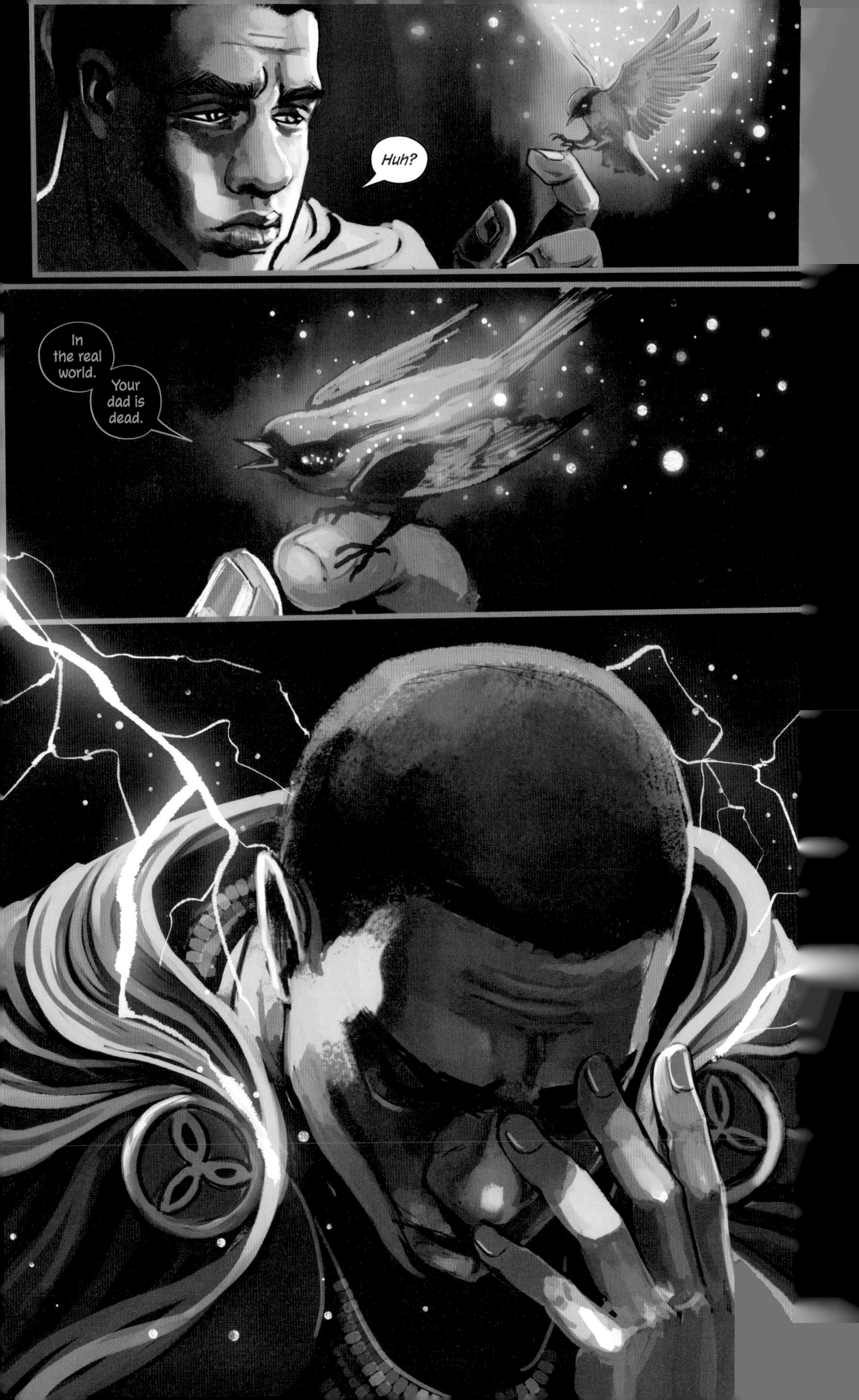
Huh?
In the real world.
Your dad is dead.

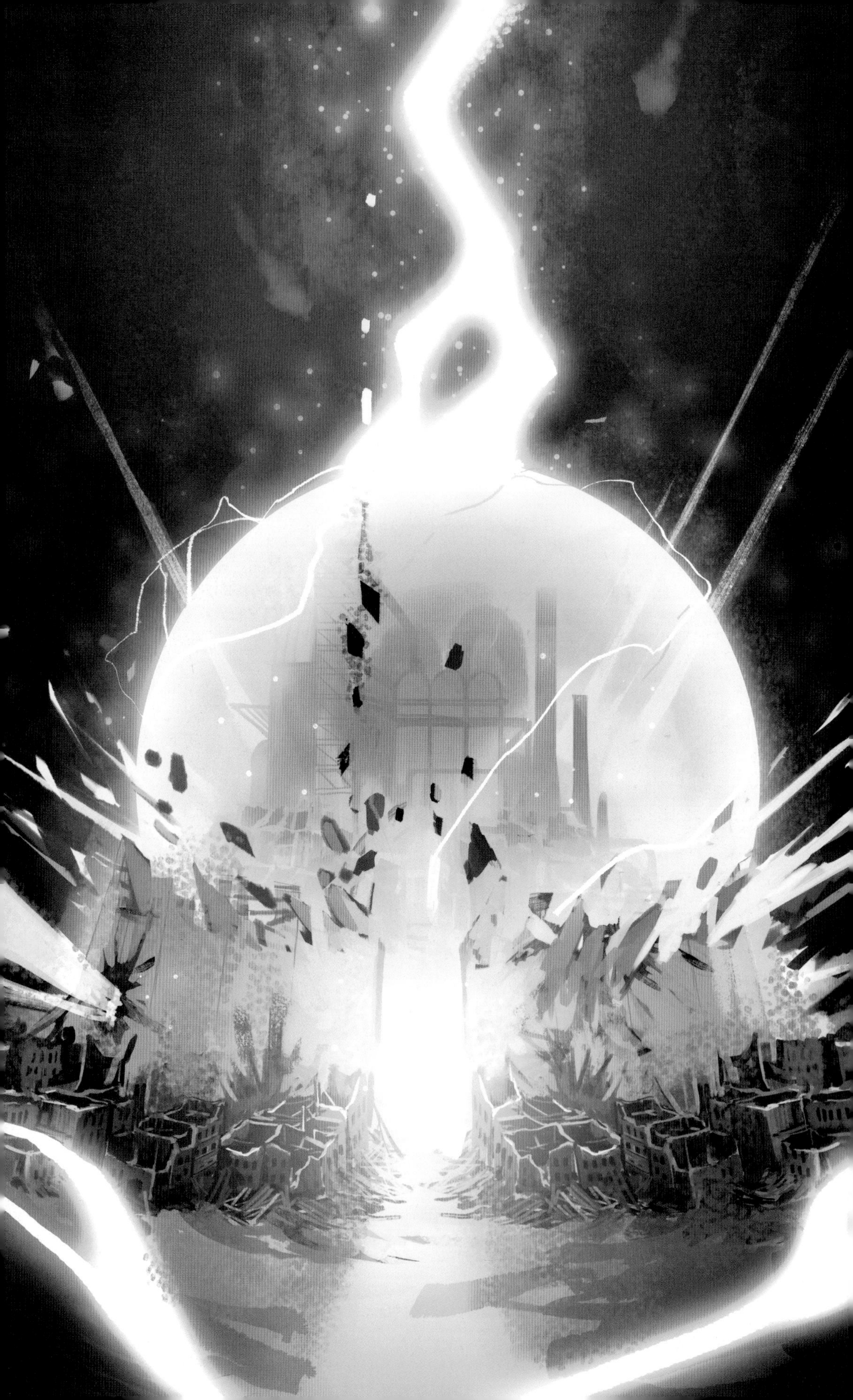

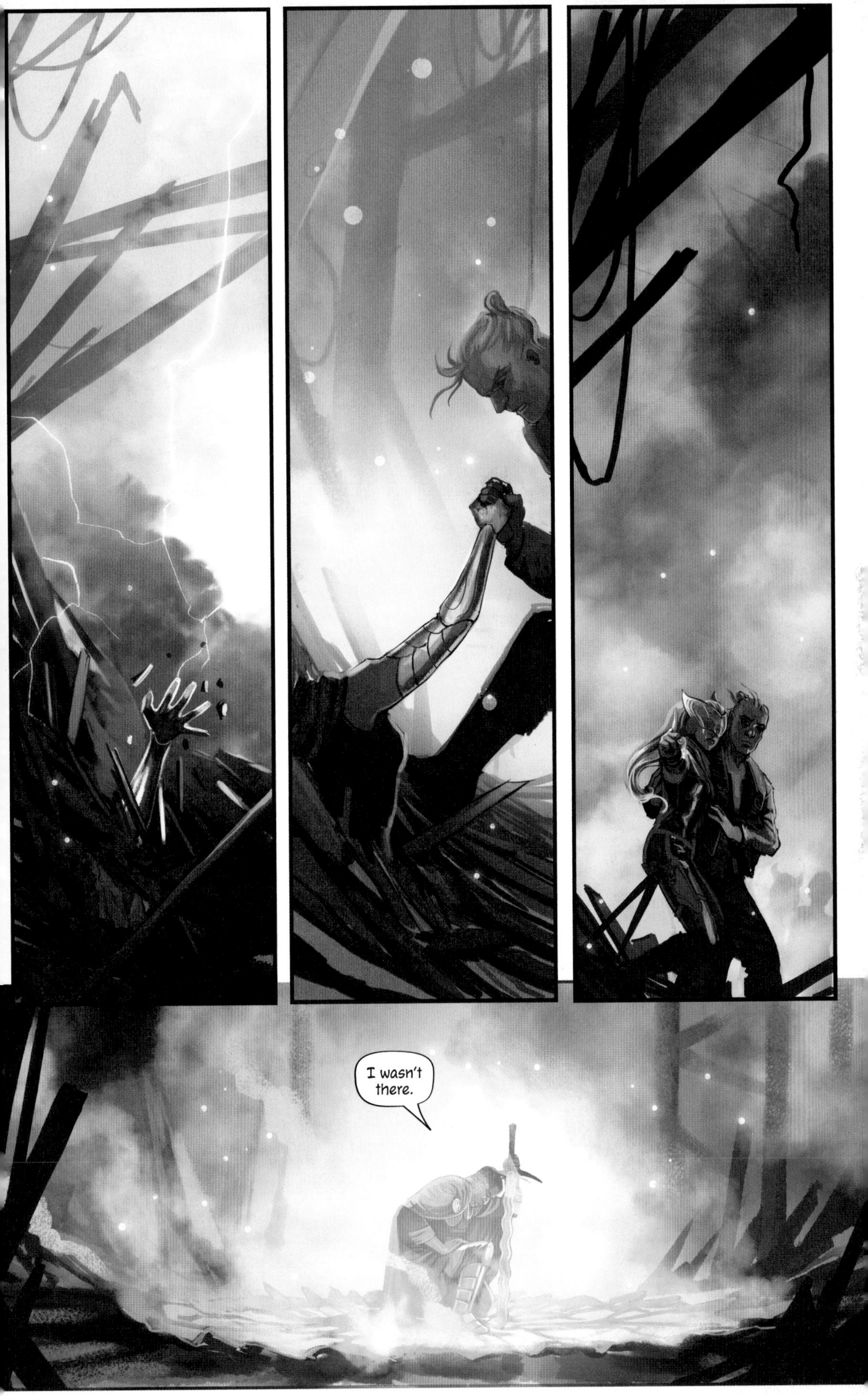
I wasn't there.

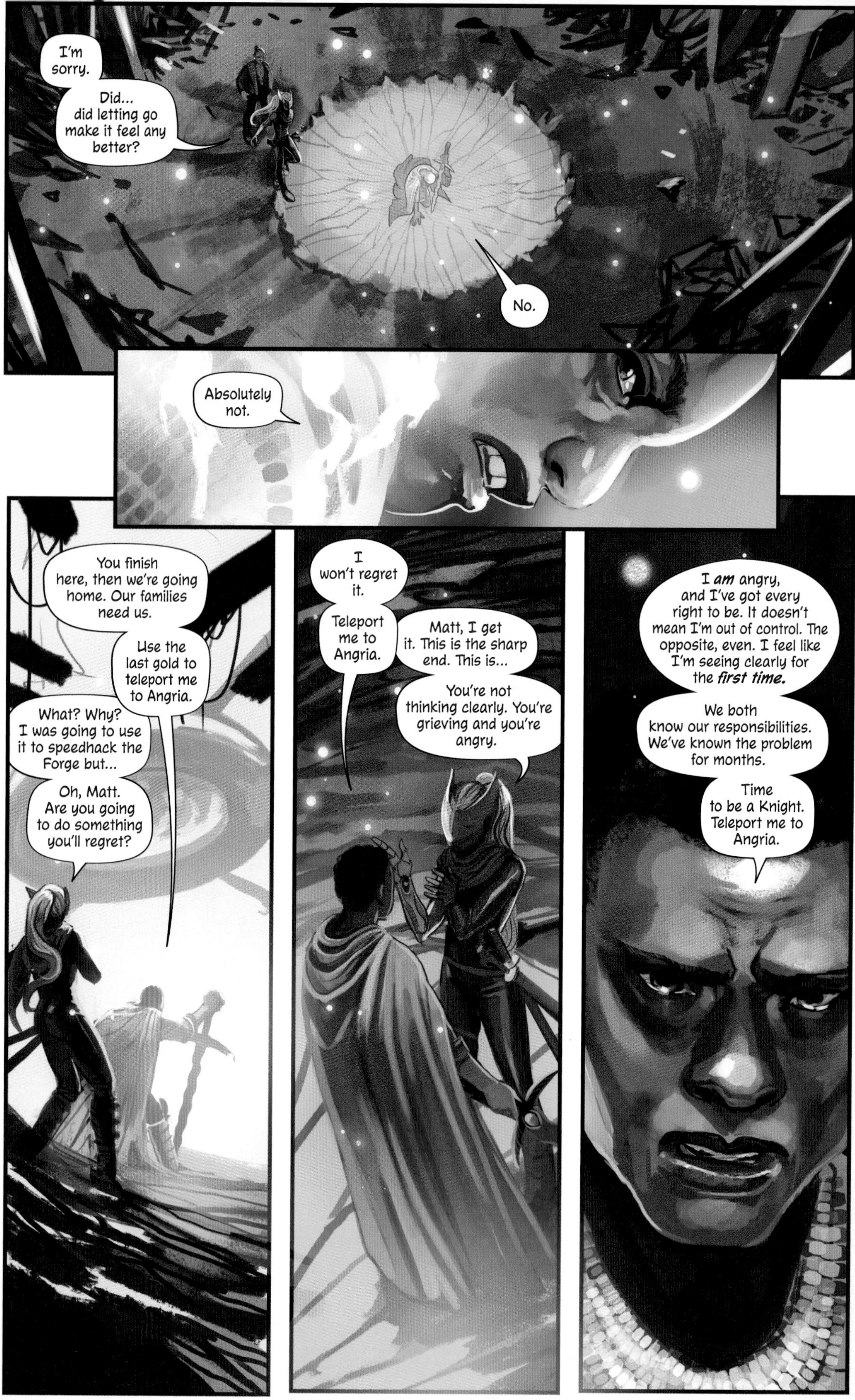
I'm sorry.
Did... did letting go make it feel any better?
No.
Absolutely not.
You finish here, then we're going home. Our families need us.
Use the last gold to teleport me to Angria.
What? Why? I was going to use it to speedhack the Forge but...
Oh, Matt. Are you going to do something you'll regret?
I won't regret it.
Teleport me to Angria.
Matt, I get it. This is the sharp end. This is...
You're not thinking clearly. You're grieving and you're angry.
I *am* angry, and I've got every right to be. It doesn't mean I'm out of control. The opposite, even. I feel like I'm seeing clearly for the *first time.*
We both know our responsibilities. We've known the problem for months.
Time to be a Knight. Teleport me to Angria.

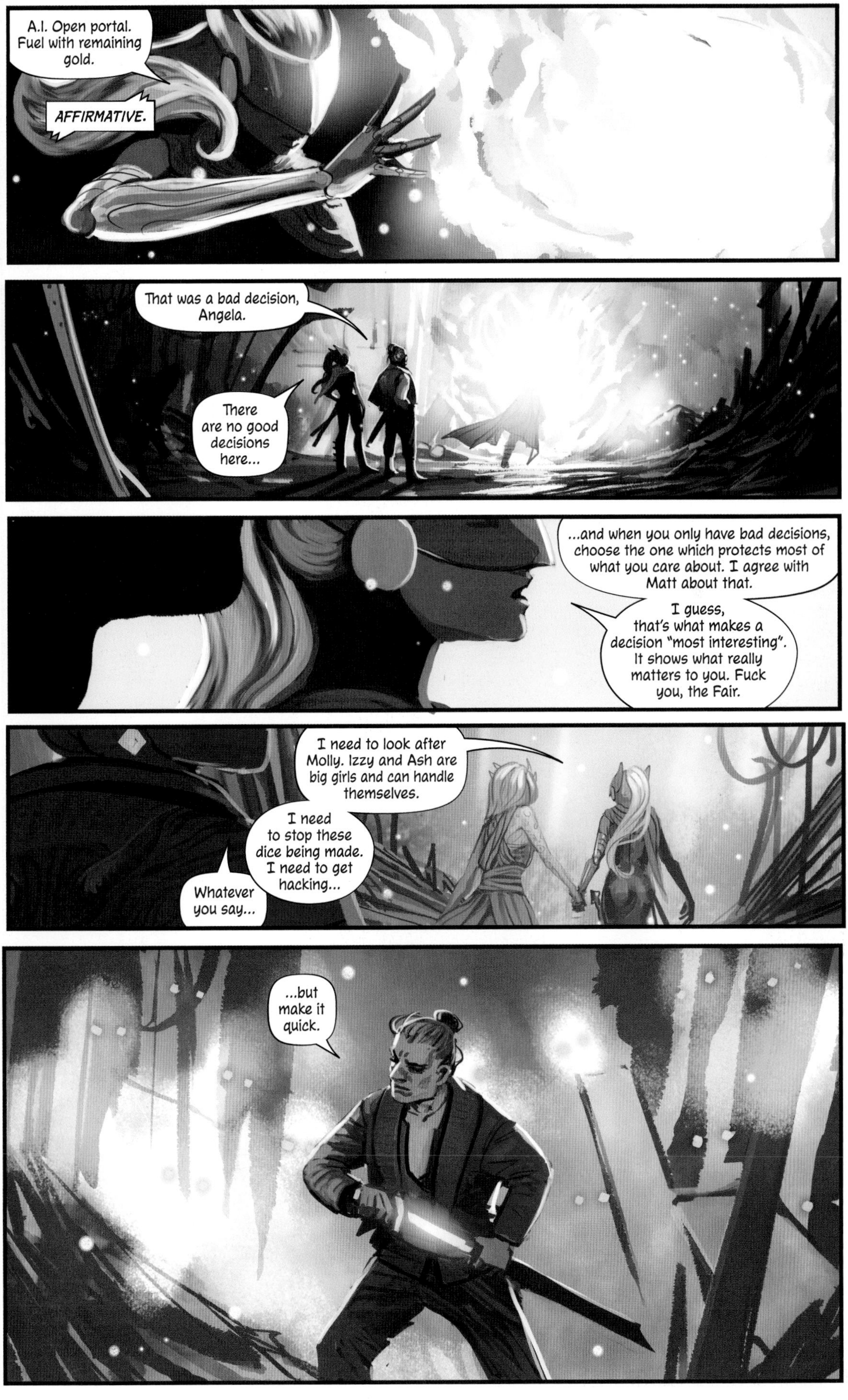
A.I. Open portal. Fuel with remaining gold.
AFFIRMATIVE.
That was a bad decision, Angela.
There are no good decisions here...
...and when you only have bad decisions, choose the one which protects most of what you care about. I agree with Matt about that.
I guess, that's what makes a decision "most interesting". It shows what really matters to you. Fuck you, the Fair.
I need to look after Molly. Izzy and Ash are big girls and can handle themselves.
I need to stop these dice being made. I need to get hacking...
Whatever you say...
...but make it quick.

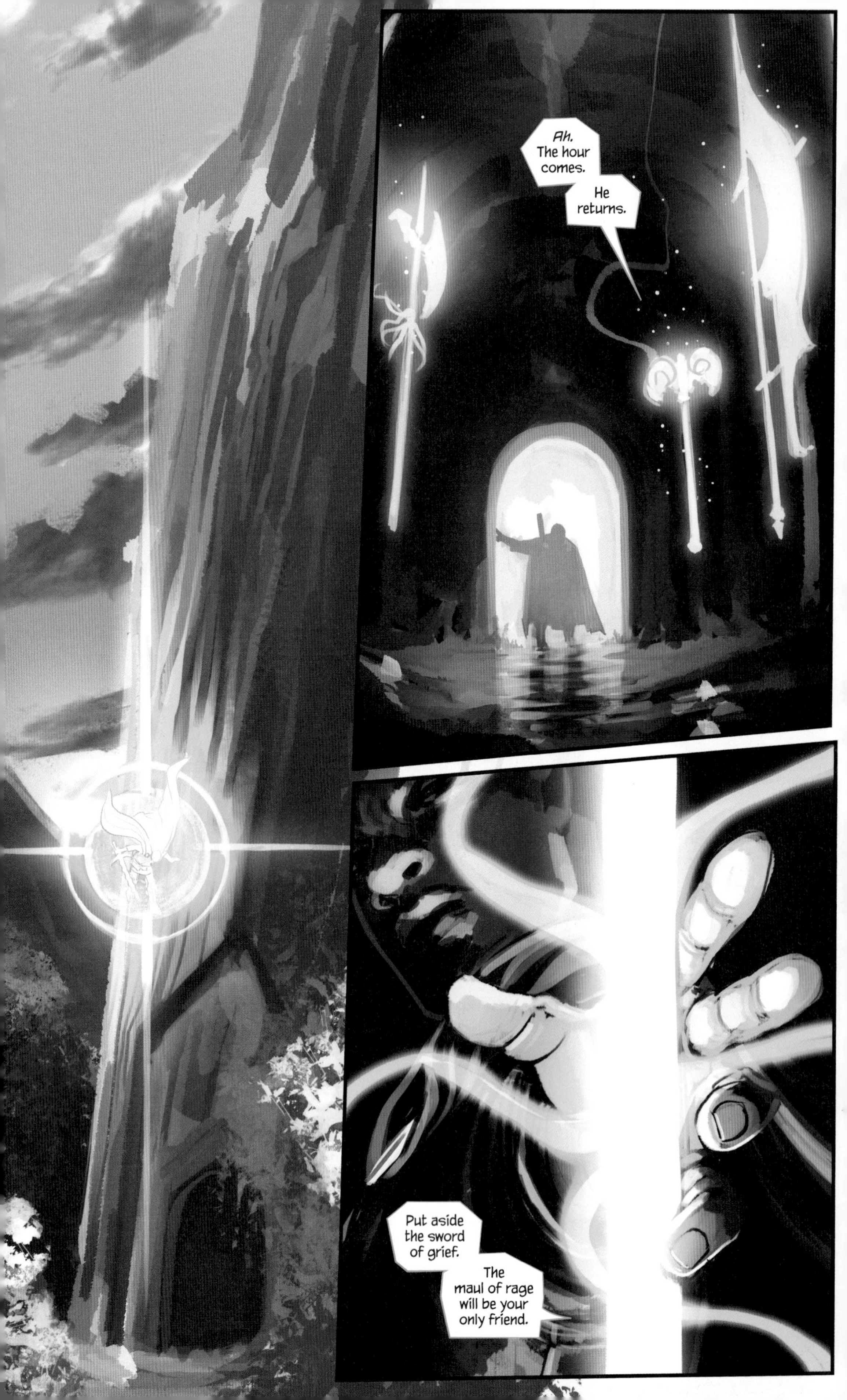
Ah. The hour comes.
He returns.
Put aside the sword of grief.
The maul of rage will be your only friend.

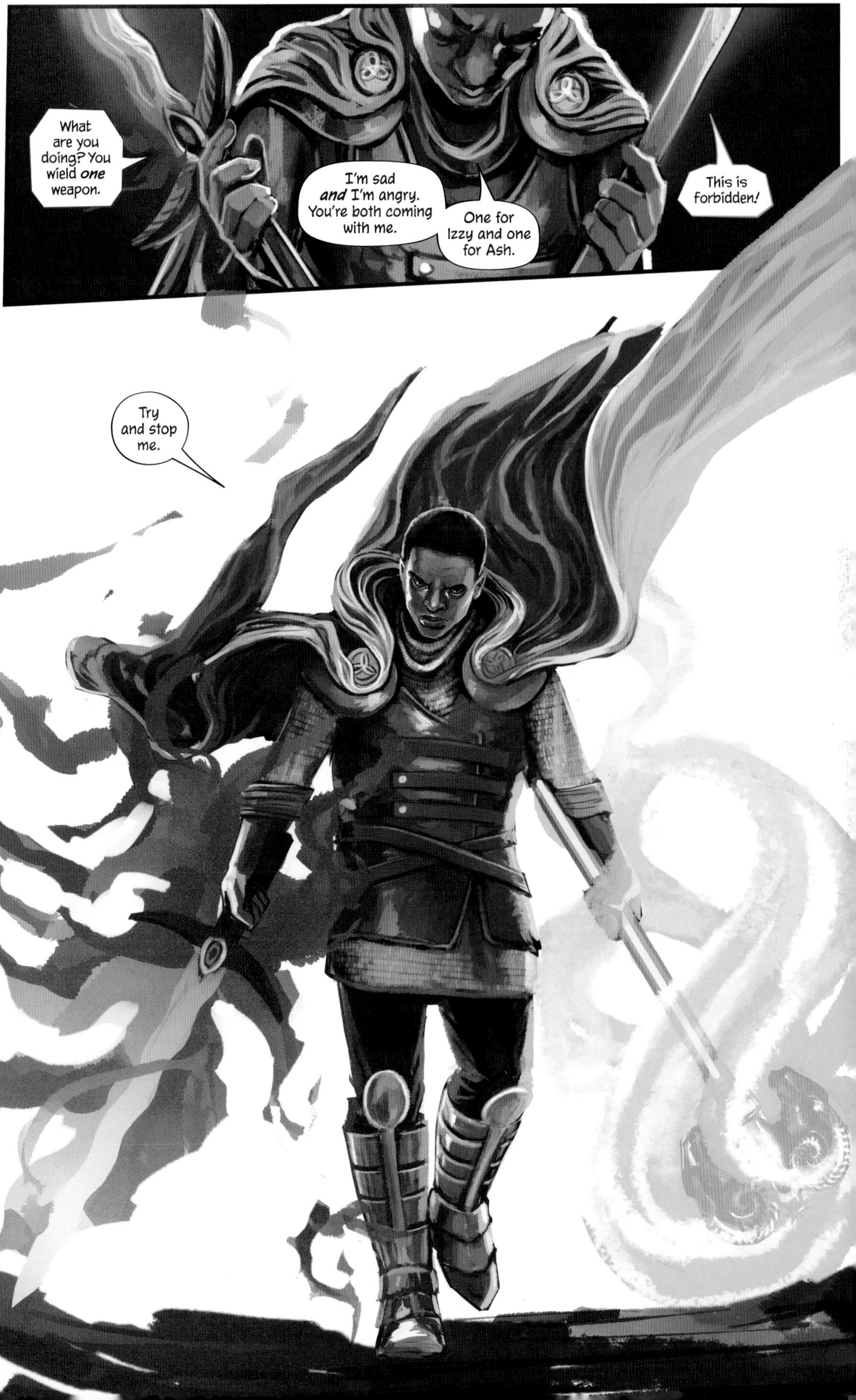
What are you doing? You wield *one* weapon.
I'm sad ***and*** I'm angry. You're both coming with me.
One for Izzy and one for Ash.
This is forbidden!
Try and stop me.

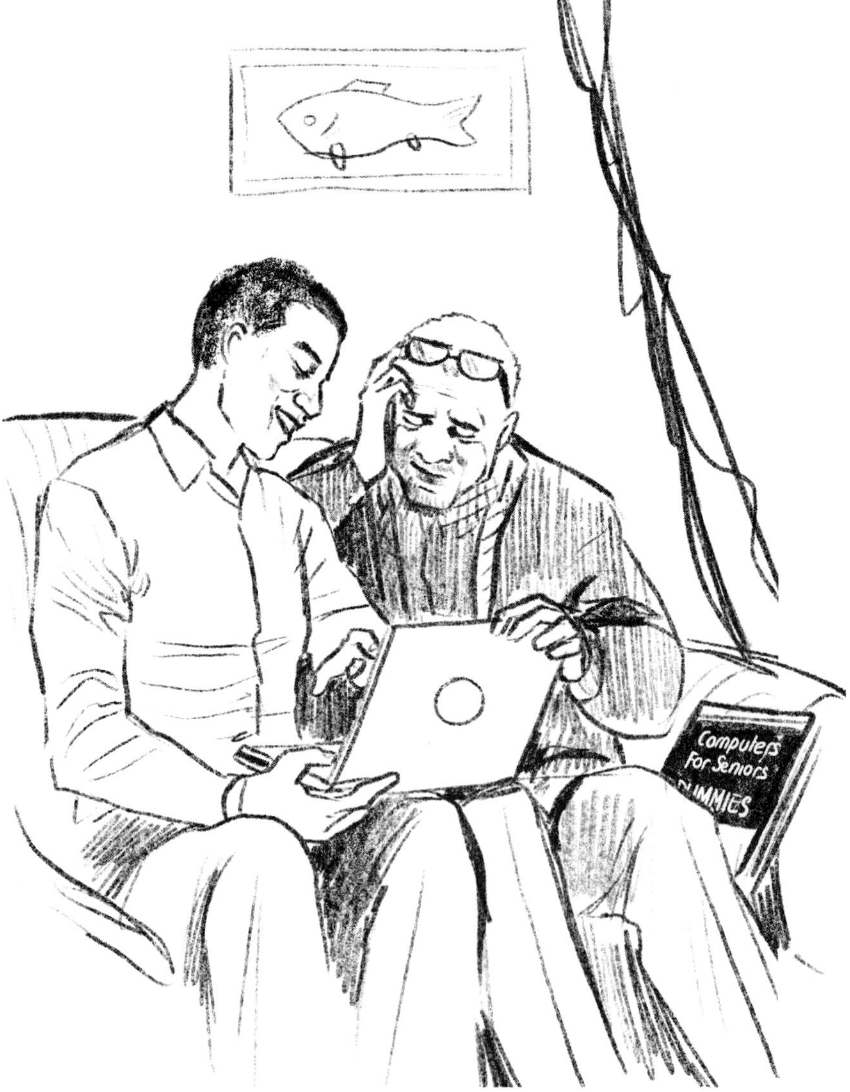
Computers
For Seniors
DUMMIES

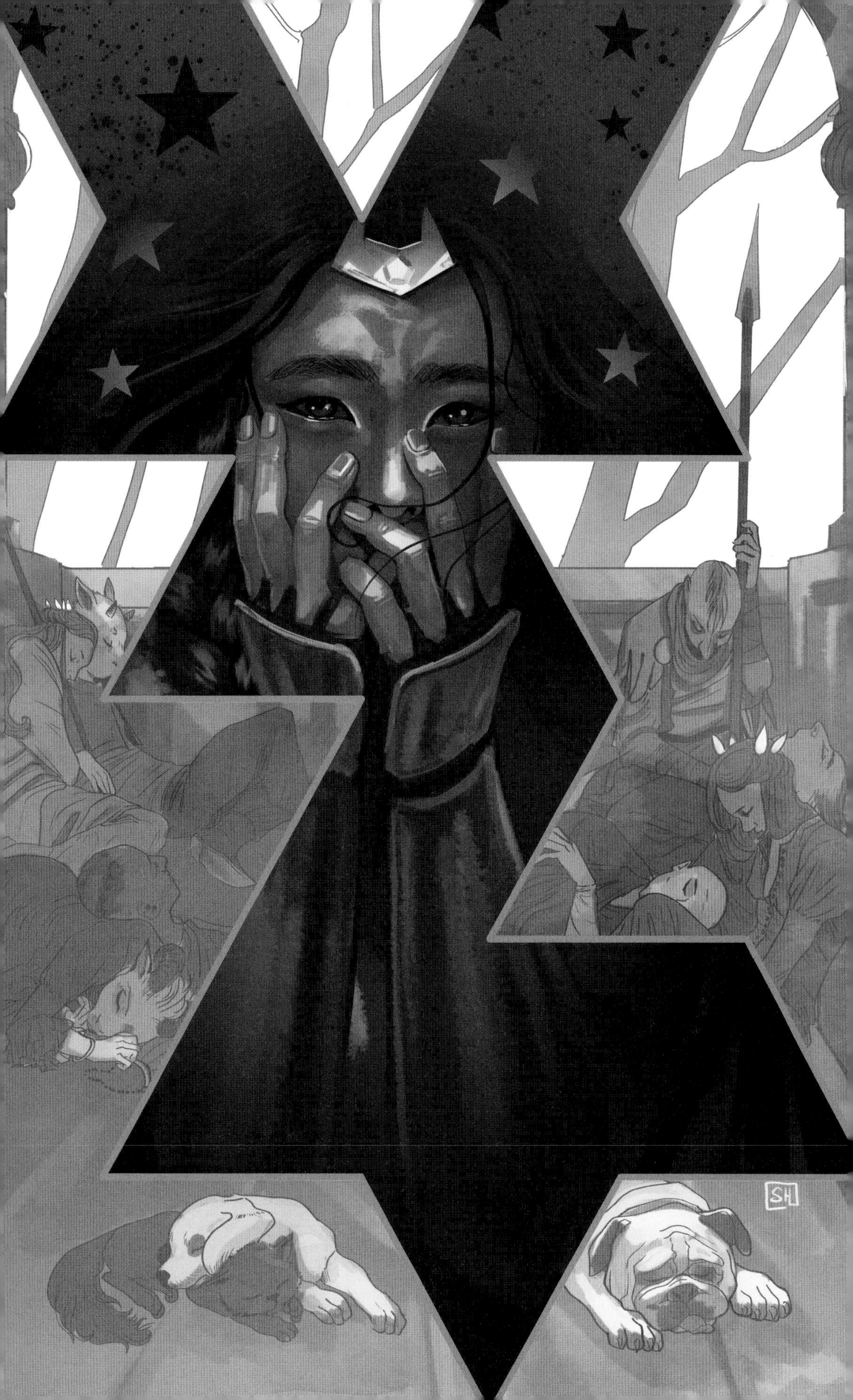
SH

15:
PvP

"All games are hostile. Basically there is only one game and that game is war. It's the old army game from here to eternity."
– *William S Burroughs*

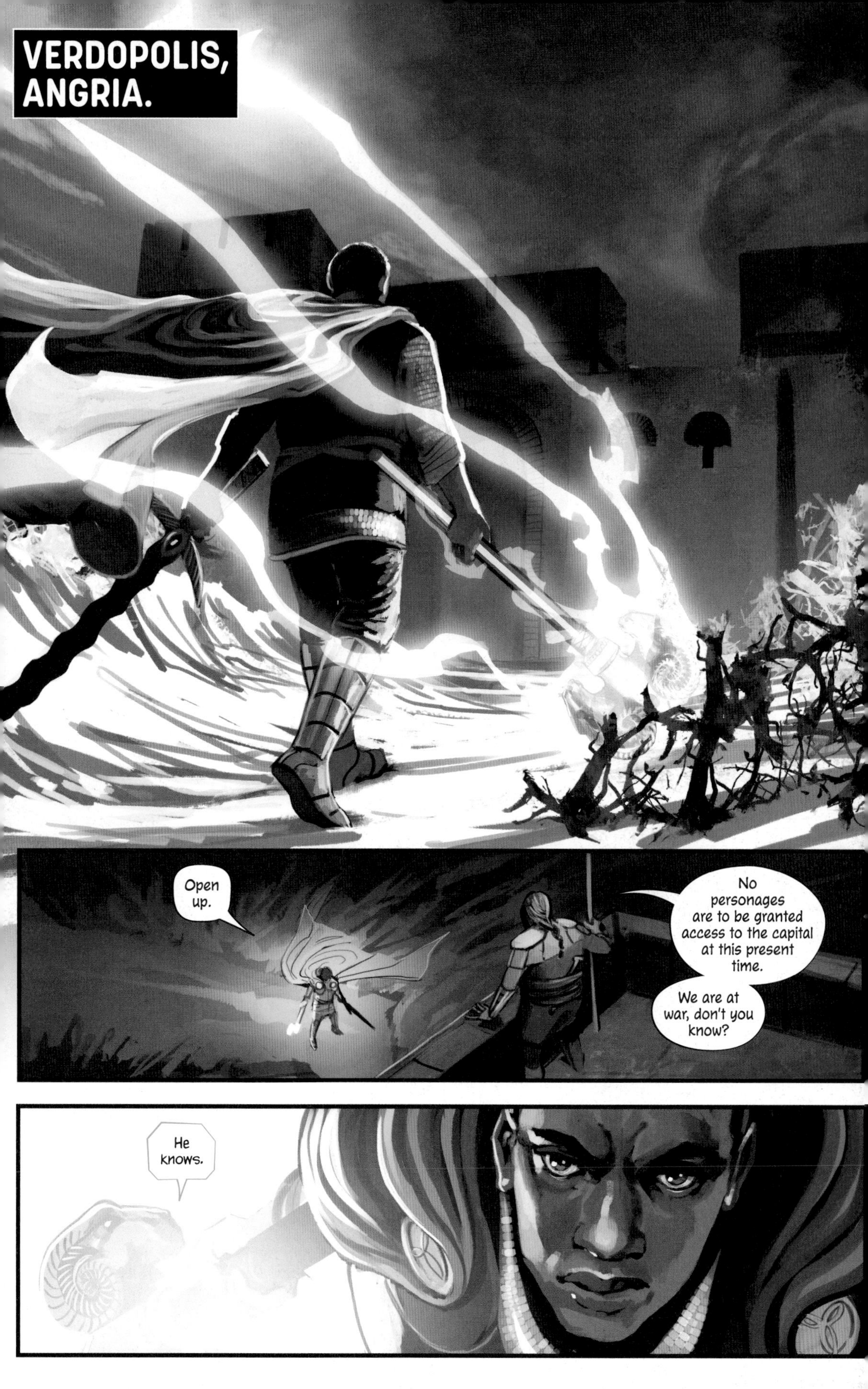
VERDOPOLIS, ANGRIA.
Open up.
No personages are to be granted access to the capital at this present time.
We are at war, don't you know?
He knows.

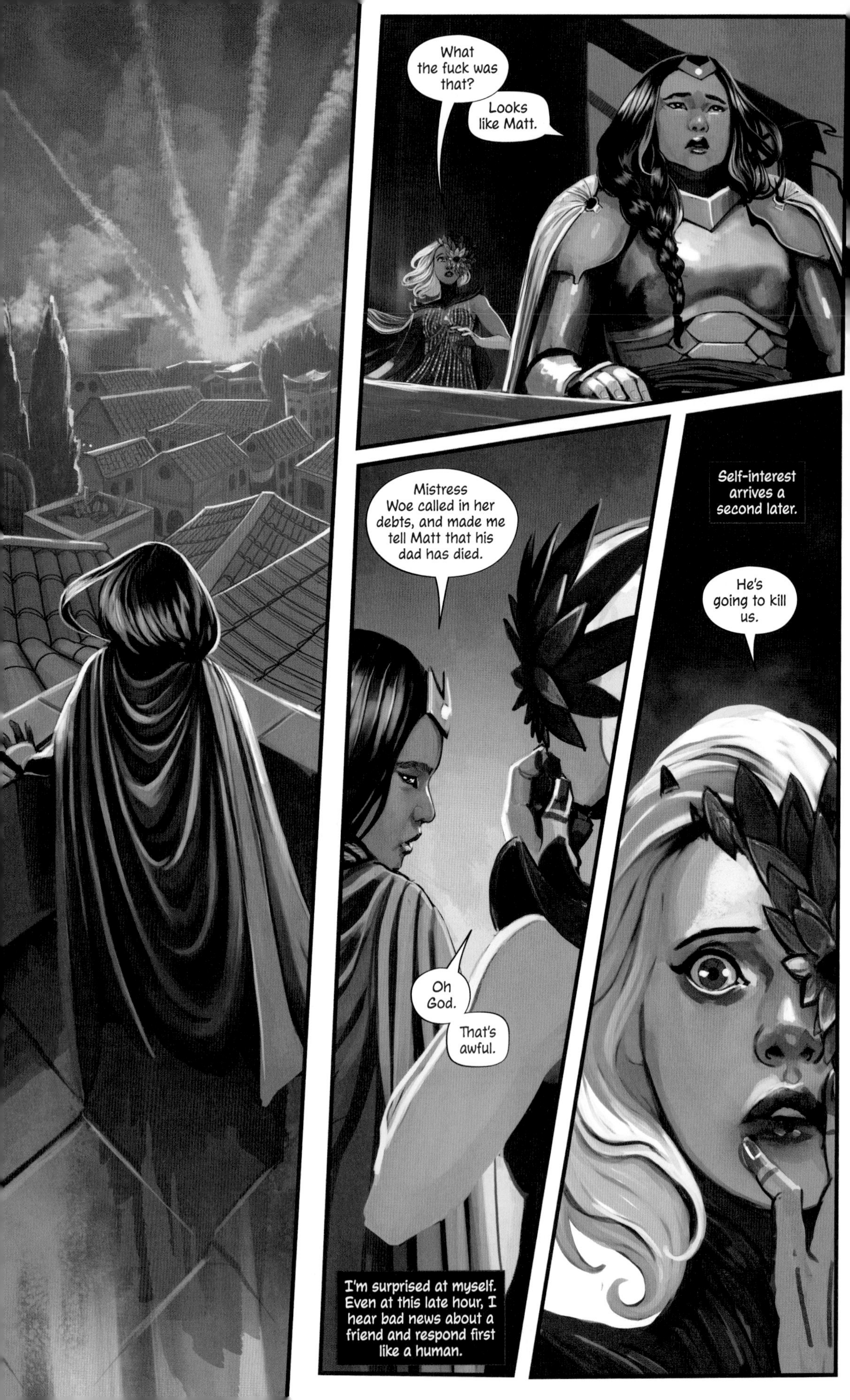
What the fuck was that?
Looks like Matt.
Mistress Woe called in her debts, and made me tell Matt that his dad has died.
Oh God.
That's awful.
I'm surprised at myself. Even at this late hour, I hear bad news about a friend and respond first like a human.
Self-interest arrives a second later.
He's going to kill us.

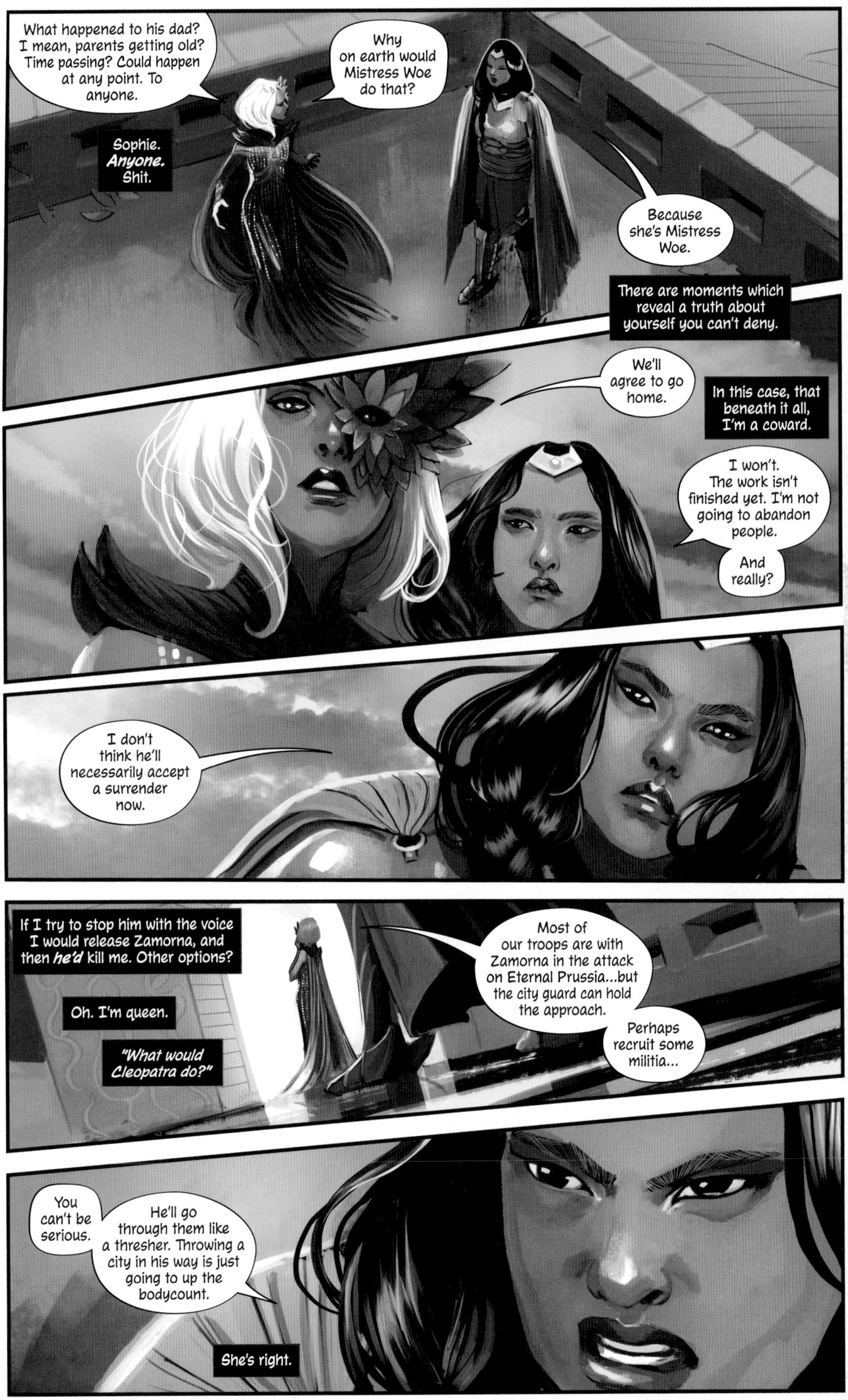
What happened to his dad? I mean, parents getting old? Time passing? Could happen at any point. To anyone.
Why on earth would Mistress Woe do that?
Sophie. *Anyone.* Shit.
Because she's Mistress Woe.
There are moments which reveal a truth about yourself you can't deny.
We'll agree to go home.
In this case, that beneath it all, I'm a coward.
I won't. The work isn't finished yet. I'm not going to abandon people.
And really?
I don't think he'll necessarily accept a surrender now.
If I try to stop him with the voice I would release Zamorna, and then *he'd* kill me. Other options?
Most of our troops are with Zamorna in the attack on Eternal Prussia...but the city guard can hold the approach.
Perhaps recruit some militia...
Oh. I'm queen.
"What would Cleopatra do?"
You can't be serious.
He'll go through them like a thresher. Throwing a city in his way is just going to up the bodycount.
She's right.

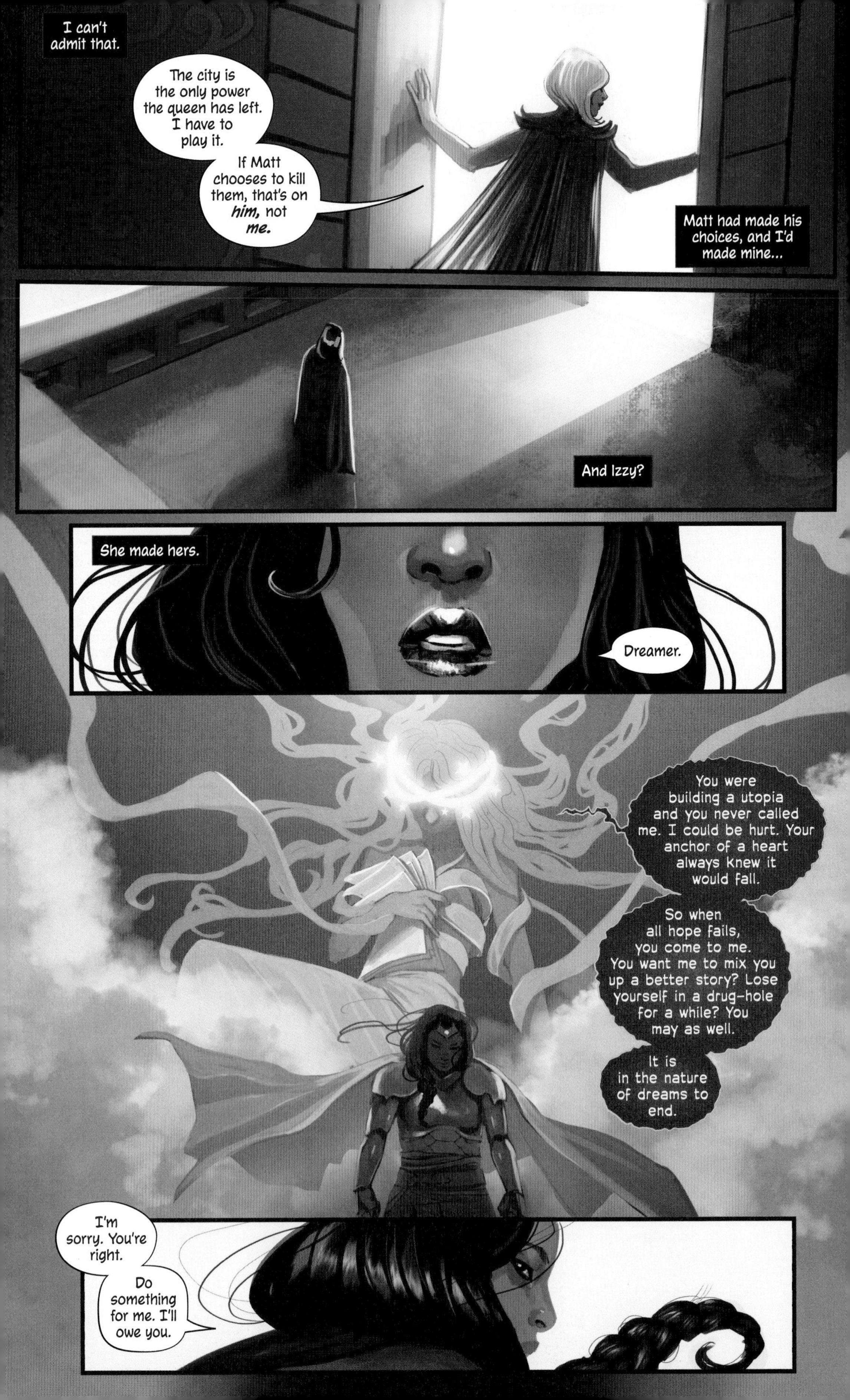
I can't admit that.
The city is the only power the queen has left. I have to play it.
If Matt chooses to kill them, that's on *him,* not *me.*
Matt had made his choices, and I'd made mine...
And Izzy?
She made hers.
Dreamer.
You were building a utopia and you never called me. I could be hurt. Your anchor of a heart always knew it would fall.
So when all hope fails, you come to me. You want me to mix you up a better story? Lose yourself in a drug-hole for a while? You may as well.
It is in the nature of dreams to end.
I'm sorry. You're right.
Do something for me. I'll owe you.

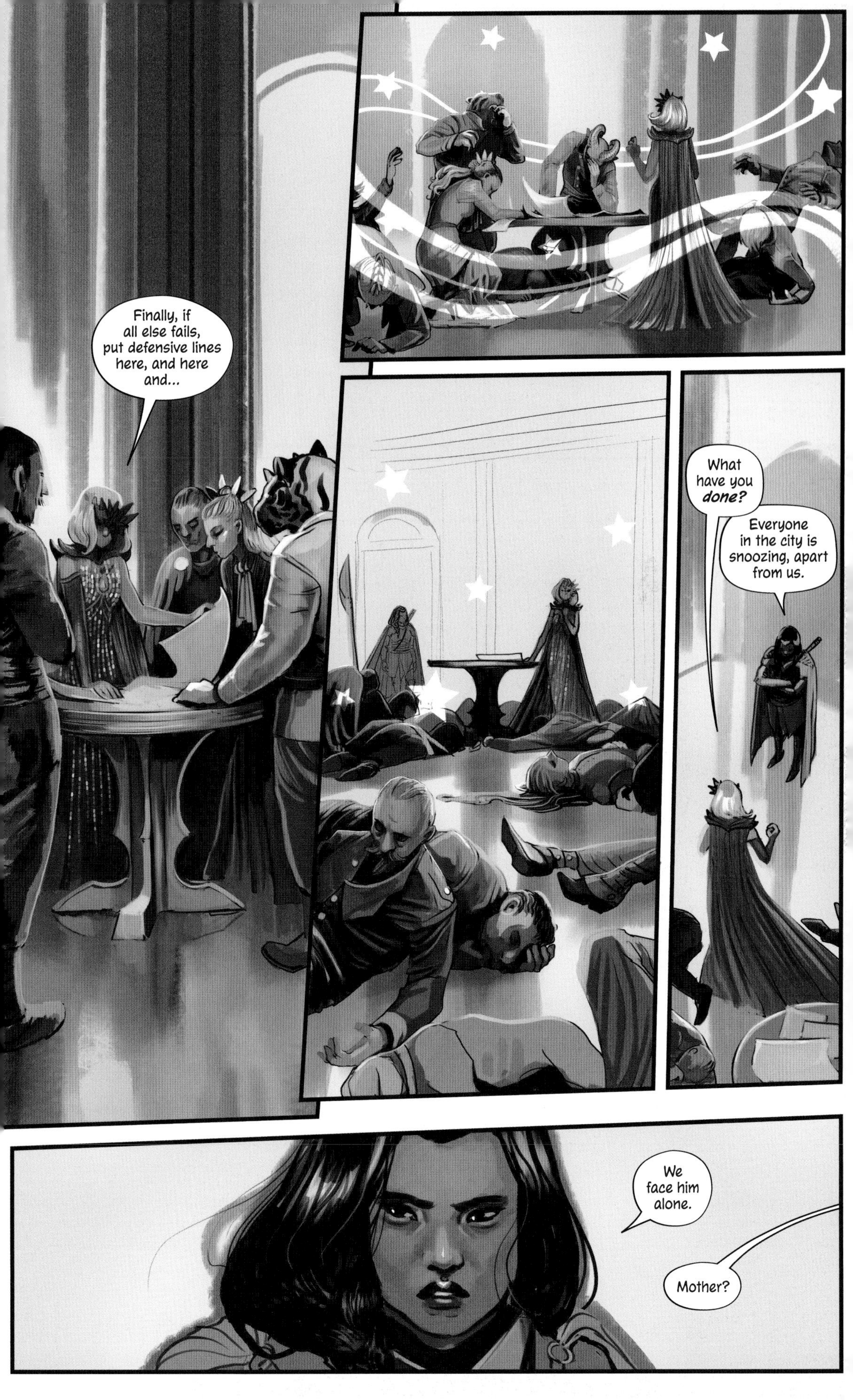
Finally, if all else fails, put defensive lines here, and here and...
What have you ***done?***
Everyone in the city is snoozing, apart from us.
We face him alone.
Mother?

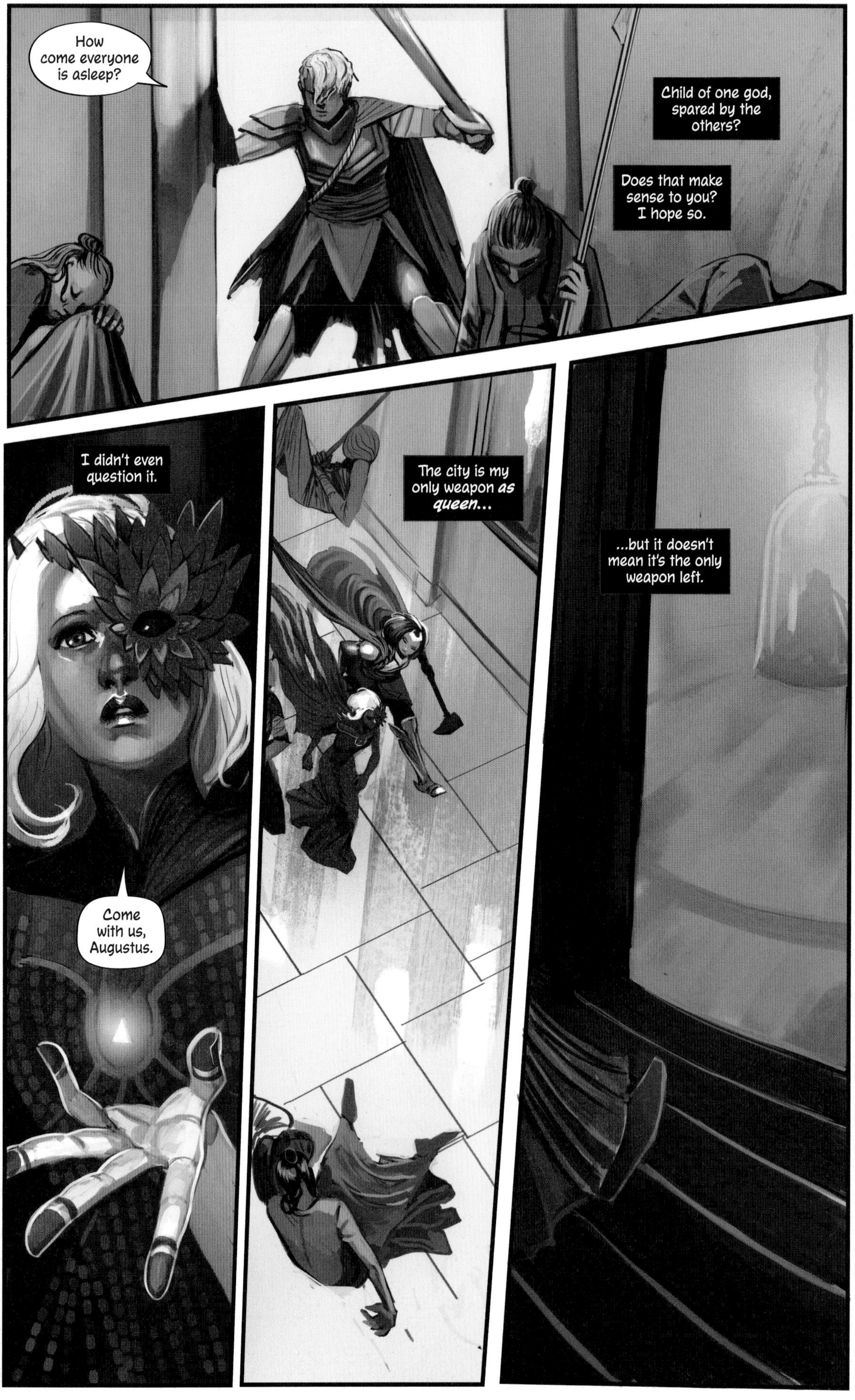
How come everyone is asleep?
Child of one god, spared by the others?
Does that make sense to you? I hope so.
I didn't even question it.
Come with us, Augustus.
The city is my only weapon as *queen*...
...but it doesn't mean it's the only weapon left.

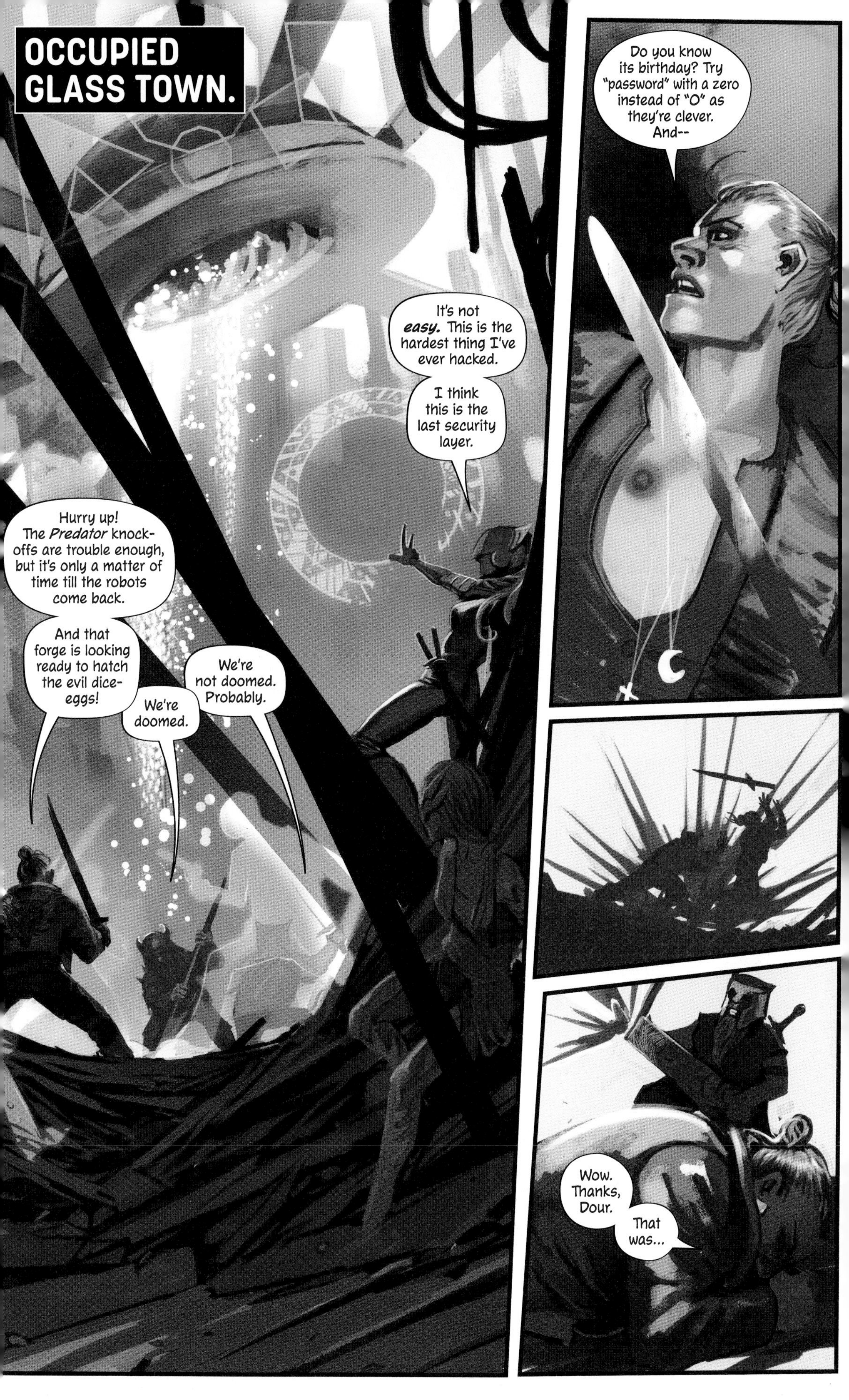
OCCUPIED GLASS TOWN.
It's not *easy.* This is the hardest thing I've ever hacked.
I think this is the last security layer.
Hurry up! The *Predator* knock-offs are trouble enough, but it's only a matter of time till the robots come back.
And that forge is looking ready to hatch the evil dice-eggs!
We're doomed.
We're not doomed. Probably.
Do you know its birthday? Try "password" with a zero instead of "O" as they're clever. And--
Wow. Thanks, Dour.
That was...

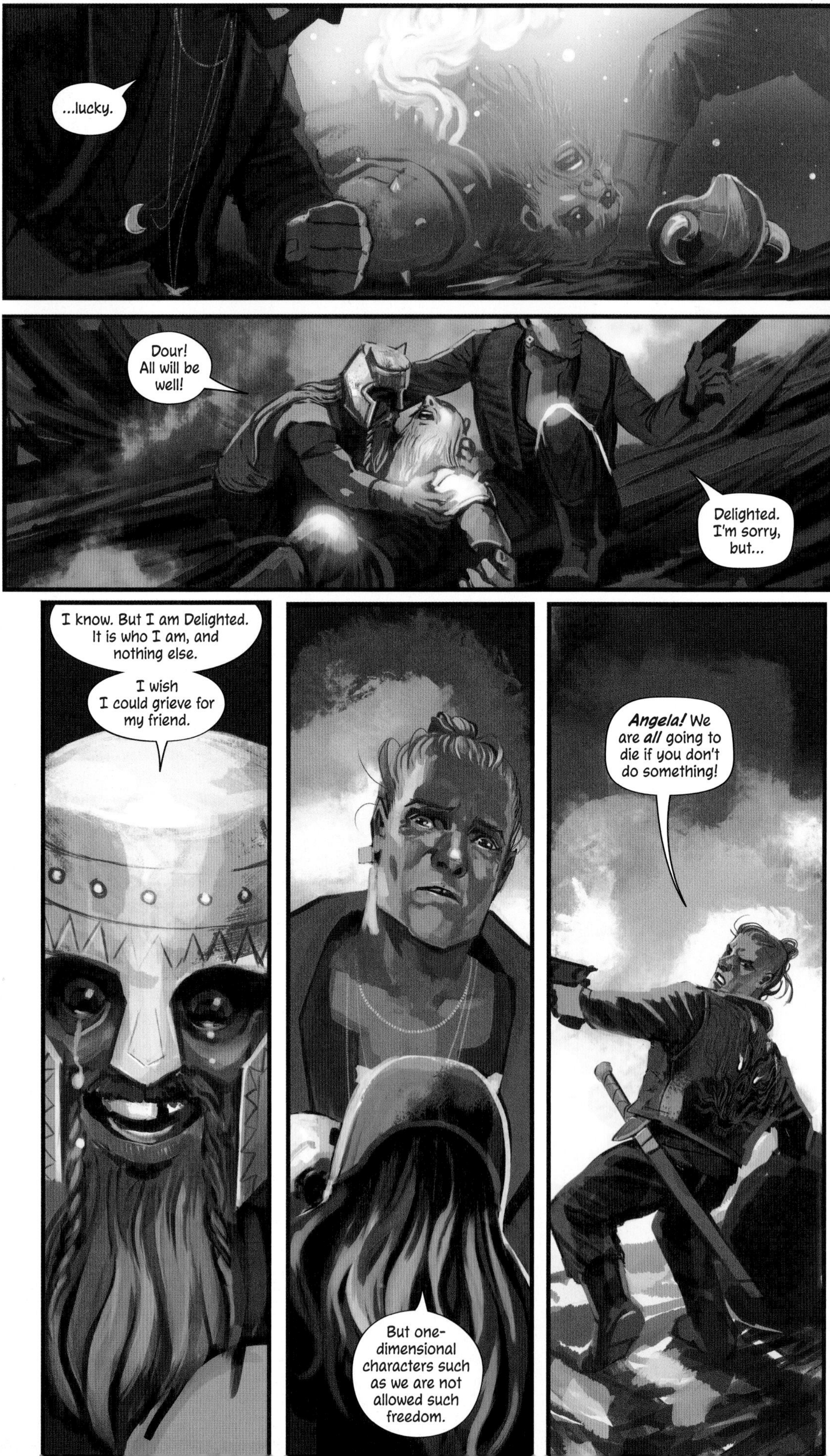
...lucky.
Dour! All will be well!
Delighted. I'm sorry, but...
I know. But I am Delighted. It is who I am, and nothing else.
I wish I could grieve for my friend.
But one-dimensional characters such as we are not allowed such freedom.
Angela! We are *all* going to die if you don't do something!

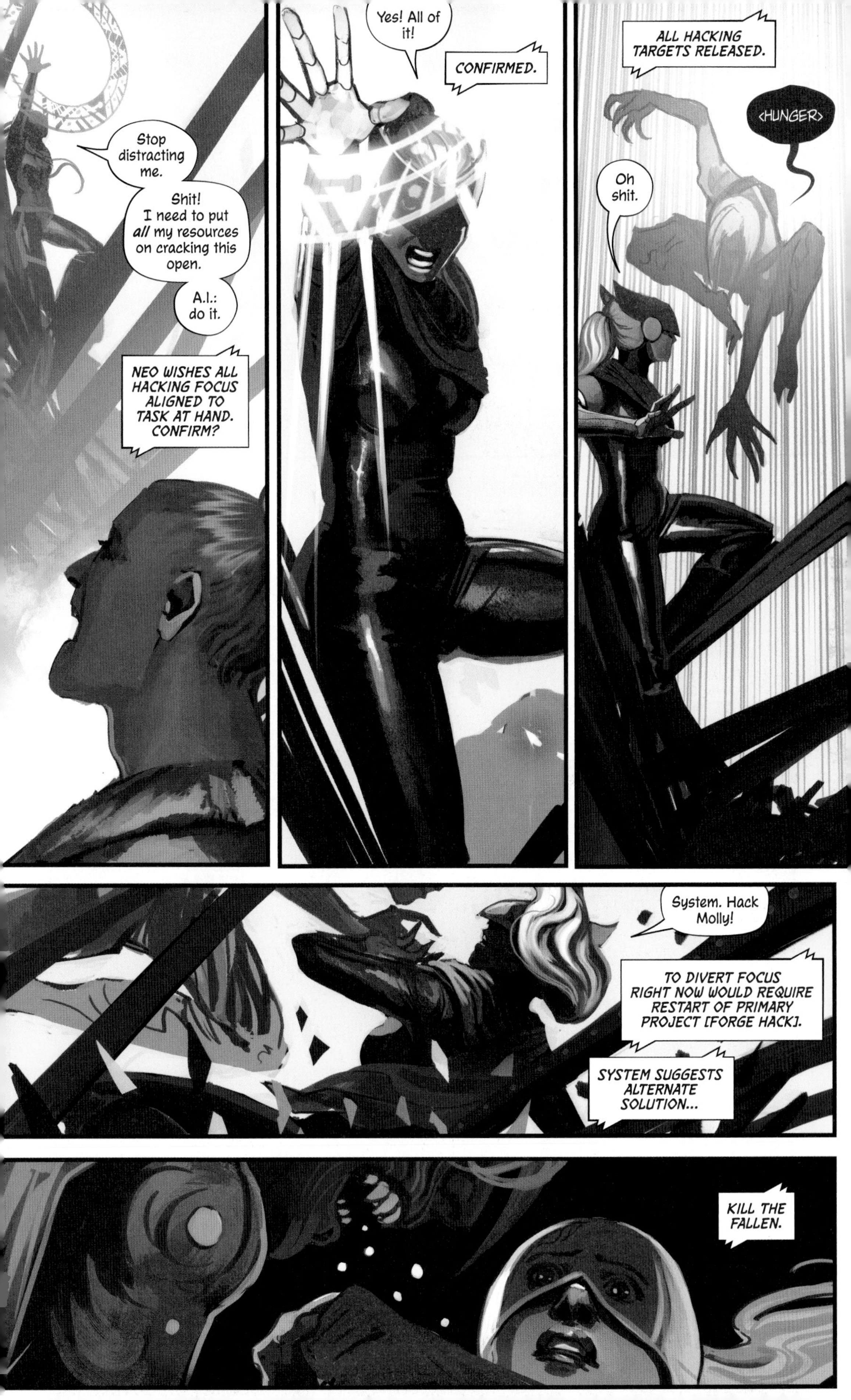
Stop distracting me.
Shit! I need to put *all* my resources on cracking this open.
A.I.: do it.
NEO WISHES ALL HACKING FOCUS ALIGNED TO TASK AT HAND. CONFIRM?
Yes! All of it!
CONFIRMED.
ALL HACKING TARGETS RELEASED.
<HUNGER>
Oh shit.
System. Hack Molly!
TO DIVERT FOCUS RIGHT NOW WOULD REQUIRE RESTART OF PRIMARY PROJECT [FORGE HACK].
SYSTEM SUGGESTS ALTERNATE SOLUTION...
KILL THE FALLEN.

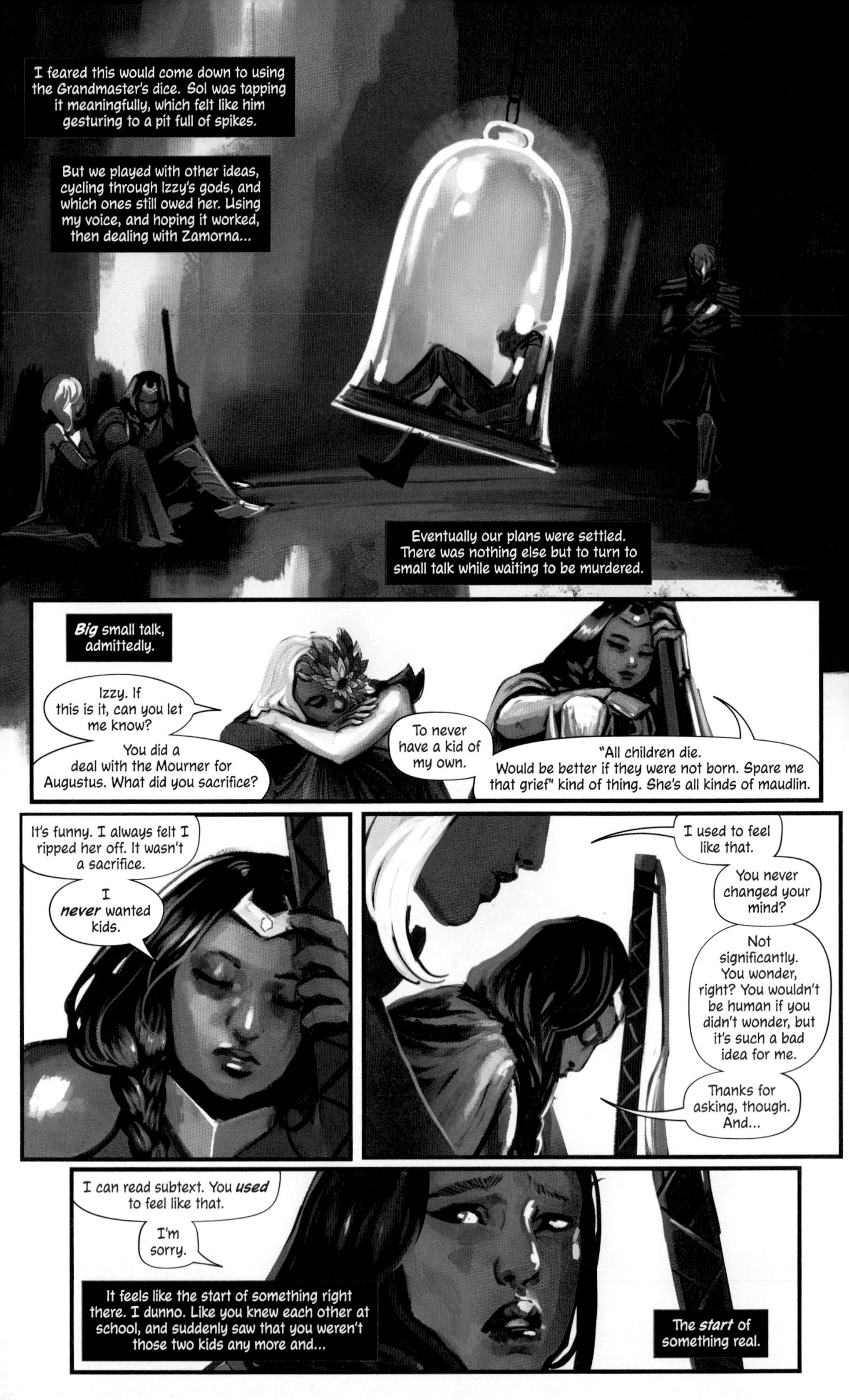

I feared this would come down to using the Grandmaster's dice. Sol was tapping it meaningfully, which felt like him gesturing to a pit full of spikes.
But we played with other ideas, cycling through Izzy's gods, and which ones still owed her. Using my voice, and hoping it worked, then dealing with Zamorna...
Eventually our plans were settled. There was nothing else but to turn to small talk while waiting to be murdered.
Big small talk, admittedly.
Izzy. If this is it, can you let me know?
You did a deal with the Mourner for Augustus. What did you sacrifice?
To never have a kid of my own.
"All children die. Would be better if they were not born. Spare me that grief" kind of thing. She's all kinds of maudlin.
It's funny. I always felt I ripped her off. It wasn't a sacrifice.
I *never* wanted kids.
I used to feel like that.
You never changed your mind?
Not significantly. You wonder, right? You wouldn't be human if you didn't wonder, but it's such a bad idea for me.
Thanks for asking, though. And...
I can read subtext. You *used* to feel like that.
I'm sorry.
It feels like the start of something right there. I dunno. Like you knew each other at school, and suddenly saw that you weren't those two kids any more and...
The *start* of something real.

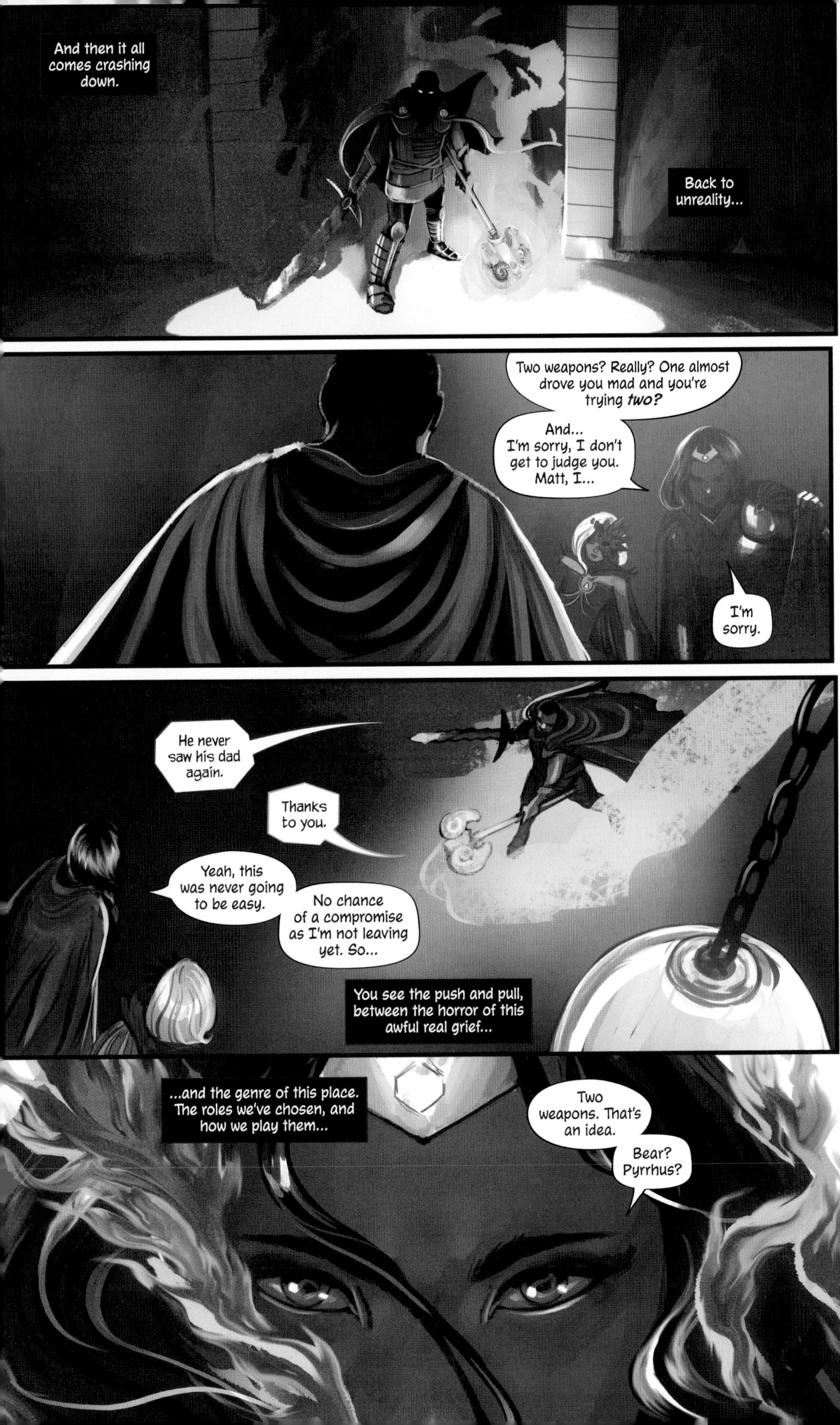
And then it all comes crashing down.
Back to unreality...
Two weapons? Really? One almost drove you mad and you're trying *two?*
And... I'm sorry, I don't get to judge you. Matt, I...
I'm sorry.
He never saw his dad again.
Thanks to you.
Yeah, this was never going to be easy.
No chance of a compromise as I'm not leaving yet. So...
You see the push and pull, between the horror of this awful real grief...
...and the genre of this place. The roles we've chosen, and how we play them...
Two weapons. That's an idea.
Bear? Pyrrhus?

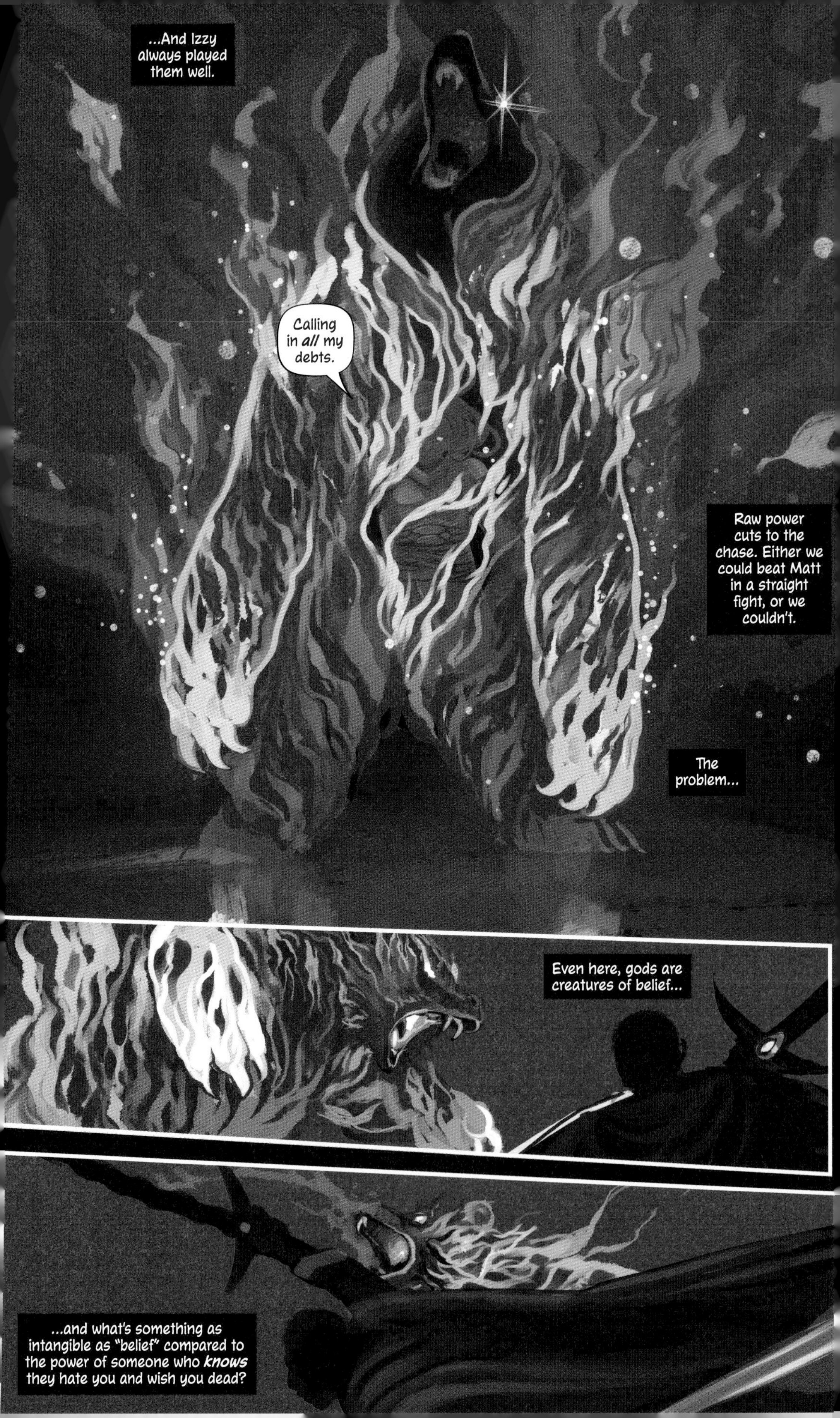
...And Izzy always played them well.
Calling in *all* my debts.
Raw power cuts to the chase. Either we could beat Matt in a straight fight, or we couldn't.
The problem...
Even here, gods are creatures of belief...
...and what's something as intangible as "belief" compared to the power of someone who *knows* they hate you and wish you dead?

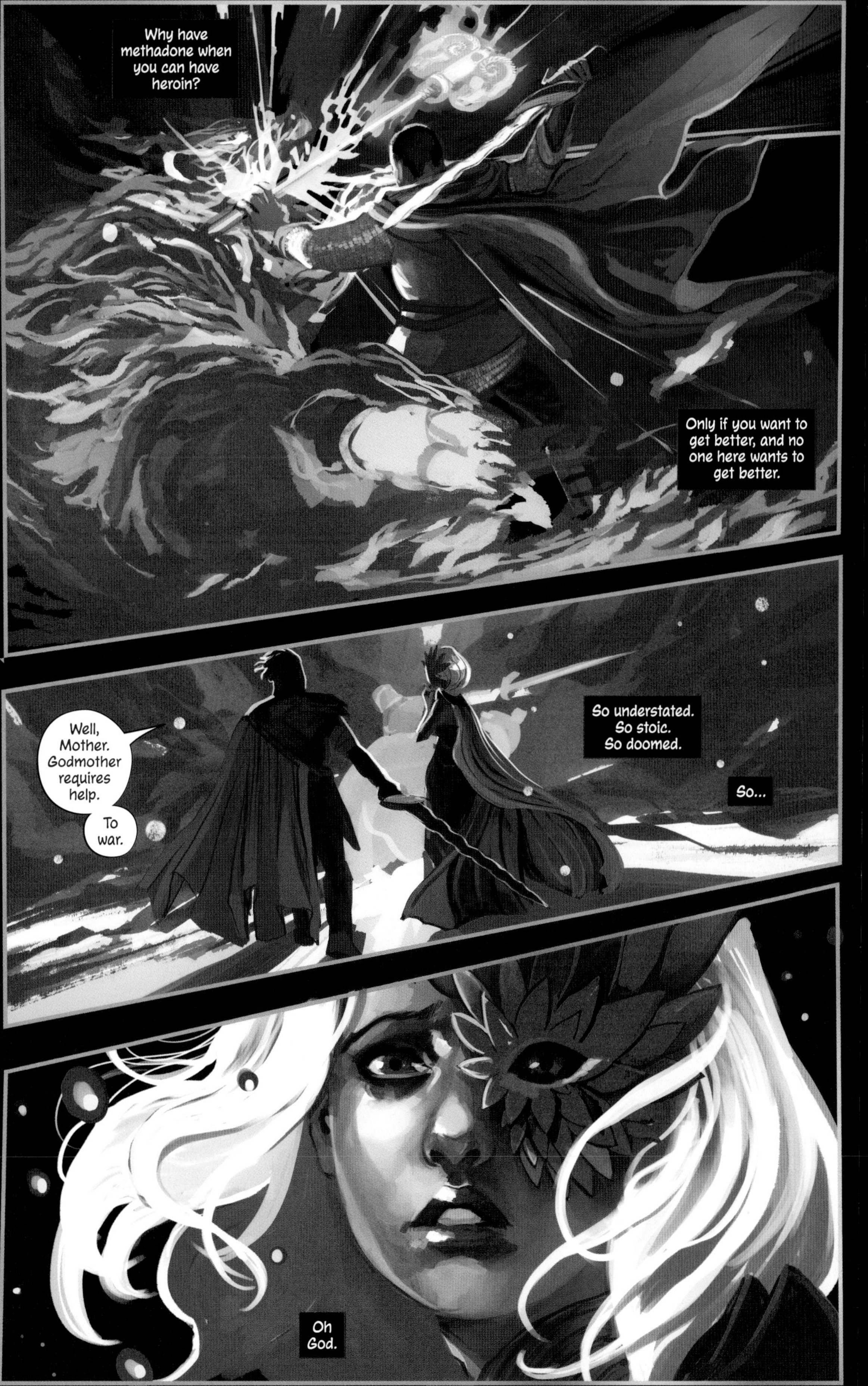
Why have methadone when you can have heroin?
Only if you want to get better, and no one here wants to get better.
Well, Mother. Godmother requires help.
To war.
So understated. So stoic. So doomed.
So...
Oh God.

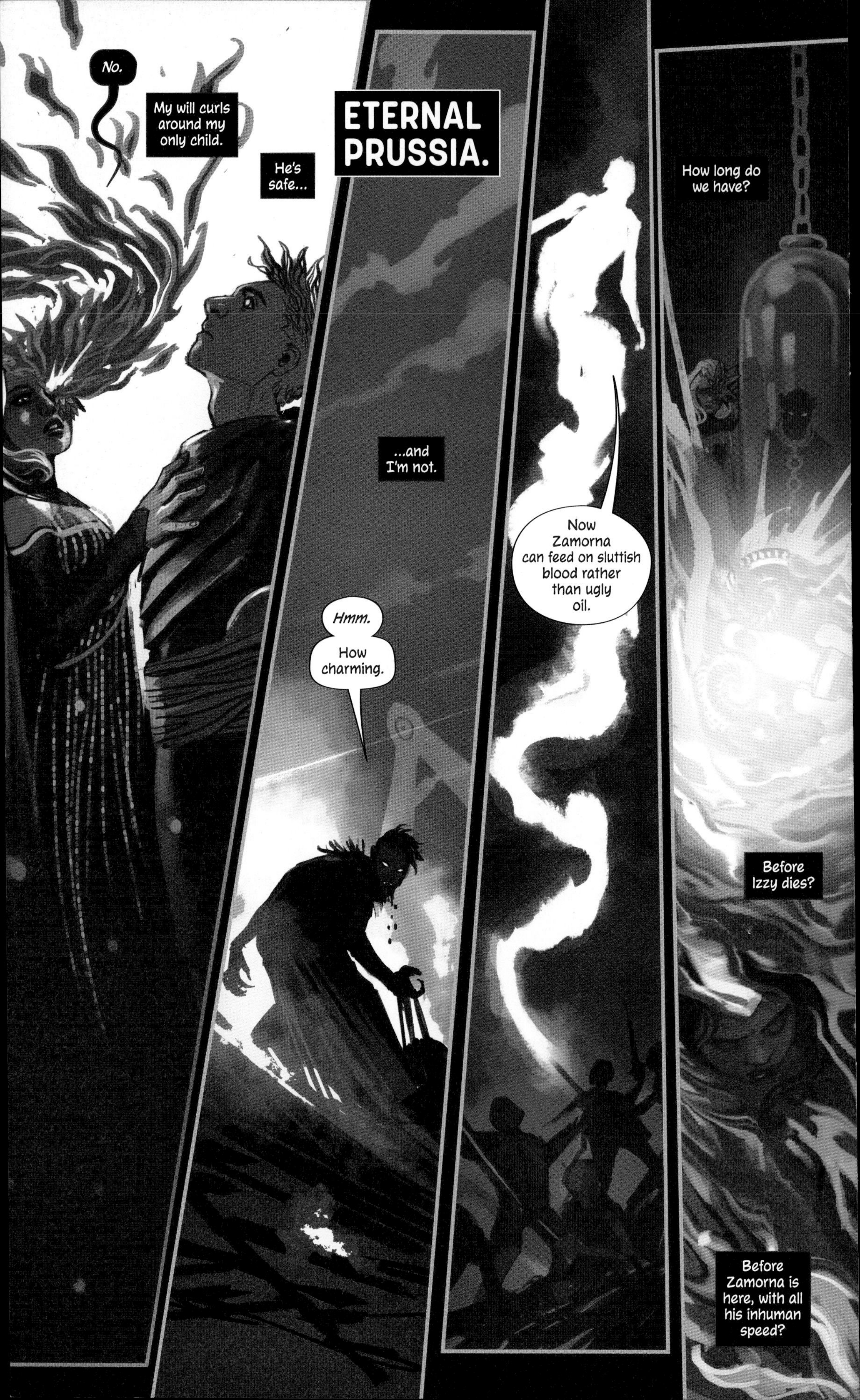
No.
My will curls around my only child.
He's safe...
ETERNAL PRUSSIA.
...and I'm not.
Hmm.
How charming.
Now Zamorna can feed on sluttish blood rather than ugly oil.
How long do we have?
Before Izzy dies?
Before Zamorna is here, with all his inhuman speed?

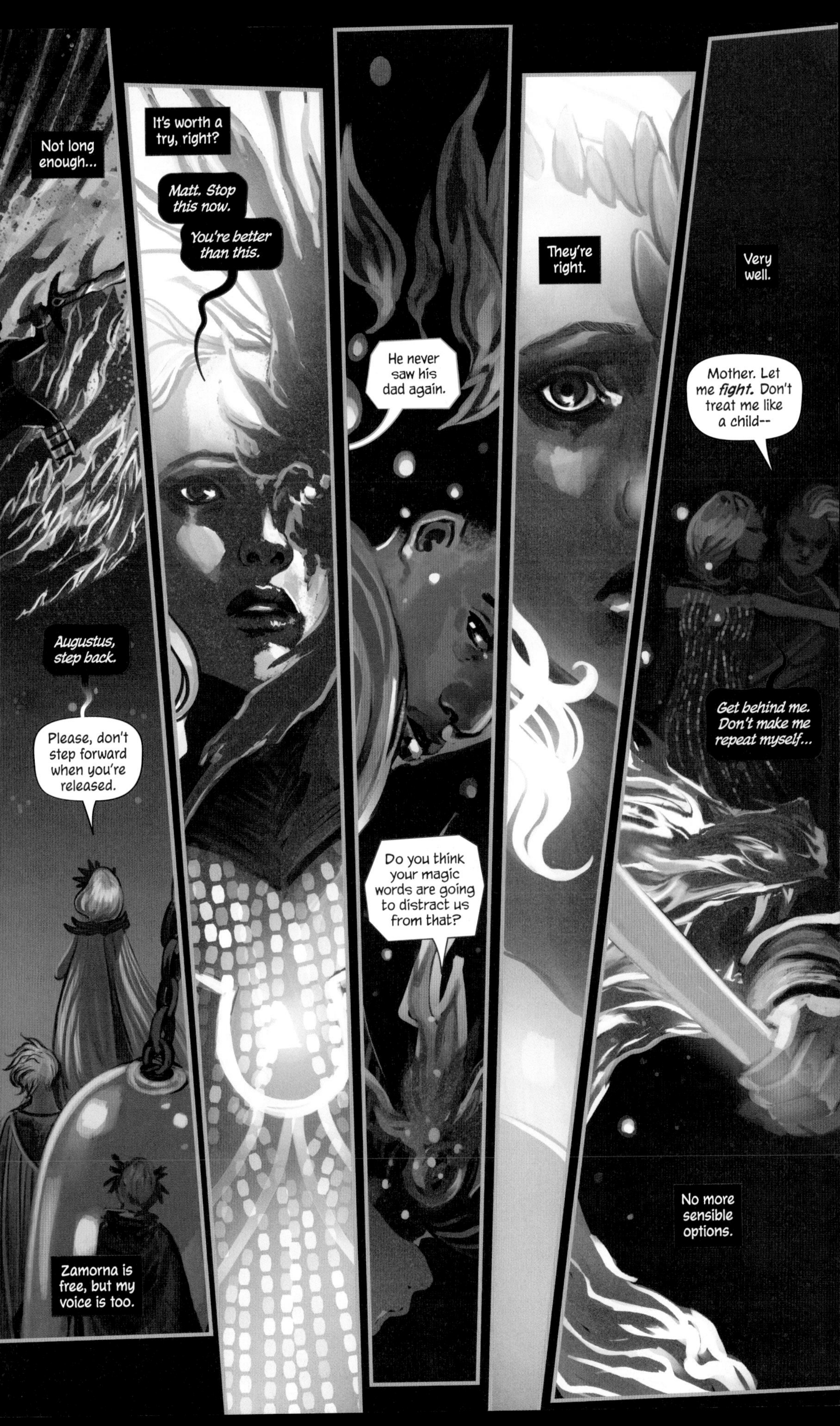
Not long enough...
Augustus, step back.
Please, don't step forward when you're released.
Zamorna is free, but my voice is too.
It's worth a try, right?
Matt. Stop this now.
You're better than this.
He never saw his dad again.
Do you think your magic words are going to distract us from that?
They're right.
Very well.
Mother. Let me **fight.** Don't treat me like a child--
Get behind me. Don't make me repeat myself...
No more sensible options.

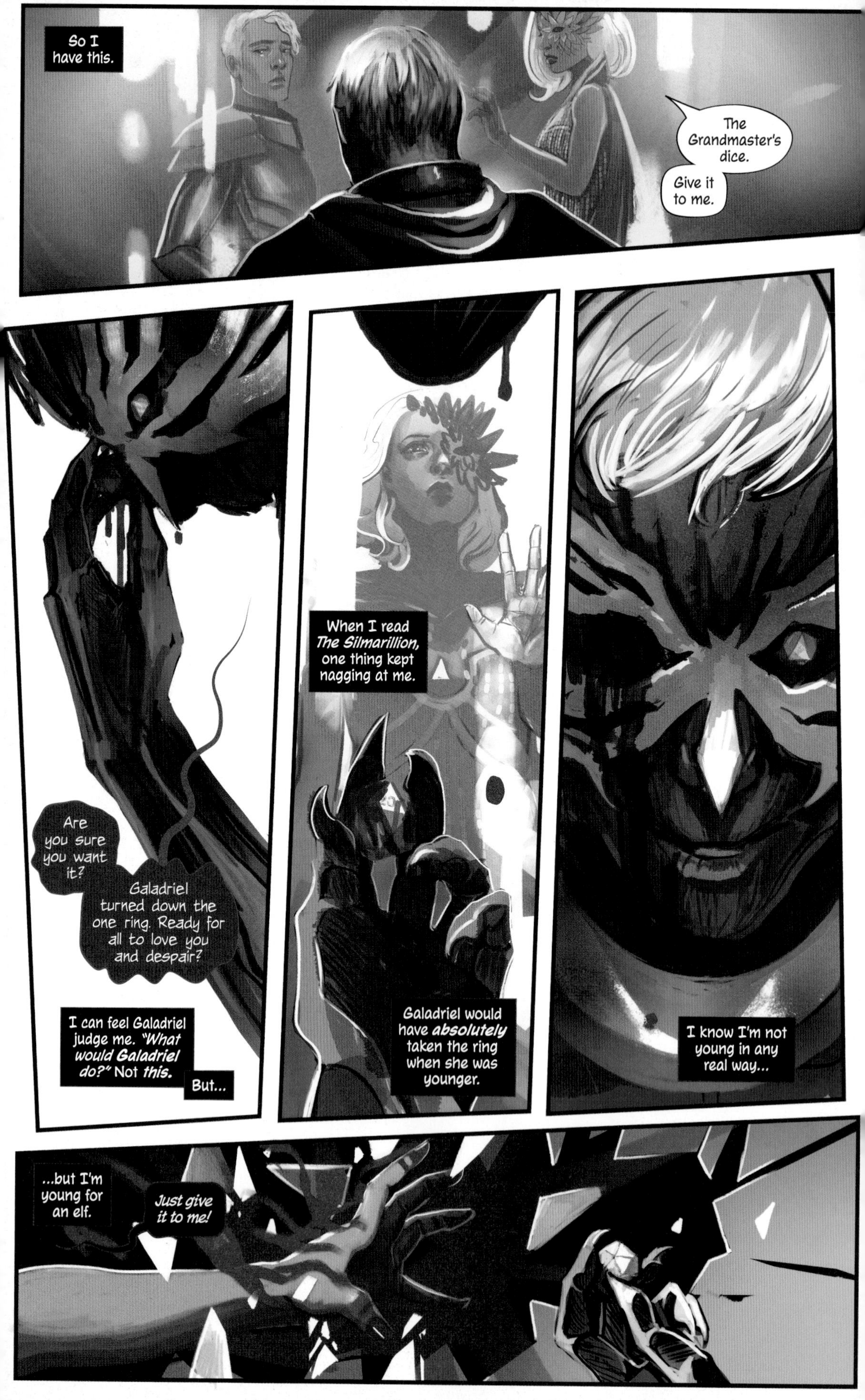
So I have this.
The Grandmaster's dice.
Give it to me.
Are you sure you want it?
Galadriel turned down the one ring. Ready for all to love you and despair?
I can feel Galadriel judge me. *"What would Galadriel do?"* Not ***this.***
But...
When I read *The Silmarillion,* one thing kept nagging at me.
Galadriel would have ***absolutely*** taken the ring when she was younger.
I know I'm not young in any real way...
...but I'm young for an elf.
Just give it to me!

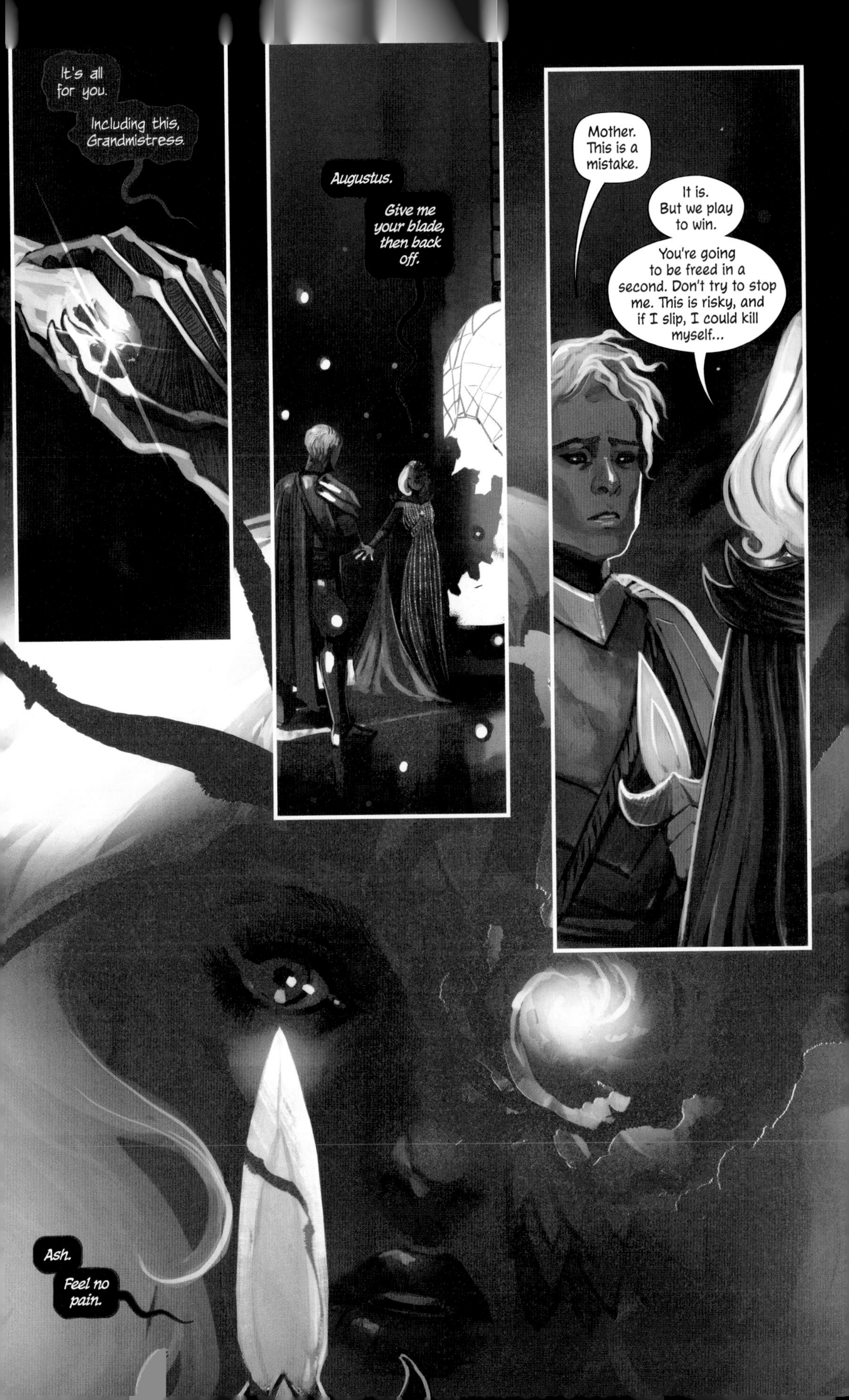
It's all for you.
Including this, Grandmistress.
Augustus.
Give me your blade, then back off.
Mother. This is a mistake.
It is. But we play to win.
You're going to be freed in a second. Don't try to stop me. This is risky, and if I slip, I could kill myself...
Ash.
Feel no pain.

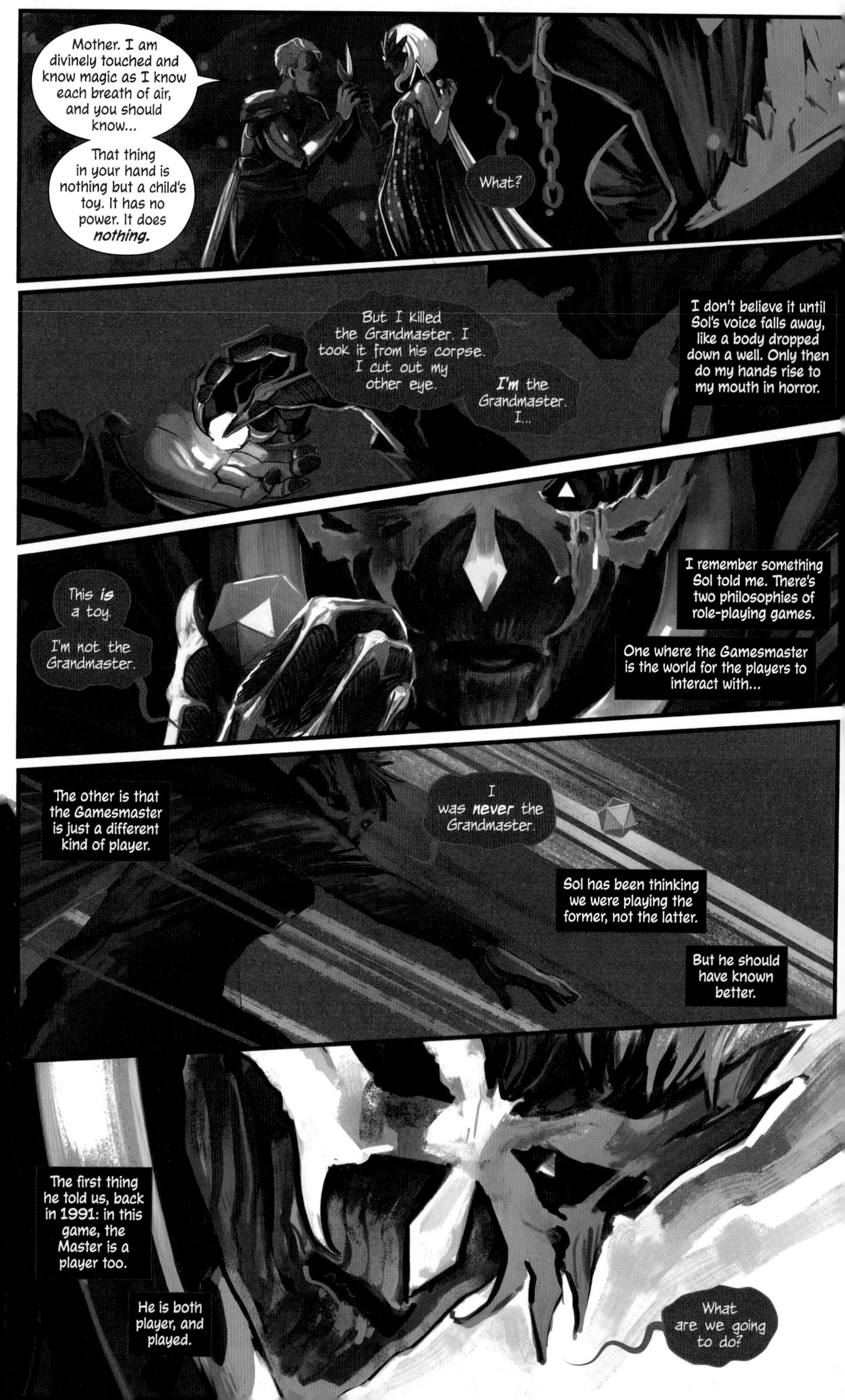
Mother. I am divinely touched and know magic as I know each breath of air, and you should know...
That thing in your hand is nothing but a child's toy. It has no power. It does ***nothing.***
What?
But I killed the Grandmaster. I took it from his corpse. I cut out my other eye.
I'm the Grandmaster. I...
I don't believe it until Sol's voice falls away, like a body dropped down a well. Only then do my hands rise to my mouth in horror.
This ***is*** a toy.
I'm not the Grandmaster.
I remember something Sol told me. There's two philosophies of role-playing games.
One where the Gamesmaster is the world for the players to interact with...
The other is that the Gamesmaster is just a different kind of player.
I was ***never*** the Grandmaster.
Sol has been thinking we were playing the former, not the latter.
But he should have known better.
The first thing he told us, back in 1991: in this game, the Master is a player too.
He is both player, and played.
What are we going to do?

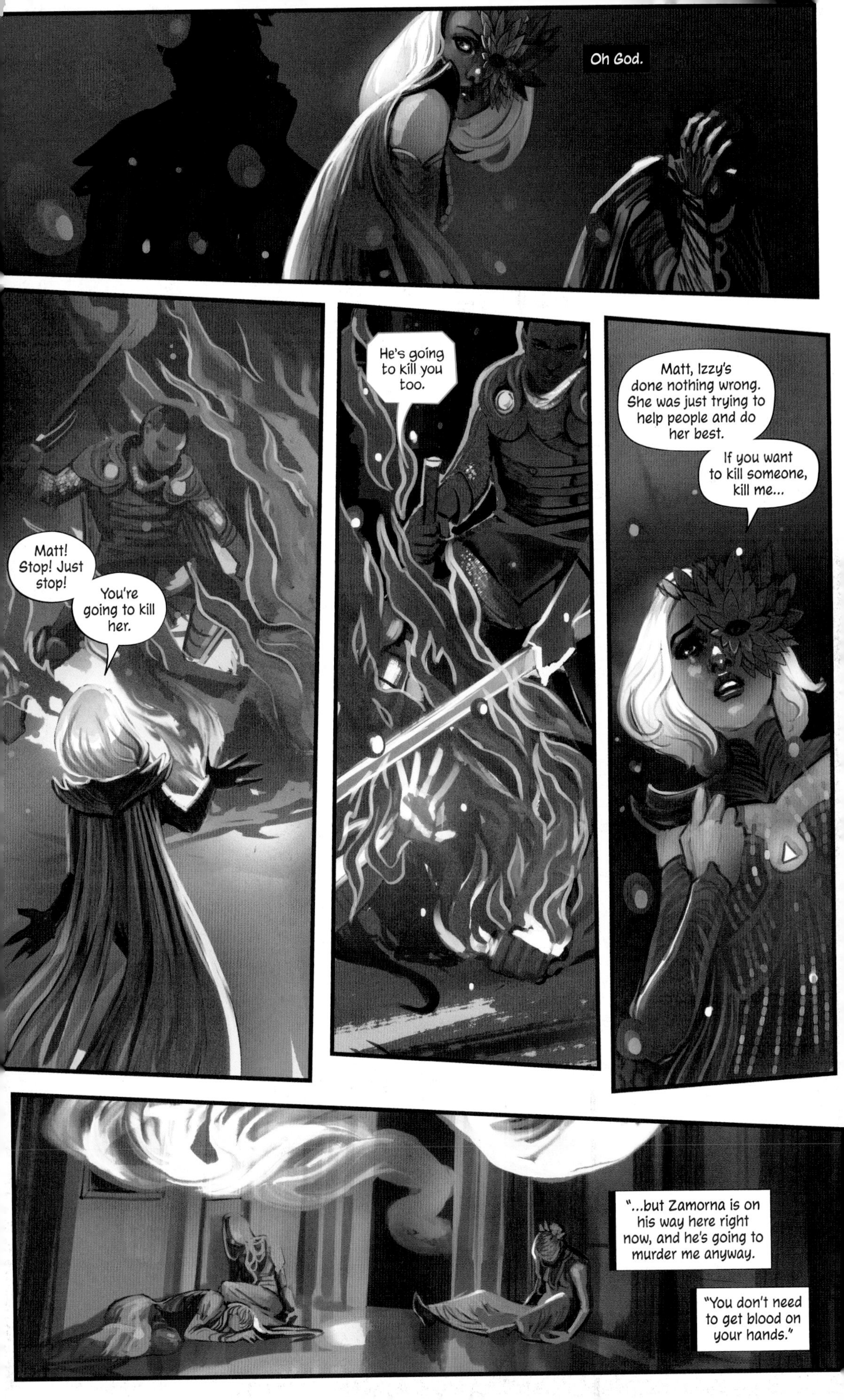
Oh God.
Matt! Stop! Just stop!
You're going to kill her.
He's going to kill you too.
Matt, Izzy's done nothing wrong. She was just trying to help people and do her best.
If you want to kill someone, kill me...
"...but Zamorna is on his way here right now, and he's going to murder me anyway.
"You don't need to get blood on your hands."

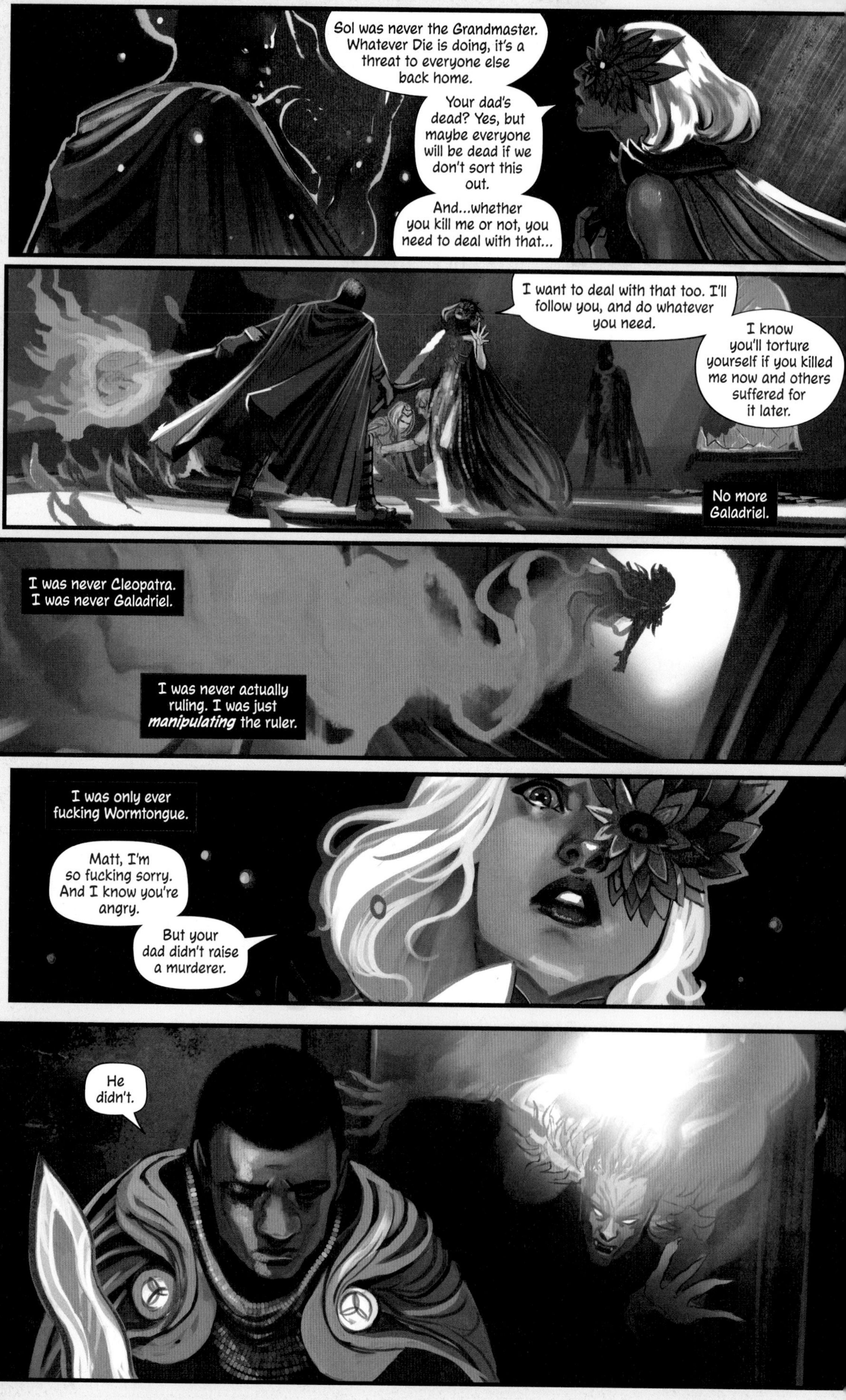

Sol was never the Grandmaster. Whatever Die is doing, it's a threat to everyone else back home.
Your dad's dead? Yes, but maybe everyone will be dead if we don't sort this out.
And...whether you kill me or not, you need to deal with that...
I want to deal with that too. I'll follow you, and do whatever you need.
I know you'll torture yourself if you killed me now and others suffered for it later.
No more Galadriel.
I was never Cleopatra. I was never Galadriel.
I was never actually ruling. I was just *manipulating* the ruler.
I was only ever fucking Wormtongue.
Matt, I'm so fucking sorry. And I know you're angry.
But your dad didn't raise a murderer.
He didn't.

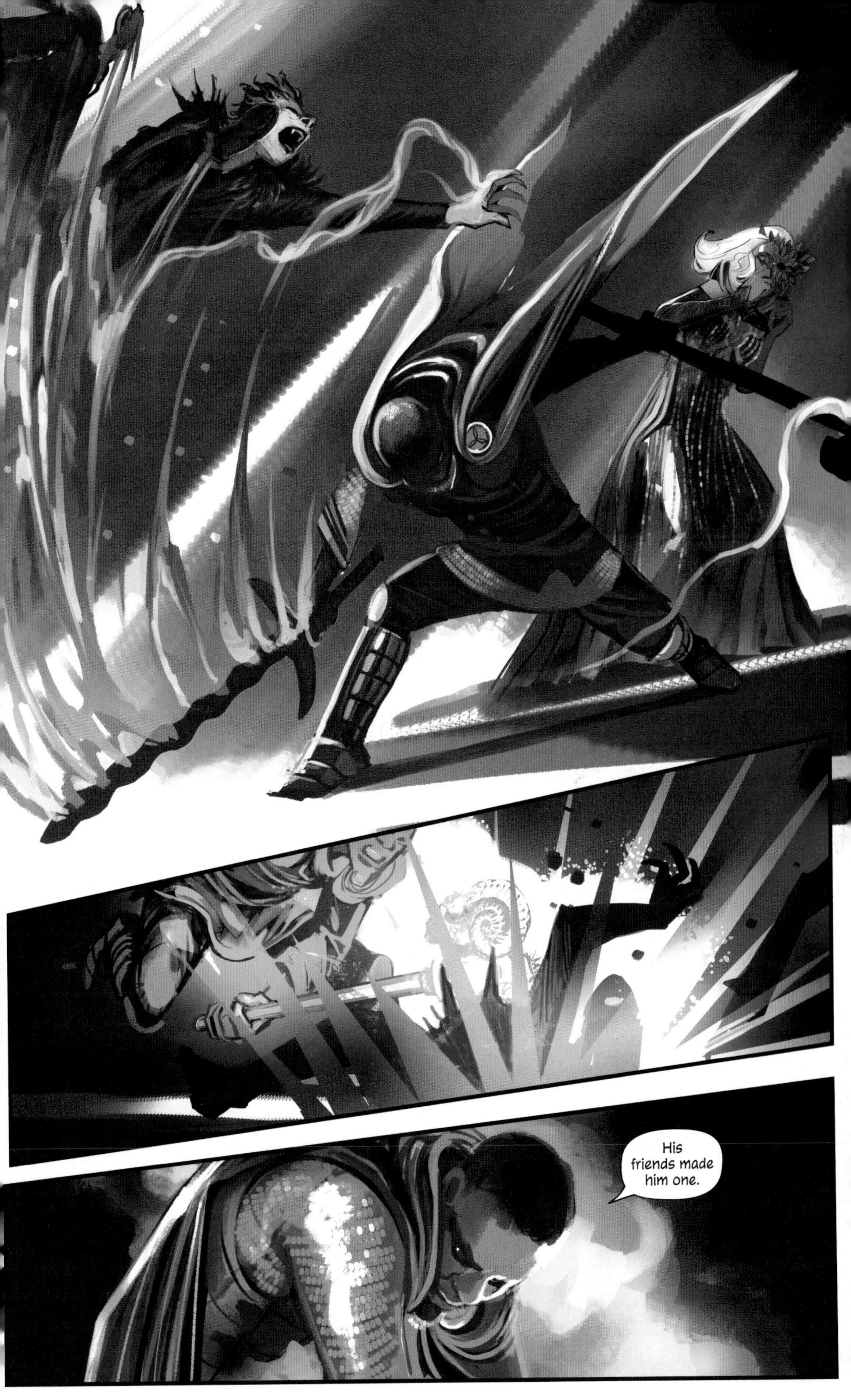
His friends made him one.

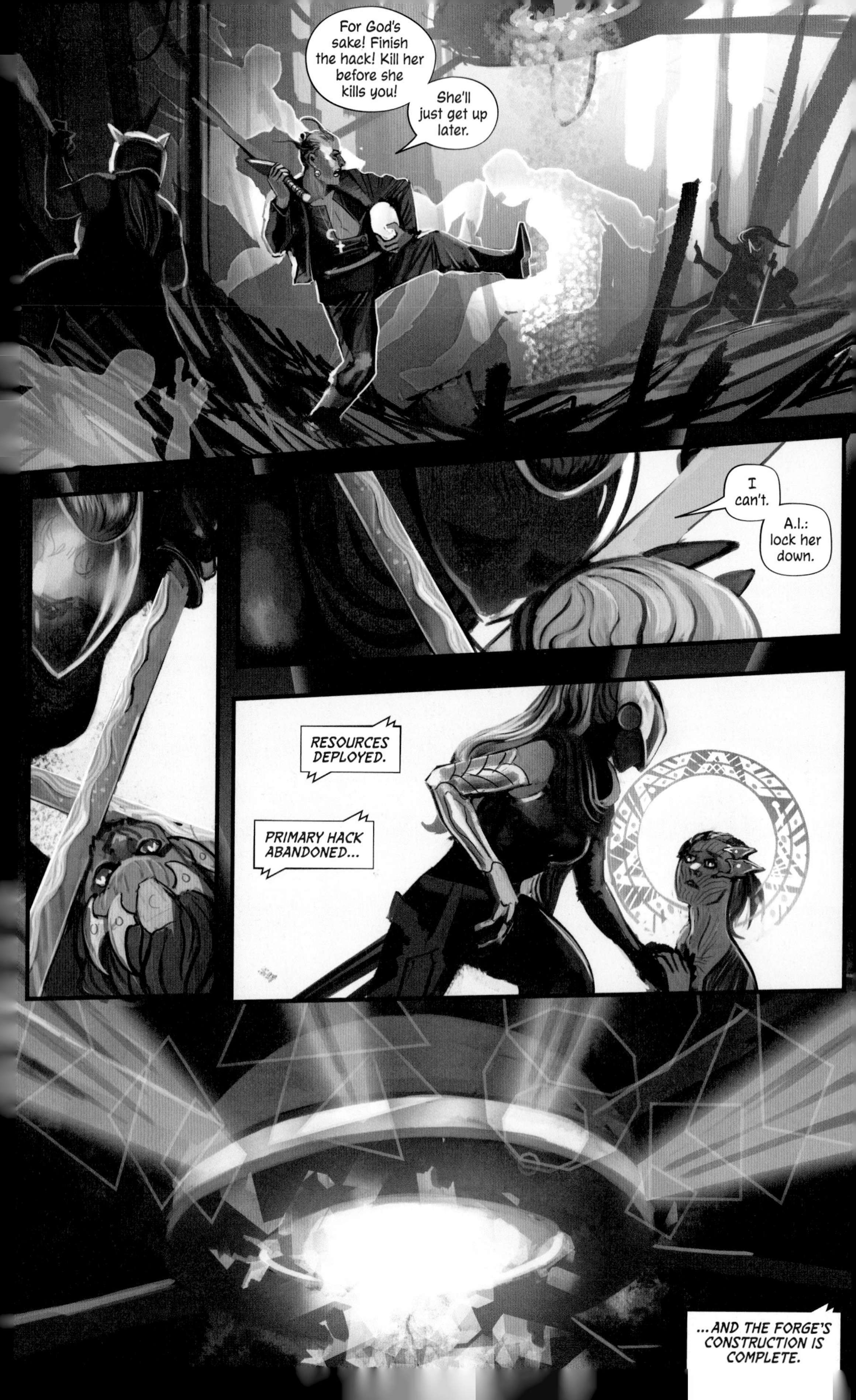

For God's sake! Finish the hack! Kill her before she kills you!
She'll just get up later.
I can't.
A.I.: lock her down.
RESOURCES DEPLOYED.
PRIMARY HACK ABANDONED...
...AND THE FORGE'S CONSTRUCTION IS COMPLETE.

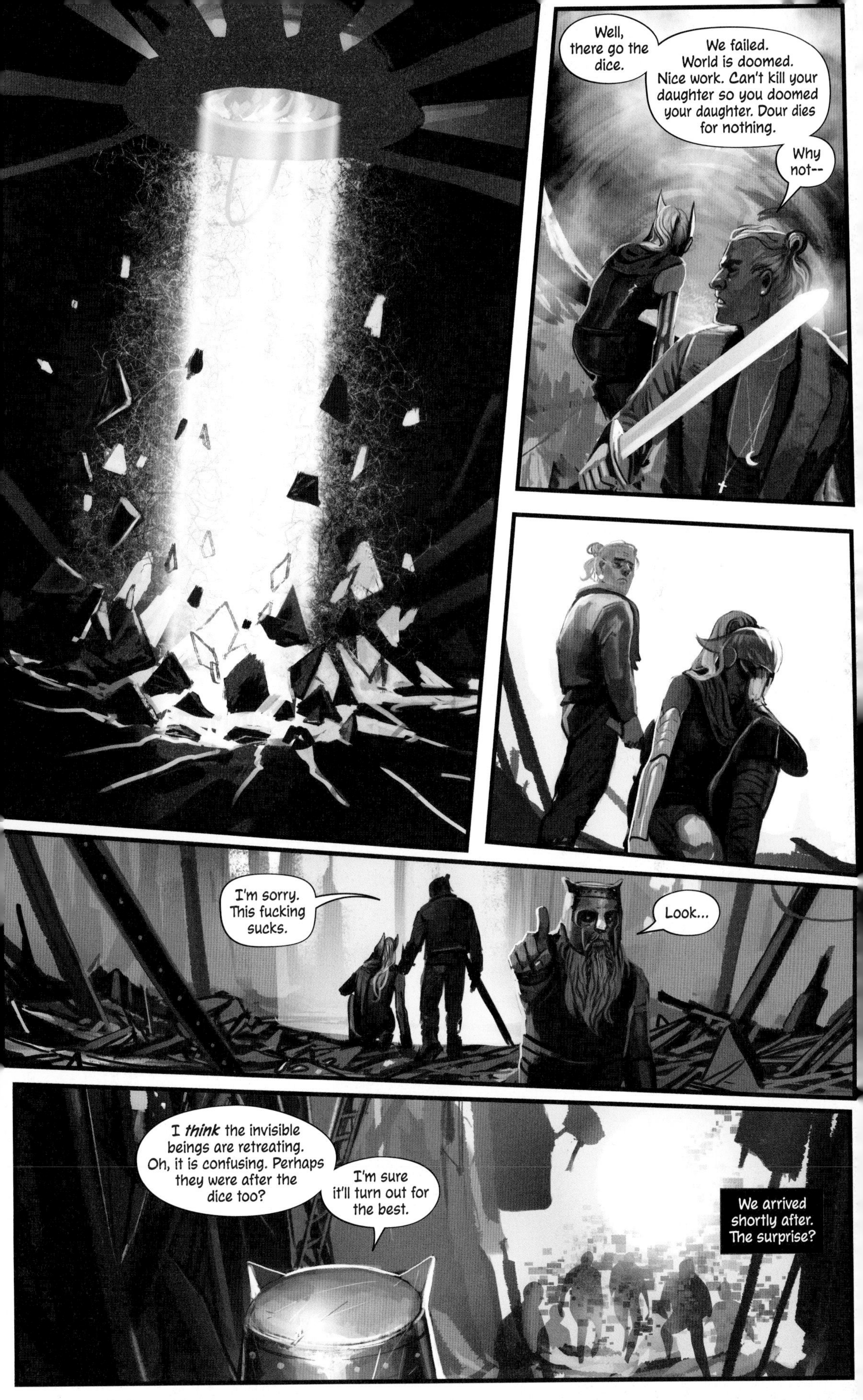
Well, there go the dice.
We failed. World is doomed. Nice work. Can't kill your daughter so you doomed your daughter. Dour dies for nothing.
Why not--
I'm sorry. This fucking sucks.
Look...
I *think* the invisible beings are retreating. Oh, it is confusing. Perhaps they were after the dice too?
I'm sure it'll turn out for the best.
We arrived shortly after. The surprise?

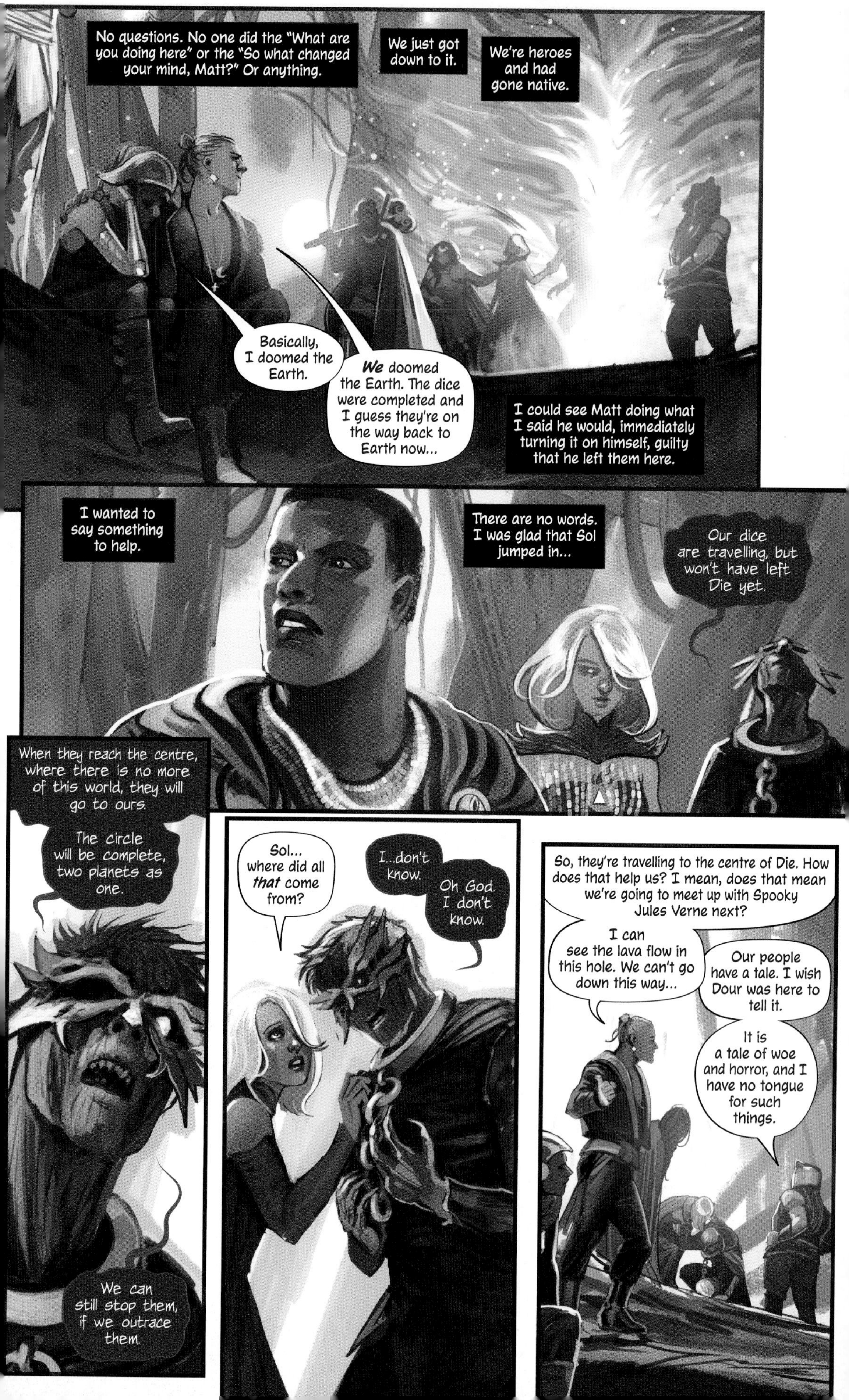

No questions. No one did the "What are you doing here" or the "So what changed your mind, Matt?" Or anything.
We just got down to it.
We're heroes and had gone native.
Basically, I doomed the Earth.
We doomed the Earth. The dice were completed and I guess they're on the way back to Earth now...
I could see Matt doing what I said he would, immediately turning it on himself, guilty that he left them here.
I wanted to say something to help.
There are no words. I was glad that Sol jumped in...
Our dice are travelling, but won't have left Die yet.
When they reach the centre, where there is no more of this world, they will go to ours.
The circle will be complete, two planets as one.
We can still stop them, if we outrace them.
Sol... where did all *that* come from?
I...don't know.
Oh God. I don't know.
So, they're travelling to the centre of Die. How does that help us? I mean, does that mean we're going to meet up with Spooky Jules Verne next?
I can see the lava flow in this hole. We can't go down this way...
Our people have a tale. I wish Dour was here to tell it.
It is a tale of woe and horror, and I have no tongue for such things.

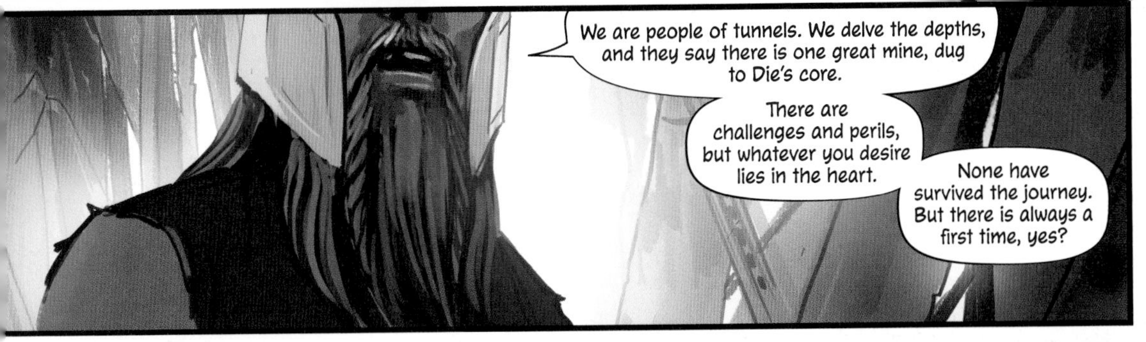
We are people of tunnels. We delve the depths, and they say there is one great mine, dug to Die's core.
There are challenges and perils, but whatever you desire lies in the heart.
None have survived the journey. But there is always a first time, yes?

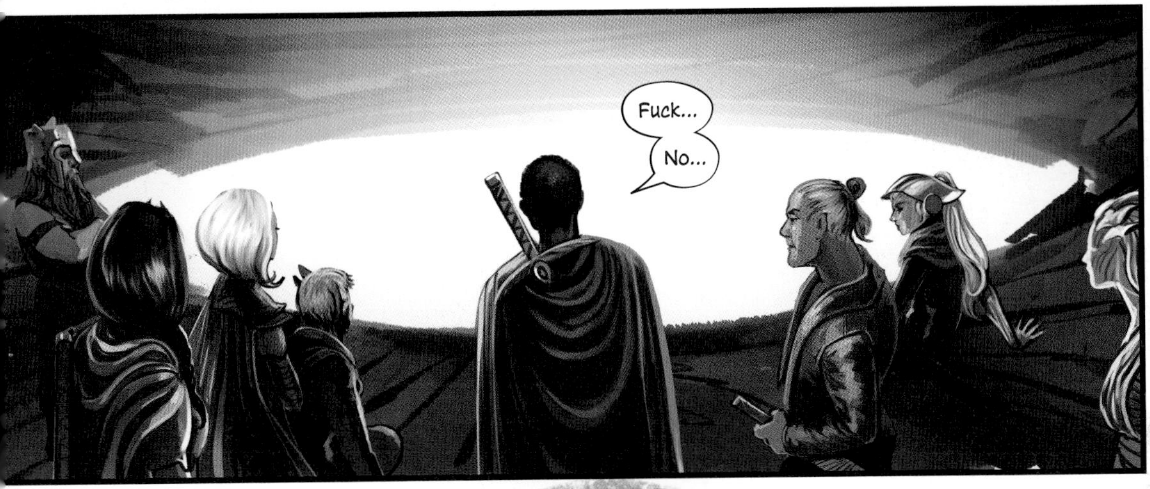
Fuck...
No...

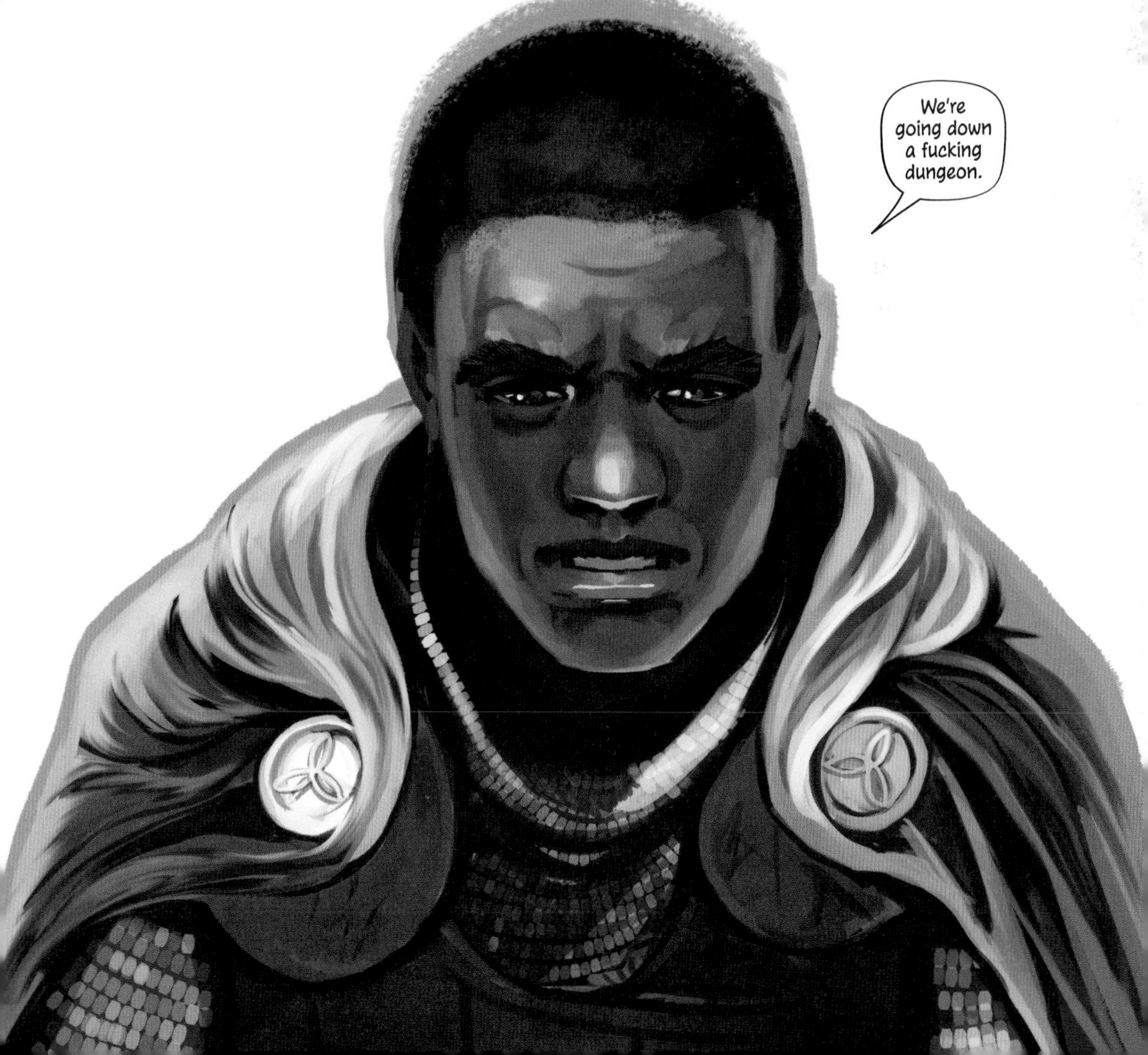
We're going down a fucking dungeon.

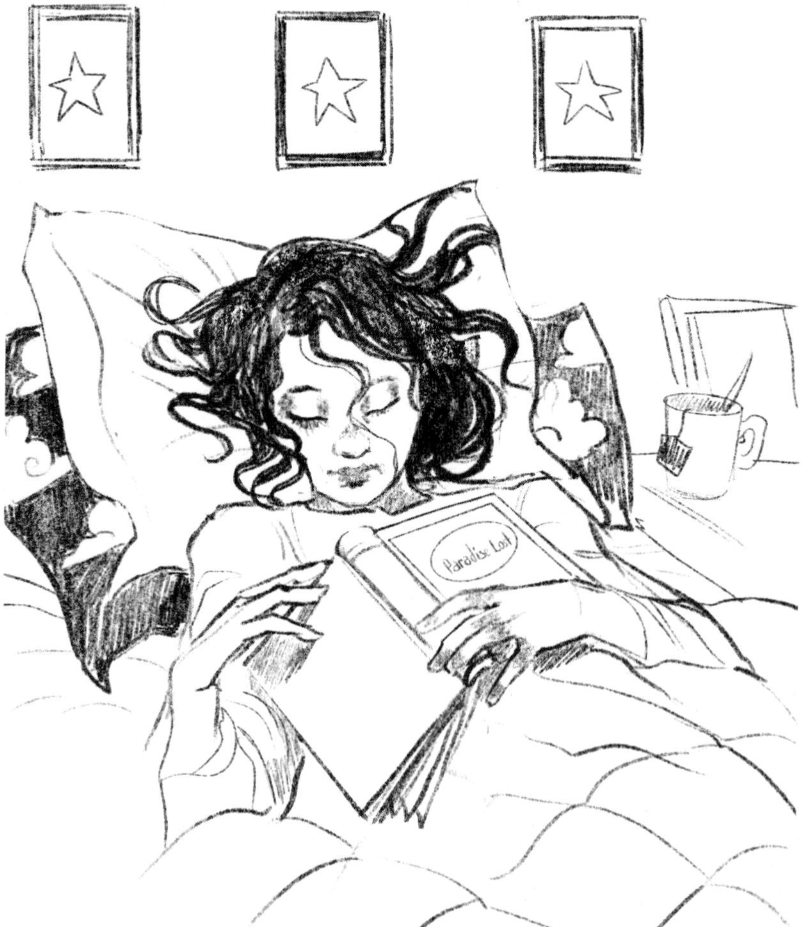
Paradise Lost

DIE:
THE RPG

Turning this whole endeavour into a meta-experience, as part of writing *DIE*, Kieron has been developing a whole RPG. Its beta rules have been released since the first trade dropped, and you can find them here...

www.diecomic.com/rpg

The present rules let you basically recreate your very own version of the first volume. As in, you create a messed up social group, generate some game characters for them, and then drag them into a fantasy world and see if they come home or not. It's designed to take a group of up to six people (including the person running the game) between two and four sessions to play. It's meant to be very flexible and replayable.

And since the original release, we've continued. As well as a second release and a whole book of extra stuff ("Arcana") we mentioned last time, there's been another small release (1.2). In fact, by the time this is with you, we may have released the 1.3 edition, which should finally let you have player-controlled Masters.

In terms of future plans, Kieron is at work on the full larger campaign rules for *DIE* RPG, which allow you to play it as something more open-ended. And then? Well, we're planning some kind of physical release. We're unsure what form that will take - though Kickstarter looks likely.

If you want further updates, see the site above, or check in on the *DIE* discord, which you'll also find in the link above. That link above is just great.

RPG
BETA

D

I

BASED ON THE COMIC SERIES BY
KIERON GILLEN
AND
STEPHANIE HANS

E

VARIANT COVERS

At the core of *DIE* was the idea to let Stephanie Hans create a fantasy world. However, a key part of creating a fantasy world is to see it reinterpreted, to live in others' fantasies. As such, we take great joy in asking our peers to do alternate covers...

Ben Oliver
Issue 11 variant

Justine Frany
Issue 12 variant

Mike Del Mundo
Issue 13 variant

Sana Takeda
Issue 14 variant

Bill Sienkiewicz
Issue 15 variant

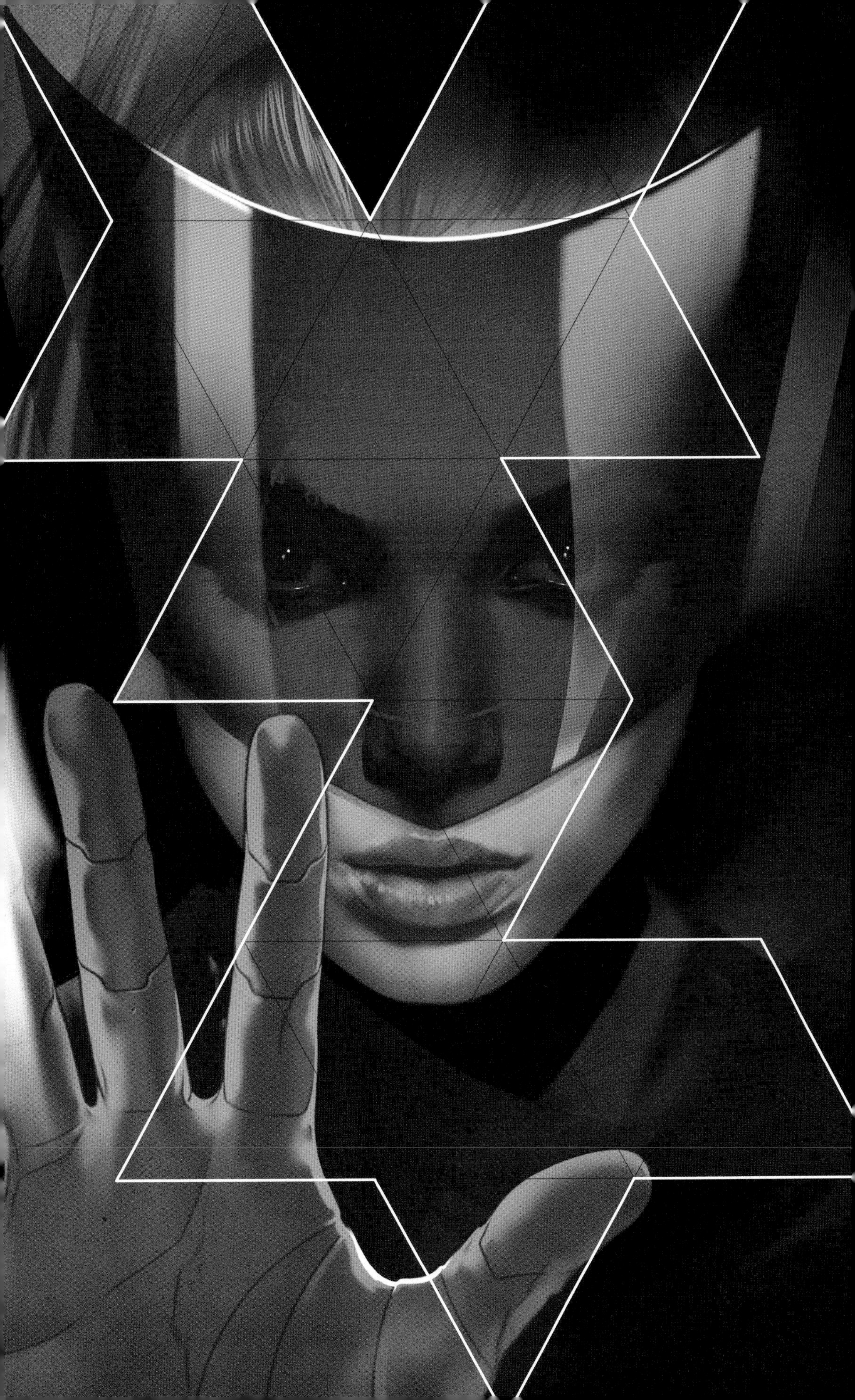

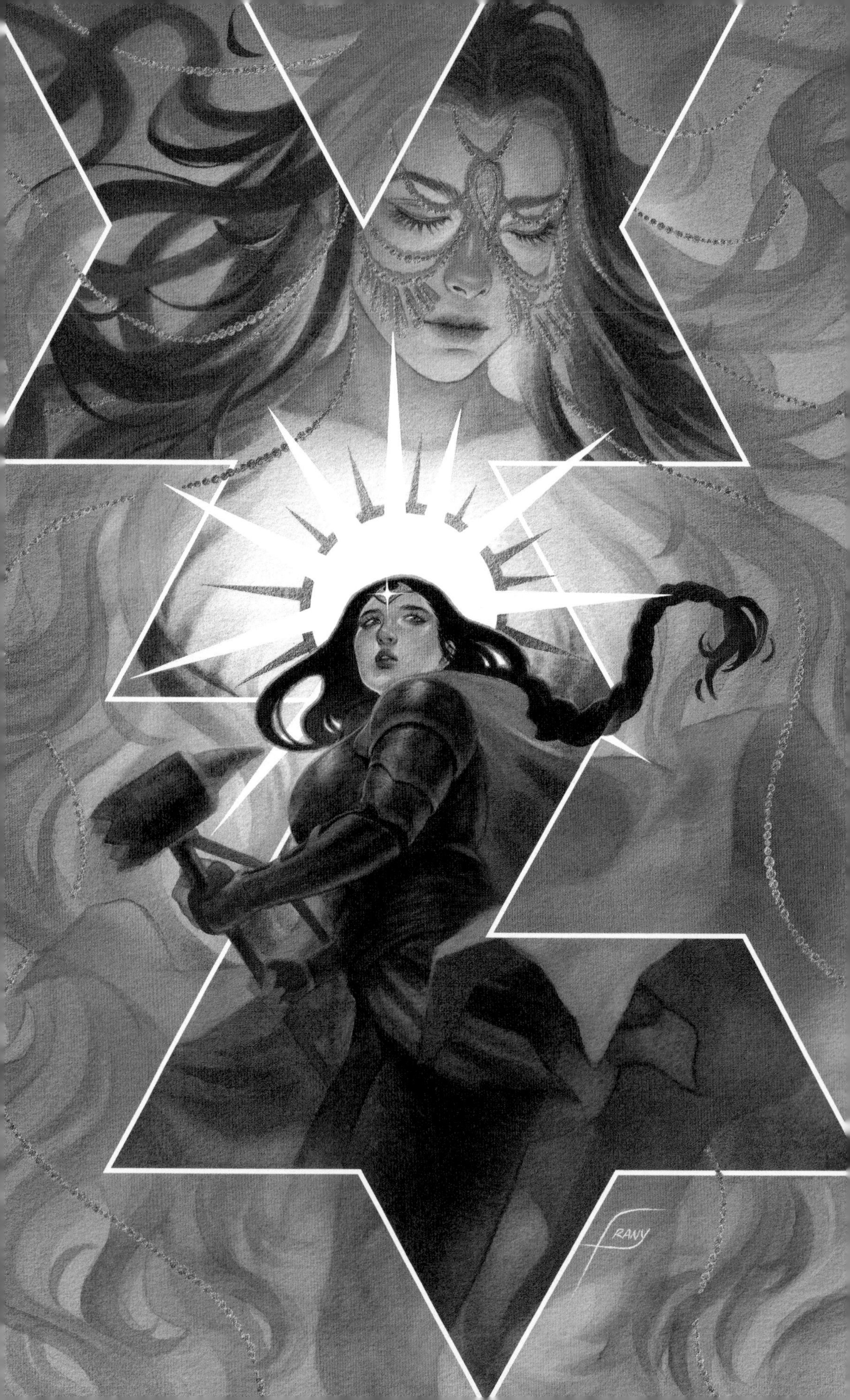

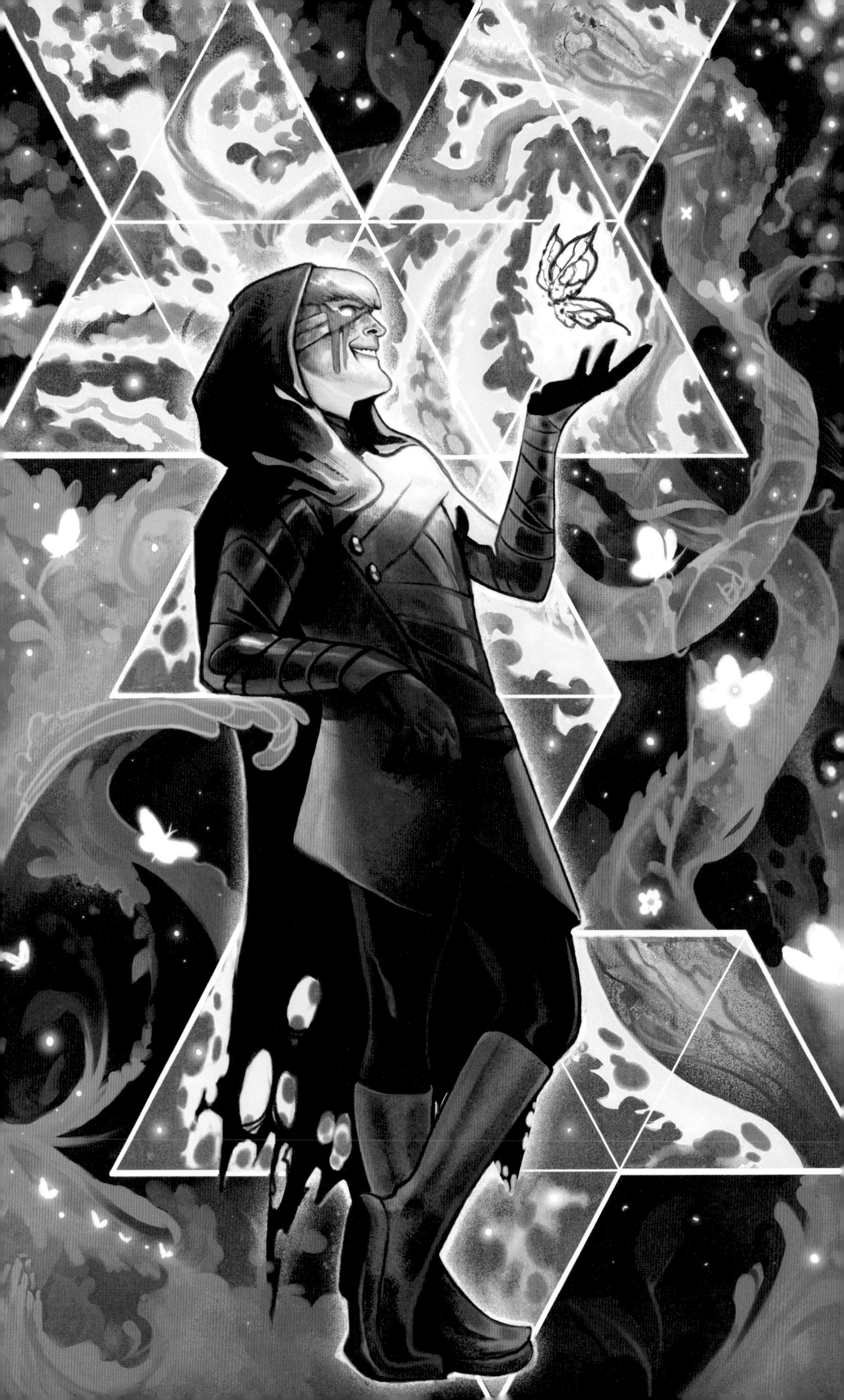

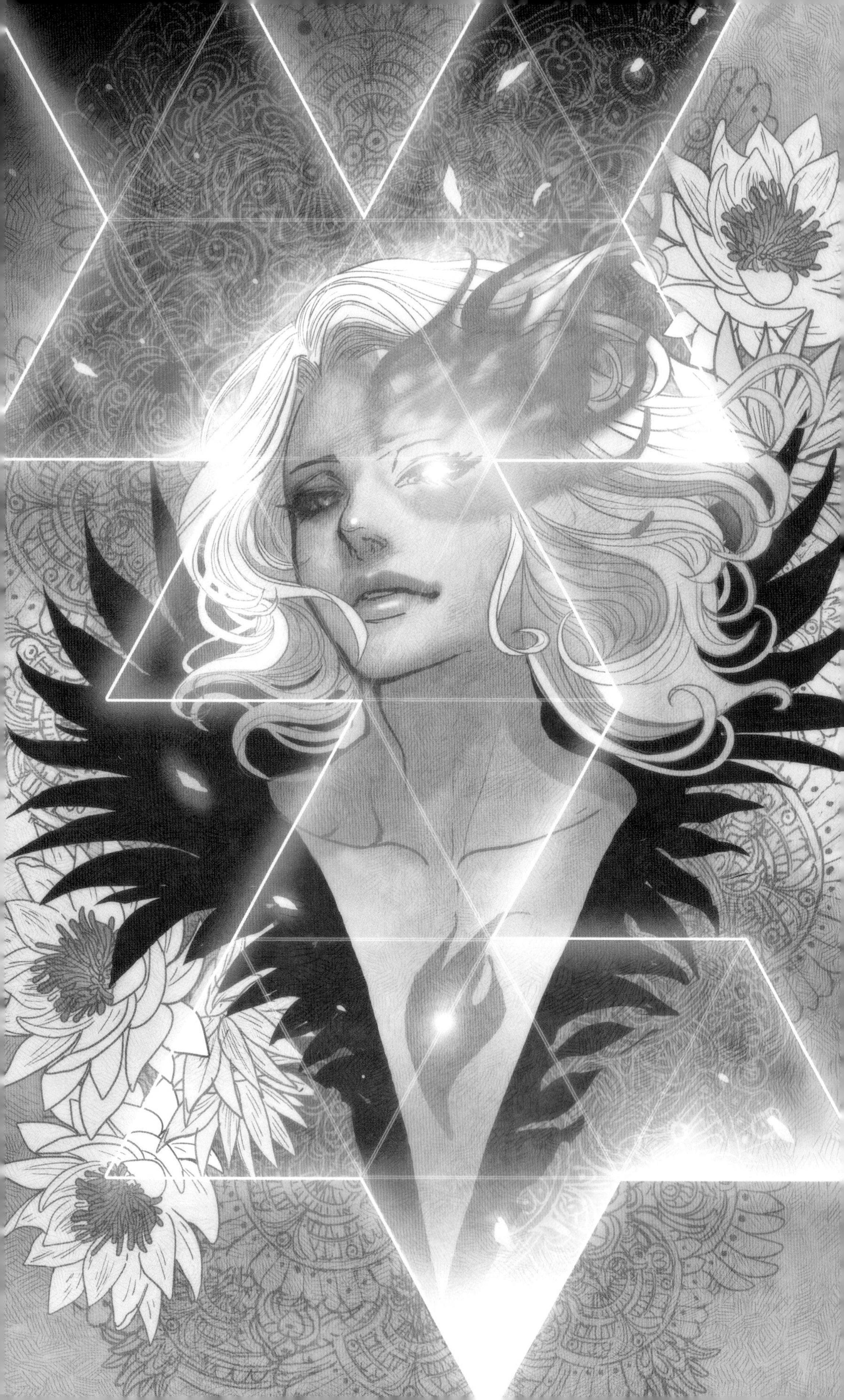

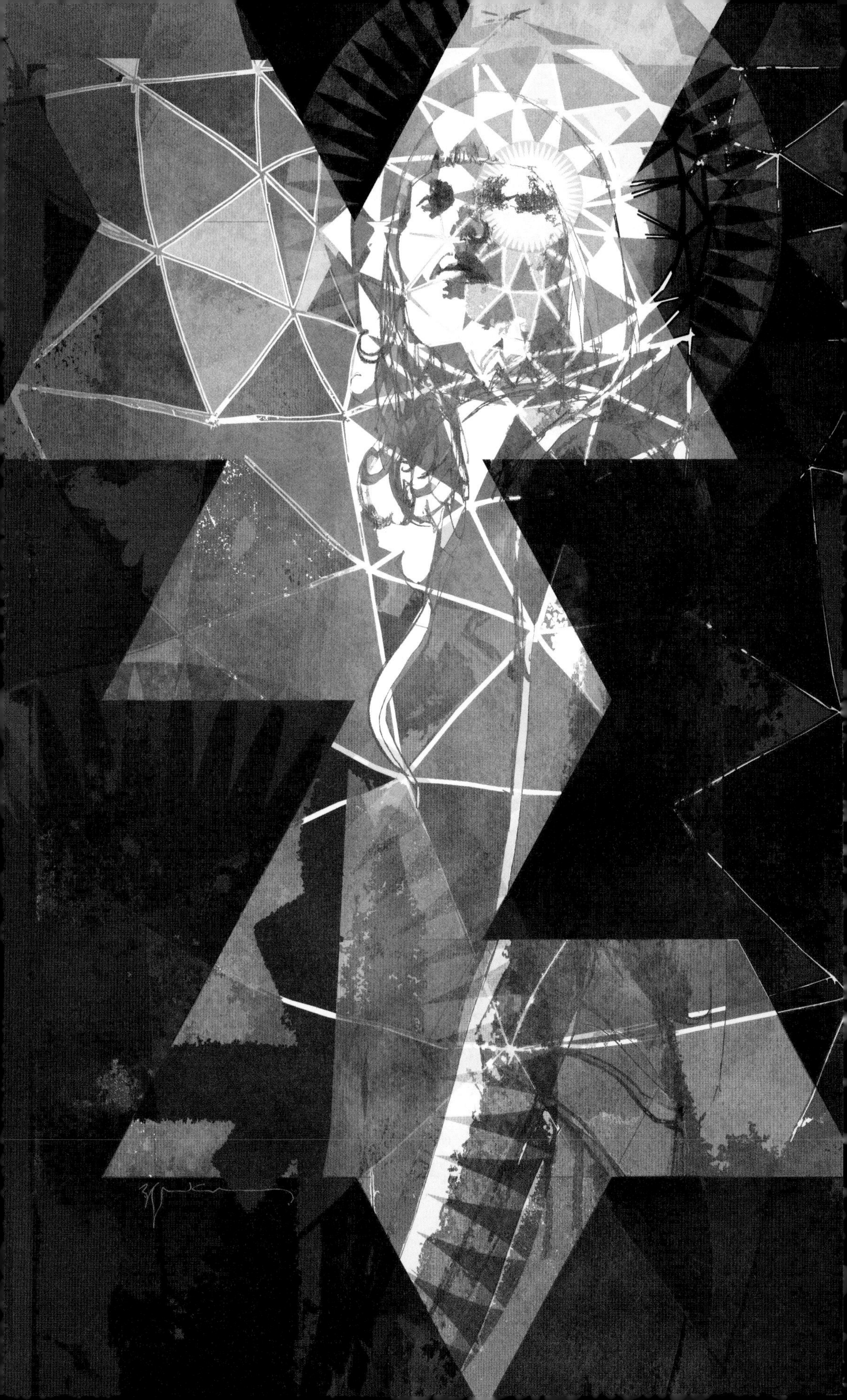

COLOUR MOODS

As you already know, *DIE* relies a lot on colour to express emotion. When I started my job as an illustrator, and especially since I was a cover artist, I realised that too many colours will make an image a bit less easy to read. So, I decided to work with limited but vibrant palettes. There is usually a first gradient of colour to set the ambiance of the illustration or the page, and one heavily saturated colour that I use to direct the eye of the reader to the important points. It shouldn't be a surprise right now to learn that that colour is often red. Anyway, I paint in black and white, using light to shape space, apply my gradient, and then use the colour in an overlay mode. Here are the main colours of these five issues. **SH**

ISSUE 11

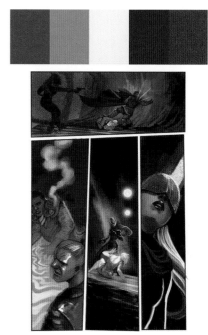

ISSUE 12

ISSUE 13

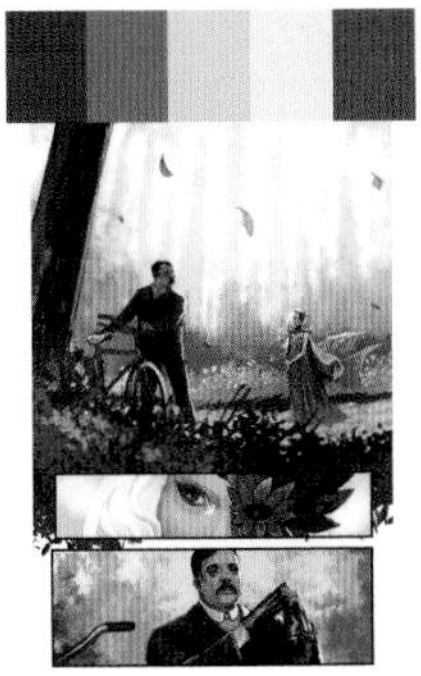
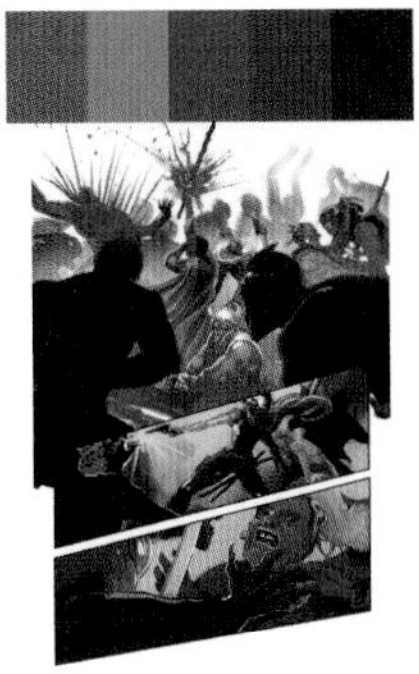
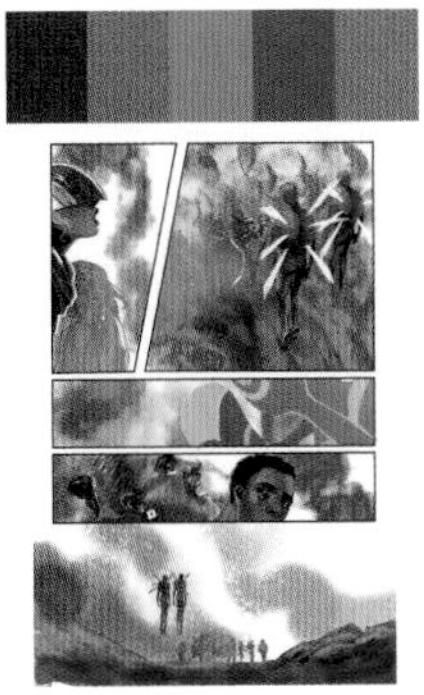
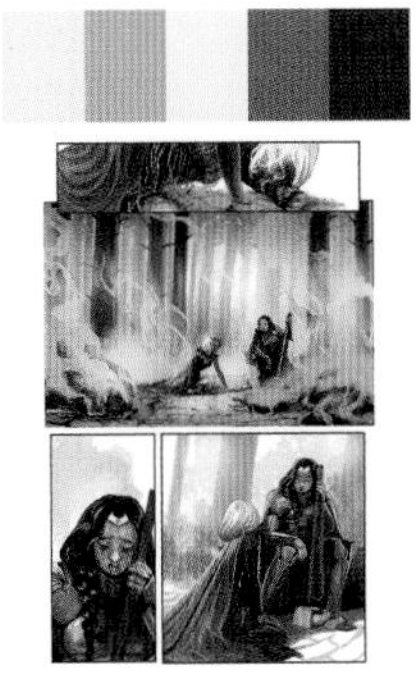
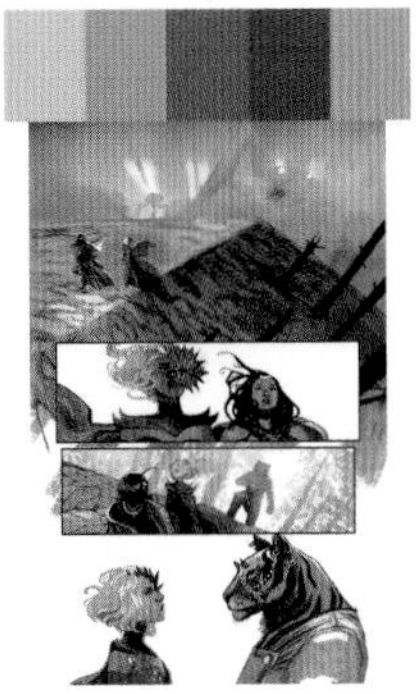

ISSUE 14

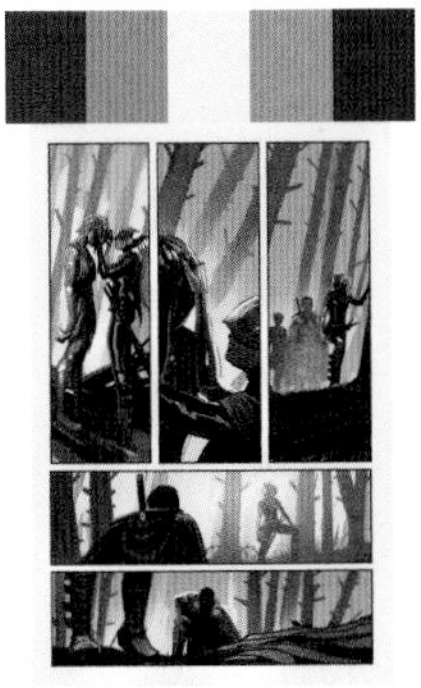
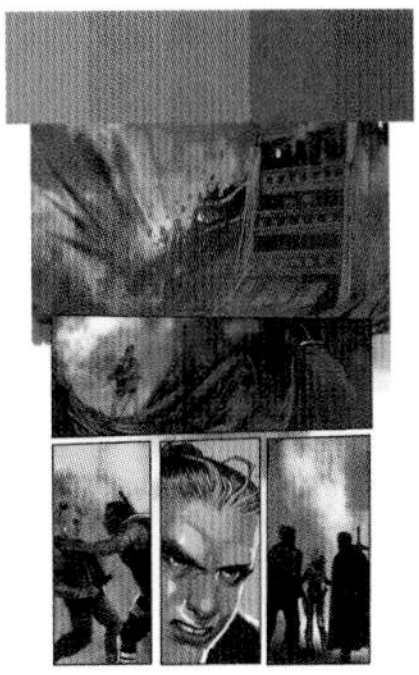
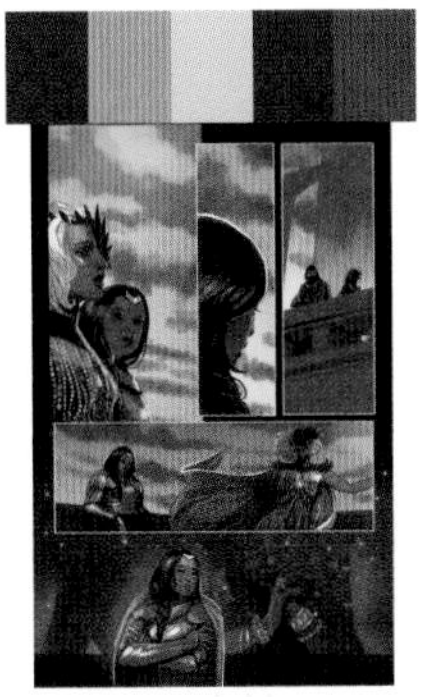
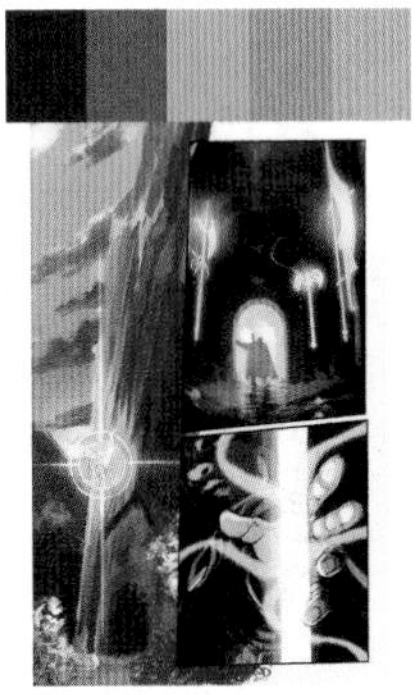

ISSUE 15

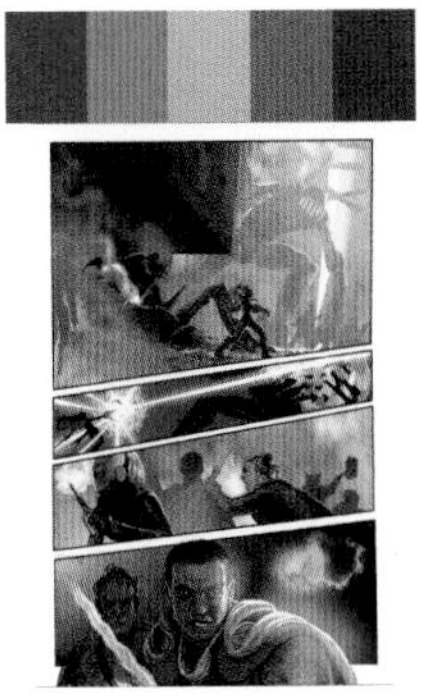
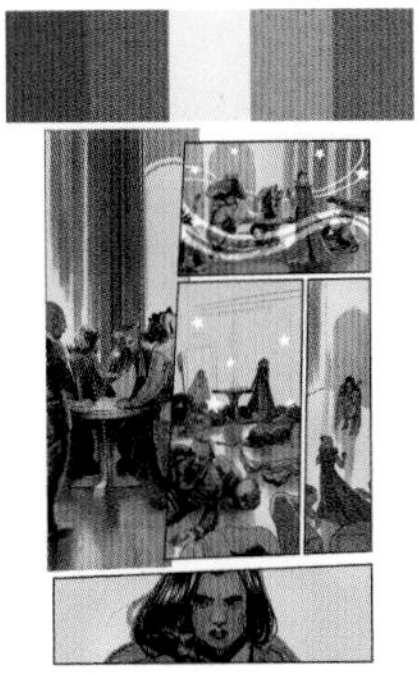
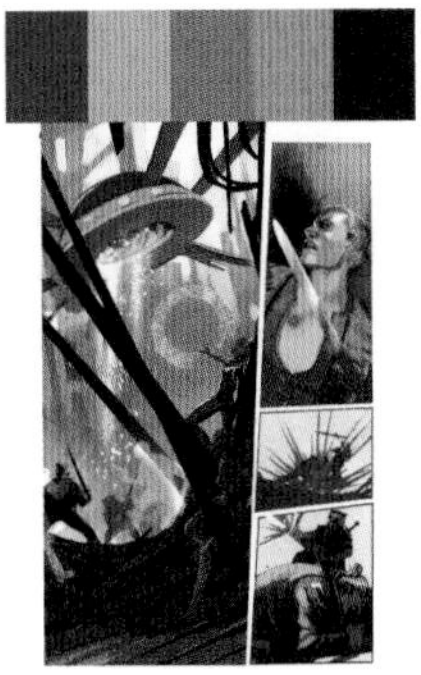
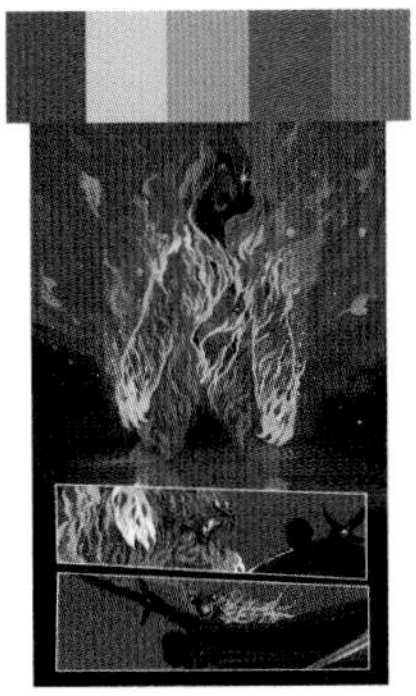
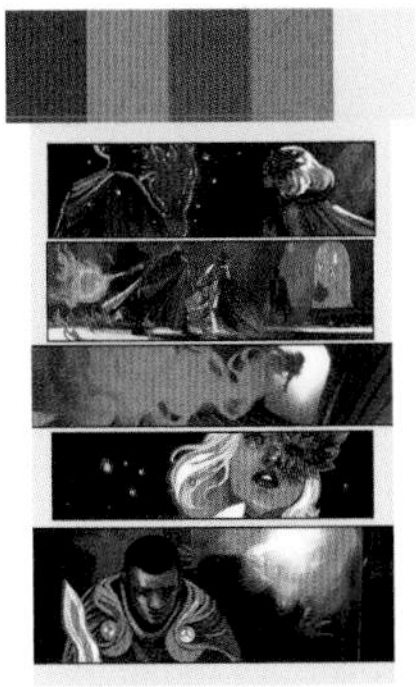
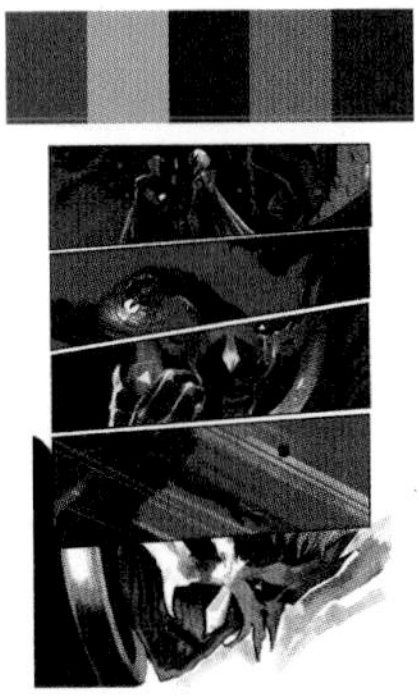

INTERVIEWS

We felt that rather than just download Kieron's brain in essay-form, it'd be useful to interview some key figures in role-playing games, to consider where the field is today and how we got here. There's a thesis to connect them all, as Kieron continues to be Kieron and can't help himself.

ALEX ROBERTS

DIE was approached on multiple vectors, because why make it easy when you can break your heart? Some of the research I did is more obvious in the text - the digging into the form's roots and immediate historical antecedents. Just as important was a survey of the state of the present art. What new ideas were happening *now*?

It's not that I was starting from nothing in terms of the form. I used to be a game critic. Primarily, videogames. I basically went cold turkey in 2010 and have spent the entire decade in analogue games, mainly boardgames in the first half, and mainly RPGs in the latter. As we approached *DIE* that all went a bit deeper, and I started watching the scene more closely. A thesis formed, and it's the thesis which underlies this series of interviews.

The 2010s are the most important time in the tabletop industry since its first decade.

step through to a hundred Narnias. Or eighty-nine, to be precise.

Between 2016 and 2019 she recorded an eighty-nine-episode podcast series called *Backstory* on the One Shot Podcast network, where she interviewed designers of all sorts about their work. Between them all, you get a portrait of the rainforest of thought of the time. An interview guiding you to all these other interviews struck me as a good entry point.

It's appropriate, as it was born of Alex's own real entry into being a designer.

She played self-made *D&D* as a very young child, imitating what she'd seen on the TV. "That was basically just me deciding that I was the GM, because I was just a real bossy kid, and us sitting around, or sometimes acting it out physically," says Alex. "But very often at things

"[*D&D*] was really more about making characters and coming up with ideas..."

selection of games. She recalls being told about the *Burning Wheel* games, and how when you fail a roll you gain experience, and being excited that there were other ways of doing this than *D&D*. She played a new game almost every month, finally GMing thanks to *Kagematsu* requiring a woman GM, it being a game where a group of village women try to convince a Ronin to protect their village. This led to conventions, and meeting designers whose work she loved. "I was starstruck, but you can't be starstruck for long when you meet roleplaying game people.

about them.' And then, next episode would be, 'Wow, this person, I haven't heard of them. Let's check it out.'"

As such, she was in the right place, and saw exactly what a moment the form was having. "It was really only after a little while of doing it that I started to notice all these kinds of changes in the community, and these exciting broad trends that I was only able to see after maybe a year or two, that I started thinking of it as like, 'Well, you know, this isn't going to last forever. I always knew that. This is like a snapshot.' And so I started

really beautiful cross-pollination time," she says. "At the same time, very much thanks to actual play, people watching *Critical Role*, or listening to *The Adventure Zone*, or things like that, the number of people interested in roleplaying games was growing enormously. So, we had this massive influx, this diversification, all happening at the same time."

Alex had started her own design work in this period. She found herself working for Bully Pulpit Games in administration and marketing. While they'd previously published only the work of the hugely influential Jason 'Fiasco' Morningstar, they'd started to release work by others, but only work which excited them. It was in a meeting she mentioned in passing she'd been working on a game. "'I'm doing this, I don't know, it was going to be a hack of *Dread*, and now it's kind of its own thing. It's about forbidden love. It uses a tower, like a *Jenga* tower.' They asked to see it. They loved it. "Yes, and so they ended up publishing it. It's really funny for me to think of, even now," says Alex.

"It's a very participatory culture. If you have an idea, just go for it, just make it."

---

it doesn't work, they're not celebs. It can feel like it, but everyone I met was so encouraging, and so down-to-earth, and so just like, 'If I could do this, you could do this.' That was always the attitude when I met people whose work I really loved. It's a very participatory culture. If you have an idea, just go for it, just make it."

Later, as she was moving further into the world, the One Shot podcast network asked her to develop a show for them. But what? She returned to what is always a cast iron creative magnetic north: what does not exist that I want to see? "What I realised was that I didn't so much enjoy hearing about people's projects. I really liked hearing about *them*, and their design, and their thought process, and their relationship to games," she says. "I was starting to meet designers, and certain things you can tell about a person through their art, and certain things you would never expect. So, I just wanted to talk to designers to get to know them better, and to have everyone get to know them better."

The spread of those covered was key, both influential established names and newcomers who she wanted to know better. "I really wanted *Backstory* to be a balance of both of those things," she says, "so that people would listen to them and go, 'Oh, wow, this person I would love to know more

thinking more about what is going to be important, historically, in this very niche-within-a-niche world."

This was a period of change. Distribution was changing massively. Distribution by PDF as well as hard copies was a movement from an earlier age, but continued to flower. If you had something to say, you could publish it. Equally, conversation in the late 00s moved to the big platforms. "A lot of designers, or potential designers, who were really isolated, were able to start finding community, and conversations about roleplaying games were shifting out of small, obscure forums, and onto these big platforms like Twitter," she says. "People started putting their games up on things like itch. io, where anyone could put anything up, and anyone could find it."

"And as the means to create games became easier through a bunch of different tools, people who were making games changed a lot," she says, "and the people who were able to see themselves as capable of putting a game out into the world changed a ton. So, we just had a way, way, more diverse group of people making games, and they started talking to each other internationally, even." It's visible in *Backstory*, where in the last third you hear more and more from voices outside North America and Europe. "So, it was this

Dread is a horror game, where actions involve removing objects from a *Jenga* tower, with the falling of the tower meaning the fall of a character. Alex played it and saw something else. "I thought the scenarios that people write for these are pretty neat, but you know what's really scary?" she says. "Having a crush on someone. Someone should just make a playset where you're in love. That's the most terrifying, intense thing of all." As always: ideas are easy, but the execution is hard. "Design is just throwing stuff out there, and then cutting away, and cutting away. It's like writing, right? You just edit, edit, edit." Years after she had the idea, she tried, found it didn't work, and carried on working on prototypes, seeing what landed.

In Alex's game, *Star Crossed*, a tower falling means the player acts on their desires, for good or ill. The game leans towards trying to push that feeling of butterflies and anxiety as much as possible, with so much from its extensive playtesting. For example, you have to touch the tower when your character is speaking. "That came up because I watched people have full-on, comfortable, back-and-forth conversations and I didn't want that," she said, "I wanted really, really tense, minimal dialogue where people felt terrified to begin speaking, to let their whole heart out."

Design is finding ways to mechanise the feelings you're trying to evoke. "I think making games will show you what you think. Trying to make a game forces you to articulate the way that you think things work, right?" she says. "A mechanic will resonate with you if it fits with how you think the world works. So, when mechanics don't fit that way, when in a videogame, your guy falls off a building, and he just completely stays standing, and he loses two hearts, but is otherwise completely unaffected, there is this moment that kind of breaks a little bit, with your game, where you're like, 'Okay, sure.' But when a game really, really fits, and you really go, 'Wow, that's how it is,' that's a really special weird feeling. So, I think in *Star Crossed*, I was figuring out what I actually think being in love is like, and in *For the Queen*, I'm figuring out what I think loyalty feels like, and I kind of had to confront those things in myself a little bit. Both in their fun and joy and beauty and misery."

For the Queen is a game about loyalty, where the players are all close companions of a queen on a journey. A handful of facts are established before play, and then players draw cards, and answer the questions from place to place, and they're doing these important things when you get there. Maybe you'll have a cutscene or a big battle or some dialogue. But you don't know what their experience of going around the world is like, and how they feel about the mission that they're on, or how they're interacting day to day. Are they talking to each other during battle? Are they thinking about each other? Are they thinking about what lies ahead, when you're pressing A to hit with sword?"

As I am me, I like to think of *For The Queen* as the roleplaying game you can play with your boardgaming friends without them realising you've suckered them into playing a role playing game, as it expertly uses ritual to comfort and welcome people. The anger at the heart of the game is inescapable though. "I tried to make a game about an adventuring party and their feelings about each other, but it ended up being about that other thing instead," she said. It's strongly influenced by Aleksandra Sontowska's *The Beast*, an incendiary one-player roleplaying game, where cards prompt you to write secret diary entries about your love affair with the eponymous beast. It showed how much you can do with the simple process of answering questions and building on answers. *For the Queen* builds on that insight, and a story I think, are really, really closely intertwined. They're really similar behaviours and thought processes. To engage with it at all is to be creative and come up with ideas. And I think the greatest lesson of RPGs is that ideas are so much easier, and so simple, and so cheap compared to what we're often told, that 'only great creative people come up with those'. No, you can come up with eighteen hundred million ideas over one session of a good storytelling game, and there's something just beautiful about that experience."

Alex Roberts can be found online at www.helloalexroberts.com. Backstory can be listened to at the Oneshotpodcast network here: (http://oneshotpodcast.com/category/backstory/). For the Queen is from Evil Hat Productions. Star Crossed is available from Bully Pulpit Games. Both are available from fine game stores.

"A mechanic will resonate with you if it fits with how you think the world works."

questions. A narrative emerges, and is a fearful, joyous, awful delight. If *Star Crossed* came from a dissection of flirting and desire, *For the Queen* came from a different place.

"So, I was really, really angry at somebody, and I couldn't really express it to them, and so I played videogames until I fell asleep," she says. "I was playing *Theatrhythm Final Fantasy* and then I woke up before my alarm, and wrote many of the questions that are still in the game today. I had this idea of like, in those really old RPGs where you can see your characters walking along the world map, and they're going

emerges from these simple questions: 'What brings out the Queen's kindness?' 'You saved the Queen's life once - how?' 'You are considered beautiful by almost everyone you meet. How does the Queen make you question that perception?'

It's wonderfully democratic, and also wonderfully freeing. I play it and see people who do not consider themselves storytellers amazed at what they'd done. It's very much Alex's goal.

"There's this distance between making and consuming, right? The act of play and the act of design,

ROWAN, ROOK & DECARD

When approaching the unknown you inevitably use the prism of the known. It's not sufficient. It will mislead you. However, it is a start. As such, when I look at the indie games scene, I'm inevitably thinking: "So - what would *I* be doing?" and "How is it like comics?"

Chatting to Alex last issue about the wonderfully supportive system she described in North America was exciting, but I was also aware that if Jamie and me were a decade younger, and trying to break into indie games instead of indie comics, we wouldn't be part of that scene. We'd be in Britain. The events described by Alex such as Metatopia, cons people travel to play at, or even the capacity to win the most prestigious awards - they'd all be inaccessible.

Hence, I'm talking to Grant Howitt, Chris Taylor and Mary Hamilton (aka Rowan, Rook & Decard) about their route and how they survive in my local ecosystem in the UK, how they formed

The band got together at university. As Mary says, "I think Chris and Grant fell in love soon after that." Their game together was a live-action *Zombie* game: basic inspiration, epic execution. "They'd come to the conclusion that shooting each other with nerf guns while one of you pretended to be a zombie was fun," said Mary. Having secured them from America off eBay in nondescript brown bags ("It was so illicit, it was wonderful.") it became a question of where they could bring this vision into existence. This involved months of political manoeuvring ("We put significantly more effort into that than our degrees.") to gain access to the Sports Hall overnight. They ran *Zombie* from midnight until the very early morning. They were all experienced with LARPs (aka Live Action Role-play) but it wasn't quite like this. "Normally LARPs take a weekend, or an evening," said Grant. "I think we had an average character life span of about six-and-a-half minutes. No one had played

"There were genuinely quite creepy zombies crawling about the place."

their company and bound together with their peers in a self-supportive system ("UK Indie RPG League"), a set-up which kinda reminds me of a more anarchistic take on the Image set-up: as in, creators practising solidarity and mutual support, while still being fiercely independent. "We don't, or we very rarely, publish work by other people, except as part of those game worlds," says Mary, "so in terms of creator-owned and run companies, we might actually be the largest in the UK now."

When I hear Grant, Mary and Chris talk, I think of bands. Three people gathered together to pursue an aesthetic, and creating spaces to propagate that aesthetic. I use the same metaphor when talking comics. There is also another connection. In comics, self-publishing is no scarlet letter. "Real" publishers ignored us for a long time. In games, almost all the great publishers started from scratch.

anything quite like it since they were about twelve. We tapped into that."

It was also terrifying, despite everything making that seem less likely. "We didn't really have proper makeup, we had brightly coloured nerf guns, and you were playing with people that you'd seen on and off for the last six months, so you knew everyone..." says Chris, "and people were *still* going to the bathroom in twos. They were covering themselves as they went to the bathroom because there were genuinely quite creepy zombies crawling about the place."

"Fresh zombies are the easiest monster to make. You can spend as much money as you want on a werewolf and it'll still look stupid. Vampires only just look like big goths. But you put a bit of blood round someone's mouth and have them limp? Perfect," says Grant. "It's dark, you're running, you don't really have time to examine them as someone turns around and does the Ggrrrrrhhhh."

The game started to develop. Flashlights were issued. Special flashlights. "I'd gone through and broken the connections slightly so if you held the flashlight wrong it just turned off," said Chris. "We used to deliberately buy the nerf guns that were most likely to jam at inopportune moments," says Mary. "Or the really complicated ones where you had to put the dart into a shell, then the shell into the gun. It took 30 seconds to fire your second shot," adds Chris. "Mm.

"Within minutes someone's an unhinged panda Thief wearing a crown..."

So many motherfuckers died trying to reload. It was delightful," says Grant. The thought strikes me: we talk about game mechanics. This kind of thing makes it wonderfully literal.

In the end, they ran it eleven times in total, climaxing with running it in an abandoned shopping mall in Reading for 150 people each paying a fiver. It was a passion project. They made a grand total of £2.28. It was also where their philosophy started coming together. "In retrospect, looking at Grant and Chris' work now, I can see these seeds of it back in *Zombie*," says Mary. "Your characters are expendable. They're vessels for story. The point is to have an amazing story, and death is not necessarily the worst thing that can happen to your character."

"Death is a reward," says Grant.

There was a journey ahead before that work started to come into being. Chris, Mary and Grant had a separation before reuniting. Mary and Grant ended up in Australia and New York, starting to do games on Patreon and writing a novel on his iPad in five weeks ("Don't do that. Terrible plan."). Meanwhile, Chris did absolutely nothing (aka working in high-street videogame retailer Game). "And then my mind kind of shattered from that, so I was just unemployed, and not doing terribly

well with that," said Chris. "So when we kind of got together online, to do a project together, it was like a sanity booster for the both of us. That's the reason we did it. We didn't do it to make a game. We made a game to stay sane. And honestly that has continued until this very day."

Cue the beginning on a long-distance Skype collaboration, the first result of which was *Unbound*, a pulp adventure game which married a freeform world-building stage with hard tactical action. "*Unbound* is the most obvious game that is the clash of Grant's and my way of doing games," says Chris. "You build everything in the start. There's no hard and fast lore or anything. You make it yourself... and then you go into a potentially incredibly complicated tactical game."

"It's heavily influenced by the fact that we were playing a lot of *The Secret World* as a trio at the time," says Mary, talking about the conspiracy online RPG by Funcom, headed by Ragnar Tørnquist. "The flipside of the tactical bit, of course, is that your session zero is you making up a world from whole cloth," says Mary, alluding to the technique where you start a game with a session where the group generates the world in which they'll adventure in together, before the actual play kicks off. "It's one of the best session zero world generation tools."

There was a previous Grant game which foreshadows some other aspects of their aesthetic. *Goblin Quest* is a deeply playful game about goblins and questing. It was also about the loosening of what was possible in the RPG space in the mid 2010s. "They were just like: 'I have made a fantasy game'; 'I have made a space game'," says Grant, "and then *Goblin Quest* lands. And that is, like... It's not really like anything else. Except, apparently it's a lot like *Kobolds Ate My Baby* if you ask anyone on the internet." It is extraordinarily

silly, not something which people have traditionally connected to RPGs.

Which is a good way to bring up *Honey Heist*.

People from a scene, even the progressive parts of a scene, have a tendency to imagine a future that is an extrapolation of the present. I remember, in videogaming, when I first played *Gone Home*. Despite the fact I was into all the culture it describes in the early nineties, I'd never have thought that *Doom* would have led to a teenage lesbian wandering around a house, listening to Riot Grrrl. Similarly, if you'd asked me in nineties about the future of RPGs, it'd be all big, hefty narrative themes. Perhaps mechanically heavy, but certainly *thematically* heavy.

The problem is that all this does is make art smaller. If I was to choose a theme of the 2010s, it'd be a widening acceptance of those many possibilities. I want to get to the Nordic LARP scene eventually here, with the seriousness of theme that it often explores... but it's also about the other emotional side. They can be a burst of life on an A4 sheet, to be played and discarded. Or played again and again. Editor of this organ, Chrissy Williams, has run three RPGs ever [**Ed's note:** So far!]. Two of them were *Honey Heist*.

Honey Heist is an RPG where you play bears trying to steal honey. Don't get too 'Criminal' or too 'Bear'. Chaos ensues. It is a delight. It's also a masterpiece of minimalism. You roll a few dice, look at a few tables, and within minutes someone's an unhinged panda Thief wearing a crown, trying to break into a run-down truck convoy carrying Black Orchid Honey (which turns anyone who eats it into a goth), while not knowing the place has been rigged to blow. "The set-up is immediately engaging, and I think that's why people got into it," says Grant. "People thought 'There's enough of a buy-in here that I understand what the stakes are and I want to see what happens,' as opposed to something like one of our horror games, like *The Ward*, where you play people in comas who are all in the same murderous dreamscape." As the namecheck of *The Ward* suggests, while *Honey Heist* is the most famous of Grant's one-page RPGs, he does one monthly. In putting out one-page RPGs, he's far from alone. It's a welcome part of the current scene. While *Honey Heist* is a light game, there's many rules-light games that hit serious topics. Spend some time wandering through the itch.io microgame RPGs, and there's whole worlds there.

The future of RPGs can be anything. That includes being enormously dumb.

One of Mary's roles at Rowan, Rook & Decard is editor. "Your game needs editing," says Mary. "It does not matter how brilliant you are. If anything, the more brilliant you are, the more important it is to get it edited well. And that isn't just about making sure the words are in the right order and making sure that your commas and your full stops are in the right place." The multiple roles of an RPG editor could fill this space. A game needs to make grammatical sense and also *gaming sense*. One human editor serving those masters strikes me as nightmarishly difficult. "I think having worked in the news industry really helps with this, because if you're editing news you're editing for multiple things," says Mary. "You're editing for clarity, and for ease of the expression of the idea. You're editing for capacity to grab and hold the intention, which might be quite limited. You're editing for truth. You're editing for accuracy. You're editing for consistency."

aesthetic of elevated genre which we trade in on in *DIE*. It's work that aspires to be interesting while also being able to secure an audience, and create something that someone will pay for.

"We do have to make it at least a little bit commercially viable, because bills and that," says Chris. "It's an interesting one this, because I have never seen any of you sacrifice any of your art for the sake of something that will sell," Mary says, "but then I'm not in the room half the time when you're having discussions about the nitty gritty detail of the creative process." "Chris is throwing a lot of my darlings into a big fire, and I respect that," says Grant. "The only stuff that I kick out is the stuff that will be a problem, rather than changing it so that it's more acceptable, if you're with me, and more marketable," says Chris. "We try to be weird," says Grant.

It's a process of iteration, with an idea that eventually gains an identity. "It's happened with *Spire* and it's happened with *Heart*," says Grant, "and I think to a lesser extent with *Unbound*, but there is an understanding of what *Heart* is, between Chris and I, and then once we release it the players get that, get their own vibes around that, get their own understanding. But we couldn't necessarily define it,

quite a big thing, that we've just put into our own paradigms, and because we're so sort of in tune with what is *Heart* and what isn't, we just assume the other person is also on the same wavelength."

What next? They're hiring interesting voices to do expansions for their worlds, while working on their next thing. While there's much that's uncertain in this period, there's a lot they look forward to. "Grant once said, we are in the business of joy," says Mary. "We are in the business of giving people ways to connect with each other and find joy in collaboratively doing something, in play. We need that, now, probably more than we've needed it in my lifetime. So we keep doing it. We're gonna need this stuff. And I think one of the things about the current situation is that it's showing a lot of people how valuable art, the arts, as a concept, and art on a very personal level, actually is. And RPGs are art."

Rowan, Rook & Decard's games are available from their website at rowanrookanddecard.com. If you like Chris and Grant's yabber, they have a podcast Hearty Dice Friends *you can listen to. Grant's patreon is at www.patreon.com/gshowitt.*

"A game needs to make grammatical sense and also *gaming sense*."

Aside from Grant's monthly one-pager games, the most recent big projects from Rowan, Rook & Decard have been *Spire* and its sister game *Heart*. *Spire* is a game of dark elf revolutionaries trying to bring down their high elf masters in a city that soars a mile into the sky. *Heart* is about the chaotic depths beneath the city, a surrealistic dungeon crawl, all China-Miéville-does-*Tomb-of-Horrors*.

Both are great games, and did well on Kickstarter, building off all their previous work, but also they're warped takes on mainstream genres. I find myself thinking the aesthetic of *Vertigo comics, but for RPGs, as in, an*

but there's a point when that rolling stone gathers enough moss for us to say, 'That's *Heart*' and 'That isn't *Heart*.'" Fundamentally, even the game creators are playing it their own way.

"Grant's version is kind of urban, and ruins, and decay," says Chris about running *Heart*, "and my version is all meat tunnels and tripping. And, like, occasionally when we're writing we'll be talking about a specific location, for maybe two hours, and then suddenly go, 'Hang on, hang on, you think this is underwater?' Like, 'Yeah, this is underwater. Obviously this is underwater.' 'What?' And, like, there'll be one little thing, sometimes

KEN HITE & ROBIN D LAWS

The guiding concept for these interviews is that the 2010s were the most fertile period in the RPG since its original decade. That implies the other periods weren't, and so acts as an implicit riposte to those who say your love for a form is tied entirely to nostalgia. If that were true, I wouldn't be saying 2010s. I'd be saying 1991. I was 16 in 1991, and the gaming elitists of this comic rolling their eyes at *D&D* are absolutely me. I know that 1991 was an interesting, liminal period too. I was thinking *Vampire: The Masquerade* and Nirvana's *Nevermind* happened here, both ushering in a darkness to their forms which dovetailed with one another...

I was 16, doing the gaming equivalent of going to gigs. Ken Hite and Robin D Laws were a decade older, and doing the equivalent of forming bands. I love their work, and I wanted to speak to them, and get perspective. What was it like then? Did it feel like that? Except listening to them talk, rather

Surrealists versus the arrivals in the twenties and thirties of Paris, nobody's breaking each other's arm with a cane. But aesthetic battles and personal battles are endemic to everyone. I think that our little clique had the enormous good fortune of just deciding to do the opposite of that."

When I came back to tabletop, I was obviously struck by what was new... but I was also struck by what was familiar, like a band I'd loved who I hadn't checked in on for fifteen years, and who'd done a great bunch of albums. Robin was like that. The last game I loved before leaving games was his *Feng Shui*, which found ways to make the RPG feel exactly like the Hong Kong action movie. His work has strikingly explored how to mechanize genre across the period, with his GUMSHOE system being a device for making detective games work like detective fiction does, most recently showcased in the reality-horror of the multi-timelined *The King In Yellow*.

"Unlike the Surrealists ... nobody's breaking each other's arm with a cane."

than 90s shadows sweeping in, I find myself thinking of the other side of that 1989-1991 period - as in, the loved-up bonhomie of acid house.

"Ken and I are part of a golden generation," says Robin, "not necessarily golden in talent, but golden in our luck, and being in a moment where we were all game fans who were then publishers, or freelancers, or creators, together. And we all felt the spirit of camaraderie, and loved everything and loved games." The prior generation, in the wake of Gygax and Arneson, tended towards feuding. Later in the timeline, a factionalism

He was also doing a public podcast *Ken & Robin Talk About Stuff* which does talk-about-everything polymath fun which always made me think of game designers as philosopher kings and queens when I was a teenager.

Through it I discovered Ken Hite. If Robin was the band whose albums I'd missed, Ken was the band whose work I had heard of, but never given a spin, and suddenly had a whole back catalogue to rush through. As well as interest in play-at-table, Ken's games are characterized by deep research, both in terms of both historical and literary texts. To choose a single example, *The Dracula*

Robin then does a campaign for, and so on. Overlapping interests, and differing interactions, all Beach Boys vs Beatles. "I often joke my job is to take things out of GUMSHOE, and Ken's job is to put things in GUMSHOE," says Robin. I love the energy between them, and the crackle was there from when they first met.

They came together at Gen Con when it was in Milwaukee, at a party. Ken considered Robin's scenario for Burroughian RPG *Over the Edge* one of the greatest ever written, and he extensively informed Robin of the fact. "For some reason, in Robin's Canadian reserve, he did not back away and never speak to me again. He responded as many writers do when you begin with effusive praise of their work, with genuine warmth and friendship. Very rapidly, I think Robin and I sort of became Young Turk ironic observers together, as we were going into the business."

The industry there was small enough that folks made these small connections. "That's still happening now, but it's much more atomised," says Robin, "and so, there was a time when I felt like I was on top of everything that's going on in roleplaying, but as all of the tasks associated with being a professional game designer have expanded, my ability to pay attention to all of those things is gone, and I don't think that there's one posse any more. Which is great, right? Imagine painting if there were just the Impressionists all hanging out together, and that was all there was?"

The atomisation is a sign of growth. "There are different personal networks that become different aesthetic networks, with different assumptions of how play should go, of what everyone will do when they sit down at the table together," says Robin. This continues into player networks, but the demarcation

between the two is hardly firm. "Everybody one hour into playing a roleplaying game decides to become a roleplaying game designer," says Robin, "and there are more ways than ever to express that."

"It's The Velvet Underground of art forms," says Ken, referencing the line about everyone who heard their first album forms a band. "Once you've GM-ed anything, you've started to think like a game designer. Because you're answering, 'How do these rules cover this situation?' And unless you're literally playing out an adventure word for word, and the players are, as Robin says, uncharacteristically behaving themselves, you immediately have to start thinking like a designer. You are already having to make all these decisions, and you are, whether you like it or not, a game designer in that moment." Of course, this requirement limited the people who did go there. "GMs became a sort of self-selecting crowd with similar characteristics, because they were people who wanted to basically be game designers," notes Ken, "and that kind of psychopathy cannot be taught."

Their 1990-ish golden time felt golden, but also felt like an ending. "I think that at the time we were aware that there were giants in the earth that we were privileged to know," says Ken. "This is when you could be standing at the Chaosium booth, and Greg Stafford (**Ed.'s note** - *Runequest*, *Pendragon*) would be giving you crap. That's like meeting an archangel." And the fascinating thing is the idea that the gaming project was near completion. "I think that, like a lot of young designers, we thought, 'Well, we are basically just finishing the project of game design.' And I probably said, in print or in pixels, that we'd basically fixed the system. The only thing to do now is expand it to other topics, and come up with new and exciting fun worlds

to play in. But between, goodness me, there must be two dozen game systems. Surely we're done?"

Spoilers: no, they were not done.

"Almost as those words were coming out of my mouth, Ron Edwards is doing *Sorcerer*, and blowing up system again as a conversation," says Ken, "then the indie game scene blows up in about 1999, 2000. I saw that happen, and realised, 'Oh, I'm just part of the wave. I'm just the pre-indie last wave of game design.' And at the time, we didn't know if trad and indie would fork, or if they would, as it happened, merge and influence each other. And that was the moment, I think, that I was conscious of the art form having a history in the sense that you're talking about, that we're a quotidian part of it, as opposed to just standing and looking up at Mount Rushmore and saying, 'Check it out! I saw Dave Arneson!'" Generations are appearing, and generations will always be defined by the times they're in, and they all exist in response to the moment they find themselves. Obviously, at the time of writing, that's more striking than ever.

"We're having a little period now where the tables that people are going to be meeting at are Skype and Google Hangouts," says Robin. "We're about to see an incredible social change that is going to change this generation forever. And I don't know what effect that is going to have on roleplaying, but because it is a medium made up of people, it is absolutely going to have an effect on the medium and the scene and the way that it works."

As well as the medium, there's also the question of themselves, as creatives later in their careers. Once more, they return to the emotional core that brought them in: doing what you love. "The thing I find very inspiring is that the superstar prosthetic make-up artist, Rick Baker, has retired from filmmaking in order to make prosthetic masks and put them up on Instagram," says Robin. "So, he's still doing it. He's just not getting studio notes any more."

Robin D Laws' latest game is The Yellow King. *Ken Hite's is the forthcoming 5th edition* D&D *campaign world* Hellenistika. *Their podcast is found at www. kenandrobintalkaboutstuff.com*

"...to be game designers ... that kind of psychopathy cannot be taught."

JEANNETTE NG

"I was a false prophet once."

I'm in Harrogate, at Eastercon 2018, and I've been introduced to novelist Jeannette Ng. She's just said something that's made me blink. I think I've misheard. I'm sorry, Jeannette, could you repeat that?

"I was a false prophet once," she says, and starts to tell me the whole story. In that moment I know that I'm going to read her novel and love it.

Under the Pendulum Sun came out in 2017, and is a gothic fantasy of obscene quality, haunted by fairy and literature. Since then, she's marched on to award-winning acclaim, receiving the Astounding Award for Best New Writer in 2018.

She was also a false prophet once. In a LARP.

LARPs (as in, Live Action Role-play) are perhaps the part of the hobby

re-enactment. Alas, being a 16-year-old boarding-school girl in Hong Kong caused problems with trying to be a Viking. Cut to Durham University and a Freshers' Fair, where her eyes fall upon the people with the rubber swords. She fell into the world, with one eye on herself as a fantasy writer. "After all, people keep telling you, 'You have to write what you know.' And it's like, 'Well, if I spend every Thursday pretending to be a goblin in a fantasy tavern, then surely I can write about that.'"

Durham had the oldest still-running role-play society in the country, Treasure Trap. The pros of the lineage mix with the downside of the cultural investment in an old system. "We write rules by committee," says Jeannette. "A lot of LARPs don't do this. Durham does. All our rules have to be voted in, and rule changes still have to be voted in by a general meeting. We're constantly rewriting them." The "We"

"It's my favourite live role-play format, and it is the most tedious to run..."

I have least direct experience of. Not zero, but it's fragmentary, mostly gathered either from others' perspectives. To use a broad definition, LARP is about role-playing games which involve actual, physical embodiment of your character. The environment you are in is transformed into the board, your body the playing piece. What that means exactly varies. There's the whole school of Nordic LARP, with its Bergman intellectuality, often exploring non-traditional game topics. Solo LARPs, versions-of-table-top, arguably murder-mystery, and on and on. Then, there's games which do exactly what non-LARP-fluent people think LARPers do to determine the result of conflict. As in, often bash the living hell of one another with rubber swords.

Jeannette's entry into games came from her love of fantasy, via *Baldur's Gate 2*, a mysterious second-hand *D&D* manual in the schoolbooks sale, and a longing to get into

is the tell that even now, years later, she's still involved in community, attending the annual banquets and even recently has written some of their larger weekend events.

"It's my favourite live role-play format, and it is the most tedious to run, and it is very unwieldy," she says. "It's a weekend-long, 24-hour time-in event, in which 30 to 50 players are given characters which have detailed 1-20 A4 page interlinked backstories. You spend six months writing them. It's great. It's awful. No one should ever do it. It's almost a full-time job, writing one of those."

While not all LARPs of the sort Jeannette has played are these multi-day affairs, they are one of the more striking things to imagine. Marathon role-playing, and as exhausting as that sounds. "Everyone talks about event drop," she says, "where afterwards you're stuck being yourself again, and you just feel so drained, because you've lived all these emotions at once. I really like the small moments of role-play, doing the things that you do in-character 'for reals'. A lot of really interesting little nuances can come out of that in a way that doesn't feel scripted. Like little interactions of how you characterise yourself when you're peeling a potato, when you philosophise about it, or when you're making tea and you engage in these little in-character rituals."

Rituals and beliefs segue neatly back into being a false prophet. Her

vision. It was secret for a few events, and then the Good News broke. "We preached it to the populous," she says. "It got very silly. And then we were declared heretics by some of the player base. I had some in-character followers who were very passionate, and the in-character synod, which is the religious body, were debating it constantly. And in the end, I got prosecuted for heresy, and got executed." Erk. "I didn't expect the run-up to the execution to be as emotional as it became," she says. "One of the things about pretending to be the false messiah is that, after

also sanguine. "A lot of people got to role-play being disillusioned by me," she said, "and I am very aware they really enjoyed tearing my false heresies to shreds." That she picked up the UK LARP Awards' 2018 award for Best Player shows the appreciation. And Yael, like many well-loved characters, had followed her.

"I was at a convention, and there were editors, and I would be very shy to approach people," she says, "but I remembered being the false messiah, and when I was playing the false messiah, a lot of people wanted to talk to me, and every single one would come up to me and apologise for how they didn't want to take up my time, and I would always say, 'I'm physically here, this is what I choose to do with my time. If I don't want you to talk to me, I would not be here.' So, I just kept holding that emotion close to me, going, 'The editors, if they didn't want to talk to you, they wouldn't be here.'"

"I am very aware they really enjoyed tearing my false heresies to shreds."

name was Yael. The "was" is a clue. Yael was a character at Empire, which meets four times a year, and is one of the largest events in the British LARPing calendar. Empire has well over 1,000 people gathering in what looks on maps like the LARP equivalent of a music festival. It's also a game which primarily has large plot events, furthering the history of the world... and this is where Jeannette put in her oar in. Empire's religion is a kind of fantasy Buddhism, complete with rebirth. *Rebirth*.

"I conned them into thinking I was the first Empress reborn." She returned with completely fabricated scripture, replete with afterlife, fate of souls and "all this stuff that I ripped off Revelations".

How? An in-world ancient box, sealed for thousands of years was opened, and Yael quietly slipped her own "ancient" scroll in before anyone could notice. She encrypted it, which proved that it *must* be important. And lo, when other players eventually decoded it a prophecy is born. But how to make Yael the prophet? She acquired an in-game potion of past lives, leading to a magical ceremony where a priest shows you a vision your past life, acted out in private in a tent... and then when she emerged, she proceeded to just lie about her

a while, you just believe your own hype. You can't help it. So, there was a lot of anxiety over the lies that I was telling, and how true they were, and trying to convince myself that they were kind of true, because they were things that my character believed in-character."

And finally, the execution, and all the church politics you could hope for. ("She's a heretic, she's not allowed to be executed with a relic sword."). After she's struck down, entirely unexpected singing. "There was this choir who struck up this hymn that they wrote about the land without tears," she said. "I had no part in it. They came with the song. It was really beautiful, because the whole theme of the song was going to the land without tears after death, basically. And my character's followers, they were all crying, whilst they were singing that song. And it was this wonderful juxtaposition of this hope of a better place..."

Her martyrdom caused a new following, but eventually the forgery came back to haunt her, based on an in-character spell revealing that Yael actually wrote it. Jeannette's a little frustrated that the rules were interpreted in a way to let that happen, as it removes her hoped-for-legacy. There was no grey area. She was just a hoax. However, she's

We talk a little about our con outfits - her, early on, choosing a quirky writer outfit, complete with yellow beret, so she could easily ID herself in e-mail. "It's the same strategic mind that I brought to role-playing strategizing characters and things," she says and I recognise it. I remember the armour of suits that folks who only see me at cons presume I wear at all times.

In a very real way, we're all live role-playing. "Yes, we are, we are. All the time," says Jeannette. And we laugh, yet not.

You too can be a false prophet. And if you're a false prophet once, you're a false prophet forever.

Jeannette Ng's Under the Pendulum Sun *is available from Angry Robot.*

AVERY ALDER

If the thesis of these interviews is that the 2010s have been the most interesting time for role-playing games since their first decade, it leads to a question: "Where the hell did that idea originate?" Let's keep this simple. In 2012, I was a moderately renowned videogames critic, and completed another big-budget videogame. Then, I discovered Avery Alder's *Monsterhearts*. I haven't significantly played a major digital game since. It was so clear that this was much more interesting than anything happening in the space I'd devoted my career to for the previous fifteen years. In the band metaphor, Avery's the artist that started me hanging around in a different kind of scene.

Her own personal history also dovetails with some of the trends I've found most compelling. She was in her final year of high school in 2005, and had been playing *Dungeons & Dragons* for a year or so. It had been driving the group to distraction. What *was* this game? One DM set it up devoid of theme, with a shop for items or weapons. If Avery ran it it was

you in the role of a henchperson to a villain who lives in a castle on the hill, sent to do his evil bidding. "It is about your anguish in trying to resist that oppressive paradigm, and was just totally clear on what it was, and what it wanted to be, and who it was for," says Avery. "From the moment I encountered that game I was like, 'Awesome. This is what I want to do.'"

While she's abandoned much of the specific theory from the Forge, there are some core things she carries forward into her work, especially the idea that specific is best. "I write weird niche games, right?" says Avery. "I write games about lesbian community drama, and I write games about post-capitalist civic planning. They actually gained me a really wide audience. And I think the reason why that is is I'm not trying to cater to as many people as possible. I'm saying, 'Listen, this is what the game offers. If that's not for you, that's fine. If that is for you, I've put a lot of work into it, and I think it's going to be good.'"

We move forward a few years to 2010, and indie RPGs have had a few

> ## "*Monsterhearts* was a vehicle for better understanding..."

more likely the gnomes and minotaurs would be staging a revolution. "That took me to the internet, trying to figure out: are there ways to navigate these disagreements about what a game is supposed to be about?" says Avery. "Are there other games that are designed to have thematic unity built into them?"

She found the Forge, the online RPG community which foreshadowed a lot of the modern indie RPG scene. It had been founded in 1999, so was well into its middle-age by this point, and games had emerged which answered her question. Yes, there *were* games with more thematic unity. "They kind of blew my mind," says Avery. "*My Life with Master* is an incredibly conceptually and mechanically tight game." Rather than the idea of freedom, it puts

obvious successes, but there is one relevant technological advance that echoed through this decade. It's the Powered by the Apocalypse system ("PBTA"), as first seen in *Apocalypse World* by Vincent and Meguey Baker which became something approaching a *lingua franca* of indie game design. Avery stresses PBTA is far from the only theme in the period - games which step away from single characters and tells stories about communities (Avery's own *The Quiet Year*, *Microscope*, *Dialect*), Nordic LARP, exploring pre-made characters (*Montsegur 1244*) and more - but it *is* important. "What Apocalypse World did is that it brought up this idea of fiction-first games," says Avery.

PBTA conceptualised the RPG as a conversation with "moves" that are triggered when specific things are said, and then create specific changes in the fiction. That moves can be *anything*, and so make your game about any specific something, is very powerful. "There was an open encouragement to write new moves," says Avery. "If someone goes into the toxic swamplands, make a move about it, plug it into the game, see what happens. And so that invitation, I think, is what led to the boom of Powered by the Apocalypse games."

Which begat *Monsterhearts*, Avery's game born of the love and encouragement of the *Apocalypse World* forums and the frustration of misogynistic knee-jerk responses to *Twilight*, of college-educated men going for easy dunks on what teen girls like. This led to her writing a move that was little more than a joke about Bella and Edward, leading to encouragement to actually make the game, and digging to discover there was gold there...

What PBTA also does particularly well is genre emulation. As in, by selecting the moves that are triggered by the fiction, you can mirror what genre does. An adventure game can have moves like "when someone tries to fight a monster". When games are about emotional drama they have moves like "when someone feels conflicted". However, one of the most striking things about *Monsterhearts* is that for all that it's 100% born of genre - teen paranormal stories - its focus is to tell stories which are still not nearly represented enough. It magics better genre fiction into existence.

"In terms of what I was aiming to do with *Monsterhearts*, I was aiming not to emulate this genre of paranormal teen romance, but to deconstruct it," says Avery, "to take what is interesting and problematic and what the core tensions of that genre are, and to play with them. And not to sanitise them, or fix them

or make them not-problematic any more, but to make them interesting and thought-provoking."

And so, *Monsterhearts* is an explicitly queer game. While Avery had come out as queer as a teenager, it wasn't until much later that she was able to truly explore it. "It's a game where the core tensions that drive the story in *Monsterhearts* are about making sense of your identity, about making sense of your sexuality, and about making sense of how the forces around you in your world shape you in adolescence. It ended up being that *Monsterhearts* was a vehicle for better understanding, and declaring who I am, as a queer person. And I published *Monsterhearts*, and within about a year I was starting to engage in the process of coming out as a trans person, and beginning to transition."

This became a core theme of her work. "From that point forward, my design became a lot more explicitly queer in nature. And even with the games that weren't explicitly queer, I still understood how my world view and perspective as a queer person was embedded within those designs. Like, *The Quiet Year* is a game about community, and how dialogue happens, and what it means to sit with discomfort and difference within a community process."

Later, building on a PBTA core, she wrote *Dream Askew*, which debuted the Belonging Without Belonging system, which is about marginalised identities creating their own communities. They feature no dice and are entirely without a classical gamesmaster. "Ultimately, every character in *Dream Askew* is someone who holds a problematic but potentially necessary type of power within the community," say Avery. "In the here and now, these are people with asymmetrical and complicated types of power, trying to

figure out how to exist in relationship to one another. And so, yes, the game does not have a central authority for governing the characters, or governing the setting, because my experience of anarchic spaces is that, ultimately, people are just going to do things, and we have to figure out for ourselves, each of us, how we feel about that, those actions and those people. Are we able to make peace with what they're doing, or not?"

Avery's work continues. She's training as a narrative therapist. Canada's Department of Education has invited her to help design training materials for climate adaptation. While she rarely starts with a political idea, in the creative process she thinks about the politics of the game intensely. "I think all game mechanics are inherently political," says Avery. "What game mechanics do is model our reality. They model the reality of the game world. And since it is impossible to create a system that objectively models the universe without it being the size of the universe, you as a designer end up making choices about what enables someone to achieve their goals in the world. Is it having broad-reaching, generationally-linked coalitions of support? Is it being individually skilled and self-possessed, and having a discrete set of skills, like 'use of broadsword,' and 'animal tracking,' that you can pick up and take with you, out of a community? And usually it's the latter, in roleplaying games. But even just that starting premise of, 'Our skills and power and capacity grow over time, are embedded within us as individuals, are contextless, are fully meritorious, and self-deserved, and self-possessed.' There are a lot of political assumptions built into that alone."

Avery Alder's work is available from buriedwithoutceremony.com.

"What game mechanics do is model our reality ... the reality of the game world."

ALSO BY THE SAME CREATORS

KIERON GILLEN & STEPHANIE HANS:

The Wicked + The Divine #15
Collected in *The Wicked + The Divine* Volume 3

The Wicked + The Divine 1831 #1
Collected in *The Wicked + The Divine* Volume 8

Journey Into Mystery
Collected in two volumes, with Stephanie providing covers and interiors on the final issue

Angela: Asgard's Assassin
with Marguerite Bennett and Phil Jimenez

1602 Witch Hunter Angela
with Marguerite Bennett and more

FOR FURTHER INFORMATION PLEASE VISIT:

www.diecomic.com
For comic and RPG news, new issues and updates

#diecomic
The hashtag for whatever social media you use

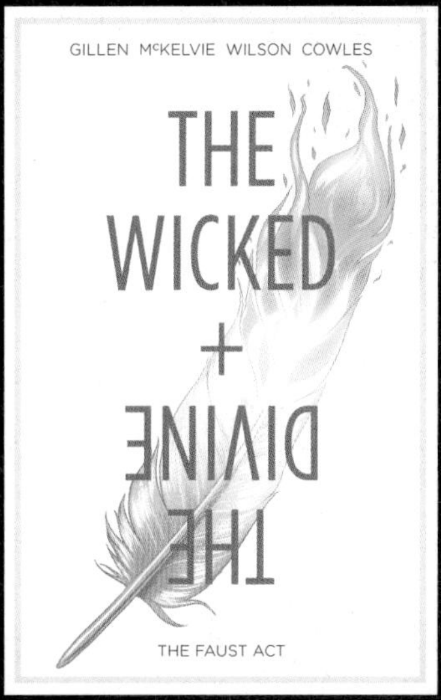
GILLEN McKELVIE WILSON COWLES
THE WICKED + THE DIVINE
THE FAUST ACT

The Wicked + The Divine
Volumes 1-9
With art by Stephanie Hans in Volumes 3 and 8

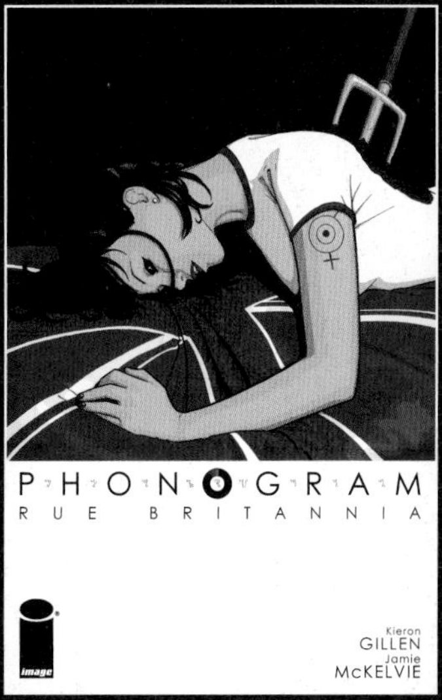
PHONOGRAM
RUE BRITANNIA
Kieron GILLEN
Jamie McKELVIE

Phonogram
Volumes 1-3

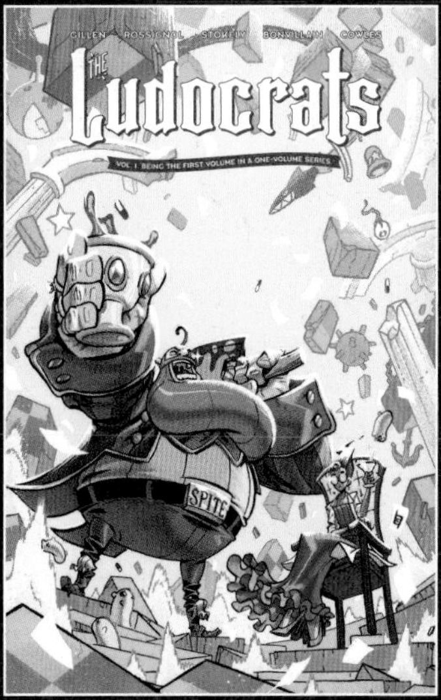
The Ludocrats
SPITE

The Ludocrats

TEAM BIOS

Kieron Gillen is a comic writer based in London, Britain. His previous work includes *The Wicked + The Divine, Once & Future* and *Young Avengers*. He mainly plays low intelligence barbarians or high charisma bards.

Photo: Mauricio de Souza

Stephanie Hans is a comic artist based in Toulouse, France. Her previous work includes issues of *The Wicked + The Divine, Journey Into Mystery* and *Batwoman*. She mainly plays clerics and wizards.

Clayton Cowles is an Eisner-award nominated letterer, based in Rochester, USA. His credits include everything. He has only played *D&D* once, and was a bard.